Praise for

'Absolutely delicious – a
which kept me guessing up until the very last moment.
This book is so much fun'
Daisy Buchanan

'It'll seep into your psyche and leave you wanting more'
Hannah Tovey

'I adored this book! It is riotously funny,
horribly familiar, and a brilliantly compelling story.
I related so hard to way too much of it, revelled
in the darkness, and can't wait for Kate Weston's
next novel. Hard recommend!'
Lucy Vine

'Outrageously entertaining'
Maz Evans

'This deliciously dark tale is an ideal summer read'
Sun

'Brilliantly plotted'
Amy Beashel

'One of those books that keeps catching your eye
before you succumb to its charms'
Stylist

Kate Weston is an ex-stand-up comedian and the author of YA murder mystery *Murder On a School Night*, as well as *Diary of a Confused Feminist* and *Must Do Better*. *Diary of a Confused Feminist* was longlisted for the Comedy Women in Print Prize and nominated for the Carnegie Medal, and *Murder on a School Night* was shortlisted for the YA Book Prize. Kate lives in London with her partner and their cat Angus.

Also by Kate Weston

You May Now Kill the Bride

HOW TO MAKE A KILLING

Kate Weston

Copyright © 2025 Kate Weston

The right of Kate Weston to be identified as the Author of
the Work has been asserted by her in accordance with the
Copyright, Designs and Patents Act 1988.

First published in 2025 by Headline Publishing Group Limited

1

Apart from any use permitted under UK copyright law, this publication may
only be reproduced, stored, or transmitted, in any form, or by any means, with prior
permission in writing of the publishers or, in the case of reprographic production, in
accordance with the terms of licences issued by the Copyright Licensing Agency.
All characters in this publication are fictitious and any resemblance
to real persons, living or dead, is purely coincidental.

Cataloguing in Publication Data is available from the British Library

Paperback ISBN 978 1 0354 1248 8

Typeset in Sabon by CC Book Production

Printed and bound in Great Britain by Clays Ltd, Elcograf S.p.A.

Headline's policy is to use papers that are natural, renewable and
recyclable products and made from wood grown in well-managed forests
and other controlled sources. The logging and manufacturing processes
are expected to conform to the environmental regulations
of the country of origin.

HEADLINE PUBLISHING GROUP
An Hachette UK Company
Carmelite House
50 Victoria Embankment
London EC4Y 0DZ

The authorised representative in the EEA is Hachette Ireland,
8 Castlecourt Centre, Dublin 15, D15 XTP3, Ireland
(email: info@hbgi.ie)

www.headline.co.uk
www.hachette.co.uk

*For Abi Nightingale and James Goodill.
Without you I'd have spent a lot more time
crying in the toilets xx*

Prologue

Bella walks away from the warm glow of the mansion and further into the darkness of the maze-like garden, twirling a long strand of chestnut hair around her finger. She reaches out to her left, her hand grazing the leaves of the box hedge that lines the path. A rustle from the other side of the bush startles her and she freezes, prickles fizzing at the back of her neck. Searching through the shadows for the source of the noise, she sighs with relief as a tiny robin hops out of the branches and skitters off about its business.

Still for a moment, Bella looks back towards the house where all the other women are, still telling their lies and playing their games. Each one of them doing things they think that no one else sees. But she does. Bella sees everything they do. She turns and follows the path round to the left, her heels clicking against the natural slate chippings on the ground. In the distance a hideous, old stone cherub fountain spews out a sudden surge of water, like an exorcism. Expulsion complete, the water settles in the fountain's stone basin, and she walks towards it.

Tom, the seller, loves the cherub but she finds it creepy,

and she reckons whoever buys the house from him will too. If it was her house, original feature or not, that fountain with its ghostly effigy would be the first to go. She stares into its cold, blank eyes, just as a loud burbling sound emanates from within, before another great gush of water is vomited into the basin.

Aggressive and disorientating, it makes her jump, overwhelming her senses so that when another noise comes from behind her, she wrenches her head round with dizzying speed. Adrenaline slams through her veins, making her feel untethered until she sees the familiar face.

'Oh, you came back,' she sighs, clutching her hand to her chest, her heart still fluttering. 'I assumed our conversation was over?'

The intruder says nothing, simply staring as though mirroring the vacant Victorian cherub. In the dim light of the fountain something shiny glints in their hand. Bella doesn't realise what the object is until the last second – when a bronze vulva sculpture is smashed into her head.

Chapter One

Hannah's jaw clenches with the relentless clang of the bell. Around the office, the women of Harrington's Estates are grinning and clapping their hands like overwrought seals. Robotically, she joins in, palms slapping together in the direction of her triumphant colleague. Lip filler stretches across her veneers as she tries to offer the perfect congratulatory smile. It's a fine line; if she smiles too widely, she might look sarcastic, but not wide enough, and someone might perceive her as jealous. And Hannah would never be jealous of that prick.

What a great accomplishment! She applauds with bitter abandon. *What an inspiring success of a woman!* Hannah's hands have become flippers. She tries to be the kind of woman who feels happy for the achievements of others but, despite what the internet memes say, success *does* feel like pie. There's only so much victory to go round, and currently Bella's gobbling it all up, like a greedy little piglet. While they're wasting time praising Bella, Hannah could be selling a house right now. Celebrating Bella's win is actively keeping her from pursuing her own. There's no thrill quite like selling a house for Hannah, and Bella's stolen more than a few of those thrills from her lately.

'I'm *so proud* of you, Bella darling!' Amanda Harrington, CEO and founder of Harrington's Estates, stands from her seat to emphasise how delighted she is with her prodigy. She likes to make sure that, as a boss, she's encouraging and inspiring the women beneath her.

'A house sale and a shortlisting for Estate Agent of the Year all in the same day. Double celebration! Honestly, I worried that flat was going to be *impossible* to sell at that price, but once again you've proved that you can do anything! BRAVA, MY DARLING!'

Amanda's tiny Bichon Frisé, Buster, stands from his throne-like bed, barking at the noise while Amanda raises her hands, performing a deskside standing ovation. A photograph of Michelle Obama hangs above Amanda's chair, in a gold frame, engraved with the quote *'There is no limit to what we, as women can accomplish'*. It sits – aptly – just below a shelf displaying years' worth of trophies to honour Amanda's work.

Amanda is a busy woman – a mother, a business mogul, a self-starter – who built her career from nothing after a childhood marred by poverty, and a voracious Instagrammer, mumfluencing her large follower count daily. She's not just a She-EO, she's a brand. And, like Michelle Obama, she's also wife to a very powerful man – the CEO of a huge television channel. She thinks her and Michelle would have a lot to talk about if they ever met, which she's sure they will. One day.

Hannah exchanges a glance with her desk mate, co-listing buddy and best friend, Olivia. It's a silent acknowledgement that they would both rather file Laurence Fox's toenails than join this standing ovation. Unfortunately – but not unexpectedly – their colleague Claire has already followed Amanda's lead, whooping and cheering in front of her desk like a crazed fan. If they don't join in now, they'll look like arseholes and Amanda will be disappointed in them. None of the women could bear Amanda being disappointed in them. Begrudgingly, the two of them resign themselves to joining the cult of Bella and stand up.

Amanda raises her phone, filming her office of women cheering Bella for Instagram, as she swings the bell pull again. When the final smack of the clapper rings out – as Bella stands next to it pretending to look embarrassed by the attention – Amanda turns the phone's camera to selfie mode.

'When women support women, we all succeed!' she says earnestly into the lens.

'Yay! Well done, Bella,' the monotone praise escapes Hannah's tight lips with a tone that makes it sound more like a 'fuck you' than encouragement.

'I couldn't have done it without my Harrington's babes!' Bella gestures around the room, her stare lingering on Hannah for an extended and uncomfortable period. 'Especially you Han, the most experienced among us! You've always been *so* supportive, and I truly value your wisdom and advice. I'm pretty shocked you weren't shortlisted for the award too, actually!'

'I've won the last three years in a row. Probably time to let someone else have a go. Congratulations.' Hannah hauls the word out of herself like a tapeworm. She's furious enough about being bumped from the shortlist, without this late twenties bitch describing her as having 'wisdom'. Everyone knows wisdom's code for being old.

Next to her, Olivia worries that if Bella keeps talking, Hannah might snap, and she'll have to hold her back. She pictures her lurching across the desk, bludgeoning Bella's smug face with her own Estate Agent of the Year 2023, 2022 and 2021 trophies.

Amanda's attention abruptly switches from the celebrations to her phone and work again, sitting back down at her desk. She chews the side of her cheek, focussing on finding the right filter and backing track to turn the video into an aspirational masterpiece. The other women take her lead and sit back down also, resuming tapping away at their keyboards. Claire turns to Bella and snaps a quick, candid photo.

'For the 'Gram. I'll caption it "When your best friend's also your inspiration",' gushes Claire.

'Aren't women great?' Amanda says to no one in particular.

A message pops up in the corner of Olivia's computer screen while next to her Hannah's fingers tap away at her keyboard with the bouncing efficiency of someone who's just expelled a satisfying snark.

Hannah: Oh god Claire. Get out of Bella's arsehole.
Hannah: She'll suffocate if she goes much further up there.

Olivia: She's probably just pleased something's distracted Amanda from dildo-gate.

Dildo-gate – one of Claire's most exciting moments at the agency, and not for good reasons – was a property tour she posted to Instagram this morning that went immediately viral due to a lurking foot-long dildo that had been casually left on a bedside table next to a tube of eight-hour cream – that Claire had failed to spot in the background before posting.

No one's sure exactly how she still has her job aside from Amanda's reluctance to fire another woman. Claire's actually only sold four houses in all her three years at the agency. But she's not sat idle the rest of the time. She's also lost six sets of client house keys, accidentally caused a small kitchen fire while demonstrating a gas hob (arguably something that didn't need demonstrating), and inadvertently caused one property to flood while demonstrating the power of a shower (as above). She sticks to Bella like glue, as if she might somehow catch success from her like a child rubbing up against patient zero at a chickenpox party.

Hannah: Bella's only sold a house. That's her job? Why's everyone behaving like she's single-handedly created the cure for HPV?
Olivia: It's embarrassing.
Hannah: And the Estate Agent of the Year Award's been done before. She should try being at least a little original.
Olivia: Next time you sell a house I'm going to make you a small crown out of paperclips – if Claire lets me have them.

Hannah: ????
Olivia: Have you not seen her email?
Hannah: I don't read emails from Claire because they're mostly either shit or annoying, often both. Also they're always far too long. CONDENSE BITCH.
Olivia: She's stationery monitor now – self-declared. It's in her email signature and everything.
Olivia: She's trying to make herself indispensable after earlier. Worried Amanda's going to give her the boot.
Hannah: Amanda's not going to give her the boot. It's not her style.
Olivia: I've been deleting aubergines from our Instagram comments ALL DAY. There need to be consequences???
Hannah: Don't worry, she'll definitely let her know she's disappointed in her. And that's gotta feel pretty bad.
Olivia: On that, someone's commented 'Love the cornicing'. Is there any way that cornicing could be sexual?
Hannah: Maybe delete it just to be safe.

'Bella darling,' Amanda says pointedly across the office as she types. 'I want to announce your shortlisting on Instagram, but I might wait until tomorrow if that's OK with you? Just to give time for the little ... incident ... to be forgotten.'

Amanda shoots Claire a disapproving look and Claire, rightly, looks like she wants to die.

'Of course,' Bella says. 'I really don't mind.'

She tilts her head in Claire's direction, giving her a kind of pitying look that Hannah can see from a mile off is so fake. Bella was the one who pointed out the dildo to

Amanda in the first place. Olivia and Hannah were just going to delete the video and sweep it under the carpet. But that was Bella all over, a snitch. Always ready to go to Amanda the moment anyone does the slightest thing wrong.

'Oh for god's sake.' Hannah nudges Olivia and points over at the window.

Outside, the slimy, shiny, blue-suited, brown-brogue-wearing estate agents of Sanders – their rival agency – are setting up for a performative game of cricket on the town green that lies between the two agencies like a battle line. The shops, the pub, Mabel's wine bar, the cafes and restaurants of Wellingden all face this small strip of green. The boys use it like their pathetic little stage.

Holding the bat is Ron, Hannah's nemesis. He pushes his floppy undercut back from his face before tapping the floor with the end of the bat. One of his colleagues, Felix, flings the ball overarm towards him and there's a light crack as Ron barely hits it, instead disguising his error with an arrogant shout.

'I'M KNOCKING IT OUT THE PARK, MATE!' he shouts as the rest of the blue-suited knobhead army cheer along.

'Stay classy, guys,' Olivia sighs.

'Such losers,' Claire chimes in while Bella and Amanda professionally tap away at their keyboards.

'It's a shame we're too busy with actual work to bother with that kind of showy ridiculousness, isn't it,' Amanda smirks, and the women all giggle.

Hannah doesn't know what's worse, that Bella's on

the shortlist and she isn't, or that Ron is, and she isn't. Actually, she does. It's still Bella. She knows that only one person from each agency can be on the list. She just hopes that Amanda didn't have a say in who was listed. Amanda choosing Bella over her would be too blatant, too painful; she can't entertain it.

Olivia: Oh god, don't look now. It's about to get worse.

Hannah looks up and out of the window where a huge bunch of flowers is travelling down the high street towards them, so outrageously massive and gauche that it's basically a garden on legs. The bouquet stops in front of the office, where being closest to the door Hannah or Olivia can easily get up and open it to help. But neither of them do.

Hannah: Do you ever wonder how he affords these constant cringeworthy displays?
Olivia: Guess the world of freelance phallic art is more profitable than either of us would have thought?
Hannah: This is going to shock you but I googled him the other day. Did you know Brick isn't his *real* name?
Olivia: Why, I am shocked.
Hannah: It's Caspian Smith.

'FLOWERS FOR MY AGENT OF THE YEAR!' An obnoxious, put-on cockney accent emerges from behind the excessive, somewhat ungainly, display followed by the grinning face of Bella's boyfriend, Brick.

Hannah: I would be mortified if someone did this for me.
Olivia: She pretends to be.

Across the office, Bella squeals in delight before putting her hand over her face as though embarrassed.

'Oh my god, BRICK! You shouldn't have! They're gorgeous!' She takes the flowers, kissing him on the cheek like she's accepting an Oscar.

A ludicrously small beanie defies gravity on top of Brick's shaved head as he advances towards Bella with the bunch, his heavily pierced ears sticking out the sides, adorned with enough gold to fix austerity. He pushes the dark, thick-framed glasses up his nose, the words 'BARE' and 'LOVE' tattooed across his knuckles. He passes the bunch to Bella who promptly places them into the vase on her desk, which is a permanent feature due to the galling frequency with which Brick finds reason to send her these vulgar displays. From behind the bunch, his white holey T-shirt becomes visible, reading 'Corporation Whore'.

'They're *so* gorgeous!' Claire gushes while Bella smiles at the flowers like a proud parent, as though she just birthed herself a reward for having a boyfriend.

'Gorgeous,' Amanda says, briefly gazing over the rims of her glasses, distracted. She didn't get anywhere by dwelling on achievements for too long. There's always work to be done.

'I gotta shoot, but I just wanted to let you know how proud I am of you,' Brick says, revealing a flash of gold tooth as he smiles. 'I'll see you later, superstar.'

He struts out of the door and waves everyone goodbye as though he were a visiting celebrity before striding down the street with his jeans slung so low that the crotch is impeding his movement.

'Oh my god, this is *so* embarrassing.' Bella grins broadly.

Hannah and Olivia smile back in the most genuine way they can possibly muster.

Hannah: I'm going to need a LOT of wine.
Olivia: Same. I'll message Matt, he can meet us across the road at the bar after he finishes.

'I've had another email from Marcus Fritton about the house. He's got a new property he wants to sell. Who's turn is it this time?' Amanda checks.

'*Again?*' Hannah sighs.

'It's barely been six months since my last listing with him,' Olivia says, looking slightly haunted. 'We almost lost the buyer on that last house … twice … thanks to him meddling and getting in touch with them directly. He's got no boundaries.'

'He's enthusiastic and particular. A perfectionist,' Amanda reasons.

Claire knows that Amanda would never put her name forward to Marcus, and that the one time she suggested herself she was brutally rejected, but she speaks anyway, boldly covering her own back.

'I'm going on holiday in about two weeks and I know

he likes things to move fast, so I'm probably not the ideal candidate. Considering I'll be on holiday,' Claire smiles.

Hannah and Olivia roll their eyes and Hannah adds another mark to the tiny five-bar-gate tally that they've got running in the top corner of a notepad between their desks for the number of times Claire can mention that she's going on holiday before she actually goes on the fucking holiday.

'Last time I sold for him, he started an argument with a prospective buyer during a viewing because they'd said the solid oak herringbone looked more like engineered laminate. The two nearly came to blows. I thought Marcus was going to slap them with a sample block,' Hannah says. 'He's too involved, a pest!'

'He is,' Amanda concurs. 'But it's only because he's so passionate about what he does. He's got high standards. And we don't want him going across the road to Sanders, do we?'

The women all shake their heads in agreement, but notice that Amanda isn't about to stick her hand up and volunteer to take on his latest listing herself.

Hannah's in desperate need of the commission so she's obviously going to tell Amanda she'll do it – she just wants her to know it's a ball-ache first. Maybe that way she'll notice how above and beyond Hannah goes for the agency. Something she hopes will be remembered by Amanda, especially if it comes to appointing a manager, which they're all convinced she's about to do. After all, Amanda's been spending less and less time in the office, instead favouring time spent on sponsored PR and ad trips for her mumfluencing career. While she's spending more time on that, having a manager who oversees things here would make the most sense. And Hannah wants to make sure that manager is her.

'I'll do it,' Bella says, stealing the words right out of Hannah's open mouth. 'I can fit it in between a viewing and a valuation tomorrow.'

'Oh darling, are you sure? You've already got so much on,' Amanda says, closing her laptop and grabbing her bag for the day. 'I have to head off to an appointment now, but I'd really appreciate it.'

'Of course,' Bella says, shooting Amanda a winning smile, her fingers tapping at her keys as she speaks. 'We all have to do our bit right? That's teamwork. I'll send him an email now and I'll make sure we get a meeting in over the next couple of days.'

'God, what would I do without you, Bella darling. You are an absolute angel. Thank you, I know Marcus isn't easy to work with.' Amanda clips Buster's lead on him before looking over and noticing the fresh sticker Bella placed on her laptop this morning. 'Love that sticker, darling.'

Hannah and Olivia squint across the office, reading the bright pink sticker affixed to Bella's rose-gold laptop.

'*Live, Laugh, Be A Strong Woman.*'

Hannah knows Bella's stuck it there purely because she knows Amanda will love it. Pathetic. It's not even catchy.

'I saw it and just found it really inspiring, you know?' Bella smiles.

'I couldn't agree more.' Amanda smiles back.

Hannah: Overachieving little cunt.
Olivia: Don't worry, she'll fuck up and end up on the slag heap with the rest of us before long.
Hannah: Incredible use of the word slag babe.

'See you all tomorrow! And congratulations again, Bella!' Amanda says, heading towards the door, with Buster trotting at her heels behind her.

'Go, Bella!' Claire whoops.

'Great work,' Olivia chimes.

'So good,' Hannah mutters, tapping away at her keyboard, her right eyebrow raised.

She knows exactly what Bella's up to. She clearly thinks she's going to be manager, but the only way that would happen is over Hannah's cold, dead body.

Olivia: Amanda's leaving early.
Olivia: What do you think? Mumfluencing or Botox?
Hannah: Botox, I think I almost saw her having an emotion.

Amanda's real age and exactly what she's had done to her face is a topic of hot discussion between the two friends. While they've had their own work (hasn't everyone?) and they suspect that their speculation is not within the 'feminist' ethos of the company, they simply can't help it. Besides, as Hannah regularly reminds Olivia, there are millions of women all over the world simultaneously wanting equal pay and opportunities while bitching about each other's botched Botox. It's human nature, an irresistible primal instinct. And where Amanda's concerned, no matter what they think of her forehead, they've never needed the respect and approval of someone so much in their life.

> **Olivia**: Fuck I miss Botox.
> **Hannah**: I don't understand why you don't just keep getting it until you get pregnant. Surely it can't hurt while you're just trying.
> **Olivia**: OMG imagine how bad I'd feel if I found out I was pregnant the day after getting some injected? NO.
> **Hannah**: Fair point . . . I guess.

Across the office Bella's enjoying the effort it took for Hannah and Olivia to pretend to be happy for her. As if she doesn't know that they hate her. But this is all part of the plan, and the plan's going very well.

Chapter Two

'Whispering?' Olivia calls over her shoulder to Hannah, her heels clacking across the black-and-white flooring of Mabel's wine bar as she rushes to get her friend a much-needed drink.

'Angel,' Hannah replies in the affirmative, slumping down into an armchair across the bar, deflated.

She misses the victorious feeling of selling a house, of selling someone their dream. She used to be in the thick of it all: works of modern architectural genius, glamorous houses done out with indoor pools, dressing rooms containing more labels than a Dymo, rolltop baths and waterfall showers in Italian-marble wet rooms. Not to mention the bidding wars – last year two women had fought over a house in a way that would make any of the *Real Housewives* look tame. Walking around houses she can't afford with purpose – the ability to judge their worth and, by extension, the worth of the people in them – makes her feel like she *can* afford them. It makes her feel secure. The more houses she sells, the further away Hannah feels from the council estate she grew up on. But her current lull in listings and sales is denting that security. Lately, she's barely even had a valuation for anything half decent. It's having a profoundly negative effect on her.

Hannah opens Instagram to unwind, scrolling the property porn on her feed. She's barely started decompressing before Ron's smug, self-satisfied voice jars her. It takes a good few seconds before all five foot eight of him, complete with short-man complex, comes into view behind the noise of his undeservedly confident 'bants'. The slicked-back hair, the undercut, the shiny shoes without socks, the man's a walking trigger on a good day. She knew it wouldn't be long before he found her to gloat about his Estate Agent of the Year shortlisting up close; she'd just hoped she would have had time to numb herself with alcohol first.

'Hannah! How's it going? Guess you saw me KNOCKING IT OUT THE PARK earlier?' Ron stands, staring at her as the other *Love Island* drop-outs from Sanders gather at the bar to order a celebrity brand of Cava like the basic bitches of estate agency they are. 'KNOCKING IT OUT OF THE PARK! GET IT?' he repeats, louder for emphasis, in case the reason that Hannah hasn't commented on his wit or offered a congratulatory giggle, is because she didn't hear it, not because it was shit. But Hannah simply takes out her phone with a thoroughly bored expression and starts jabbing away at its screen, hoping that he'll eventually get the message and move on.

Olivia watches from the bar, worried that if she doesn't get the wine over to Hannah soon, she's going to end up spending the night in a police cell on a GBH charge.

Although there's probably a long line of people who would congratulate Hannah for decking Ron. She doubts it would be the first time a woman's punched him in the face.

'I was surprised not to see you on the shortlist this year Han ... Hannah ... Hannah banana ... Spanna, do your friends ever call you that?' Ron's teeth glint at Hannah from under the lip flip he had three months ago that he seems to be under the illusion was subtle. Hannah thinks the money would have been better spent on getting Botox in his sweat glands, the way his shirts seem constantly flooded around the pits.

Olivia catches the end of what he's saying as she heads back from the bar, leaving the rest of the Sanders boys alpha maleing over who's going to pay for the cava. It's a veritable scramble for the first person who can hit the card machine with their Apple watch.

'I think your friends are calling, Ron.' Olivia points over towards the bar where his colleagues are asking the bar man for the biggest knife he has to open the bottle with.

'Looks like you should hurry up. You don't want to miss being showered in cheap fizzy piss, after all.' Hannah briefly glances up to him, only to look straight back down at her phone.

As predicted, Ron skips off in the direction of his friends like the little fake-tanned squirrel he is. The barman hands one of his buddies a blunt butter knife, which he starts desperately rubbing at the bottle with like a grubby little wanker. Olivia can't help but think there's a metaphor around penis size somewhere in there.

'MATE, SHE WAS,' one of the Sanders guys gestures at his chest as if holding a massive pair of melons. 'AND ALL ORIGINAL FEATURES.'

'No way,' one of them smirks. 'No extension? Or renovations?'

Olivia's disappointed that the barman didn't give them something they could actually maim each other with.

'Oh good, I haven't missed anyone making a tit of themselves.' Olivia's tall, blond husband Matt appears next to her, kissing her on the cheek. 'Hope you don't mind, I brought Tom with me?'

Olivia tears her eyes away from the Sanders team in Tom and Matt's direction.

'Not at all!' Olivia waves to Matt's friend behind him, while Hannah continues to jab grumpily at her phone.

She's so deep in misery scrolling she's barely aware of the two men's arrival. Her eyes fix on a video Bella's just posted to Instagram about her great day, the hideous flowers from Brick taking centre stage next to her. She tried muting Bella once, but she just seems to seek out the posts anyway. Obviously hate-following someone isn't healthy, but she can't seem to stop herself.

'Bad day, grumpy guts?' Matt teases, going round to give her a kiss on the cheek.

'Some people are just such pricks,' Hannah sighs, scrolling past the video so Matt doesn't mock her for watching it.

'God, tell me about it,' a male voice she doesn't recognise chimes in, piquing her interest.

Hannah's head whips upwards, her lips instantly pouting

as she takes in the trousers without a hint of shine, the hair without undercut and the rolled-up white shirt sleeves displaying the area of a man's forearm, which is her – and every other millennial woman's – kryptonite. She looks directly into this mysterious stranger's brown eyes and immediately feels everything becoming less shit.

'Hi, I'm Hannah. Do we know you?' she asks, tilting her head in a way that she hopes is playful and flirty but enquiring. She wants this dark-eyed, hot stranger with his expensive suit and wavy brown hair falling perfectly over his forehead to tell her everything about himself immediately.

'Tom.' The stranger reaches out a hand. 'I'm Matt's friend.'

'If you're Matt's friend, how come I've never met you before?' Hannah asks, detective mode officially activated to work out what's wrong with him. She narrows her eyes to Olivia behind him.

'I lived in Australia until a year or so ago,' Tom says, matching her playfully official tone. 'I missed the wedding because of Covid, and I'm really sorry?'

'What do you do for a job?' Hannah continues her investigations.

'Same thing as Matt but for a different company,' Tom replies.

'Hedge funding?' Hannah asks, cocking an eyebrow towards Olivia to let her know that she's been slack. She should have introduced this man to her immediately.

'That's the one,' Tom says.

'Tom also develops property in his spare time. He's been doing up that massive old, neglected mansion by the park for the last year or so. It's looking great,' Matt says.

'The Welling Estate?' Hannah asks. She knows exactly the place. Huge, hidden behind wrought-iron gates and fences, but sprawling; she's been dying to see the inside of it for years.

'Yeah, that's the one. I think it's time to think about selling, though,' Tom says. 'Before I get too attached and can never leave. It's a beaut.'

Hannah can tell Olivia's avoiding her eye contact, and she's right to. A handsome man with a massive house to sell? Why wouldn't she have introduced them? Unless Olivia has been trying to keep this house sale for herself? It's the size of project they'd normally co-list on.

'Wow,' Hannah says, averting her gaze from her lax friend and back to the hot stranger. 'I'd love to take a look some time.'

'Of course,' Tom smiles back at her.

They're interrupted by Matt's phone ringing. He presses reject, silencing it immediately, but Olivia sees the screen light up again straight away with a text from a random number.

'I'll get the drinks in.' Matt nods in the direction of the bar, looking at his phone again as he heads towards it.

'You guys want another?' Tom asks, walking backwards in pursuit of Matt, keeping smooth eye contact with Hannah.

'Love one,' Hannah says, downing her large glass of Whispering Angel so fresh the condensation is still dripping down its sides.

She tries her best to hold his gaze, aside from when she's actually mid-gulp – that's creepy. Tom nods and cocks a questioning eyebrow in Olivia's direction.

'I'm OK for now thanks!' Olivia says, raising an almost full glass of rosé in his direction. She's been trying to drink less to help them conceive, although she's not sure what use it'll do if Matt isn't making the same effort.

Hannah waits for the men to move out of earshot before turning to Olivia, eyes sparkling.

'I can't believe you didn't introduce us sooner! My own best friend, trying to keep a mega mansion and a hot man all to herself!' she accuses. Her tone's jokey, but she's also somewhat disappointed by Olivia. 'Is he single?'

Olivia looks from Hannah to Tom and screws up her face a little in surprise and confusion.

'He's single,' Olivia confirms.

'So why no introducing Hannah to the hot man?' Hannah pouts at her.

'He's just ... he's a bit of a player ...' Olivia says. 'Like, he's a nice guy, and obviously I get on well with him for Matt's sake, but I dunno. I think he can be a bit of a dick where women are concerned. There's always a revolving-door situation going on with him, never with the same woman twice. And he always has a shitty reason why he's ended it with the last one.'

'Commitment-phobe.' Hannah nods sagely, staring at Tom's arse.

'Also, you always said hedge funders were profoundly

boring people.' Olivia recounts just one of the extraordinarily offensive comments Hannah made about her husband's profession to his face, when Olivia and Matt first met.

'I'll take boring job for hot and rich with a massive ESTATE,' Hannah declares. 'Also how can he be boring and a player? Actually, don't worry about it. I love a challenge. Shhh, they're coming back. Oh my god, he's so fit.'

Hannah looks like she might be about to expire with lust. She doesn't seem to realise that Olivia wasn't even saying anything.

'God, those guys are such planks.' Matt points towards the gaggle of Sanders' bellendry that's still going on at the bar as one of them loudly orders a second bottle of shit cava and threatens to 'open this one properly though, mate'.

Matt's phone starts vibrating again and he looks at it briefly before cancelling the call for a second time.

'You can take it if it's work?' Olivia says. She doesn't understand why he doesn't just answer whoever it is and then they'll finally stop calling.

'Nah, it's fine. It can wait till tomorrow.' Matt shrugs, putting his phone back in his pocket, where it immediately starts buzzing again.

'Who *are* those dickheads?' Tom asks, appearing behind Matt and leaning forward to give Hannah her second large Whispering Angel of the night.

'Sanders.' Hannah's teeth set on edge as she says the name, her eyes narrowing.

'The other estate agency in town,' Olivia explains. 'Our biggest competition.'

'Except they're not really, because they're literally the worst estate agents ever,' Hannah says.

Olivia chuckles. 'I mean they're dicks, but at least they're not selling murder houses.'

Hannah shudders, remembering a particularly grisly case from the noughties. 'Wouldn't surprise me,' she snorts.

'I'm guessing they're the ones that have those hideous budget Audis?' Tom suggests. 'Anything that comes in that colour has to have been a mistake sold off at cost.'

'Oh my god,' Hannah giggles. 'Budget Audis, that's so funny. Like a Bicester Village Audi. Hahahaha.'

Tom laughs, slightly perplexed, as Hannah lays a hand on his arm, her fingers curling around it, vice-like, as she yanks him down onto the seat next to her.

'So, tell me, Tom, if you're planning on selling, what will you do after that? Do you think you'll stay around Wellingden?' Hannah bats her extended lashes, hoping to cast some kind of spell over him with her blue eyes.

'I'm not quite sure yet,' Tom says innocently. 'I usually go wherever there's an interesting prospect. Definitely time for a new challenge, though.'

'Last time we spoke, I thought you were considering staying a bit longer?' Olivia furrows her brow.

'You know me. I never stay too long in one place,' Tom says. 'The house is done. Time to recoup my investment and find a new project.'

The words 'recoup my investment' give Hannah the immediate horn.

'Well, like I said earlier, I'd love to take a look. Maybe

me and Olivia could give you a valuation at the same time. Kill two birds with one stone?' she offers, purely professionally.

'Hannah and I co-list on a lot of bigger projects so I'm sure we could sell it for you quite quick,' Olivia agrees. 'Not to brag, but we're good at this.'

'It's true,' Hannah says. 'We're deadly.'

Hannah can't help but feel relieved. Olivia clearly just didn't think he was selling yet; it wasn't that she was trying to cut Hannah out. Of course, she wasn't. Olivia's a far nicer person than Hannah, and Hannah knows it. She shouldn't judge her by her own 'every woman for herself' standards.

'And there I was thinking Sanders would be the way to go,' Tom teases with a cute smirk.

'With their level of competency?' Hannah points to the bar – using it as an opportunity to get closer to Tom – where Sanders are still trying to open their second bottle of cava, each stroke of the butter knife becoming more inept than the last.

'Fair point. Why don't you guys come tomorrow around eleven? I'm working from home so I can give you the guided tour,' Tom says.

'I'd love that,' Hannah says, almost breathless. Maybe they'll grow close while she sells his house then, at the wedding, they can tell everyone how Hannah impressed him with her incredible property prowess and, before they knew it, they were buying their own luxury house together, in a great deal brokered by Hannah.

'I can show you some pictures now if you like. A sort

of amuse-bouche before tomorrow?' Tom offers, reaching for his phone.

'Oh, don't tease,' Hannah says, playfully patting his bicep, getting a small thrill from its solid form under her fingertips.

Olivia feels a wave of anxiety watching her friend throw herself at Tom with so much vigour.

'Oh, I wasn't teasing . . .' Tom says, slightly puzzled. 'I've actually got some on my phone. Do you want to see them?'

Hannah clears her throat, brushing away a sheepishness that she desperately wants to ignore. 'Yes. Please,' she says.

'I'll take a look at those too,' Olivia says, squishing in on the other side of Tom.

Olivia can hear Matt's phone buzzing constantly in his pocket. He finally takes it out, the same unrecognisable number that was ringing before flashing on the screen.

'Someone really wants to talk to you,' Hannah comments.

'Yeah, I think it's spam,' Matt says, cancelling it.

'Why don't you just answer or block the number? Get them to stop?' Olivia asks.

'Good shout,' Matt sighs as the phone rings again. 'I'll be back in a sec.'

Olivia watches him walk out the door. She trusts her husband, but if it's just a spam call, why's he being so weird? Why does he have to take it outside? She feels an uneasiness in the pit of her stomach that's been cropping up far more frequently than she'd like lately.

* * *

Hannah runs her finger along her top lip, hoping to draw attention to it while leaning seductively against the toilet door. She tells herself it wasn't creepy to follow him down here into the basement, pretending that she needed the toilet too, then wait in the shadows for him to emerge so that she could engineer a surprise crossing of their paths in a more private setting. Not creepy, just using her initiative.

'It's been so nice to meet you. I'm disappointed Olivia hasn't introduced us before,' Tom says.

'Yeah?' Hannah replies, her inflection rising at the end like a question as she tilts her head. She can literally feel her pupils dilating the more he talks.

'Yeah,' Tom confirms, smiling at her. 'Especially because it sounds like you're going to sort my house sale for me.'

She knows Olivia called him a player, but having seen his house she finds that hard to believe. This man's created a family home. Sure, he's selling it on, but it's still giving her sensitive vibes rather than man-whore ones. Maybe Olivia just doesn't know him well enough to understand him? He has been on the other side of the world all this time.

'Oh, definitely.' Hannah leans closer to him, the gap between the two of them rapidly closing, just like she planned.

She looks up, into his dark eyes. It's not professional to bang a client, but he's also a friend, right? The lines are already blurred. She reaches out to touch him playfully on the arm just as the toilet door behind them opens. A woman stands in the doorway for a second, glaring at the two of them for blocking her way, before barging carelessly between them. The magic's broken and all because some selfish twat finished their wee.

'Better head back up,' Tom says. 'They'll be wondering what we're up to down here.'

'Oh, right, yeah,' Hannah says, following him.

'Didn't you need the loo?' Tom turns to her.

'Oh yeah,' Hannah slaps her forehead and immediately hates herself for it. 'Duh.'

Rumbled.

'See you in a bit,' Tom says, heading upstairs.

'In a bit.' Hannah waves, not knowing why, and hates herself.

She ducks into the toilet in shame.

Hannah emerges from the toilet and walks down the long, dark, empty basement corridor towards the stairs. When Tom was down here, it felt romantic: the candles in the brickwork offering a dim, flickering light, the tinkling of classical music masking the sound of flushing toilets and the cloying smell of reed diffusers covering the aroma of piss. Without him here, it's just a creepy sewer. She knows it's kind of a vibe in these bars to have atmospheric toilets, but she's always wished Mabel's could be a bit less Jack the Ripper. As she races for the stairs on high alert, a hand reaches out from the darkness, grabbing her arm.

'ARGH!' she screams and jumps away, before Matt emerges from the shadows.

She breathes a sigh of relief, clutching her fluttering chest as he becomes fully visible.

'Fuck's sake, Matt. You scared me!'

'Sorry. Just figured while you're down here . . . we should probably talk, about . . . stuff,' he whispers vaguely, but Hannah knows exactly what he means.

'I'm assuming you still haven't told your wife what's going on?' Hannah glares at him.

Matt stares down at the floor like a naughty child, but Hannah's got no time for his sulking.

'I don't like keeping secrets from her. The only reason I haven't said anything is because it's you that needs to do it. She'd be so much more devastated if it wasn't even you that told her,' Hannah hisses. 'Look, I wish I didn't know, but now I do, I need you to tell her, or I will.'

'Can't you just pretend you don't?' Matt says. 'Just wait for me to sort it out.'

'Believe me, I'd rather bury my head in the sand like you seem to be doing, but how exactly are you planning on sorting it out? It's not something that can be *'sorted out'*. Actually, fuck it, I don't want to know, Matt. Just tell your wife so I don't have to. Stop being such a knob.'

She starts to walk away, just as Felix from Sanders emerges from the toilet, sniffing and wiping his nose. She can tell Matt's immediately anxious, worried someone else might have heard his little secret. But Hannah's sure Felix is far too into himself to notice what anyone else is doing.

Chapter Three

@Amanda_HarringtonsGroup
Backing track: Hustlin', Rick Ross
Video begins with Amanda Harrington corralling two small children into putting their shoes and coats on ready for school as they cause havoc. A jar of chia seeds teeters dangerously close to the edge of the marble kitchen island, about to spill onto the floor, but Amanda stops it. A small chocolate-covered hand heads towards a white sofa, but Amanda stops that too. And a petrified bichon frisé races into Amanda's arms away from a child that's trying to make it wear a wedding dress.

Amanda: Us women know what it's like to be *Hustlin'* every single day. I hustled my career, building my business from nothing, and now I'm a successful working mum, I'm hustlin' my kids out the door in the mornings before hustlin' at work to achieve my goals. So that's even more reason not to be hustlin' when it comes to house organisation. Am I right ladies?

Amanda smiles to the camera gesturing around at her perfect life, perfect house, and perfect existence. Her nanny is just out of shot.

> **Amanda**: Keep an eye on my feed for a tour of the PERFECT family home later. It's coming on the market soon but I'm giving you guys – my special mummy followers – a sneak peek before it hits. Because imagine how much easier all this could be . . . with a bit more space and organisation. One of *you* lucky people could be about to buy the solution to all your mummy problems.

Amanda gestures to what she pretends to think is carnage around her as one child plays neatly on the floor with some Lego bricks in her very own perfect house.

'Kids! Let's go!' Amanda holds open the door to the four by four with the Harrington's Estates logo printed on its door while pressing 'post' on the video.

She's nervous because she actually recorded the video at 3pm on Saturday afternoon, but she just can't get them done in the mornings at the moment. Both kids need extra help with their maths so she's had to hire a tutor, meaning that they have to practise their Duolingo in the mornings now. She's barely got time to do her essential morning sun salutations as it is. Recording the video at another time seemed the only option and, fortunately, the kids thought getting ready for school at 3pm on a Saturday afternoon was a fun game. She's exhausted. She can't keep this up, running the business and doing all the mumfluencing. But this is everything she's always wanted. She's a brand. Finally, *she's* the dream she's been selling to people for years. People come to her for help achieving their fantasies because they think she's living it. They're hardly going to do that if they find out the truth about her, are they? She can't slip up now, not when she's built so much for herself to lose. She needs to maintain perfection and keep being someone who's envied. But something's going to have to give.

Sometimes, Amanda thinks perfection's a cage she desperately wants to break free from, and just sit around eating Ferrero Rocher in a velour tracksuit all day.

Chapter Four

Hannah peers over the rim of her sunglasses at the house in the distance, the tyres of her lilac convertible BMW crunching down the long gravel driveway as she lets out a low appreciative whistle. Next to her in the passenger seat, despite it not being her first time at the house, Olivia's finding its beauty in this morning's light almost biblical: the perfectly manicured sprawling lawns, the sun glinting off new wooden sash windows framed by lilac wisteria and the centred double black front door complete with antique brass knocker.

It's the sort of house she's always dreamed that her and Matt would have one day. With their future children playing on its lawns or having epic rainy-day games of hide and seek around the house's copious rooms and floors. They could easily make a tennis court and swimming pool with all this space too, then they'd be the stars of their summer camps. She could raise the next Andy Murray. Matt's secret phone calls from last night drift into the picture, ruining her fantasy and setting Olivia on edge again.

Instead, Olivia remembers when she'd first walked into

her kitchen a year and a half ago, to see Tom, sweaty and fresh from a squash game with her husband, drinking a glass of ice-cold water from their fridge. She'd almost dropped the vase of flowers she was holding. She was used to Matt bringing people back after various sporting activities, but she generally knew them and had thus far been unmoved at the sight of them in their sports kits (though some of the Lycra ones had moved her to leave the room). Tom, however, was properly handsome, and she knew just from looking at him that Hannah would be all over him. Especially when Matt had told her about the house – or rather estate – that Tom had bought at auction to flip. But Matt had already told her what a womanizer Tom was, and she didn't want Hannah getting into another bad situation with someone who wasn't worthy of her. Men with high-value property and ambition were Hannah's catnip, but they often tended to come with a moral greyness.

'Jackpot,' Hannah breathes next to her as if reading her mind. 'It's even better than those pictures he showed me last night. I was beside myself.'

'Yes, I think half the bar could tell you were enjoying them,' Olivia says before doing an impression of Hannah fawning over the pictures. 'Oooohhhh, ahhhh, oh my god, is that a rolltop bath? ... Oh, Tom ... tell me that's an Aga!'

The two women giggle as the car comes to a stop. They just about manage to contain themselves, putting on professional faces before they open their car doors, each sinking a stiletto heel into the white gravel of the driveway.

'My god, it's an orgasm made of bricks,' Hannah breaths, shutting the car door and aiming the key fob with a bleep.

'Please don't use Brick and orgasm in the same sentence,' Olivia winces as the two of them walk towards the house. 'It's bad enough that Bella posted a shirtless picture of him this morning.'

Both women baulk at the memory, which really put Hannah's hangover to the test.

'Besides, we've been here before; it never works out when you date a man for his house. In the end, the man never matches up to the bags of potential,' Olivia warns.

'You're right, I should be careful. Besides, you can never tell what horrors are lurking outside of the camera shot,' Hannah says. 'At least we know from the pictures last night that he doesn't think black's a neutral decor colour. And there are no mirrors on the bedroom ceiling.' They shudder slightly as they walk to the front door, both of them remembering a house they sold for a couple in their eighties who were moving into a retirement home.

'Bella's going to be *sick* when we go back to the office with this listing,' Hannah whispers, pulling the brass door knocker back and bringing it down with a gleeful thud.

'If we throw a massive open house and make everyone in the office come, we can really rub her nose in it,' Olivia whispers back.

'This pisses all over anything she's ever listed.' Hannah grins up at the three storeys of original period features and restored charm that lay ahead of them. 'I can't wait to see her gutted face.'

'Now, what would Amanda say if she could hear you?' Olivia chastises. 'Competition is the thief of feminism. Other women are not the enemy.'

'Bella is the thief of feminism. Bella is the enemy,' Hannah quips. 'The way she dobbed Claire in yesterday, her own "best friend", the absolute snake. It's so obvious she thinks she's going to become manager.'

Hannah quickly whispers the end of her rant as a click sounds behind the door and it begins to open. She replaces her bitching face with that of a smooth and enigmatic smile.

'Hey, To—' Olivia stops dead, cut off by a sight so hideous that if she and Hannah weren't seeing it with their own eyes it would be inconceivable.

Hannah thinks this might be the first time she's ever fully understood the phrase 'blood running cold'.

'Oh my god! It's you! Hey, guys!' Bella smiles back at them from the wrong side of the door. Olivia and Hannah stand frozen in horror, mouths gaping.

'Are you . . . ?' Olivia hears Hannah muttering the words, but she feels like they're far away.

She does some equations in her head. Where did Bella say she was going when she left the office earlier after the morning meeting? *Did* she even say? What's she doing here in Tom's house? How does she even know him?

'So, *you* must be the other agents that Tom was talking about!' Bella's voice is excited, jovial, the opposite of everything that Olivia (and she's pretty sure Hannah too) is feeling right now. 'Such a relief!'

She's giving the impression that whatever the situation

is here, even if they're going for the same listing, it doesn't trouble her at all. That arrogance alone is extremely troubling to Olivia, and it's like a giant, red rag to Hannah.

'I was worried I'd have to fight one of those boys from Sanders for it. It hadn't occurred to me it could be someone from our agency! How lucky! There's no competition at all!' Bella grins with shark-like confidence.

Hannah digs the pointed acrylics of her left hand into the palm of her right one. Next to her, Olivia's face is performing a series of acrobatics in an attempt not to look bothered.

'Gosh, well come in and take a look! *Mi casa su casa!*' Bella grins and opens the door more widely, as if she were a troll guarding the entrance bridge to the castle.

Hannah is ready to take this woman down. She will fight her to the death for this house.

'We could all work on it together!' Bella says as if she's just thought of it.

Hannah would rather fellate Donald Trump than work on a listing with Bella.

Olivia takes Hannah's arm, trying to prevent incident. With a gentle hand, she supports the weight of her contained (for now) rage and follows Bella inside. The pristine front door closes behind them with a click, its brass door furniture now feeling more like a trap than a blessing.

Inside, Hannah looks around the hallway, becoming more and more tempted to physically and aggressively take out Bella somehow so there's no way she can get her paws on this listing. The house is impeccably decorated with a sharp eye and expensive touches. If she's not mistaken, there's even a Constable hanging opposite the front door by the console table. And she's pleasantly surprised to see the walls painted something other than the usual Jitney or Setting Plaster from Farrow & Ball, the two colours that people use when they think they're not being basic, but they're actually basic as hell. Instead, it's a warm, rich, putty-like colour that exudes a rare luxurious style. Hannah already thinks Tom's hot, but a well-decorated home is her love language. She's in danger of breaking her own very strict rules about relationships with clients: no bone before you sell the home. Much like the manager's position, Bella will have to prise this house from Hannah's cold, dead hands. She will stop at nothing to make sure that smug twat doesn't get it. And what the fuck is she even doing here anyway?

'Tom's just downstairs in the kitchen making coffee,' Bella says, stalking across the herringbone flooring as if she owns the place.

Jealousy rises in Hannah like bile. She feels foolish for her earlier smugness, but she doesn't understand how this could have happened.

'How do you know Tom?' Olivia asks before Hannah even gets the chance to open her mouth.

'It's the funniest story!'

Hannah and Olivia both doubt there's any humour involved.

'I was leaving the gym this morning after spin, looking like an absolute *mess* in my workout gear,' she says, her tone implying she looked anything but. 'Anyway, I had my

Green Goddess smoothie and I wasn't looking where I was going obviously, because I was reading all the lovely comments on my Instagram post about the award shortlisting. As you can imagine, there were literally hundreds of them. I was totally distracted!'

Hannah and Olivia exchange constipated smiles.

'Anyway, I bumped straight into Tom! Poured my Green Goddess all down his T-shirt. I offered to drive him home so he didn't have to walk about with a massive green stain down himself and then when we got here I saw the house and we got to talking and, well . . . now here we are. I was saying I could list this for him no problem! And we were just talking terms. How do you guys know him?'

'He's my husband's best friend,' Olivia says flatly.

At the top of the stairs, both women have thoughts of pushing Bella down them but hold themselves back. Hannah follows behind without violence, but she won't let this continue. There's no way Bella is getting this listing because of a fucking Green Goddess smoothie. Her jaw clenches tighter than ever before. At least there'll be no need for gua sha this week. She can simply tense her way to a snatched jawline.

At the bottom of the stairs, Hannah stops herself from gasping. Sunlight pools in through the kitchen via two open Crittall doors that lead out into the garden, which she can see is stylishly wild and perfectly complemented by the sound of birds tweeting in the trees. In the centre of the room, a huge, marble kitchen island is spotlit by the golden mid-morning sun, and it's not the only thing. Tom pours coffee from a glass pot, the outline of his biceps peaking from under the sleeves of his white T-shirt as he moves. Hannah swallows, her mouth a little dry with thirst. Tom looks up from his coffee, his furrowed brow loosening into a smile as he puts down the glass container onto the island top.

'Here he is! The man himself!' Bella gestures to him as if he's a trophy to be presented.

Of course, in Hannah's mind, he sort of is, well, at least part of a trophy. Him and his house. Either way, if anyone's going to be presenting the trophy, it'll be her.

'Tom! Hannah and Olivia are here!' Bella sweeps to him like lady of the sodding manor.

'So great to see you again, Tom!' Hannah 'accidentally' elbows Bella out of the way.

Olivia considers whether she should be keeping Hannah away from the knife strip on the other side of the kitchen. Out of the corner of her eye, she spots the boiling-water tap, convinced that if Hannah really wanted to she'd easily find a way to weaponize that too.

'Hey! Good to see you again, Hannah.' Tom steps out from behind the island and kisses her briefly on both cheeks. Hannah feels a warmth akin to smugness spreading through her body. She considers the double kiss a win already. Good *can* triumph over evil.

'Hey, Liv.' Tom goes to give her a hug, and kisses her on the cheek.

Hannah notes that Olivia only gets one kiss.

'Heya.' Olivia air kisses him back.

'This is even better than the pictures you showed us last night!' Hannah says, eager to make it clear to Bella that they have been hanging out and talking about the house already – and that photos have been exchanged. She will not take the back foot. 'This is going to be such an easy sale.' Her sale.

She also wants Tom to know that she's a professional. A businesswoman eager to impress him and sell his house. It just so happens that she would also happily ride him like a spin bike.

'I hope you don't mind?' Tom gestures towards Bella. 'We met this morning, and she was very convincing. I figured there's nothing wrong with a bit of healthy competition!'

'I bet she was,' Hannah mutters.

'Oh my god, Tom! You're going to love this.' Bella's girlish giggle echoes around the house as she places a hand on his arm. 'It's the funniest story. We work for the same agency. So you see, it's no competition at all!'

Hannah and Olivia wince again at Bella's repetition of this phrase, her hand still resting on Tom's arm as though staking her claim. Olivia wonders how exactly Bella thinks she knows what Tom's going to 'love' having spent precisely ten seconds with him.

'Well, I mean, for your sake, I should think that you'd want to pick which one of us you work with, just because it might get a bit confusing if you have too many point people.' Hannah chooses her words carefully. She doesn't want to come across as too desperate or too forceful. 'With me and Olivia, though, you would be getting two people, and you already know Olivia very well!'

'Obviously, it's completely your choice,' Bella says, finally removing her hand from Tom's arm where it had lingered for so long that Hannah thinks she may as well have just rubbed her crotch against him. 'Like I said, if speed is of the essence, I can do it quickly. Open house in the next couple of days. I bet we'd have offers the day after.'

'Well, I am looking for a quick sale,' Tom says.

'More hands make light work!' Hannah cuts in as Bella's mouth hangs open, ready to say something.

'We're all very efficient. And we're great team players,' Bella interrupts. 'Amanda only hires the best.'

Hannah knows this is bullshit. None of them are team players, especially not with each other. And Amanda also hired Claire. She watches Bella run her hands through her long, chestnut hair, making doe eyes at Tom.

'God, you may as well get Claire down here too, have the whole agency working on it,' Olivia jokes to try and ease the tension.

'Oh, Claire wouldn't do something this big,' Bella dismisses without thinking. 'This is a little more top level than she usually deals with.'

'Wow, I thought Claire was your best friend?' Hannah whispers.

Hannah and Bella lock eyes. They're in a stalemate, staring-off over what Hannah's identified as a £60,000 marble kitchen island.

'Why don't I show you round before we make decisions?' Tom asks, a hint of fear in his voice.

'Sounds great!' Olivia smiles.

'Obviously, you've already given me my own private tour, Tom, but I'd love to see it again.' Bella smiles at Hannah who almost vomits in her mouth.

'Right, I think maybe we'll start in the garden, then, because I haven't shown you that bit yet,' Tom smiles. 'It's quite a beast! Absolutely huge. It was just an overgrown field when I got here.'

Tom leads them through the Crittall doors into a garden that's been separated into maze-like sections with hedges and paths. A lot of work has clearly gone into the design and it's the perfect day to see it with birds chirping and bees flying around tamed wildflowers. Tom directs them to the left where there's a path winding away from the house through some bushes.

'So along here is something kinda cool. An original feature, I believe. I think I've told you about this before, Olivia,' Tom says, his face a sort of smirk.

'Oh my god! You kept it!' Olivia squeals.

'Kept what?' Hannah asks, torn between hating not being involved and loving that neither is Bella.

'You'll see.' Tom leads the women quite literally down the garden path.

They come out to a small clearing. In the centre gurgles a large white, rustic-looking water fountain. It's a confusing sight at first: a stone statue of a small naked cherub, its mouth open, water spewing out of it in huge quantities at varying intervals. To Hannah it looks like the angel is vomiting.

'OH MY GOD! You got it working as well? This is amazing! He looks like he's having some kind of exorcism!' Olivia chuckles, leaving Hannah and Bella staring in confusion.

'Wow,' Bella exclaims.

'It's the original fountain from when the house was built in the 1800s. Something I believe that in your line of work you'd call an original period feature,' Tom says proudly. 'The pressure's a bit off so it's a little inconsistent, but that adds to the charm I think?'

As he says it, the statue stops, makes a small babbling noise and then proceeds spewing water again with great force.

'Oh, we do love an original period feature,' Hannah nods.

'Anyway,' Tom says, 'I could spend forever in this garden, watching that little guy chucking up over there, but I should show you the rest of the house.'

The women follow as he leads them back towards the house. Once inside, Bella grabs his arm and points to the island.

'I can't wait for you to tell them about the marble, Tom!' Bella brags, clutching his arm again before facing Olivia and Hannah, both gritting their teeth at her words. 'He has the most incredible story about the marble!'

Olivia wonders if she might weaponize the boiling water tap, actually.

Chapter Five

'There's no way he's going with her, not with the way she was manhandling him. It was actually starting to feel a bit #MeToo in there,' Hannah says, sipping on her matcha iced latte as she and Olivia totter down the high street to the office. 'If we hadn't been there, god knows what she would have attempted in front of the spewing cherub.'

'Whereas you definitely weren't drooling over him last night?' Olivia questions.

'Very different,' Hannah says. 'We weren't in a professional setting and it was mutual, don't you think?'

Olivia tries to speak, but is drowned out by pumping bass coming from one of the Sanders' cars as the 'lads' all stand around admiring Ron's new 'deep subwoofers, man'.

In a further assault to their senses, when Hannah and Olivia turn back around, they find themselves face-to-face with Brick, holding a massive A0 canvas with a face on it. It's been distorted with two bacon rashers for eyes, and a slice of ham for a mouth.

Olivia audibly gasps while Hannah blinks, indignant. Brick never wraps his artwork when transporting it.

Hannah can only assume he considers it more important that everyone sees the art rather than it arriving at its destination safely.

''Sup.' He nods to them from under his cap.

'Hey.' The women recoil from the image slightly.

'Just taking this bad boy to the framers. I've sold it to this billionaire art collector. God knows why he wants my self-portrait on his walls.' Brick shrugs as if someone had actually asked him about it and this is his humble answer.

The women tilt their heads and squint at the canvas. Of course it's a self-portrait, Hannah thinks. Who else could it be with the bacon for eyes? Brick's one of those people with too much confidence to ever develop an ounce of self-awareness. No matter what they say at this point he'll only ever hear praise and adoration, so they choose to stay silent.

'Catch you!' He turns and leaves again.

'Isn't the framer's the other way?' Olivia asks.

'He has to do a loop of the town first to make sure everyone's seen it and heard that someone's bought it,' Hannah replies.

'Ah, of course. Good point.' Olivia nods.

'I find it amazing considering all his chat about being anti-capitalist and evil corporations that he'd sell to a billionaire. Or have an estate-agent girlfriend, for that matter,' Hannah says. 'Where does he draw that moral line?'

'Around himself,' Olivia replies, her blonde ponytail bobbing. 'Wonder if Bella's back in the office yet from that important meeting she left Tom's for.'

'Pleeasse, there was no important meeting.' Hannah rolls

her eyes. 'She just wanted him to think she was in demand. Like he'd be lucky to have her or some shit.'

'She's responded to five of Amanda's emails since we left the house. I think you could be right,' Olivia says, eyeing her emails on her phone.

'Oh god, I hate the way she does that,' Olivia says.

'Great idea, Amanda!' the two of them mimic.

'And have you noticed that Claire's started doing it too?' Olivia says, showing her phone to Hannah. 'Look at this one.'

From: Claire@harringtons.co.uk
To: Amanda@harringtons.co.uk
CC: All @ Harringtons
Subject: Re: Re: Toilet paper

Such a good idea, thanks Amanda.
Cx

------------------------Original Message------------------------
From: Bella@harringtons.co.uk
To: Amanda@harringtons.co.uk
CC: All@harringtons
Subject: Re: Toilet paper

Great idea, thanks Amanda.
Bx

------------------------Original Message------------------------
Hi Team,
As we seem to be constantly buying toilet paper, I've

pulled in some influencer contacts and signed us up for one of those subscription services. We're getting these free of charge (look after the pennies and the pounds take care of themselves!) as long as we post about them. So next time you go for a tinkle, just add a little #ad to your feed for me please guys? Thanks so much.

Appreciate you,
Ax

'That's so gross,' Hannah says.

'So needy,' Olivia nods.

They stand in silence for a bit.

'Do you think we should have said something?' Olivia asks. 'Does it look bad now that we haven't?'

Hannah thinks for a bit. 'No, that's fucking ridiculous. It's an email about toilet roll. I don't need Amanda's approval that bad.'

Both women are typing their replies to the email as they push through the glass door to the Harrington's office. Although the door has been left unlocked, when they look up from their phones, neither woman can see anyone in the office.

'Hello?' Hannah asks cautiously.

'Hi!' Claire pops up from underneath Bella's desk to the sound of a drawer slamming shut and goes racing across the room towards her own desk.

There's a forced smile on her face as she lunges at her chair like she's in the middle of a particularly feisty game of musical chairs. The seat's wheels are set in motion by her incredible velocity, and she goes careening across the room before eventually coming to a stop against one of the bouclé sofas. Claire is unable to hide the expression of great alarm on her face as she catches her breath.

'You OK there, Claire?' Olivia asks as she and Hannah stand in the doorway, viewing the spectacle.

'Fine!' Claire says, hanging half off the seat.

She straightens herself up and uses her feet like flippers to wheel herself back across the office at a much more controlled pace. Within seconds she's back behind her desk, still wide-eyed but now staring at the computer screen.

'You sure?' Hannah imitates her wide-eyed stare as she and Olivia take their own seats with care, deeply affected by the cautionary tale they just witnessed.

'Oh yeah, totally fine!' Claire says. 'Coffee, anyone?'

Both women shake their heads and Claire shuffles towards the kitchen like an Olympic race walker, still eager to brush off whatever embarrassment just went on there.

'Where are the others?' Olivia asks.

'Bella's out at an appointment. Amanda's out to lunch.' Claire sets off the coffee machine and forces a casual lean against the Smeg fridge.

Olivia and Hannah exchange a look, annoyed that despite their theories Bella might have had another appointment, after all.

'Bella's had this amazing bit of luck on a massive house. She knocked a smoothie on some really hot guy this morning and then within, like, thirty minutes apparently he was showing her his house. So cool,' Claire says. 'I wish stuff like that would happen to me. I never meet hot guys.'

Hannah and Olivia nod as Claire speaks, their fingers moving at lightspeed across their keys.

> **Olivia**: I feel sorry for Claire. She actually thinks they're friends but the way that Bella was just talking about her at the house was terrible.
> **Hannah**: We should tell her.
> **Olivia**: Oh my god no, it would break her heart. I couldn't bear it. Poor Claire.
> **Olivia**: I'd never talk about you that way.
> **Hannah**: I'd push you into oncoming traffic if you did.
> **Olivia**: We should really try and be nicer to Claire you know. She tries really hard.
> **Hannah**: 😩 It's because she tries so hard that I can't be nice to her though . . . It's like . . . nature or something?

The door to the office springs open and Bella races in with her phone held aloft.

'OH MY GOD YOU GUYS DID YOU GET AN EMAIL FROM TOM TOO?' she shrieks, making Claire jump so that she spills the freshly made coffee all over her desk.

'What's going on?' Claire asks, dabbing at the coffee puddle with a tissue from the box of Kleenex that lives permanently on her desk for when she has her cries – an almost scheduled part of her day.

Hannah's head whips up from her keyboard so fast it

looks like it's just been snapped back onto her body. She scans her inbox, frantically pressing refresh, but nothing comes. Olivia does the same to no avail. She contemplates that he could just be letting Bella down gently first. He's a nice guy, after all. Surely, he'd understand what a slap in the face it would be for her not to get the listing.

'Nothing,' Hannah concedes, trying not to show she's outwardly bothered by this, even though inwardly she wants to scream, cry and throw up.

'Me neither.' Olivia tries to keep her face neutral so as not to alert Bella to the fact that she may have won some kind of contest here.

'Oh my god, I'm almost too scared to open it!' Bella fusses, standing in the centre of the office between the desks. 'I'm sure he'll go with you guys. He knows you, after all.'

The false modesty of it almost pushes Hannah into a rage. An instant message pops into the corner of Olivia's screen just as she contemplates whether she can do a stealth vomit into the wastepaper basket under her desk.

Hannah: You're the only one who got an email you fanny.

'This is so exciting, and I don't even know what's going on!' Claire cheers. 'It feels like when they announce the results in *Britain's Got Talent* or something.'

Hannah: Shut up Claire.
Olivia: Shut up Claire.

Claire hovers excitedly around Bella, desperate to try and make herself part of whatever's going on, completely unaware that there's more hate in this office right now than there was between Coleen Rooney and Rebekah Vardy at the Wagatha Christie trial.

'OK, I'm going in! Good luck, guys! I know that whoever gets it will do an amazing job. We're *all* great agents after all,' Bella taps at her phone with one hand and shoves almost her entire fist in her mouth with the other.

Hannah hopes she chokes on it.

'Oh my god! Wait! You guys went to see the house that Bella went to too?' Claire finally twigs, but everyone ignores her.

'I got it!' Bella squeals, her hand flying to her mouth as Claire leans over to give her a congratulatory hug only to receive an excited punch to the cheek. 'Oh my god!' Abruptly Bella's expression changes, her head tilts to the side as she looks over to Hannah and Olivia. 'Oh no, guys, I'm so sorry.'

Hannah tilts her head too, mirroring Bella. 'Congratulations,' she says, imagining throwing her through the plate-glass window.

'Well done!' Olivia smiles, her eyes shimmering with spite.

The two women's fingers are on their keyboards in a flash, their faces still putting on a good show.

Hannah: I don't understand it, how?
Olivia: She's done something dodgy, must have.
Hannah: I'm going to find out what.

'I can't believe it,' Bella says while Claire hovers around her, still trying to get her to notice that she's there, celebrating the good news.

'Gosh, it feels exciting in here! What have I missed?' Amanda sweeps through the glass door into the Harrington's office.

Her face is a little swollen, her lips plumper than yesterday and she's wearing a set of lululemon workout gear that remains unsweated.

'I just got a new listing!' Bella fan girls over her own work. 'It's this big mansion over by the park! I think it'll be our most expensive yet. I've said that we should start around £10 million.'

'Oh, marvellous! Congratulations, darling!' Amanda looks positively glowing at the prospect of so much money on one of her listings. 'How clever of you! Always my star agent!'

Amanda walks over to Bella's desk, peering over her shoulder at pictures of the house in excitement and Hannah's heart sinks. That should be her with Amanda. She's always prided herself on being good at her job. She'd worked hard to get where she is, and leave the past behind her, just like Amanda has done. The two of them are the same, coming from nothing and building their careers. It used to make Hannah feel special, knowing Amanda was proud of her. But now, watching her with Bella, celebrating the house that should have been hers, Hannah feels like an outsider again.

Lately, it seems like everything's slipping away from her.

Gradually, piece by piece, the life that she's spent years building is starting to fall apart. Her finances are dwindling fast, and she's already had to make cutbacks. She can no longer afford some of the things that she used to be proud of, the symbols that had distanced Hannah from her upbringing. She can feel the walls she built between her and her childhood crumbling and worries she's not far enough away from the teenage girl who was constantly picking up after her drunk mother. The teenage girl who was bullied for how she looked, how she dressed, for being poor. She's terrified of sliding back any further and Tom's house gave her hope that things might pick up again. She can't work out why he hasn't even messaged to apologise or explain himself. Did she imagine their connection? How could she have got it so wrong?

Olivia stares at her phone screen. There's a text from Tom there now, offering an explanation, but it's too little, too late. It doesn't matter what he says. He's embarrassed and betrayed her, and she'll never forgive him for that. Her eyes glaze over as a new email pops up on the right-hand side of her screen.

From: Claire@harringtons.co.uk
To: All @ Harringtons
Subject: Come and give Stress the AXE (LOL)
Hi Team,

While we're all sharing achievements, I'm delighted to let you know that after a bit of negotiation, I've got us a 50% off deal to do company AXE THROWING for our work social this month! Just fill in the doodle poll with your dates and I'll get it all booked in!

I know we're all busy but please don't forget like last time. I think you would have all really loved that felting workshop; it's such a shame that I was the only one who got to experience it.

Just to remind you, I'm off on holiday in a couple of weeks so it'd be good to get this nailed down before I go.

Let's Get Social!

Claire xx

Social and Stationary Manager

Harrington's Estates

Hannah and Olivia delete the email immediately. Now feels like a bad time for the women to be in a room together throwing fucking axes.

Chapter Six

'I actually can't believe you just said that!' Bella blinks at Brick across the open-plan kitchen, wishing – not for the first time – that he would agree to put up some curtains in their huge floor-to-ceiling glass living room. Just so they aren't constantly on display.

'I just think maybe you've taken this all a bit far. You started this because you said you wanted to make a change, take down capitalism and make the housing market more ethical. But what you're doing now feels like something *they* would do. You've gone from despising those women and wanting to teach them a lesson, to becoming one of them,' Brick says. 'I can't remember the last time I heard you even mention the plan to take over and make the agency more ethical and supportive of the poor rather than a disgusting symbol of capitalist greed.'

'Yeah, bit hard to focus on the plan when you lost a huge chunk of our money playing big bollocks with the boys. Money that *I* earned, by the way,' Bella snaps.

'Don't do that,' Brick says, giving her sorrowful puppy-dog eyes. 'You can't tell me that you don't mind me not earning as much money as you and then use it against me like that. It's not fair. Besides, I was doing it for the greater good! So we could double our money and fight the yuppie pigs faster. But it feels like that's not even top of your agenda any more.'

'How dare you! I work hard all day every day to give us this life – you don't seem to hate this capitalist-funded house and its contents, by the way – and you can't stand it, can you? You're just like all the other men when it comes to it. You couldn't stand that I was earning more than you, so you pissed it all up the wall in one moment of arrogance and male pride!' Bella shouts. 'How does that exactly fit in with your 'mission'?'

'This was *for* the mission! I thought I was doing a good thing!' Brick yells back.

'You thought you were doubling our money without doing anything? *You're* the problem – you and your privilege. You can't just expect money to fall in your lap like it did when you were growing up! That's not how life works, Brick. You want to double our money? Make some more art that actually fucking sells,' Bella shouts again.

'My art isn't a fucking commodity!' Brick cries. 'It's so much bigger than the value that our capitalist society places upon it!'

Bella shakes her head, realising that she's never going to win this. There's no way she can make him understand.

'You say I've lost track of what I'm doing it for, but you're not exactly hating the perks. And selling your art to billionaires is hardly morally superior, is it?' Bella sighs.

'At least I'm not trying to take people down for being corrupt while becoming just like them. You've become so ugly,' Brick replies, quieter. 'An eye for an eye is so not zen.'

Brick walks over to the fridge and takes out a can of brightly coloured craft beer. It's expensive, but it's also a large part of his personality. Even while they're struggling financially, he's not been willing to sacrifice it.

'That's my beer,' Bella says. 'If you want to be zen you can get your own.'

'You don't even drink beer.' Brick opens the can, ignoring her.

'I paid for it, so it's mine,' Bella says. 'You may have it now that you've opened it, though.'

'See, this is what I mean! Ugly! You're better than this – deep down you know you are. You've been brainwashed by the people you're trying to take down. You need to remember why you're doing this in the first place. You're only working there to take them down. This obsession, this –' Brick points towards a Cath Kidston box that he'd found earlier, the source of the argument – 'this bitterness and targeted behaviour ... it's not you.'

Bella slams her rose-gold laptop shut, the inspirational quote sticker on its top glaring back at Brick like proof that she's changed. The old Bella would never have stuck something so cringy to her possessions.

'Maybe it's time you left, then. If I'm not who you thought I was, maybe I need someone who accepts me for who I am and appreciates everything I do for them. Clearly that's not you.' Bella slumps down on an Eames recliner.

'Let's see how you get on without my money. Where will you live then? How will you make a living? Because I can tell you now your art alone isn't going to cover all of this.'

Bella gestures at the house around them as Brick slams the can of IPA down on the kitchen counter, his eyes wide with anger and panic at the thought of having to fend for himself.

'Of course I don't want to leave! I love you! But what am I supposed to do? Just sit here and watch you tear people's lives apart? You can stop this. You can stop it all now. Leave the agency, we can go back to how and who we were. You can get another job – work for Oxfam or Greenpeace or something. Extinction Rebellion! Building a future and lives, rather than tearing them apart.'

'They're tearing their own lives apart, Brick. I'm just helping them do it faster. In some ways, what I'm doing is a kindness. Ripping off the plaster,' Bella says. 'Stopping people from having to live a lie.'

'You're not even just going after the person who hurt you any more, though, are you? You're going after all of them.' Brick takes an infuriated swig of beer.

'Yeah, well, they're awful people! They constantly screw each other over! They lie and cheat and do awful things and yet still have all this money and power. Why shouldn't I go after them all?' Bella asks.

'Because everything you're doing is as bad as the things they've done. In fact, some of it's worse.'

'How *dare* you,' Bella shouts, standing abruptly. 'Get out of my house.'

'You're kicking me out for telling the truth?' Brick asks.

'I'm kicking you out because you're not on my side. You've let me down. I can't trust you, so it's over.' Bella stomps over to the wine fridge, grabbing a bottle from it and slamming the door so the glass bottles inside jangle together.

'You're *actually* breaking up with me?' Brick asks, wide-eyed with shock. 'Just like that? Being as heartless with me as you are with everyone else?'

'Yep, I guess so.' Bella takes a slug from the bottle and sits on the sofa cross-legged, staring at him with vacant eyes.

'Oh yeah, and what are you going to tell everyone about that? Why will you say we've broken up?' Brick says. 'You can't break up with me. I'm the only person who really knows you. Not even the people you work with know who you really are. They just know the awful person you became while you were pretending.'

'I'll just say it didn't work out.' Bella shrugs. 'Break-ups happen. Besides, it's none of their business. These people aren't my friends, Brick. They're my work colleagues.'

'What about tomorrow? My art's all over your open house. You *need* me to make that place interesting. And the seller loved it. He said it was "truly unique", remember? How would you explain taking it out now? I'd say that'd be a bad look,' Brick says. 'I *will* be there. With my work.'

'Fine. We do the open house together, but that's it. You've got till the end of the week to find somewhere else to live,' Bella shouts to him across the living room without moving from her spot on the sofa.

'Do you know how much rent is these days? How am

I supposed to afford it? I can't move back in with my parents after what happened with Granny's portrait. It's not my fault they didn't understand that painting her as a giant boob was a societal comment on matriarchs and motherhood,' Brick sulks.

'Not my problem, Caspian,' Bella says. She can see Brick trying hard not to rise to that.

'How do you know I'm not going to tell everyone what you've been up to?' he asks. 'Without you it's not as if I've got anything left to lose?'

'You've benefited from everything I've done so far tooh you know. If you tell people about me, you're incriminating yourself as well,' Bella says.

He stares at her, mouth open in shock at the fact that she could turn on him so spectacularly.

'Maybe I'm wrong. Maybe you haven't changed. Maybe I've never known you at all and you've just been this person all along.' Brick grabs the beer and storms out of the kitchen/living-room space towards the bedroom.

'Fuck you,' Bella shouts after him.

'FUCK *YOU*,' Brick shouts back, slamming the bedroom door.

The walls shake with the force of the slam, and one of Brick's own portraits of Bella comes crashing down from the wall, landing with a thud and smashing all over the floor.

Chapter Seven

Olivia feels the first twinge of pain at her desk, just half an hour after sitting down to start work for the morning. She looks at the beautiful sun streaming through the plate-glass window of Harrington's and does a few deep breaths, telling herself that it's nothing. She tries to ignore it when it comes again, making the same excuses she's used dozens of times now. It could be implantation pains, or something she ate – it doesn't have to be cramps. But it still comes again, harder this time. Like someone's pulling her pelvis in two separate directions. By the time she stands up and walks across the office to the toilet, there's no mistaking it. She passes her colleagues, feeling the fog of disappointment settling around her, their faces turning to distant blurs as they continue responding to emails like normal, oblivious to the crushing pain and disappointment coursing through her.

Locking herself in the cubicle, Olivia tries to tell herself she could be imagining it, but on the toilet, the bloody, rust-coloured streak glares back at her, harsh and unyielding against the bleached white of the toilet paper. She'd hoped this time they'd cracked it; she'd even stopped off on her way to work this morning and got a digital pregnancy test for her and Matt to do tonight when they were home. She wanted to be able to see the word, flashing back at her from the little screen. The joy and positivity of every letter, in bold, making it even more real. But now that won't happen. The image she'd longed for of the two of them huddled in the bathroom, jumping with joy – Matt steadying her, so she didn't jiggle the bean-sized baby – fizzles away.

She stands and flushes the toilet, then washes her hands briskly, as if soaping away the hope, watching it slip down the plughole in the foam.

Shaking her head, Olivia roughly slathers her hands in Aesop hand balm and stares at herself in the mirror, checking for visible signs of what's just happened on her face. It feels impossible that there isn't something more distinctive, more obvious, for people to witness. But the face staring back at her is the same as it's always been. She pushes back her shoulders and leaves the toilet.

Walking through the office, a crackle of numbness settles over her. She takes her seat next to Hannah, but everything feels further away than usual. The sound of Hannah's fingers click against the keyboard, echoing in stereo. She looks around, watching the other women as though removed from the situation. All of them are going about their business. Even Claire's looking dangerously productive, which can only be a bad thing. Then there's Amanda, clearly getting ready to leave the office for something no doubt very important and likely not at all related to the agency. And

Bella, her back straight, fingers grazing the keys with effortless efficiency. The picture of perfection.

Olivia tries to focus on her inbox, debating what she should be replying to first. But each email feels unattainable, just a collection of pointless words. She grabs her phone and texts Matt. At least she can get that disappointment over with.

Olivia: My period came. Not pregnant this month.

She watches the screen, expecting an immediate response to something that's been consuming so much of her thoughts and her life. She knows Matt doesn't feel the failure as keenly, but it's as though he's stopped even dreaming about it with her now. They used to discuss names, or characteristics their children might have. Now he's distracted when she mentions it. She swallows back tears, knowing that there were other reasons she needed the test to be positive this month. She'd hoped it might fix whatever's going on with them. The calls, the silence and secrecy. It felt like a permanent way they could resolve it all, and now she's failed them again.

Guiltily, Olivia remembers the picture she'd taken last night of Matt's phone when it was ringing yet again with that same number. She knows taking it was wrong, and that if she does call the number in the picture that's even worse. It's as bad as saying she doesn't trust him. But part of her thinks if she did it might put an end to her worries, set her mind at ease.

'Guys, seeing as we're all here, does anyone want to

go for lunch today?' Claire's optimistic voice intrudes on Olivia's confused haze, irritating her.

What does Claire have to be so perky about? Olivia's spent the majority of her morning fielding DMs of a sexual nature because of Claire. And now she's suggesting fucking lunch?

'Afraid I've got an appointment,' Amanda says, glancing up from her phone where she's uploading a video about how she maintains balance in her life as a business owner and mother. In other words, ninety seconds of pure lies. 'But you go ahead.'

'I should really go round and see Tom, get the house ready for tonight,' Bella smiles.

Olivia feels her left hand ball into a fist over her keyboard at the cheek of Bella, swanning about like she's more important than the rest of them, planning her open fucking house. She watches Amanda smiling fondly at her and wants to scream that Bella's a snake. A property-stealing little bitch.

'Liv and I have another valuation,' Hannah says hastily.

Olivia stares at the wide-open space on her calendar over lunch and wonders what she's talking about.

Hannah: We'll go for lunch somewhere on our own. I don't want Bella thinking that we're not doing anything while she's flouncing around at the open house.
Olivia: Good plan.
Olivia: I got my period so I could use some comforting carbs.
Hannah: Ahh, sorry dude. Maybe it's just not the right time? It'll happen when you're ready.

Olivia knows she's only trying to help, but Hannah's response irks her even more. She knows it's just something people say, but it *is* the right time. It *IS*.

> **Hannah**: If it helps any, I got my period this morning too! We're synced!
> **Hannah**: Carbs and a hug for lunch, maybe even an afternoon treat too.
> **Olivia**: ♡ Thanks love. What would I do without you? 🫂

Olivia's grateful to Hannah for trying to cheer her up, but she doesn't think carbs are going to cut it. There's no way Hannah can understand what this feels like, although that's not her fault. The more the cramps attack her abdomen, the more her anger grows. It's not just Bella or Claire – currently hitting her keys with irritating performative force, like she wants applause for actually doing some fucking work for a change – it's the injustice of how hard she tries at things – work, a baby – and yet she can never quite get there. Why *can't* she have a baby? People get pregnant accidentally all the time. Why when she's putting so much time, energy and good vibes into it, is it not happening for *her*? And why can't she have a husband who's not behaving weirdly and getting constant mysterious calls he's lying about? She's sick of it. She opens the picture on her phone and switches to the call app, tapping in three digits at a time, flitting between the image and the keypad until her phone makes a suggestion.

'*Maybe: Bella Radcliffe?*'

Olivia feels the world freeze around her, her stomach dropping. Even the cramps briefly cease. She blinks in disbelief, going to Bella's number in her contacts and checking it against the number in the picture, but it's the same. No matter how many times she searches for a difference. It's still Bella's number. Why is Bella repeatedly calling her husband?

The ping of an email hitting Olivia's inbox startles her out of her fog. She stares at the preview for longer than usual, trying to make sense of it. It looks like spam, just a series of letters and numbers in the address and a coaxing subject line of 'Something I thought would be of interest'. The preview text lists an attachment that Olivia knows better than to click so she deletes it and puts it straight into trash just as an instant message appears from Hannah again.

> **Hannah**: Someone's just sent me something you're going to want to see.
> **Olivia**: What is it?
> **Hannah**: I've just forwarded.

Olivia sees an email popping into the corner of her screen with the same subject as the one she's just deleted, except this time because Hannah's the sender she opens it. The email must be the same as the one Olivia discarded because it's not only got the same subject line, it's sent by the same address, with the same attachment too.

From: Thingsyououghttoknow@gmail.com
Subject: Things you ought to know
Begin forwarded message –
From: Bella@harringtons.co.uk
To: Amanda@harringtons.co.uk
Subject: Team structure
Hi Amanda,
Following my brief message to you earlier, this is what I was thinking re: the structure of the team. This would definitely free you up and give you more time to pursue other projects while still maintaining ultimate control of the business. It's a win-win!

Harrington's Manager: Me
Lead Agents: Olivia and Hannah
Office Admin: I wonder if we want to consider recruiting for this role?

With regards to Claire, I do think a restructure provides the opportunity to make her redundant and recruit someone new in that role with a little more experience. It would be great to get someone who fits the Harrington's ethos a little better, but also someone who can do the job.

I've long wanted to take more of a managerial role within the company and I know it's an opportunity I'm more than ready for. I appreciate it might be tricky with Hannah and Olivia having worked here longer than me but I do also think it makes sense especially with them being so close. Promoting one over the other might cause problems.

Separately, I have also heard that Olivia's trying for a baby. You know more than anyone it's hard to keep on top of a family *and* a career. Of course you make it look easy, but I'm sure there's plenty we don't see, a few skeletons under even your exposed original floorboards. While I know you'll always support her career alongside her burgeoning family, it's surely better to put someone in the role who you know will make it their top priority.

I've long admired your work, and the way you've really made yourself such a success and inspiration to so many. Yours is a true triumph-over-adversity story! I really value everything you've taught me and would love the opportunity to show you what I can do. And more than that, as a manager you can consider me a safe pair of hands, a confidant, a paragon of discretion. Someone to help you keep those skeletons hidden.

Let me know your thoughts.

Bx

Olivia: What the fuck?
Hannah: I can't believe she's done this.
Hannah: OMG THE WAY SHE TALKS ABOUT CLAIRE?
Hannah: She's a truly shit friend.

Olivia: I'm pretty sure it's illegal to deny me a promotion because I'm trying for a baby. And how does she even know about that anyway?
Hannah: Do you think Claire's seen it?

The two women peer over their computer screens to where Claire's sitting at her desk typing away. Next to her, Bella's putting her laptop into her Longchamp bag and standing from her desk. Olivia assesses this woman who's been calling her husband endlessly. Is that how she knows Olivia's trying for a baby? Did Matt tell Bella? The thought of the two of them even talking is so disorientating, but the evidence is right there on her phone.

'Right, better go. See you all later at the open house!' Bella walks towards the door with the wave of a woman on a mission.

'Let me know if you need anything,' Claire calls after her. 'I can come over and help you set up if you need?'

Bella shoots back a winning smile. 'Thanks, babe, I'll let you know!'

Hannah: Oh she doesn't know.
Hannah: We should tell her. We could forward the email.
Olivia: I dunno . . . I mean . . . oooh I don't know.
Hannah: Amanda won't go for it will she? Like she'll see through her? She's trying to shaft her friend. That's not women supporting women is it?

Olivia finds it hard to think about Claire right now. She's got her own Bella issue. What could Bella and her husband possibly have to talk about? She tries to remember any situation where she's seen them talking. Any time at a work event or something where the two of them have said more than just a hello, but she's drawing a blank.

> **Hannah**: You're never in my shadow either babe.
> **Hannah**: The cheek of the bitch saying that.

But then, if there was something going on between Matt and Bella, would they be seen talking in public? Surely, they'd avoid it. She's always trusted her husband. It's Matt, after all. She wonders if she should tell Hannah. Maybe she'll be able to help. Tell her she's being stupid.

> **Olivia**: Hey, can I talk to you about something?
> **Hannah**: Who sent it do you think? That email address could be anyone?
> **Hannah**: They've just set it up to send that haven't they?

Olivia can see talking to Hannah about anything other than the email right now is going to be impossible. She's a woman obsessed. To be fair the email is fascinating, for a start, someone needs to have got into the Harrington's email accounts to see it in the first place.

> **Olivia**: Whoever it was had to have been able to hack into either Amanda or Bella's email accounts.

Olivia wouldn't mind hacking into Bella's email account herself right now, and her phone.

Hannah: We know it's not Claire then.
Hannah: A couple from *Married At First Sight* are more likely to reach their ruby wedding anniversary than Claire is to hack something.

The two of them look over at Claire, staring intently at her screen, her tongue poking out in concentration. She can sense them looking at her as she types, so maintains laser focus, tapping away with intent as though she's doing vitally important work.

Truth be told, though, Claire's just opened the desktop version of Instagram, hoping that if she carries on watching the successes of strangers it will somehow translate into some kind of internet osmosis. Besides, if she can be happy for everyone, surely fate or karma or whatever will smile on her and then she'll get everything she wants too?

Claire's computer dings and she can hardly believe her luck, maybe all her manifestations and good vibes are going to amount to something after all. But it's just an email from some weird Gmail address. Probably someone asking to view 'the dildo house' and enquiring whether the owners will be home when they do so. She'll read it in a bit.

She goes back to Instagram where a video of Amanda talking about balance pops up. Claire congratulates herself on her balance right now: she's working and she's manifesting all at the same time. So why isn't she the one selling massive houses like Bella?

Positivity and light. You get what you put out into the universe, Claire recites in her head while smiling vacantly into her computer screen.

Chapter Eight

Passers-by of the £10 million mansion watch as sports cars drive through its gates, disappearing down the long gravel driveway into the fading pink evening light. Dog walkers and joggers crane their necks, trying to see what the sudden spurt of activity at the long-empty estate could be. The town's already buzzing with gossip about the 'For Sale' sign that's just gone up. Hopefully, when pictures of the house's interior go on the website tomorrow, and everyone can see the spectacle for themselves, it'll be the most talked-about house that Harrington's has ever sold. A voyeur's dream. People are finally going to see inside the massive house that has been wondered about by everyone in Wellingden at some point or other.

Hannah and Olivia pull up behind a very expensive Lamborghini in a bafflingly disgusting puce colour with a personalised number plate containing the name 'Ron'. The only surprise really is that it took Ron from Sanders so long to get something so hideous.

Hannah guesses he's only here because Bella just wanted

to rub Sanders' faces in the new listing. It's unlikely any of that lot know a buyer who could afford this place.

'Christ, look at her,' Hannah mutters to Olivia as the two of them step out of the car in fresh summer dresses, wedged heels crunching on the gravel. 'Is she hosting an open house or the next series of *The Traitors*?'

In the doorway, Bella stands between two dramatic flaming torches, wearing a long, dark silk dress, heels and red lipstick, greeting her guests.

'She'd be terrible at *Traitors* if that email's anything to go by. She's far too transparent.' Hannah looks her up and down with disdain.

'She really shouldn't stand so close to naked flames in that dress. It's so cheap it'll go up like a match,' Olivia tuts.

Every time she looks at Bella, Olivia can't help wondering when Bella last spoke to her husband and if it was more recently than her.

'Maybe we'll get lucky and one of those torches will fall on her,' Hannah mutters dryly.

'Hannah . . .' Olivia chastises. 'Remember, we only wish harm that's trifling or transient. No life-changing injuries.'

Olivia steers Hannah away from the flames lest she accidentally nudges one towards Bella in her flammable accoutrement. It's probably for the best that she hasn't told Hannah about the phone calls. It would only fuel her rage from the email. She thought about telling her a few times this afternoon, but somehow it felt like that would make it more real. Confronting.

* * *

Bella spots them straight away, smiles plastered on their faces, saying that they're happy to be there when she knows the only thing they're really looking forward to is judging everything she's done.

'Oh my god! Hi, guys!' Bella launches herself at them both with overzealous cheek kisses, as if they're reunited old friends and not colleagues who spend almost every day together staring daggers at each other across an office. 'I'm so pleased you could make it.'

'Not at all!' Hannah says, a metallic taste growing in her mouth with every false word.

'Any time!' Olivia concurs, still especially stung and confused by Tom's decision to choose Bella over her. Matt's take on the whole thing – that Tom probably wanted to shag Hannah so didn't want to 'muddy the water' only made it worse too.

To Hannah, it feels like she's been dumped for another woman. She's relying purely on her bitterness and spite to power her through this evening without curling up in a corner of this beautiful house and loudly crying her eyes out at its loss. All three women know that Amanda said attendance was compulsory; there was no option but to be here.

'We'll let you get on and welcome the other guests!' Olivia says.

'Bye, guys! Have a great time! There are drinks in the kitchen!' Bella shouts after them as the two women walk side by side, stifling smirks, in through the doorway of the mansion.

Hannah knows that most of the people are just here to be nosy. It's highly unlikely any of them will actually make an offer. Especially at this price. People love to snoop around houses. It was partly her own voyeurism that made her want to be an estate agent in the first place. Walking around lovely houses like this, it's easy to get caught up in a different world. You start to see yourself as part of the elite that can actually afford them and she likes that.

'*Bye, guys! There are drinks in the kitchen and a stick up my ar—!*' Olivia stops imitating, her breath literally taken away by the sight of a small sculpture on the console table underneath the Constable painting. At first and second glance, it looks like a bumhole next to a Diptyque Roses candle.

'Wow . . .' Hannah trails off, as the two of them stand and stare at it, quite literally stopped in their tracks.

'Sorry, I'm not hallucinating, am I? That's actually an arsehole, isn't it?' Olivia whispers.

'I'm assuming it's one of Brick's,' Hannah whispers back. 'Arsehole by arsehole.'

'Oh god, there's a note from the artist next to it.' Olivia points to a small bit of card next to the abomination.

The two women lean in to read it.

This sculpture represents the arse of the world. The roses candle next to it is a visualisation of the way that we're all papering over global warming with luxury and material goods, distracting ourselves from our part in the earth's murder.

Both women stand for a minute, taking it in before

wordlessly heading for the kitchen with the certainty that a lot of alcohol will be needed if they're going to make it through the evening.

Claire watches Hannah and Olivia's arrival in the kitchen, sipping on her third glass of prosecco as she leans against a cabinet. They both look reasonably composed so she's guessing they can't have seen the *Suck My Dick* portrait over the bed in the master suite yet. They don't understand Brick's art – they make fun of it. But then they make fun of everyone.

Claire is trying not to stare too much at Brick, but can't help admiring the way that his Artslut T-shirt clings to him. She takes another sip of her prosecco, realising that she might be on the cusp of dribbling a little bit. Earlier, when Bella told her that she and Brick pretty much broke up last night, Claire really had to work to hide her glee. She knows she needs to bide her time before making a move, but she feels she was born ready to swoop in and mop up Brick's tears.

Draining her glass, she congratulates herself on not going straight over to Hannah and Olivia. They've been downstairs for almost two minutes now and she's stayed put. She's trying to be more aloof, a little cooler. Especially in front of Brick. Even if that means that instead of speaking to anyone, she's been drinking her feelings and already feels a little tiddly.

Her eyes are drawn to the guys from Sanders. They've never really looked at her. They're always too busy trying to get Hannah and Olivia's attention. She feels kind of invisible to them. It figures that they'd be interested in women who are conventionally beautiful, though. They're all quite basic. But she wouldn't mind it if they'd look at her just once. Attention from a basic bro is still better than being completely irrelevant. Sometimes Claire wonders if she's a figment of her own imagination. Until, of course, she does something wrong and then she's suddenly very visible to people, for all the wrong reasons. But that's all going to change. She's going to hoick up her disappointing breasts and become very visible to Brick.

Amanda's car pulls up outside the mansion. Behind its tinted windows, Amanda and her husband, Alastair, sit staring out of opposite windows. They haven't spoken a single word since leaving home. She guesses some people would call it a companionable silence after all their years of marriage. But, at least on her part, it's actually a seething silence. Not that Alastair's noticed. Amanda's barely spoken to him since yesterday morning when she saw a notification on his phone.

'We're here.' She only says it because Alastair has yet to look up from his phone and register anything around him. If it weren't for her, he'd probably spend the whole night in the car staring at the screen without even realising.

'Crikey.' He blinks at the vast house, with the expression of a newborn lamb seeing the world for the first time. 'I've never noticed this place before.'

Leaving the car, Amanda doesn't mention that she's

unsurprised by this revelation. As they walk towards the house, Alastair places a gentle hand on the small of her back, a supportive gesture that's muscle memory more than a sign of affection. To Amanda his fingers feel like bugs, crawling over her skin. She longs to shrug them off and she would if they weren't in public.

'Welcome to the mansion, guys!' Bella's voice pushes into Amanda's consciousness like a steel girder.

'Oh, Bella! Look at all this! You've done such a brilliant job getting all these people together in such a short time.' Amanda plasters on a smile. 'Any interested parties yet?'

'A few have requested a more detailed tour already and we've had plenty of questions, so it's looking hopeful!' Bella exaggerates.

'Brilliant! I know you'll work your magic and get this sold straight away!' The praise furs Amanda's tongue.

'Gosh, isn't this lovely?' Alastair says, shaking Bella's hand. 'You must be the Bella I've heard so much about!'

'And you must be Alastair,' Bella exclaims.

A chill hits Amanda as the two of them lean forward to air kiss. She hates watching people treat her husband as though he's some kind of royalty just because of his position in the media and money. She's built her business and brand from scratch, achieving something without generational wealth or the protection of the patriarchy.

Everything Alastair's achieved in his life was cushioned by his family's position, reputation and class. Marrying Amanda, someone without what his mother called 'proper breeding' was probably the biggest risk he ever took. Even now, years after Alastair's parents' death, she can still feel disapproval from the younger family members about him marrying someone who once used the word 'toilet' instead of 'loo'.

'We'll let you get on! Come inside soon, though, darling. You're the face of this. People will want to talk to you.' Amanda stretches out a smile.

'I will, thanks, Amanda,' Bella says with pride.

As Amanda and her husband head into the hallway, she feels him place his hand round her waist, claiming her, prompting waves of claustrophobia.

'Alastair!' A man in a suit that looks like all the other men in suits Amanda sees her husband talking to shouts over to them.

Amanda smiles vacantly to the acquaintance while scanning the interior. This seller has done a good job. She remembers when she valued this place for the old owner years back. Even then it was a bit of a mess and she'd been relieved they chose not to sell. She can't imagine what it was like by the time the new owner took over. He's certainly got taste, whoever he is. Although ... is that an arsehole on the console table?

Without question, Amanda already knows whose arsehole it is and she wonders, not for the first time today, what the hell Bella's playing at. For now, she's simply going to have to wait until there are fewer people in the hallway then she'll evict the arsehole to somewhere outside, where it might be more fitting. Perhaps the bin. Recycling, obviously.

Chapter Nine

Brick's voice is ear-piercingly loud, an inescapable grenade going off every five seconds in people's faces as he gives sermons on his art to anyone in the kitchen who'll listen. Olivia grabs her and Hannah a second glass of wine to help them ride out the irritation, while Hannah judges him as a prime example of the privately educated cosplaying poverty. She watches him constantly pushing his thick-rimmed spectacles (without prescription lenses) up his nose as he speaks.

'The first body here represents the chemicals and bad gases we put into the world. The second body is the earth. The hand is a representation of us – society, the inhumane race – shovelling shit into the earth every time we don't recycle or when we contribute to the massacre that is fast fashion.' He points to a very questionable acrylic statue that's been placed on the marble countertop.

He pauses for a second, allowing a moment for people to marvel at his intelligence.

'So, is it just a statue of someone being fisted next to the fridge, then?' Olivia whispers to Hannah.

'Yep, seems about the size of it,' Hannah replies, taking another sip of wine and using the glass to hide her twitching lips.

'Fascinating,' another bespectacled man in jeans, loafers and a shirt says as he makes a swift retreat.

Brick immediately starts talking again, explaining the significance of a piece of art on his website that is just the word 'fuck' written in small black ink on a postcard. The woman he's explaining it to looks scared, like she'd never even say the word 'fuck', let alone want it on a postcard in her house.

'It's like fuck man, you know? There's just so much nuance in that one word. You know? It can either be, like, fuck yes! Or fuck. You know? Fuck? Like FUUUUUCCCCKK!' Brick makes passionate hand gestures as the woman looks equally as passionate about getting away from him. 'Fuck. It's just four letters, but they say so much.'

'Hannah?' Hannah's attention is torn from Brick's one-man play by a familiar voice that sends a shiver up her spine.

She freezes in recognition. If she were a weaker woman, she'd drop her wine glass or run away. But she's never been one to shy away from her demons. It's just that this one she was fairly sure she'd never see again. How and why is he here?

Olivia watches with curiosity. Hannah looks sheepish, and it's not an expression she's ever seen on her before, her face paling slightly as though she's seen a ghost.

Hannah turns slowly, taking in the watch, the hair, the

brown eyes, the expensive suit. She's always carried an anxious niggle in the back of her mind that they might bump into each other again one day. But she'd hoped that, if they did, it would be in a situation where she could simply pretend to be someone else and tell him he must be mistaken. This is not that situation, though. Too many people in this room know her. What's he even doing here?

'Hannah! It *is* you!' The man looks happy to see her, a winning smile spreading across his face before his brow lifts in an inquisitive manner. 'How are you? I think last we spoke you were dead.'

Hannah's lips and eyes set, steely, her cheekbones jutting out defiantly in the face of such exposure. She keeps it steady. It's happened. The worst has happened. And it's happened in front of everyone.

'So sorry I couldn't make it to your funeral, it was the same weekend as the Monaco Grand Prix. I guess I didn't miss much, though,' he continues, tilting his head.

She can feel eyes on her, Olivia's, Claire's — when did Claire get here? — the guys from Sanders, even Amanda's from across the room. The only person still talking is Brick, oblivious to anything happening at which he isn't the helm. She can't believe that in a room full of the richest people in the country — a room containing her dream marble island for god's sake — she's going to have to address the most unhinged thing she's ever done. She pulls herself together, trying to think on her feet.

'Um ... what?' Olivia whispers, leaning towards Hannah. 'Who's ... what?'

Hannah focuses on maintaining brazen eye contact with her target.

'John! So lovely to see you! Not sure what you mean about the dead thing? I think I'm probably alive? I'm standing here right in front of you, after all. Unless I've imagined it . . .' She reaches for a wooden spoon from a nearby jar of utensils and whacks herself on the forehead with it. 'Ouch! See! Definitely alive over here! Feeling pain and everything.'

Olivia winces and Hannah reflects that probably smacking herself in the head with a spatula in front of everyone isn't exactly a shining example of sanity, but she doubts things can get much worse anyway. She really hoped she'd take the secret of what happened between her and John to the grave. (Again.)

'I mean, I got a message from your number saying that you'd died,' John says, brow furrowing. 'I can only really go off what . . . well . . . what you yourself apparently told me.'

He smirks at her victoriously. She's trapped. Rumbled. Caught in the lie. She can't believe this is happening. It feels especially unfair because the only reason she'd been driven to faking her own death in the first place was because he was such an irritating, smug shit of a man, who was also somehow as clingy as a limpet. She'd sent the message in a fit of drunken desperation at his constant WhatsApping and inability to take the hint. The next morning, she'd obviously woken up filled with shame and regret, aware that her behaviour was flawed both morally and logistically.

For starters, who texts from their own phone when they're dead?

Olivia's confused. Why does this handsome man with a £25K vintage Rolex on his wrist think Hannah's dead? She tries to place him in the long list of men that Hannah's dated over the last few years, but can't.

'I mean, there was even a date and time for the funeral in the text,' John says, his eyes sparkling with amusement as the boys from Sanders huddle in closer, trying to make sure they catch all the gory details.

That *had* been one of the *most* flawed bits in Hannah's drunken logic. Nevertheless, she found herself casually strolling past the church on the day of her 'funeral' at the time she'd given him, and he wasn't there.

She'd waited a while to see if he would show up, becoming especially nervous when she realised there was another funeral happening at the time. One he would have known wasn't hers, thanks to the flowers on the side of the hearse spelling out 'N A N'. She'd actually been a little offended and hurt when he didn't show. She may not have liked him, but she assumed he liked her enough to at least mourn her properly. It had felt pretty disrespectful, actually. Especially in light of how many blow jobs she'd given him before she 'died'.

'Definitely wasn't me,' Hannah says, loud with shamelessness. He deserves what she's about to do. 'Maybe it was another Hannah you were dating?'

Finally, and savagely, she's confident she's diffused the situation. John's smirk vanishes.

'I'll leave you to get on with looking round the house,' Hannah smiles as people resume their conversations around them. 'It's a beautiful property. Lots of storage space. Ideal for all your baggage.'

She knows she's just being mean to him to save face now. It's a defence mechanism, but it's worked. He walks away.

'Who was that guy?' Olivia whispers to her friend.

'Oh god.' Hannah puts her head briefly into her hands. 'John – I was dating him for a bit last year. I kept trying to end it because he was so clingy do you remember?'

Olivia tries to remember, but sometimes the men Hannah date all kind of blend into one. She has a type – twats with money – and she mostly repeats the same unhealthy cycle with them over and over again.

Hannah shakes her head. 'Anyway, he was clingy as fuck. Just would *not* take the hint. In the end I had to ghost him – quite literally.'

'Poor John,' Olivia giggles.

Sometimes Olivia wonders if her friend even really wants to be in a relationship. She definitely doesn't fall in love easily, self-preservation has her walls so far up that even Olivia had to abseil into her periphery. Even the smallest misdemeanour results in Hannah getting the ick.

'He's absolutely nuts. I'm telling you. Total clinger. Really controlling too, and we can't have two of those in a relationship haha.' Hannah rolls her eyes and takes a gulp of wine.

'It's called *Bella's Vulva* because it's inspired by my muse.' Brick's voice travels across the kitchen. He's trapped a poor unsuspecting man who made the mistake of momentarily leaning next to a bronze sculpture of a vulva, displayed on a plinth-like chopping board, and he's talking at him like it's a punishment.

Hannah and Oliva shudder just as Hannah catches sight of Bella heading towards them.

'Sorry, Hannah, I should have warned you he was coming!' Bella says, complete with fake smile. 'I met him a while ago at an industry thing. When I told him which agency I worked for, your name came up. He seemed surprised. I had no idea why, though, or that him being here would cause a scene. I'm so sorry.' Bella looks up to where Tom is, as if too busy checking on him to really engage in the conversation.

Hannah smiles. She knows it was no accident; she's sure Bella knew exactly what she was doing. The last thing she's going to do is show it's rattled her.

'I think I heard Tom asking where you'd got to,' Hannah says, pointing to where Tom's talking to a newsreader and his wife. 'Better get to it. This is your night, after all.'

'Oh yes, I think those people want to make an offer. This could be the fastest a Harrington's property has ever sold.' Bella smiles again like she's just made a winning chess move, and Hannah downs the last of the glass of wine in her hand.

Claire observes Hannah and Olivia looking furious with Bella across the kitchen. She pours herself a fifth glass of prosecco before making the decision to sidle over there. It takes her a while, weaving through the guests, but she reaches them, triumphant. She leans in towards them, ready to share her trump card and Hannah immediately leans away from her, but she won't be deterred.

'I know a secret,' Claire slurs, taking another swig of prosecco. 'Bella and Brick are ... finished ...'

She slashes across her throat haphazardly as Hannah and Olivia swiftly move from a position of disgusted disinterest to great interest at Claire's news.

'Claire?' Hannah whispers. 'I can't believe I'm asking this. But I'm going to need you to tell us more.'

'Same.' Olivia leans in.

Across the kitchen, Bella stands listening dutifully to the newsreader and his wife discussing if this would be a good area for their children to become teenagers, and whether moving them out of London now, before they reach secondary school, would be wise. She's thrilled by how much she's shaken Hannah. When she'd trawled through Hannah's Instagram, googling everyone who was tagged in her posts, John had interested her the most. He no longer followed Hannah's account and Hannah no longer followed his. One swiftly engineered meet-up taught her why. One down, one to go. Claire was always going to take care of herself, after all.

The women of Harrington's Estates wave the last open house guests off into the darkness, and Amanda watches them retreating up the drive. She finds it's always the ones that aren't going to make the offer who hang on the longest. They linger because they know it'll never be theirs. It doesn't bother her, though, because Bella's in the garden now on the phone to someone who's making an offer. With any luck, the house is as good as sold. She can't deny that it's impressive.

'Thanks so much for all your hard work,' Tom says, closing the front door.

'All Bella,' Claire hiccups slightly.

No one had realised quite how drunk she'd become until the end of the night. Amanda's disappointed in her to say the least. What is she thinking getting so drunk at a professional event? Maybe Bella was right about her.

'Right, Alastair!' Amanda shouts through to the living room, and Alastair emerges. 'We should head off, make sure the kids are playing ball with the babysitter! See you all in the office bright and early tomorrow. I've a feeling we'll be starting the day with a bell ringing!'

'Great house!' Alastair says, shaking Tom's hand before the two of them sweep out of the front door and into their waiting car.

Tom, Olivia and Hannah stand in the hallway closer to the arsehole than Hannah would have liked, with Claire awkwardly hovering beside them.

'Are you sure you don't need help cleaning up?' Hannah asks Tom.

'The caterers have done pretty much everything.' Tom raises his hands in surrender. 'Nothing for me to do.'

'Has anyone seen Bella?' Brick comes up the stairs from the kitchen.

'Thought she was down in the garden?' Claire says. 'Amanda said she was on the phone getting an offer?'

'I was just in the kitchen and couldn't see her out there,' Brick says.

'Maybe she's behind the bushes, in one of the side garden-y bits,' Hannah says, sure there should be a technical name for them that she should know in her line of work. 'There's a lot of different areas down there. Maybe we should all go and take a look?'

Hannah secretly wonders if this could be her chance. She's obviously still fuming and confused about why Tom didn't choose her and Olivia to sell the house. But, if Bella's already sold it anyway, she may as well get something out of tonight. And why not a snog with Tom? Maybe that's *why* Tom didn't choose her, because he fancies her. He's clearly got taste, after all.

'Good shout,' Tom says. 'We can split up and take different areas.'

Hannah couldn't have put it better herself.

Outside, the garden is peaceful aside from the occasional bird tweeting or rustling of leaves. The group stands directly in the middle, a spot marked by a large stone sundial with five paths leading off it to separate sections of the garden. Moonlight bounces off the bushes that line each path, adding to its maze-like quality.

'I'll take the first on the right,' Olivia says.

'I'll head straight up the middle towards the shed,' Hannah says.

'I'll come to the right with you, Olivia,' Tom says. 'It can get a bit dark around there. I haven't got the lights working in that part of the garden yet.'

Hannah feels herself deflate. She'd been sure that he'd go with her, as eager as she was to have a bit of time alone, in the darkness. She'd thought the shed might hold some kind of romance for her, but maybe all it would hold was a rusty old lawnmower, after all.

'I'll go to the left,' Claire says, staring at Brick.

'I'll figure out which area of the garden no one's covering,' Brick says, like it's completely confused him. 'Maybe I'll wait here in case she comes back. Oooh, or maybe if I whistle, it'll attract her attention.'

The group stare at him for a second, wondering if he's lost a girlfriend or a dog. Hannah would love to know what Tom makes of Brick. She's pretty sure they'd have similar views on him.

'OK, meet back here in ten if we don't find anything,' Tom says.

'Plan,' Hannah says, loving Tom even more for taking charge.

Olivia and Tom head into the darkness of the right-hand side of the garden. He was right, the lights in this area aren't working so she's glad of his company even if she's still cross with him about the listing. The silence between them almost seems louder in the darkness. She wonders if she should just come out and ask why he did it. But he starts talking before she has the chance.

'Livvy, I just wanted to exp—' Tom's cut off by a piercing scream from the other side of the garden, slicing through the night.

'That's Claire.' Olivia squints into the darkness.

The two of them exchange a glance briefly before running towards the noise, their feet pounding against the stepping stones. Olivia's dress catches on a box hedge, the silk ripping as they reach the small part of the garden that Tom had taken them to the other day.

'Claire?' Olivia asks.

Claire is rocking and keening on the ground, crouched over the up-lit fountain with the small Victorian puking cherub that had caused so much amusement. She turns to them, her face pale, and raises a shaking hand to one of the lights around the fountain, a wet, red sheen visible on her palm.

'What the—?' Tom starts.

There's a gurgle from somewhere deep within the cherub as Claire steps back to reveal Bella, inelegantly tipped in the fountain, her calves and feet flopped over the edge, a bloody streak across her head. There's a gushing sound as the cherub expels water onto Bella's prone body.

Olivia lurches forward, hauling Bella's body out of the fountain. She'd thought she might try CPR, but as she frantically searches for a pulse she starts to realise there's no point. She's already dead.

'What's going on?' Hannah shouts, arriving behind them.

'It's Bella,' Claire whispers, sobbing into the darkness as Brick arrives, charging past them all.

He pushes Olivia away with an animalistic scream, scooping Bella into his arms, and shaking her. But her body stays limp in his arms.

'FFFFFFFUUUUUUUUUUUUUUUUUCK!' he screams.

Chapter Ten

The women sit around the kitchen island, shivering despite the summer night, as police and paramedics go in and out of the back doors. They've barely said a word since coming inside apart from gratefully accepting glasses of whiskey from Tom for the shock.

Hannah takes a sip from a crystal-cut tumbler and stares out of the window. She watches as a uniformed officer pulls police tape across the garden, cordoning it off.

'It can't be real,' Claire sniffs next to her, her eyes red and puffy.

'What happened? How?' Olivia asks no one in particular.

'Is there any way she could still be alive?' Hannah asks, surprised to find the words catching in the back of her throat.

'I'm afraid not,' a detective in dark suit trousers replies, emerging from the garden, his shirt untucked and tie loosened, hair messy as though he's just been dragged out of bed. Next to him, a uniformed police officer gives them all a sympathetic look. 'I'm Detective Inspector Clive Knight. This is my colleague Police Constable Croft. We're going to need to take some statements from you all covering the time before and after the event.'

The women sit silently staring at him, none of them able to offer coherent sentences. There's a commotion across the kitchen as Amanda comes racing in.

'I came back as soon as Hannah messaged!' she cries to them.

Her face is blotchy, like she's already been crying, and there's a wild, panicked look to her that none of the other women have seen before. She's usually entirely unflappable.

'Are the rest of you OK?' She moves over to Claire first, embracing her in a way that makes her cry harder, a cashmere blanket falling from round her shoulders.

Eventually extracting herself from Claire's tears, Amanda moves over to Hannah and Olivia, enveloping them both in a hug that Hannah barely feels.

'Where's poor Brick?' she asks.

'Upstairs with the officers,' DI Knight says. 'He's in a bit of a bad way, I'm afraid.'

On cue, they all hear Brick screaming four-letter obscenities once more from upstairs, making the detective wince.

Amanda notices the detective, a golfing friend of her husband's. 'Oh, Clive, sorry, I didn't see you there. What do you need us to do?'

'I was just explaining to the ladies here that we'll need to talk to them all one by one to take statements,' DI Knight says, puffing his chest out slightly with importance.

'Do you need somewhere to talk?' Tom asks. 'I can show you to my study if that would help?'

'Great, thank you,' DI Knight replies.

'I'll come up with you,' Amanda says. 'I feel I should probably speak to Brick.'

The two men walk off up the stairs with Amanda and PC Croft. Hannah, Olivia and Claire find themselves alone, staring numbly out into the garden at all the strangers swarming around with jobs to do.

'What was she even doing out there?' Olivia asks. 'I just assumed she was in the house somewhere like the rest of us.'

'She said someone wanted to make an offer on the house, so she went outside to take the call. That was the last I saw her,' Hannah says.

Bella's dead and yet still she feels a glimmer of jealousy about the house and the fact that she got an offer on something so expensive, so quickly.

'That was the last I saw of her too,' Claire says.

The women continue to stare into the garden, silently sipping their whiskey. Surprisingly, it's Hannah who reaches out first, taking Olivia's hand and giving it a squeeze, prompting Olivia to do the same to Claire. Claire, Hannah and Olivia all look to the gaping empty space on Claire's left-hand side where Bella would have been. Even Hannah can't help but feel a tear run down her cheek. Despite petty resentments, and jealousies, Bella was part of their team. They may not have necessarily liked each other, but, by default, whether they liked it or not, they were a sort of unwanted family. Now one of them was gone without any of them even getting the chance to say goodbye.

Chapter Eleven

Hannah's scrolling on her phone in bed, reading the two articles that have already been posted about Bella's death, when the sound of loud, thumping music shakes her paper-thin walls. Exhausted after very little sleep, Hannah accidentally drops her phone onto her face in surprise. Since moving into the property guardianship – very reluctantly – ten weeks ago, Hannah has spent very little time here. But, thanks to Amanda closing the office until Monday as a mark of respect for Bella, she's experiencing its daytime delights for the first time.

She rolls over and shoves her duvet over her head, the faint smell of weed already drifting under the door before eight am. It's a wonder no one's rumbled her secret, with that scent constantly in the air. She's had to keep all her shoes, bags and clothes in tightly closed suitcases, only bringing them out and steaming them with rose water right before leaving for work in the morning. Even when one of her property-guardian neighbours isn't smoking weed, the smell of mildew is everywhere. She can't risk anyone finding out she lives here now; she hasn't even told Olivia. She's too ashamed about letting things get this bad. Besides, who would want to buy a house from someone who couldn't afford their own home?

The plan was always to stay here for a month tops, just so she could get back on top of things again. Keeping up with her lifestyle, her car payments, her rent, her exercise classes and Botox isn't cheap. And she wasn't about to lose face (quite literally) just because Bella was stealing all her commission. Living here means she can save on rent while she gets herself back on track. And, because it's temporary, she doesn't need to tell anyone anyway. But, as the weeks and months wear on, things are starting to look less and less temporary. Now she'll do anything to get out of this situation.

Tented under her duvet, pretending to be literally anywhere else but here, Hannah goes into her emails and reads one of the last ones Bella sent her.

From: Bella@harringtons.co.uk
To: Hannah@harringtons.co.uk
Subject: Libraries
How come you've never told anyone that you're living in the library? I saw you going in there the other day. It's a property guardianship, isn't it? Do you not want people to know?

She hits delete on the entire email chain then texts Olivia. She really needs to get up and out. She can't just lie here all day stewing on things.

Hannah: Yo, what you up to today?
Olivia: Not sure thought I'd just kind of hang out you know? Wanna do something later?
Olivia: Have you heard from Claire by the way? Do you think she's ok?
Hannah: I literally never talk to Claire, why would I hear from her?
Olivia: Ah good point . . . Maybe I'll text her.

Hannah knows what she wants to do today, and she also knows it might be a little insensitive. But she has a plan to get herself out of this dire housing situation and back to her old life.

Hannah: I was thinking. Have you heard from Tom? Maybe we should *all* hang out tonight? It's been such a shock for him. Probably needs people to cheer him up.
Olivia: Ahhh so you do have a heart! Or do you just want to hang out with Tom? 😉
Olivia: Good idea though. We could all head round yours? Drinks on the balcony? Feel like it's been ages since I came to you, I'm always making you come over here.

Hannah feels her throat tighten up. The balcony at her old flat had an incredible view. She was always having people round for drinks. She'd hoped that Olivia hadn't realised they were always hanging out round at hers or at Mabel's these days. She feels panic set in. There's surely only so much longer she can keep this up.

Hannah: Dunno, mine feels a little small for the four of us.
Hannah: How about dinner in the garden at your place? A lovely, chilled evening to help him forget his woes?
Olivia: Sounds good. I'll get Matt to invite him.
Hannah: Sweet. I'll see you later. 7 ok?
Olivia: Sounds great.

She breathes a sigh of relief. Now she just needs to make sure that she's an irresistible proposition for Tom later because he's her key to getting out of here, especially now Bella's gone.

Almost without noticing she's done it; she opens Instagram and the first post on her feed is from Brick. It's one of many progressively unhinged posts he's made about Bella since last night. This one was of the *Bella's Vulva* sculpture he'd been foisting upon people in the kitchen all evening. It was a posed shot of him with it from 'happier times' with the caption 'RIP MY QUEEN, MY MUSE'. Normally Hannah would take the piss, but she can't help feeling a pang of sadness at the sight of the sculpture today. The poor guy is distraught. She really feels for him and even Claire. Despite the fact they're both so fucking annoying.

Rolling out of bed, she gets ready to go to the gym, selecting all black lululemon as a mark of respect. Hannah's gym membership's been such an essential – not once has she needed to use the communal showers in the library where she was sure she'd encounter someone else's pubes. At the gym, they're cleaned every two seconds and have Le

Labo shower gel and Dyson hairdryers. What more does she need?

Olivia swipes the last message from Hannah and continues with the task at hand. At first, she'd only really tentatively started checking pockets of shirts and trousers in the wash basket. She told herself she was doing it because she was putting on a load and Matt might have left things in there that could fuck up the washing machine. But she'd really got stuck into the clothes that Matt had been wearing last night when he got home, checking each pocket over and over again, staring at every loose thread in detail.

The more she tells herself that she's being silly, the more she feels unsettled. Olivia just can't get Bella's smug face from last night out of her head. She'd gone out to the garden to confront her while everyone else was busy sweeping the house for last hangers on.

It had felt to Olivia like Bella had been just waiting for her, thrilled that she was asking why Bella had been calling her husband. She'd revelled in Olivia's anxiety. Telling her that she should ask her husband, and questioning why, if Olivia's marriage was so great, she hadn't just asked him in the first place. Eventually, Olivia stormed away, full of rage, furious that not only was Bella now fucking up her career, but she was fucking up her relationship too. She should have known Bella wouldn't tell her, choosing instead to enjoy the power of knowing something about Olivia's marriage that she didn't. And now Bella's dead, so the only way she'll ever know is if she throws a grenade at her marriage and asks Matt.

The thing was when she'd got home he wasn't in. He'd said he had a work event, but he was still due home hours before her. She'd sat in the house, shaking with shock and confusion, calling and texting him over and over again, trying to find out where he was. But he hadn't picked up. And when he did eventually arrive home – hours later than he said he would be – he was flustered.

Olivia wondered if the answer could be on his clothes and she'd find something that answered her questions so she could lay the whole thing to rest. But even after intense scrutiny they're offering no clues.

She wants to trust her husband again, to feel like she can just ask him about Bella's calls. But the more she stayed awake last night, tossing and turning, going over all the possible reasons for his secrecy, the more Olivia is convinced she can't ask him. Whatever it was that was going on had to be over now Bella was gone. Ripping apart her marriage for a dead woman wasn't worth it. Besides, this is Matt, her dependable husband. The man she's going to spend the rest of her life with, in their perfect house and, one day, with their perfect children. There has to be a normal, harmless explanation for it all, and to let on that she'd been spying and snooping and not trusting him might break them. Is it really worth it now? She tells herself it isn't, but she can't settle, curiosity getting the better of her.

Determined, Olivia puts the clothes back into the washing basket. She leaves the ensuite and goes into the bedroom.

Throwing open the wardrobe doors, she grabs three hangers containing his various suits and chucks them onto the bed. Plonking herself down next to them, she thrusts her fingers into pocket after pocket, reaching around in their silk linings. But all she finds are receipts and loyalty cards for coffees. It's not until the last pocket that her fingers hit against something solid, a smooth plastic card. She's underwhelmed at first, sure it's just one of his credit or debit cards. When she pulls it out, it's a grubby off-white plastic key card with a garish logo on the front, the name Welling Inn printed on the cheap, scratched plastic. The hotel next to the station in town. Not particularly nice or classy, the sort of place where you might catch a glimpse of someone checking in mid-afternoon just for a few hours or someone who needs somewhere very cheap to stay the night last minute. The sheer number of calls from Bella, the way she smirked at Olivia, the superiority in her voice. It all starts to add up.

Olivia's phone beeps with a message from Claire in the Harrington's group chat. She picks it up, feeling dazed. Her mind's racing with the ways Matt might have betrayed her, disorientating her. She'd had other boyfriends in the past who she suspected of cheating, but Matt? She's always been safe with him. There was an unspoken certainty that he'd never be the guy checking into hotels with other women. It's why she married him. She wanted to find something because she needed answers, but now she wishes she could take it all back. Bella's dead. She didn't need to know anything. Why hadn't she just left it alone?

Harrington's Office Chat

Claire: I wonder if we should do some kind of united memorial posts for Bella on Instagram. We could post it on the Harrington's profile and then on all our personal pages. It feels like it might be appropriate.

Amanda: A great idea Claire. Do you want me to draft something for us all and then you can change it as and when you want to?

Claire: Yes please, I just can't think clearly. I think it's all the crying. It's exhausted me.

Amanda: I was also thinking that we could hold a vigil/memorial in the town on Monday night. Once we're back in the office and open again, feels only right for the town to come together and honour Bella's memory.

Claire: Such a great idea. Thank you.

Olivia: Sounds good.

Hannah: Yeah.

Olivia watches another message from Hannah – this time one just for her – popping into the top of her screen. She ignores it, trying to focus and work out what she should do about the key. On the screen, the word 'typing' keeps appearing and disappearing over and over again next to Hannah's name, like a threat. She turns her attention to the key that might ruin her marriage. Could she put it back? Pretend she never saw it? Could she really live with it, though? Knowing that it was there and never mentioning it? Another message appears, but this time it feels like relief to talk to Hannah about something else, something that means less.

Hannah: Absolutely fucking not.
Hannah: I'm not posting about Bella on my Instagram. She hated me.
Olivia: You hated her.
Hannah: We had a mutual hatred. It would actually be disrespectful to the dead for me to post pretending to have liked her, I think.
Olivia: The way your brain works is so . . . unique.
Hannah: I will go to her memorial but I will not post some affected, gushy, bullshit about her on my Instagram. People will know it's crap. She was a sly, underhand prick.

A sly, underhand prick who Olivia worries may have been fucking her husband. She looks around their house, the marks of their life all around her. She's never once questioned her husband's loyalty to her. Never once worried about what he was up to or who was calling him. He was so predictable, dependable. And yes, as Hannah said, maybe a little boring, but you had to take the whole package, didn't you? She got stability with him, or so she'd thought. That Bella's making her question this, and now she's not even here, rankles Olivia. She wonders at a logical reason for the key. Maybe it was for someone at work? Or a surprise for her? Who keeps a hotel room key in their pocket when they're not staying there?

Olivia shakes her head. Bella's dead and still somehow winding her up. Still winning from beyond the grave. It stops now. She's not going to let Bella derail her life any more than she already did when she was alive. She's gone now; Olivia's safe from her. There's nothing else Bella can do that can hurt her marriage or her life.

> **Hannah**: Still, Claire must be pleased that finally someone other than her is posting in that fucking WhatsApp group chat that she started.
> **Olivia**: Go and do a spin class or something, try and get some of that bitchiness out before we're back in the office next week and you have to deal with Claire's grief face to face.
> **Hannah**: Oh god, I hadn't thought of that.

Olivia slides the hotel key back into the pocket of her husband's suit jacket and puts all his clothes on their hangers exactly where they were before. When Matt comes home later, he'll have no idea that Olivia's pulled their life apart and put it all neatly back together again.

Chapter Twelve

Claire sits in the lawn chair looking over the gardens with a reproachful eye. There used to be so many flowers here, roses, chrysanthemums and peonies too, even if it was only for a small part of the year. But since Tony the gardener died, a new, younger gardener's taken over and implemented his own taste for Japanese minimalist gardens. Claire's great-aunt Esme said it was good to have someone breathe young life into the place. But to Claire it feels as though someone's come in and torn up her past from the roots, replacing it all with something stark and meaningless, as if all Claire's childhood memories were nothing. And they're not nothing.

Claire's the only one of the family who really makes the effort with Aunt Esme now. After her parents' divorce when Claire was twelve, the family just shattered, everyone moving far away from here; she doesn't have any happy memories after that. Just her mum throwing things at her dad and her dad telling her mum that she was mental and that it was her fault, that he'd been driven to having an affair by her craziness. This house is the last place she remembers her life having stability as a child or as an adult.

She looks over at Esme, who's fallen asleep again. She's sleeping more lately and seems older to Claire. This is the second time she's dozed off since Claire got here. The first time, Claire had been telling her about Bella's death, so had to repeat the news when Esme woke up.

Claire had cried her way through the story for a second time, while Esme looked on from behind the huge Dior sunglasses that she thinks stop people from realising when she's drifted off to sleep. To be fair, if it weren't for the indelicate snores and the way her mouth hangs open, her head lolling to the side as she slumps in her wheelchair, the glasses would really work.

Claire breathes in the scent of the afternoon summer air, listening as the birdsong juxtaposes with Esme's snores and speckles of golden light glint off her white hair. People are always trying to put Esme under a parasol these days, but she won't have it, saying that by her reckoning she'll be dead soon anyway. So what are they protecting her from? She wants to get her vitamin D while she still can.

Claire stands up quietly, not wanting to wake the old lady. She gently takes the empty teacup and saucer from Esme's lap before heading up the garden path towards the flaking French doors that lead into the cottage's kitchen. Usually, she'd alert Esme's carer that she's asleep, but today she just wants to enjoy her time with the house while both women are preoccupied. She likes to potter around, picturing herself living here one day when Esme's left the house to her. Not that she's willing Esme's death or anything, but Esme did tell her a few years ago that it's in the will: everything goes to her favourite great-niece.

She rinses the two cups in the old Belfast sink, noticing, as she does, a splash of bright red sauce streaked across the glazed terracotta tiles and reaching over to wipe it off. She dries her hands on one of the brown-and-white tea towels Esme's had for as long as Claire can remember, slightly holey but still functional. Like the rest of the house.

Creeping into the hallway, Claire glances through a crack in the living-room door to check that Sarah, Esme's carer, is still distracted. She watches the young woman for a few seconds, sitting with her noise-cancelling headphones on, her face aglow with the filth of *Bridgerton* on the screen in front of her. Claire doesn't understand why the carer watches *Bridgerton* in secret. She'd only have to look at the bookcases – wall-to-wall Jilly Cooper and Mills & Boon – to figure out that Esme's a huge fan.

Claire knows Esme's already watched the whole thing at least twice and one of those times was with her. She made Claire rewind the filthiest parts so that they could rewatch them, claiming that she'd fallen asleep the first time. Sometimes she had, but often she definitely hadn't. It's probably what keeps her going. Esme runs on the yearning, burning and pining of a period romance. Claire had delighted in the old woman's cackles every time one of the suitors or *Bridgerton* boys got their bum out. At one point, Esme started wheezing so hard with her cackles that Claire had been afraid it was the end.

At least she would have died doing what she loved, though. Claire wonders if by next season she'll be watching it alone, on that very same sofa. Great-aunt Esme having passed over to the great romance novel in the sky. Of course she would be sad – you must be, mustn't you? – but she was sure that the house and its massive garden would be of great comfort to her.

Walking through the hallway past the original oak staircase – only slightly defaced by Esme's installation of the aesthetically jarring stairlift – Claire runs her fingers along the William Morris-papered walls, covered in portraits of earls, ladies, viscounts and dames. All jumbled and hung in a haphazard manner, where Esme had tried to fit as many as she possibly could onto the cottage's walls. Claire knows Esme amused herself with the hope that visitors would think them her family members and maybe consider her to be as grand as they were. But most of them had come from junk shops or were simply painted by her. Esme found it all terribly funny to watch people think she in her small-but-perfectly stunning house was aristocratic, declaring it all a load of made-up nonsense anyway. Especially if those people were men who might have underestimated her.

Taking a moment, Claire opens the oak door to Esme's old study. Back in the seventies and eighties, Esme and her two best friends, Fliss and Saff, had run a successful modelling agency from here, representing some of the greats. She was a shrewd businesswoman, as were Fliss and Saff, and it always seemed to Claire that they were just having a great time together.

After selling the agency in 2010, the only thing the three women entertained themselves with these days was excitedly messaging each other when a new sexual predator in the industry was uncovered and taken down. To Esme, Fliss and Saff, it was a sport worthy of the OAP Olympics. The only meetings held in this room now were for secret whiskey drinking, strictly forbidden by Esme's medical team, but also strictly essential to her two partners in crime.

Claire liked to sit in the study and imagine all the great and stunningly beautiful women who'd spent time here. She'd always wanted Esme, Fliss and Saff to consider her a businesswoman just like them. She wanted them to like her. She always wanted people to like her, whether she cared about the person in question or not. She came here often, hanging out with them, running their errands, ferrying them to their busy schedule of funerals ...

Walking across the room, Claire inhales the scent of Chanel No5 and cigarettes, now ingrained in its walls. Golden sunlight pours in through the black-rimmed squares of the leaded windows. She sits on the wooden chair at Esme's desk. A layer of perfume-scented dust covers the green leather top and everything on it, including Esme's golden Montblanc pen and cigar cutter. Esme didn't like cigars herself, but she didn't want men to have anything that she couldn't. She much preferred a Vogue cigarette, and she suspected that actually, if they were to be honest, so did most men. Claire slides open the desk's top drawer. Old packets of cigarettes, Chanel lipsticks in 31 Le Rouge and a gold, inscribed lighter with someone's initials in curly letters sit next to a pile of papers she'd first found a few weeks ago.

Claire takes out the papers. A modest stack of A4, the top page features a picture of the house's exterior with an insulting price tag listed above it. She flicks through the pages, the shiny paper catching the light and creaking under her fingertips. Phrases pop out at her like they did the first time: 'in need of modernisation', 'good transport links', 'close to schools'. Her neon manicured nails flick through the pages for one last time before she closes the brochure. She unclips the Harrington's Estates business card from the front page, staring at the name across its white front, the betrayal still as fresh as when she'd first found it.

Papers in hand, Claire walks over to the fireplace, being sure to take the golden lighter with her. At the mantelpiece, she places the A4 papers in the grate, flicking the lighter open and touching its orange flame to the corners of the pages. It goes up in seconds and she stands watching as the image of the house distorts and crinkles. Still clutching the card in her hand, she takes one last look at it before tossing that onto the flames too. Claire stands back, watching as the paper turns to ash, the flames licking around the name on the card: Bella Radcliffe.

Chapter Thirteen

'Babe!' Matt calls into the kitchen from the garden. 'Could you bring out some tongs? I forgot!'

'No worries!' Olivia shouts back, throwing down her knife onto the marble counter and wiping her hands to go and grab the tongs for him, because, surely, he can't stop what he's doing and just come back in and get them himself.

She walks out of the large glass doors into the garden and heads round the corner to where they've set up a barbecue and L-shaped sofa area.

'So what are you going to do about selling?' Matt asks, distractedly sipping a beer and staring at the barbecue. 'Surely it's going to have an impact?'

On the sofa, Tom and Hannah appear to have settled themselves, waiting for dinner to be served like children while Olivia and Matt do all the work. The way Hannah's twirling her hair and touching Tom's arm in a giggly manner suggests to Olivia that she's going all in. And she didn't listen to Olivia's word of warning about Tom being a player. Of course, Tom doesn't seem like he hates it at all. But she worries about Hannah in this scenario.

'Matt!' Olivia says. 'She's literally *just* died.'

'Savage, Matt.' Hannah nods earnestly.

Matt shrugs, sheepish, as Olivia passes him the tongs. He starts poking at the warming coals, oblivious to how much his wife's keeping in right now. She made the decision to put everything behind her and not to mention anything to him. But the moment he came back she could barely stand to look at him. His presence just seems to make her angry. She can only hope it passes.

'Too soon, Matt,' Tom says. 'Besides, I can't exactly just throw it up for sale straight away now, can I?'

'When *can* you sell a house after a death?' Matt asks, shoving round, bloody burgers onto the barbecue's grill.

Olivia watches him. If he was having an affair with Bella, he seems awfully cavalier about her death. Surely this is proof that he wasn't. She tells herself that this is enough to put it out of her mind. But she knows it's not.

'You can sell as soon as the coroner's finished their report,' Hannah says, matter-of-fact.

'Surely that's got to be straightforward for this, though?' Matt asks. 'They think she fell into the fountain and hit her head, right?'

Olivia can't stop staring at her husband. Not a tiny shimmer that he was receiving up to ten calls from this woman a day is visible.

'That's what the police were saying last night,' Tom says. 'They seemed to think it was just an accident. That she'd drunk too much, and taken an unlucky tumble.'

'Wow,' Hannah says, taking the word right out of Olivia's

mouth. 'It's so random ... like, it could have happened to any one of us ...'

Her voice cracks slightly and Olivia refreshes her wine from the bottle of Miraval on the table.

'You OK?' Olivia puts the bottle back down, putting a reassuring hand on Hannah's shoulder.

'Yeah, fine,' Hannah says, blinking away her surprising urge to cry.

Hannah hadn't expected to feel as emotional about Bella as she had today. She keeps telling herself it's just the shock, but there've been a few times now where she's thought of Bella, dead, just like that, no longer around to plague her existence, and she's felt herself start to well up. Tom touches her arm gently and her thoughts immediately turn to excitement. She's pretty sure he fancies her and she knows what Olivia said about him being a fuckboy, but he's never met a woman like Hannah before.

'Really makes you think about how short life is,' Olivia mutters, taking a long and inappropriate glug of the glass of Miraval in her hand. She already feels pissed; she wouldn't normally drink this much. It feels like the only way to try to counteract the weirdness of the past twenty-four hours. It's not just Bella that's gone – normality seems to have been completely shattered too.

'I guess my hands are tied somewhat on that until the coroner's report is done,' Tom says. 'But it feels a little crass to be annoyed by someone's death just because it fucks with my plans.'

There's a moment of silence between them all as they

deliberate over this, the profoundness of how short life can be and how easily it can all be taken away.

'But will you still get the same price?' Matt asks, gesturing towards Tom with his tongs.

Olivia can't believe he's still pressing this.

'Should be fine,' Hannah says. 'You don't need to tell the buyer about accidental deaths. You only legally need to declare murders. Obviously, if that was the case, you'd be looking at slashing the price by millions in your case. Fortunately, it sounds like that's not something you need to worry about. Selling is going to be harder though, obviously it'll be emotionally hard for whoever takes over . . .'

Olivia eyes Hannah as she speaks. She knows exactly where she's going here. She thinks she's being smart, but Olivia can see right through her and she can't believe it.

'But I'm happy to take over in Bella's absence, when you're ready to sell, of course,' Hannah says.

'Hannah! She's not absent . . . she's dead, babe . . .' Olivia says, shocked at her friend's candour. A minute ago, she was almost crying – now she's leaping right into Bella's dead shoes. She knows Hannah's driven, but shouldn't there at least be *some* mourning period?

'I know!' Hannah says. 'And it's going to be hard whoever does it. So I'm just taking it off people's plates! I'm trying to help!' Hannah throws her hands up. 'Tom still needs to sell and I know it's going to bring a lot of stuff up for people so I'm saying I can handle it. And I'll do Bella's memory justice.'

Olivia's unconvinced. Hannah's never really displayed

much selflessness in their time as friends. She tries to think the best of her, but can't help wondering if this is just a way for Hannah to get the listing she desperately wanted. And – Olivia notices – cutting her out as a co-lister at the same time.

'Are you sure?' Tom asks. 'I know it'll be emotional.'

Olivia narrows her eyes in her friend's direction, but Hannah doesn't notice.

'Definitely.' Hannah puts on a brave smile.

'Stick with our Hannah,' Matt says, pointing at her with his tongs. 'She knows what she's doing on this one.'

Olivia remembers Bella's email. Maybe she was right. Olivia was in Hannah's shadow and Hannah didn't even care. It's as though Bella predicted this very moment.

'I'd better go and finish the salads,' Olivia says, walking away.

'Do you need any help?' Hannah asks.

'Nope! You can't chop a salad for shit anyway, babe! You leave the chunks too big!' Olivia shouts back.

'It's true,' Hannah giggles. 'But Olivia does have very exacting salad chopping rules.'

Olivia listens to them all discussing her very precise salad skills as she walks back into the kitchen, shaking her head.

At the counter, Olivia cuts tomatoes roughly, hacking into them with drunken anger. She pounds at the chopping board with an unusual inaccuracy, bringing the knife down on the tip of her finger. Blood spurts from the cut immediately.

'Ow!' She drops the knife and sticks the stinging finger

into her mouth not wanting to spray blood all over their white shaker-style kitchen.

Now even more annoyed, Olivia walks over to the enamel butler sink, sucking at the nick like a vampire, and turns on the brass tap. She sticks her finger under the stream, feeling a jolt of pain as cold water rushes into the wound. Luckily, the knife hadn't been sharp enough to slice too cleanly through her flesh and, despite the bloody water, it's just a superficial wound. She stands for a moment letting the water wash over her fingers, a surprising calmness engulfing her as she stares at her plaster-coloured walls, remembering that, whatever else is going on, she has this house. This house is hers. This life is hers. Bella is gone. She can't touch it.

'You OK?' Tom's voice startles her. She turns off the tap. 'Matt said I could come and grab another wine.'

'Of course.' Olivia nods to the fridge, drying her hands and noticing that the cut has almost stopped bleeding – it's actually only small. It's always the tiniest cuts that hurt the most, she finds.

'Top up?' Tom asks, standing at the fridge.

'Yes, please.' Olivia downs the rest of her wine and leans against the marble countertop. 'You and Hannah seem to be getting on well.'

'She's nice,' Tom says, his tone non-committal in a way she's heard when he talks about other women.

'She's selling your house for you now, then?' Olivia asks, eyebrow raised in question, although she dare not look directly at him.

Tom closes the fridge, trying to make sheepish, apologetic eye contact, and walks towards her with the wine bottle. He places the bottle down on the counter next to her and her empty glass and tries to catch her eye, despite her best attempts to look anywhere but him.

'She asked. I said yes,' Tom says.

'Fair enough.' Olivia shrugs.

He leans closer to her, picking up the bottle again, his arm brushing against hers as he reaches for it.

'Problem?' he asks, moving closer towards her, his head in the space between her head and shoulder as he pours her more wine.

'Not at all,' Olivia whispers, her lips close to his cheek.

She knows she should move, but the warmth of him so close to her is comforting. There's silence aside from the glugging noise of the liquid hitting the glass and her shallow breaths, close to his ear. He stops pouring and moves to put the bottle on the counter, but stops short, resting it against the bare skin of her upper arm. She gasps as the condensation tickles against her skin.

'You seem hot,' he whispers, his breath on her cheek.

Olivia glances down at the glass pressing against her flesh with an aching chill. When she looks up again, her eyes meet his. She wants to reach up and graze his stubble with her fingertips. But Matt's just outside – she can hear him laughing at Hannah's jokes.

'I should go,' Tom whispers, but he doesn't move. His face stays just millimetres from hers.

Her mind goes back to the hotel room key. How many

times has her husband slept with Bella while she tried to bury her own feelings? She reaches up to his face, her fingers lightly brushing his cheek.

'You made a choice. You chose him,' Tom says, the lashes of his brown eyes fluttering against her fingers as he looks down at her.

'I did what I thought I should,' Olivia replies. 'Things change.'

Condensation starts to drip from the bottle still pressed into her upper arm. With his other hand, Tom runs a finger slowly along the wet lines on her skin. She watches the clear liquid sliding from her, down onto him. He parts his lips as if to speak, but instead he leans down, pushing the cold glass harder against her skin so it stings. His hair falls against the stickiness of her cheek. She feels almost angry with want as he leans further down.

She feels his lips gently kissing her bare shoulder, grazing her collarbone, softly biting her neck. He lingers at her jaw, pausing and pulling away. But she leans forward, their lips meeting, his fingers sliding through her hair, the strands of blonde twisting and knotting around them as he grabs at it, yanking her closer to him, the two of them inhaling each other like oxygen they've deprived each other of for months. He slams her against the counter, grabbing for her waist while his other hand loses grip of the bottle. It slides down her body before smashing to the floor, breaking the two of them apart. There's a second of calm before realisation hits.

Breathless, Olivia turns away from him, back to the counter and her salad.

'I should take this outside. Before Matt wonders where we've got to,' she says.

'Please don't,' Tom says, trying to catch her arm.

Olivia stares down at the salad in her shaking hand. She can't do this again. She just got carried away with everything that happened. Fell into bad habits. She knows he can't give her what she wants; Tom knows the moment's passed.

'I'll clean up in here,' he says, gesturing to the floor. 'I made the mess, after all.'

'We both did,' Olivia says abruptly, grabbing a platter of mozzarella-and-tomato salad and heading for the door.

Hannah knows what's coming when Matt sits next to her and she really wishes he'd stop it. The more he talks about his situation, the more she has to confront the fact that she's still keeping a secret from her friend. She doesn't know how many ways she can tell him to just tell Olivia the truth and leave her out of it. She wishes more than anything that she'd never gone on a Tinder date with Dan, the guy who'd told her about it in the first place. She will never again swipe right on a man who lists his occupation as 'finance bro'.

'Look, I know you don't want to talk about it, but I just wanted to say thank you for not telling Olivia,' Matt says.

'ARGH, Matt, I said stop it. Stop talking to me about it. I didn't ask to find out. If I could go back in time, I wouldn't have gone on that date, for multiple reasons, but the main one being that I wish he hadn't told me any of this. Please don't make it worse by repeatedly mentioning it,' Hannah hisses at him. 'I'm trying to pretend I don't know because it's literally the only way I can reason away not telling Olivia at this point.'

'I still maintain that he shouldn't have been sharing that information with someone he'd only just met,' Matt says. 'He's a total weasel. I can't believe you went out with him.'

Hannah rolls her eyes, because, yes, he was a weasel and she was never going to see him again anyway – especially because he referred to himself as having 'rizz', but that wasn't what this was about.

'He looked hot and rich in his bio. How was I to know he was a total loser or that he worked with you? And, besides, come *on*, Matt! You can't blame *him*! You're the one in the wrong. Dan didn't know that I knew you! He was just a guy telling his date a story about his work. It just so happened that I figured out it was you from the details. And we wouldn't even be having this conversation now if you'd just told your wife in the first place. I went on that date weeks ago,' Hannah whispers, staring anxiously towards the house. 'Just tell her.'

'I will!' Matt says. 'I just feel like she's really shaken up about Bella. I don't want to add another stressful situation on top of that. Besides, I'm just trying to make things a little better before she finds out. Is that so bad?'

'How?' Hannah shoots back at him. '*How* can you possibly make the situation any better? And this has got nothing to do with Bella. Stop hiding behind that as an excuse, and just man up and tell your wife. I'm not keeping this secret much longer.'

'Mozzarella, tomato and basil salad!' Olivia trills, rounding the corner with a platter of salad in her hand. 'There's a feta-and-olive one in the kitchen too. I think Tom's going to bring that out in a minute.'

Hannah and Matt shift away from each other in a way that would be subtle if not for the fact that Olivia's already watching her husband like a hawk.

'Everything OK?' Olivia asks.

'Yeah, course,' Matt says, going back to flipping the burgers.

Olivia puts the salad down on the glass-topped table next to the sofas as Hannah glugs her wine, trying to hide her anger.

'Feta salad!' Tom follows close behind.

Olivia can't help noticing there isn't a trace of guilt or fluster on his face. He's a seasoned pro, which is the exact reason why she should never have done it.

'Was Hannah telling you about the guy she went on a date with who was a hedge funder too?' Olivia asks.

Hannah chokes on her wine, coughing and spluttering, tears pricking her eyes. Embarrassment sets in as they all look at her.

'I'm so sorry ... I was just ... overcome ... with ...' The tears run down Hannah's face. She knows they're from choking on her wine, but she's going to style this out. 'Poor ... Bella ...'

Tom puts the salad on the table and goes straight to

Hannah on the sofa, putting a comforting arm round her shoulder. The jealousy hits Olivia like a sledgehammer.

'I know what you mean,' Olivia says, finding herself surprisingly genuinely choked up and not for the first time today. 'It's hard to think that she's just gone?'

Matt copies Tom's gesture and puts his arm round Olivia and she tries not to throw him off, her shoulders tensing at his touch. She worries that he can smell Tom on her, sense what she was just up to.

'I didn't like her, but I've never known someone just die like that before? Like, there one minute, gone the next?' Hannah's voice breaks, and she finds herself more genuinely now, fighting back tears. 'It just doesn't seem right, or fair? She was younger than us.' The last bit comes out as a whisper.

Tom pulls her in close to him.

'You cry, have a good cry,' he says, grabbing a napkin from the table and dabbing at her face before pulling her in tightly to him again.

His eyes meet Olivia's as she watches on, jealousy raging while Matt pats her shoulder tentatively. She feels her own tears start to come, but she can't say they're all for Bella.

Chapter Fourteen

Amanda's surprised by Alastair coming from behind and placing his arms round her waist. He brushes her hair back over her shoulder and kisses the bare skin of her neck while she hurriedly locks her phone screen and places it face down on the marble countertop.

'How was your day?' he asks. 'How's everyone doing after last night?'

'It was OK, rather not talk about it. How was your day?' she asks almost as a reflex to keep things normal in front of the kids, while he buries his nose further into her neck.

'Long, boring, frustratingly full of old men,' Alastair says, his words muffling against her skin.

'KIDS! DINNER!' Amanda shouts, brushing him off to put the plates of pasta on the table.

'Where's the nanny?' Alastair asks, taking off his tie and following her over to the table.

'She left early, wasn't feeling well,' Amanda says, wondering why the nanny always calls her when she has to leave early, never him.

Amanda has had a very full-on day, writing posts about

Bella, answering calls from concerned friends. And it's not over yet – she still has a video that she needs to record with the children for a kids' clothing brand, but she couldn't get them to sit still long enough to film it earlier. The last thing she'd needed was the nanny crying off sick this afternoon.

'She had a bloody meee-grain, actually,' six-year-old Rupert states, walking into the kitchen, with his snuffly little voice.

Amanda thinks he might be getting a cold again. If he is, then they definitely need to do the video tonight before he gets all snotty and uncooperative.

'Mum! Rupert's been licking the remote again,' eight-year-old Maisie shouts, racing in behind him.

'Rupert, don't do that, darling,' Amanda says gently. She sets down their plates and goes back into the kitchen to get Alastair's and hers. 'Especially if you've got a bit of a cold coming.'

'I don't!' Rupert protests, but a small snot bubble gathers at his nose to scupper him.

'Boys are gross,' Maisie says, putting her hands on her hips before strutting to the seat that Alastair holds out for her as if they're in a fancy restaurant.

'Madam,' he says, tucking her in.

'Don't worry, I'll get my own,' Rupert sighs, fatigued by life, aged six.

The kids begin to eat, but Rupert is swinging his legs and scooping pasta with his fork a little too gleefully for Amanda's liking. He only does this when he's got a secret, usually one that's about to get his sister in trouble. She's amazed but delighted to have raised two children who are such incredible snitches. He's probably been waiting for this moment, with all of them round the dinner table, to reveal it for maximum impact. On the breakfast bar Alastair's phone vibrates; Amanda doesn't need to see the screen to know what it's a notification for.

Alastair used to be the kind of man who left his phone lying around, with message previews turned on, the font on large so that everyone could see he how important he was, receiving important messages. But over the past few years, as their marriage has progressed, he's had reason to turn off the previews, make the font size smaller and hide the screen from his wife and children's prying eyes.

Amanda catches sight of her reflection in the darkened window and feels rage at her husband. She spends every day of her life trying hard to be good enough, only for him to barely bother.

'Maisie got into trouble today,' Rupert practically sings.

'Dobber!' Maisie mutters.

'What happened?' Alastair asks, taking his seat. Amanda knows he's going to sit at the head of the table, resolving their arguments, then congratulate himself on his cracking parenting before retreating to his study to spend the night staring at his phone.

'She said a swear,' Rupert answers before Maisie gets the chance to reply.

'I didn't!' Maisie says. 'It was a blustremey.'

'A what?' Amanda asks, taking her seat next to Alastair and purposefully not looking at him.

'A blusteamy?' Maisie tries again.

'Blastercine,' Rupert says.

'Blasphemy?' Alastair ventures.

'YES!' Maisie says.

'What did you say?' Amanda asks, half distracted by her anger ramping up another notch while Alastair's phone vibrates again on the counter. The more it buzzes away the more she feels the walls closing in on her.

'I said . . . GoooooooDDA,' Maisie says. 'Because someone was being reallllly annoying.'

'Fair play,' Alastair says.

'Al,' Amanda says, raising her eyebrows. This is not the way they've brought up their children. Fair enough if he wants to behave in a haphazard and careless fashion towards their marriage, but when it starts involving the kids it's not OK. She can tell how easy his childhood was compared to hers by his lax attitude to discipline. She thinks by now the kids can too. He's never had to worry about things not going his way – his family could always pay for the odds to swing in his favour – and it really shows.

'What? Are there not worse crimes? Besides, we don't believe in Goddaaaa so I'd rather my children weren't getting in trouble for "blasphemy". I'll send an email tomorrow.'

'See, told you,' Maisie says, sticking her tongue out at Rupert. 'I knew Daddy would be on my side.'

It's amazing, Amanda thinks, that despite everything that's gone on in the last twenty-four hours the children are completely unaware of it all. Although she's aware the news will have already made it round the parents and will very soon filter through to the children by some kind of careless osmosis and she needs to be ready for that.

'MUM! SHE DID A TONGUE POKE OUT AT ME!' Rupert says.

'OK, maybe let's just eat dinner without any more tongues or fictional religious figures?' Amanda says.

'Can we watch iPads?' Maisie asks.

Amanda had hoped that she would be able to use some of this dinner for content, showing the kids having a messy-and-casual pasta dinner. If they're using iPads, it fucks it right up. She can hardly post a video of them having a great family time with Rupert in the background watching sodding *Is It Cake?* or whatever it is that she keeps catching a glimpse of over his head. She wouldn't mind so much if it were at least educational. But she doesn't think being able to guess correctly whether or not a fucking frying pan is actually cake is going to get him a Pulitzer Prize in later life.

'Actually, I was thinking we could have a bit of family time after dinner,' Amanda says.

Both children screw up their faces at her like she's just suggested two hours of Bible study before bed.

'What?' Amanda asks.

'You want to video us again for your instanet thingy and I do not want it,' Rupert says, his lips pursed in concentration, eyes focused on his iPad.

'Yeah, I've had a hard day at school.' Maisie tilts her head and does a small yawn, rubbing her eyes and looking at her dad.

'Maybe not tonight, hey, Amanda?' Alastair suggests

gently. 'They've worked hard at school – they don't need to be worked into your Instagram career as well. Besides, should you be posting ad content so soon after . . .'

Amanda's eyes narrow and she feels rage building inside her. The children sit silently, speed-eating pasta to get released from the table, both of them sucking at the strands of spaghetti so hard that their eyes widen and they look like small fish. Amanda wonders if having fish would have been a better idea than children.

'I've worked hard too, you know. I work hard every day for this family,' Amanda mutters. 'So sorry for trying to create a future and a name for myself so that I can be an inspiration to the family. Maybe I should be more like you, just wilfully striding around the place, fucking it all up.'

She spears the gooey flesh of a roasted cherry tomato, and it spurts across the table. There's silence aside from the noise of the children inhaling the last of their pasta, then Maisie's fork clatters against her plate shortly followed by Rupert's.

'May I get down now, please?' Maisie asks.

'Of course.' Alastair nods. 'I'll bring some ice cream to you both in a bit.'

They rush out of the room and Amanda wonders if she should be left alone with her husband; she fears she may do something she'll regret.

'Don't take it out on the children,' Alastair says. 'I know you've had a hard day, but we always agreed we'd only do content with them if they were still enjoying it. And it doesn't look as though they are.'

'It's all well and good saying that, but we've signed contracts. There are things we need to deliver,' Amanda sighs.

'Contracts can be broken,' Alastair says.

'Don't you just know it?' Amanda stares at him as his phone vibrates again on the kitchen counter. 'Hadn't you better get that? Some poor woman's probably on the edge of her seat waiting for you to wank over her cleaning the bathroom.'

'Don't be so fucking crass,' Alastair says.

'Me crass?' Amanda asks. 'I'm not the one that gets a boner for bleach and a fucking feather duster.'

'You agreed when we married that you'd make allowances. That there were certain things you wouldn't do and I would be able to go outside the marriage for,' Alastair says.

'I guess I just didn't realise that me refusing to do the housework would involve more than us employing a cleaner once a week,' Amanda tuts. 'It's almost every night these days I sit alone while you watch some stranger scrubbing at a pan with a bit of fucking wire wool. I've seen the bank statements to prove it.'

'You know it's more complex than that!' Alastair shouts.

'Evidently. After all, you never do any of the cleaning in your own fucking house, do you?' Amanda says. 'If I masturbated while putting the dishwasher on of an evening, would that help you remember to unload it in the morning?'

'That's unfair. We employ someone for that,' Alastair says. 'Besides, it's not like I haven't ignored enough of your indiscretions, is it?'

'Oh, here we go, it always comes back to that, doesn't it? Doesn't matter how many times I think we've left it in the past!' Amanda shouts.

'I took a risk with you!' Alastair justifies.

'Now I'm taking one on you!' Amanda hisses back, leaning into his face. 'What do you think would happen if anyone ever found out you get a hard on for Mr Fucking Sheen!'

'You know Mr Sheen doesn't do it for me – you can't give the cleaning products people names. It's not right! Besides that, it's not the products. It's how they're used and who uses them,' Alastair whispers.

'Oh, believe me, I know there has to be a person attached to them. I know only too well,' Amanda says.

'On that,' Alastair says, his voice softening with a tell-tale smidge of humility that rings immediate alarm bells for Amanda. 'I think I might have rather fucked up, darling.'

Chapter Fifteen

'Right!' Tom slaps his thighs and stands up from the sofa where he and Hannah have become cosier as the night's worn on. 'I think I'd better be heading back home.'

Fairy lights dotted around the seating area illuminate Hannah's disappointed face as Matt and Olivia stand too. Three bottles of assorted rosé, several beers and some gin and tonic later, the small impromptu garden party that Olivia never really wanted seems to finally be coming to a close, much to her relief.

She's barely looked at Tom, his closeness with Hannah reminding her exactly why she chose Matt over him. Solid, dependable Matt. She was going to forget whatever happened with Bella and move on with her life. She's not about to let either of them – Bella or Tom – fuck up her life.

'Are you getting a taxi? I'll come with you,' Hannah says, hating herself the moment she realises how needy she sounds.

'Don't you live across the other side of town?' Olivia asks, furrowing her brow in confusion.

'Oh yeah,' Hannah says. Actually, the library is right by

Tom's place, but Olivia doesn't know that; Hannah can't believe she nearly slipped up.

'I think my Uber's outside,' Tom says, frowning at his phone. 'Lovely to see you all! Thanks for a wonderful night!'

Neither Hannah nor Olivia remembers seeing him book an Uber.

Matt slaps him on the back. 'Good to see you, buddy.'

'I'm going inside to the loo anyway, so I'll see you out,' Olivia says. She actually does need the loo. She's not drunkenly trying to spend more time with him. Definitely not. She is resolute.

'Cool,' Tom says, leaning down to kiss Hannah on the cheek.

Olivia spins on her heel and heads towards the house. She needs a wee and it's rude of him to make her wait.

'I'll pop round Monday morning so we can come up with a plan of action,' Hannah says.

'Great,' Tom says, winking. 'Get home safely.'

He follows Olivia through the garden to the kitchen. She can feel him behind her as she tries to make sure it's not obvious by her walk, by the way she moves or speaks, that she secretly wants to spend any fraction of time with this man she possibly can, no matter how hard she tries to tell herself she doesn't.

'We need to talk,' Tom whispers to her once they reach the hallway, grabbing her by the wrist.

She stares at his hand with disapproval, but enjoys every second of his touch, disappointed when he lets her go.

'Why are you doing this? You want me as much as I want

you. I can make it work. I know he'll hate us, but I promise it'll be good. Isn't it better than living a lie?' Tom says.

'What about Hannah? It looked like you'd rather be with her tonight,' Olivia says, avoiding his eyes.

'Is that why you're so cross? Hannah? I was comforting her!' Tom's whisper has more than a hint of exasperation to it.

'I don't trust you,' Olivia says. 'You really think you can give up all the other women and just be with me?'

He looks at her for a second before grabbing her hand again, pulling her towards him. He kisses her softly, his lips barely brushing hers at first. He tastes of gin, wine and the three cigarettes that Matt and him smoked, claiming each time that they'd be their last ones ever. She pushes him off, coming to her senses. Matt could come in at any time.

'I don't know what I can do to show you ... I ...' He stumbles backwards, thinking for a second, reaching into his pocket and pulling out his keys. He slides a brass-coloured key from the ring and presses it into her hand.

'What's this supposed to prove?' Olivia asks, staring down at the key in her palm.

'I'm giving you the key to my house,' Tom says. 'Come any time. You can see for yourself. I don't want anyone else. I want you.'

'I've got a husband,' she says, trying to give the key back to him, but he slinks away, heading for the door. 'I don't want it.'

'I'm not taking it back.' Tom holds his hands up as

though in surrender, whispering to her, 'I'm not taking any of it back. Give me a chance. I can show you.'

'You need to go,' Olivia says.

'Fine.' He opens the door, but hesitates before stepping out. 'I love you. You love me too. This isn't kind to him, you know. You think you're doing the right thing, but you're not.'

Olivia watches Tom head out into the night, closing the door behind him with the key still in her hand. Annoyed with herself, she pushes against the door hard, making sure there's a firm barrier, her in here, in her house with her husband, and him outside. Locked out of her marriage. She pauses for a moment and rests her head against the cool wood.

'Do you think he likes me?' Hannah's voice startles Olivia from the kitchen doorway and she spins round, feeling winded, trying to hide the key in her fist.

'Christ, Hannah, a little warning!' Olivia does a fake laugh. 'How long were you there spying for? You little weirdo.'

'Only just got here. I'm not Claire, I don't lurk about the place like a little sneak.' Hannah turns and walks back into the kitchen with Olivia following. 'Anyway, what do you think? You reckon it's on?'

'I'm not sure, you know,' Olivia says. 'He knows I don't approve of his slutty behaviour so there's no way he'd tell me.'

'Oh, very supportive, thanks!' Hannah says. 'You could just lie and tell me that he thinks I'm hot?'

'I'm just being realistic! I don't want to get your hopes

up,' Olivia says, walking through the kitchen past all the clearing up that she's dreading doing later. Hannah never offers to help. In fact, she's actively unhelpful when Olivia tries to clear up with her still here. These days, Olivia just waits until Hannah's gone so she can get on with it by herself. 'I'm sure he thinks you're hot, though. Obviously. I mean look at you.'

The two women walk towards the back door, Hannah's head getting higher with every step, while Olivia's gets lower.

'MATT? MATTY? MATT? What do you think? Do you think Tom likes me?' Hannah shrieks into the garden as they head out to join him.

'God, yeah!' Matt says, slumped on the sofa. 'He was all over you!'

'See!' Hannah tilts her head towards Olivia, beaming.

Matt smiles at them both, pleased to have clearly said the right thing. He pops a cigarette in his mouth and lights it, leaning back to exhale the sweet first drag.

'Babe,' Olivia says. 'Cigarettes affect your sperm, you know?'

'On that note ...' Hannah says. 'Lovely night! I'm off! Bye, guys!'

She hugs her hosts and leaves, walking out into the night on a journey that's far shorter than Olivia realises.

Chapter Sixteen

No one's sure exactly when it happened, but at some point over the weekend while the office was closed Amanda's put a larger-than-life black-and-white photograph of Bella in the window. Passers-by have been using the picture like some kind of shrine, leaving flowers on the pavement in front of it, so that by the time she reaches the office this morning, Hannah has to wade through a sea of tributes in honour of her arch-nemesis. Despite herself, she feels choked up by it. She thinks it might be the sheer number of people who wanted to commemorate this one person and wonders whether something similar would happen if she died.

'She wasn't sodding Princess Diana,' Hannah mutters, waving humbly from her seat as another well-wisher lays down flowers.

'People grieve in different ways,' Olivia says, knowing that deep down Hannah's sad too and just as shocked as everyone else. 'When someone just dies like that, it's hard to process. It's OK not to know how to deal with it.'

Hannah's surprised to feel a wave of emotion again and aggressively pushes it back down. If Amanda's brand is being the perfect mother, wife and businesswoman, Hannah's is being hardnosed and able to cope in a crisis; pulling herself together when everyone else has fallen to pieces.

No one knows the things she's had to overcome to get to this position in her life, not even Olivia. She'd rather imprison her emotions to keep it that way. When her mum died ten years ago, she'd been her only family. She was devastated, but she pulled herself together then and she's not about to fall apart over someone she didn't even like now. The other night was as much of a slip up as she'll allow in public. Besides, it would appear other people are falling apart enough for everyone.

Hannah points to the window. 'Oh good god. What *is* she wearing?'

'Is that Claire?' Olivia spins round in her seat and leans forward, squinting.

They watch as their colleague struts down the high street in a black dress, black sunglasses – which Hannah thinks might actually be Prada, disturbingly – and what looks like a dyed black net curtain draped over her head and tied round her chin. She keeps turning and looking over her shoulder, as if she's being followed or watched, her top lip pushed out in a pout each time she does so.

'She looks like a mafia widow. Oh god, she's going to milk this, isn't she?' Hannah sighs. Today was going to be weird enough without Claire showing up to work in costume.

'Hannah! I can't keep reminding you, her best friend just *died!*' Olivia chastises.

'Yeah, I know. But,' Hannah says, gesturing to Claire through the window. 'I mean ... Come on.'

Olivia's just relieved to be in the office this morning after a weekend flitting between guilt and anger at Matt, but never mentioning – not even once – the hotel keycard she found in his pocket. She's glad of the distraction of Claire's outfit.

After creeping along the high street as though she were taking part in some kind of funereal mime act, Claire bursts through the door, shutting it behind her dramatically like she's being pursued.

'Oh my god!' she gasps, pressing herself against the closed glass door.

'You all right, Claire?' Hannah asks.

'It's wild out there.' Claire keeps her sunglasses on even as she walks across the office. Able to get a better look, Hannah can confirm they are Prada. But they could still be fakes. After all, how would Claire afford Prada sunglasses? To Hannah's knowledge, she's not made commission since 2023. Hannah can't even afford Prada sunglasses right now. She knows she's doing badly, but she's surely got to be doing better than Claire. Hasn't she?

'It is?' Olivia peers out of the window, trying to see the imaginary wildlife.

'Didn't you guys get it as well? Everyone staring and whispering as you walked down the street?' Claire asks. 'Like we're the death agency or something.'

Hannah goes to stand at the window with Olivia, the two of them baffled by Claire's account of what looks to them to simply be an empty street. They've both been down the high street over the weekend too, and although there were a few people standing outside Harrington's looking sad and gossiping – adding to the flower pile – things certainly don't feel quite as intense as Claire seems to think they are.

'No, but then I'm not dressed like my husband's just been killed by a rival faction,' Hannah mutters. Olivia takes in Hannah's outfit for the first time: a black skintight Reformation dress and sky-high Louboutins. Not a mafia widow, no, Olivia thinks, more of a grief vixen. She hasn't forgotten that Hannah's got an appointment at Tom's this morning. Hannah won't have chosen an outfit that clings to her perfect figure by accident.

Olivia has tried so hard to keep Tom off her mind this weekend. But it feels impossible. Things were especially bad when Matt tried to initiate sex on Saturday night, only for her to picture both Bella and Tom in turn until she simply pretended to have a headache and dodged him.

'Who was looking?' Olivia asks Claire, genuinely curious.

The only person Hannah's felt watched by is Bella; every single shop on the high street's put up a similar black-and-white image of her in their window as a mark of respect.

'Honestly, who wasn't? Every shop I walked past I felt like people had stopped what they were doing to have a look at Bella's best friend, now that she's gone. Seeing how I'm coping, and—' Claire stops abruptly in front of the late Bella's desk, everything left exactly as it had been the last time she left the office. 'Oh god.'

Claire finally takes off the sunglasses and Hannah finds

herself squirming to get a better look inside them. Gutted, she spots a serial number. It's such a slap in the face for Claire to have new Prada sunglasses, given Hannah's current predicament. They must have been a Vinted job.

Olivia notices how red and puffy Claire's eyes are and immediately feels bad. The two of them need to support her more. They were shaken and they hated Bella; she can't imagine how hard it must be for someone who was her friend. Why is Hannah just staring at her sunglasses?

'How are you doing?' Olivia asks, attempting a bit of compassion.

'It's exactly the same as it was when she ...' Claire crumples, kneeling on the floor at the side of the desk as if praying at an altar. She looks up again and surveys the scene. 'Even her coffee cup ... with ... She never finished it ... She never finished the coffee I made her ...'

Hannah looks towards the door with longing, wondering if she can just leave and come back when Claire's chilled out a bit.

Olivia bends down, placing a hand on Claire's back, and looks over to Hannah who rolls her eyes but comes forward to sit with her. She wonders how long after someone's death it's appropriate to tell their 'best friend' that they were really mean about them behind their back and chatted shit about them in front of a client. At least when Hannah belittles someone, she does it to their face. She's never pretending to be someone she's not. Is she?

'Someone's going to have to throw that out eventually. It's kind of already starting to grow stuff.' Hannah winces at the congealed coffee. She considers it a kindness that she's preparing Claire for the future, and the inevitable separation between her and the mug, but Olivia still glares at her.

Olivia wonders if Hannah would be this callous if she'd died. She imagines her now, heartlessly tossing out the dregs of an iced matcha latte, not even taking time to notice Olivia's lipstick still on the straw.

'NO!' Claire practically screams.

Startled, Hannah steps away.

'You can't ... This is all I have left of her ...' Claire crumples again, her tears splashing into the stale coffee at the bottom of the cup.

'Ohhkay...' Hannah walks backwards towards her desk, her hands up and eyebrows raised as Olivia shrugs back.

'Ahh, thank god, Amanda's here,' Hannah mutters, pointing out of the window to where Amanda is disembarking from her Range Rover in all-black Chanel, brown hair pulled back into a demure ponytail.

'There you go, what if we have this meeting with Amanda – I'm sure she'll help – and then maybe you can head home if you're not feeling great, Claire? Maybe it's too soon for you to be back in the office after everything?' Olivia suggests.

Claire does a brave sniff and nods. She gathers herself and begins walking slowly over to her desk as if every move were its own funeral march. Hannah tries not to get too wound up, but Claire's behaviour's a bit like the grief version of someone putting on a fake limp to get a seat on the train. If Olivia died, she'd be distraught, she'd have no idea what to do with herself. She certainly wouldn't be together enough to dress herself like a pantomime widow.

'Morning, darlings,' Amanda says, sweeping into the office with Buster galloping cheerfully in front of her. Her eyes immediately rest on Bella's empty seat and she pauses with an expression of pain. She looks round to the other women. 'Oh, loves, I'm so sorry. This all feels so weird, doesn't it? Why don't we all grab a chat on the sofas?'

Amanda drops her things at her desk and Buster takes up residence on his dog bed. She hugs each woman, spending longer with Claire, who she feels must be struggling the most. Eventually pulling away, she puts her hands on Claire's shoulders and looks at her.

'We're all here for you, darling. I know it must be the absolute worst for you. The two of you were so close, inseparable,' Amanda says.

Claire does another brave sniff while Amanda steers her over to the sofa area. Hannah and Olivia are already seated on one of the bouclé sofas, and Amanda settles Claire on the other. On the coffee table between the two sofas, Amanda lights the scented candle marked 'Reflection' and picks up the singing bowl that lives next to it. She takes a seat next to Claire and perches cross legged, her feet under her bum, placing the singing bowl in the diamond-shaped space created by her folded legs.

'Darlings, how are we doing?' Amanda asks.

She starts running the brush from the singing bowl round the edge of it in a way that makes Hannah wince. She's never understood why people like that noise. There's silence aside from the noise of Claire's sniffing, everyone reluctant to try to speak over the high-pitched sound.

'I think it's important you use this time to express yourselves in whatever way feels most comfortable to you. I want this to be a moment of sharing, of feeling safe. I know things are hard right now, but that's exactly why we must all stick together. We're a family that's been broken. We need to heal from this together. No woman left behind.' Amanda lightly taps the side of the singing bowl, having finished her speech.

'May ... I ... share ... first?' Claire asks, her words separated by tearful gasps.

'Of course, darling.' Amanda puts a hand on Claire's arm.

'Bella came into my life two years ago and she changed it for the better. Everything about her made me want to be a better person and a better friend. She was an inspiration and I'm going to miss her ... every day.' Claire breaks down again. 'I'm sorry.'

'Cry it out, darling. Sit with those feelings.' Amanda rubs Claire's back. 'I've been in bits myself ever since it happened. She was so talented. There was so much promise in her future. I was so proud of her.'

'Thank you,' Claire says so quietly that they can barely hear it, although the sniff she does next is loud enough to be heard all over the home counties.

Amanda looks at Hannah and Olivia expectantly, but they both stay silent. Olivia begins twitching her leg because she feels so award. Hannah thinks that the intensity of this situation feels more uncomfortable to her than when they discovered Bella's body. Accepting that neither of them wants to speak, Amanda decides that she should take the mantle.

'I've had an idea and I hope you'll be on board with it,' Amanda says, putting the singing bowl down so they all know she must mean business.

Claire stops sniffing and looks up from the ratty tissue that she's been weaving in and out of her fingers.

'We've obviously got the vigil tonight. It's so lovely to see Bella's picture in all the other shop windows. It really demonstrates how well she was loved, and they're all on board with tonight. But I'd like to put something extra together for the Estate Agent Awards. Maybe a video to celebrate and honour her work? Perhaps later in the week when you're feeling a bit stronger you might be able to help me, Claire? What do you think?' Amanda asks.

Claire looks up at her, eyes glassy with tears. She doesn't speak for a while. Hannah wonders if she might be stretching out her response purely because it's the first time anyone's paid her this much attention in her whole life.

'Bella would have loved that,' Claire sniffs. 'It's such a beautiful idea, and I know she'll be watching down on us, enjoying every second.'

Hannah feels a slight shiver up her spine as she realises no one knows where Bella is now. If she's watching them from some other spiritual plane. She looks around shiftily before giving herself a stern talking to. She doesn't believe in any of that woo-woo shit and why would Bella choose to watch her of all people if she could anyway. Unless she wanted to fuck with her ... She hopes Claire's not going to be crying this much all day. Maybe it'd be better if she took the day off if she can't stop.

Claire wonders how much longer she can keep the crying up, but she really doesn't want to alert anyone to the fact that before Bella died she found out what an absolute shit she was. A shit friend and a shit person really. Screwing over an old lady, chatting shit about her to Amanda in that email, trying to get her fired. Of course, she's still a *bit* sad.

Bella was a shit, the shittest of shits. But it's still shocking to think that she isn't going to be here any more. On the bright side – although obviously not her main focus – her grief seems to be bringing her and Amanda closer. They've never had a chance to work together on something before. This thing for the awards could finally be her chance to show Amanda how trustworthy and efficient she is. Although obviously she can't be *too* efficient. She's still grieving.

The door to the office opens and the women turn round. For a second, Hannah worries it's Marcus the developer, never missing an opportunity to talk about his beloved property. He probably cursed them when they were shut for two days. But instead, it's Ron, Dave and Felix from Sanders, walking in with a bunch of lilies. Hannah's stomach turns. She actually might have preferred Marcus.

'We just wanted to pay our respects,' Ron says, straightening the jacket and cuffs of his cheap suit. 'These are from us and also Pam and Joan from the bakery and Cathy at the post office.'

'Thank you, that's so kind,' Amanda says.

Hannah observes that considering so many people chipped in, Ron's offering quite the modest bunch of flowers there.

'Bella loved ... flowers ...' Claire starts crying again.

'We're so sorry for your loss,' Ron says. 'Bella was ... well, she was one in a million.'

Hannah notes that even when talking about a dead woman he comes across as lecherous.

'If any of you need anything, we're just across the road,' Felix says, and the other boys nod behind him.

Claire blinks, hoping that she's pulling off crying attractively and that her make-up setting spray is as effective as it promised on the can.

'Thank you, that's so kind.' Amanda smiles weakly. 'As you can imagine, we're all just supporting each other through this the best way we can.'

Olivia stands and takes the flowers from them, spotting a half-picked-off Asda label. They all stand in awkward silence for a bit.

'Hannah, if you need to talk ...' Ron points a thumb towards himself. 'This guy's your man.'

'Same,' Felix adds in hastily.

'Totally, man,' Dave concurs.

Hannah grimaces. 'I'm washing my hair. Forever.'

'Bit rude,' Ron mutters. Next to him, Dave pats him on the back in a show of bro solidarity.

Claire can't believe it. Why are they offering Hannah a shoulder to cry on? Hannah wasn't even friends with Bella, and she's so clearly not bothered by her loss. She hasn't shed a single tear since coming in this morning. If anyone's getting a man's shoulder to cry on in all this, it should be her. She's furious and lets out a grief-stricken gasp, holding a tissue up to her face before amping up her emotions to more of a wail. She feels an arm round her shoulder, but unfortunately it belongs to Olivia. Peering through her tissue, she attempts meaningful-if-watery eye contact with Felix. But he's staring only at Hannah. They all are.

'We really appreciate you coming in, boys. And thank you so much for the flowers,' Amanda says gratefully, trying to distract from poor Claire's wailing.

She's not sure Claire's going to be able to cope with many more well-wishers popping in today. She might have to send her home until the memorial later, at least it'll give her the dignity of crying in private.

'No trouble,' Dave says. 'We're all one big family, after all, aren't we. It feels like losing a sister.'

Amanda certainly hopes Dave doesn't look at his sisters the way that he used to look at Bella.

'I assume we'll see you all at the memorial later?' Amanda asks. 'Seven pm start.'

'Of course. And just let us know if there's anything you need. We'll get on and leave you to it now,' Ron says sincerely, ushering the boys towards the door before turning back round with a last-ditch focus on Hannah. 'I really meant it, any time. I know I'm an alpha, but I can show you I've got the sensitivity of a beta.'

'Thanks, so much,' Hannah says, voice brimming with sarcasm.

'No problem,' Ron replies earnestly, backing out of the door in his shiny suit, hands clasped, smiling to her as though he's already provided her with a service.

Hannah thinks he might be about to bow to them. She braces herself for it, but when one isn't forthcoming, she begins to relax, assuming he's found some self-respect and thought better of it. Then he does it. A bow in the doorway on his way out. She'd cringe for him, but her empathy levels are already at a low ebb.

'OK, loves,' Amanda says, uncrossing her legs. 'I've got a meeting that I need to get to, but if any of you aren't feeling up to it today, just let me know and head home. Your emotional and mental health is more important than selling houses.'

'I think . . .' Claire nods.

Amanda's relieved. She didn't want to mother Claire – she believes in women making independent choices for themselves – but Claire's in no state to be here today.

'Go home, darling. We'll see you tonight.' Amanda clips the lead on Buster and heads for the door, blowing them all a kiss. 'Look after each other. I'm here if you need anything.'

Olivia goes over to Claire, helping her leave the office, while Hannah busies herself with the lilies. Hannah waits patiently for Claire to leave but she's making a real meal of it. Finally, she's at the door when she sniffs and turns back round.

'I was thinking, actually,' she says. 'Maybe we could get a little condolences book. People could come in and sign it.'

'A lovely idea,' Olivia says while Hannah focuses very hard on cutting the ends off the lilies and arranging them in one of Amanda's stone vases. 'I'll get that started today. Just go and take a bit of time for you. Do whatever you need to do to get through.'

Hannah distracts herself because she's itching to scream that Bella didn't even like her. Their friendship wasn't real. She was actively campaigning to get her fired in that email. She knows Olivia thinks she's being kind by not telling her, but Hannah believes it's better to be honest.

'Thanks, guys,' Claire says, tilting her head. 'I know that Bella would have really appreciated this too.'

Hannah can't hold it in any more. She snorts at the flowers and has to pretend it's a sneeze.

'Bless you,' Claire mutters, weeping, before leaving the office.

The moment the door shuts, Hannah lets out a small laugh and brings the lilies over to the coffee table, arranging them between the singing bowl and the scented candles for every occasion.

'Probably best not to tell her you've taken on Tom's place yet,' Olivia says.

'God, could you imagine,' Hannah says. 'She's unstable enough as it is. I'm going to email Amanda now and tell her, though. I need to ask her if she knows who made the offer on the house before I start trying to sell it again. Maybe they still want it?'

Olivia winces at her.

'I know it's unlikely ...' Hannah says.

'That's a polite way of putting it ...' Olivia says. 'Literally everyone is talking about what happened. There's no way that they'll still want to buy the house. It's all over the news.'

'It has to be worth a try, though.' Hannah shrugs, typing out the email to Amanda as she talks.

'What have you got today?' Olivia asks.

'I'm round at Tom's this morning and then catching up on admin this afternoon,' Hannah says. 'How about you?'

'I've got an appointment this morning,' Olivia says, deliberately keeping it vague. 'And then also catching up on admin this afternoon. Shall we grab lunch?'

'Sounds good. Around one?' Hannah asks, scrolling through her inbox.

'One, perfect,' Olivia says, putting her laptop in her bag and heading for the door. 'I'll see you at Mabel's.'

'Great,' Hannah says, looking out of the window and seeing Claire on the town green, sunglasses back on, in full wailing grief flow with a fresh bunch of white roses. She walks over to get a better look. 'What's she doing now?'

'Huh?' Olivia joins her at the window. 'Is she just going to leave them there on the corner of the green?'

'Oh god, you know what she's trying to do, don't you?' Hannah says. 'She's trying to expand the sea of flowers. As if it's not bad enough that we struggle to get through the office door, we don't need to be wading through the grief on the green too.'

'Oh, for god's sake, Claire,' Olivia says, rubbing her eyes, exasperated. 'We're all sad Bella died, of course we are. But I can't cope with people behaving like she was some kind of saint when she wasn't. At the very least she was a flawed human like everyone else.'

Hannah's so relieved to hear her friend talk like this. The last few days have been a muddle of shock and confusion, but being back in the office today has reminded her of exactly the sort of person Bella was.

'I just keep thinking about the things she said in that email last week,' Hannah says. 'She was such a fucking prick and death doesn't change that she was a fucking prick.'

'Agreed.' Olivia nods.

The two women stand quietly watching Claire. They've each spent more time thinking about Bella's bid for management in that email than they can ever admit. Especially during such a terrible time for the agency. And both women have wondered at various points how long they need to wait before speaking to Amanda about the role. Hannah was thinking she'd say her and Bella had discussed it before she died – a small white lie never hurt anyone – and then she'd offer herself as an alternative.

'Anyway, I'd love to stay and watch the martyrdom of Bella Radcliffe, but I'd better head off,' Olivia says, the first to break their silent contemplation as she grabs her bag from her desk.

'And people think you're the nice one of the two of us,' Hannah says.

'I'm not. I just hold it in better than you, sometimes,' Olivia says, aware that Hannah has no idea exactly how much hatred Olivia has towards Bella and how much she pissed her off, right before she died.

'Harsh but fair,' Hannah says.

'OK, see you in a bit,' Olivia says, heading out of the door.

'In a bit,' Hannah says, waving her off.

She waits until Olivia's a little way down the street and then heads over to Bella's desk. She wants to see if there are any brochures for Tom's place knocking around. Not that she's going to use Bella's work when her own would obviously be much better, but she can at least repurpose the basics.

Not finding anything on the desk aside from the hallowed coffee cup, she opens the top drawer of the desk. It's predictably very neat and boring in there – just stationery. She closes it and tries the second drawer down, but it's locked. Hannah knew they had keys to their desks, but she didn't realise anyone actually ever locked them? For what purpose? What was Bella keeping in there that was so important?

Grabbing a thin metal ruler from the top drawer, Hannah slides it in the gap between drawers just above the lock. She has to do a bit of jiggling, but the lock comes free – not exactly state of the art.

Yanking the drawer free, she sees it's full of papers. On

top is the brochure for Tom's place. Bella's wanky wording leaps off the page at Hannah as she picks it up.

She's about to close the drawer, sales particulars in hand, when she sees what was underneath them. A picture of a small cottage with a hefty price tag and the words 'off-market sale only' underneath in bold red. She pulls the curious brochure out and starts flicking through. The house itself looks lovely, and the blurb states it comes with a large amount of land perfect for development. But Hannah's most taken by the house. It's not high spec or done out like all the others that they get through the agency. And it's certainly not luxury living. But it's got character and charm. It looks cosy and homely, all the things she craves and would race towards if she had the money. But also the things that people with money tend – in her experience – to tear down and replace with their own obnoxious tastes.

'Ahhh, Hannah!' Marcus's voice trills from the front door. She's been so distracted she didn't even hear it open.

Hannah's head pings up from the papers and she springs away from Bella's desk, slamming the drawer shut.

'Sorry! Gosh! I've surprised you. I thought you saw me there,' Marcus gasps.

'Not at all.' Hannah smiles, walking across the office towards him. 'What can I do for you, Marcus?'

'Just popping in to collect Amanda for our meeting,' Marcus says, looking around, pretending to search for Amanda in an over-the-top way that Hannah knows is just him covering up for his own snooping.

Marcus isn't only the biggest developer in the area, he's also the biggest gossip, although he claims keeping his ear to the ground is important in his line of work.

'Oh, I think she's already left,' Hannah says.

She'd assumed Amanda was going out to some kind of ad or brand partnership meeting. She's surprised that she was meeting Marcus – that would mean she was actually doing some work related to the agency for a change.

'Oh gosh, silly me! I must have got things mixed up,' Marcus says. He continues taking a good – somewhat unsubtle – look around the office, his eyes settling on Bella's desk.

'Anything else?' Hannah asks, moving to stand in his eyeline and tilting her head.

'Oh yes!' Marcus smiles at her. 'I've sorted the sound and music for tonight.'

'You have?' Hannah's confused. When did Marcus get involved in the vigil?

'Of course, I wanted to offer my expertise. Bella was part of our big family. I'll do whatever I can to honour her memory,' Marcus says. 'We can't have any old shit playing her out now, can we.'

'Right, yes,' Hannah says. She wonders if Amanda even knows he's done this. 'Thank you. We appreciate that ... I've just got somewhere I need to be.' Hannah picks up her bag, stuffing the papers into it and walks towards the door, Marcus trailing after her. 'I'm guessing you need to catch up with Amanda?'

'Oh yes, I'll be late!' Marcus says. 'And we can't keep Miss Amanda waiting, now can we!'

Holding the door open, Hannah ushers him out of the office, takes a quick look around, double checking that she's left Bella's desk as she found it, and locks the door behind them.

Chapter Seventeen

Olivia sits in the window of the cafe opposite the Welling Inn. She's popped her bag with the hotel room key inside it on the seat next to her to discourage anyone from sitting there. The last thing she needs is someone catching her watching her husband's little head in a bubble moving around the map on the FindMy app and gossiping about it.

Olivia is obviously not proud of using Matt's sleeping face to open his phone and give herself permission to track his every movement, then disabling notifications from the app to hide her crimes. It had been a night-time moment of madness. When she woke up this morning, she'd been ashamed of herself for doing something so sneaky, so untrusting. But ten minutes into her working day when she'd checked the app and seen that he wasn't in fact at work, but was at the hotel, she thought she may as well use her little moment of madness, after all.

Not wanting him to spot her, she'd sat with her sunglasses on, hiding behind the French cafe curtain in the window of Le Lard but she needn't have worried. He hasn't emerged yet and the app's shown him stationary in the same room of the hotel for an hour now.

Holding her phone with one hand, she takes a sip of her latte and Googles the hotel's phone number. She's been flip flopping between going in there and trying to work out which room he's in, or simply going to the reception desk and asking which room he's checked in to. But both options feel too scary. Instead, with shaking hands she presses the call option on the Google listing for the Welling Inn and listens to it ringing, staring at the hotel's entrance, poised in case her husband emerges from it. Though she's unsure exactly what she might be poised for.

There's a click on the other end of the phone and a chirpy, young-sounding female voice. 'Hello, Welling Inn! How may I help you?'

Olivia is flustered. This isn't all just in her head any more – it's happening in real life, and she's instigating it. She hasn't thought through what she'd say when they answered.

'Hi.' Olivia's voice is croaky as she speaks, thick with hangover and the foam from her coffee. 'I was just wondering ... I think my husband's a guest with you at the moment, Matthew Honeyman? I just wanted to send him a little surprise, but I've completely forgotten which room he's staying in. I was wondering if you would be able to help me out?'

'Of course,' the voice says.

Olivia holds in a sigh of relief. There's a tapping of fingers on a keyboard on the other end of the line, but then she hears an older voice in the background and the tapping stops. She can't hear exactly what they're saying because the receiver must be muffled, but it sounds tense. There's a click and the song 'Agadoo' starts playing for a few moments before another click connects her back to reception.

'I'm so sorry, Mrs Honeyman. I'm new so I didn't realise, but we're actually not allowed to give out information about long-term guests,' the voice says.

Olivia's taken aback by the words 'long-term guests'. She can hear someone talking in the background again, telling her off for sharing even that much information.

'Oh, but I'm not asking for information about him. I already know him quite well. I'm married to him, ha! I'm just wondering his room number – I'm so forgetful,' Olivia says. 'I just wanted to send him something, because I'm missing him terribly. He's been away for so long.'

But when she finishes speaking the phone's been handed over to the someone else, clearly the voice she can hear in the background.

'I'm so sorry, Mrs Honeyman,' a firmer, more mature female voice replies. 'Unfortunately, this just isn't something we can do over the phone. I'm sure you understand, and I doubt you'd want us giving your details to someone, either.'

'Of course,' Olivia says, feeling deflated. 'I'll just wait for my husband to finish his meeting and ask him then. Sorry to trouble you.'

'No worries at all. Take care, Mrs Honeyman,' the woman says brusquely, before placing down the receiver.

Olivia stares at her phone, wondering if the girl on the other end has it right. Why is her husband a long-term guest at this hotel when he sleeps in bed next to her every night? What could he possibly need the room for? Bella's dead. If he got the room to spend time with her, then what's he doing up there now? Sniffing the sheets where she once was like some kind of creep? He's barely seemed bothered about her death when they've spoken about it. It would be quite the double life.

She stands up, eager to leave the cafe before her husband comes out of the hotel and catches her. She's scared that the more she learns, the less she realises she knows him at all.

Chapter Eighteen

Hannah switches off Pharrell's 'Happy' as she turns into Tom's driveway. The hood of the car's obviously up (you can't be 'grieving' with your hair blowing in the wind, really, can you?) but it still probably wouldn't be the greatest look if anyone heard the song blaring from her speakers. She's thoroughly enjoyed a little dance to it on the way here, though. She smiles at the house as her lilac BMW crunches along the drive.

She knows that some people – Claire – might consider her taking over this listing so soon as insensitive. But it's not as if they could sell the house now anyway. After all, there will be a period of waiting while the coroner finishes their investigation. But she's had some resourceful ideas for things she can do to help speed things up when the time does come. After all, it wasn't Tom's fault Bella died on his property and he still needs to sell. It's beneficial for everyone if Hannah can minimise the trauma of the listing hanging around too long. Really, what she's doing – stepping in like this – is a kindness. No one else needs to know how much she needs the commission.

Hannah swings open the door of her BMW, stretching out a leg, the heel of her Louboutin sinking into the gravel. She'd settled for an all-black outfit when she was getting ready to come here, but put the red-soled shoes on as a finishing touch with just a dash of red lipstick. Nothing too bold though. She's not about to roll out the Lady Danger or wear fuchsia or anything – she's not a monster – but she does want him to think she is hot. Although she's quite sure he already does.

It's not disrespectful to flirt with Tom, and Hannah should still be allowed to have fun – after all, it wasn't her that died. She stalks towards the house trying to look sexy while the gravel swallows her heels with every step like quicksand. Hannah hopes to catch a glimpse of Tom in the windows, but all she's getting is the glare of the sun bouncing off the glass. It feels awkward not knowing if he's watching her right now, or if she's trying to be sexy for absolutely no one.

She works hard to keep her movements and facial expression very controlled just in case. When she finally reaches the door with aching calves from wading through the gravel sea, she raises the knocker, checking her reflection briefly in the well-shone brass of the letterbox. Within seconds, a click sounds and the door creaks open. Tom looks like he's just woken up, dishevelled in a sexy way, his hand on the back of his neck as he stands slouched in a pair of relaxed fit jeans and a grey T-shirt. Hannah wishes she'd been there to do the waking.

'Hey, come through!' Tom holds open the door for her.

'Thanks.' Hannah walks in and debates taking her shoes off, but really what was the point in wearing them if he's not going to see them. He turns to her, with piercing brown eyes and dimpled smile and she knows for certain she's leaving the heels on. They make her legs look ten percent longer.

'I've set up in the living room,' he says, pointing through to the main room, aptly painted in Dead Salmon.

'Brick's arsehole's still here, then,' Hannah observes as she passes the console table.

'Oh yeah,' Tom says, rubbing his eyes as if only just noticing its presence. 'With everything going on, I'd forgotten about that abomination.'

Entering the living room, Hannah looks around in what she hopes is a professional manner. Simply assessing the surroundings of a house that, if she could afford to live in it, she would probably never leave, in a detached and business-like manner.

'How are you doing?' she asks, tilting her head with compassion.

'Honestly, I've had better weeks. It's a bit of a struggle to sleep here knowing someone died just out there in the garden,' Tom says, gesturing for her to take a seat on the sofa. 'Can I get you something to drink? I've got some iced tea if you fancy? It's so hot today.'

'Isn't it?' Hannah tries to make her voice a sort of sexy purr, but it catches in her throat as she lowers herself on to the sofa and instead she sort of falls down on the cushions with a cough. 'I'd love some.'

'Great, I'll go and get those, and you make yourself at home,' Tom says, walking out just as his phone rings.

She hears him answer it and stands up from the sofa to take a better look around. *Don't mind if I do*, Hannah thinks, stalking around, imagining herself in different scenarios. Curled up reading the paper with Tom in the morning, wearing one of his shirts and cradling one of those earthenware mugs of coffee. Or late at night, with a glass of wine, her bare feet wrapped around his, binge-watching the latest Netflix thriller. She tiptoes over to the fireplace, so Tom doesn't hear the clip of her heels on the wooden floor, trailing her fingertips against the shiny grey marble surface.

Just as she's feeling extremely smug, Hannah's shoe catches on a huge wicker basket of firewood, throwing it and her forward. Wood spills out across the floor and, about to faceplant veneers first into the fireplace, Hannah throws her hands forward, catching the edge of the mantelpiece just in time. She freezes, nervous that Tom might have heard her stack it, but he doesn't call out or come rushing to her aid.

Recovered and relieved, Hannah straightens herself up and scowls down at the offending wicker basket and its contents strewn across the herringbone floor. She bends down to fix it before Tom comes back and sees how clumsy she's been. Picking up the lavender-scented logs, she hastily goes to put them back in the basket but sees something bronze and shiny peeking through the pile of wood from the bottom of the basket.

Curious, Hannah sticks her hand into the basket. Her fingers curl round a piece of cool, hard metal and she pulls the object from the basket. It's only when she's prised it entirely free from the wood that she realises what it is. Gasping, she throws it into the basket and backs away, leaving Brick's original sculpture, *Bella's Vulva,* lying on top of the wood pile, half covered in what looks very much to Hannah like blood.

She freezes, staring at the red stain on the tip of the vulva. She tells herself she's being dramatic, that the stain could be anything, a trick of the light, or paint. It was, after all, one of Brick's ideas. He probably added paint as some kind of feminist symbolism. He's just the type of man to do something performative like that, probably to try and cover up something problematic from his past. And she bets there's plenty to choose from there.

Shaking, she leans towards the basket and sniffs at the sculpture's red-tinted end. She's not sure what she's expected to resolve by smelling it. She guesses she'd hoped it might smell of paint or ketchup – but all she gets is a metallic whiff, which certainly doesn't do anything to ease her worries. Hannah stands, staring at the vulva in the basket, and remembers the blood on Bella's head as she lay in the fountain. Could it be Bella's blood? Could someone have whacked her with the vulva and then buried it in the logs? But that would make it murder? And, sure, Bella was annoying, she rubbed everyone up the wrong way and she fucked people over, but murder? Whoever put it there had certainly meant to hide it and it's not as though

Tom would be using firewood in this weather. What if it was Tom himself who had left it there?

The sound of Tom's feet on the stairs makes Hannah's head spin. Still shaking, she scrabbles to place the logs back into the basket, covering the bronze sculpture. If she buries it well enough, she can pretend she never saw it in the first place. She feels like Lady MacBeth scrubbing out the blood, trying to make the log basket look like it did before. If Tom put it there, he'll be aware, he'll know something's up. What if he heard her knocking it over?

Placing the last log on the pile, Hannah tries to calm herself down, breathing in and out as Tom crosses the hallway. She flings herself back towards the sofa. Her bum hits the velvet cushions just seconds before Tom enters the room and she tries her best not to look at the basket any more. There's nothing to be scared of. It's been a weird week and her imagination's running wild. That's all. It's just a silly sculpture.

Besides, Bella was far too boring to be murdered anyway. And Tom couldn't have done it, surely? What motive would he have? Why would he have just hidden the murder weapon in a basket in his own living room? He's had days to sort it out. He wouldn't have left it there this long. She shakes her head at herself and smiles up at him, like nothing has happened.

'Sorry, bit of a long one there! Work call! You know how it is.' He enters the room with two highball glasses of iced tea in his hands, looking as stone-cold handsome as he was when he left.

Too handsome for a murderer. Is that a thing? She's pretty

sure she's seen true-crime podcasts about hot murderers. So probably not. But she looks in his eyes, anyway, searching for firm proof that he couldn't have done it.

'Oh, have I got something on my face?' he asks, taking a seat next to her and handing her a glass.

She realises she's been staring him with quite a weird intensity and laughs.

'God no! Sorry, just exhausted! I don't think I've slept since Bella . . .' She feels herself tensing as Tom sits down next to her on the sofa.

'I bet,' Tom says. 'I just keep thinking, wondering if we'd got to her sooner, or one of us had realised what was going on, if we could have saved her? I feel somehow responsible considering it happened in my garden.'

'Oh no, it wasn't your fault!' Hannah says.

She stares at the glass in her hands as though it were a poison chalice. What if he heard the logs fall and knows she found the weapon? What if he's put something in her drink? Was it arsenic that smells of almonds? She takes a sniff, but can only smell sugary iced tea. She needs to stop this. Besides, when would he have had time to murder Bella? Hannah is pretty sure she'd kept an eye on him almost the entire night. Nevertheless, she puts the glass down on the table, untouched.

'Look, between you and me, business person to business person, I need to confess something, but I really don't want anyone else finding out, especially Matt. It's kind of embarrassing. I know we can't control when we can put the house back on the market, but I do really need a quick sale. This place cost more than I thought it would. By about £3 million.' Tom looks down at his glass. 'I'm waiting for some investments to come to fruition, but, while I wait for that, there's kind of a cash-flow issue that I need to address. Selling this place would fix that.'

Hannah almost sighs with relief right in his face. It's the final piece of the puzzle that she needs. There's no way he'd kill someone on his own property when he needs a quick sale. Especially one he had absolutely no reason to kill in the first place. She looks at Tom's tired, stressed face and feels closer to him than ever. She knows exactly what it's like to have money issues, after all.

'Please don't tell anyone,' Tom pleads, his eyes meeting hers. 'A man who works in finance with financial issues isn't a good look. It's embarrassing.'

'Don't worry,' Hannah says, reaching over and squeezing his hand. 'I've got this. We'll sell as soon as we can plus I'll do everything in my power to get you the asking price.'

'Thank you. I knew you'd help. I just sensed that you were a good and kind person. Bella promised such a quick sale that no one ever needed to know how bad things have got. When she said she'd got an offer right away, I started to feel like I could finally relax,' Tom continues.

'That was why you went with Bella over us?' Hannah asks.

'Yeah. I got lucky, I guess. Bumped into Bella, and I knew she could do the job and I wouldn't have to tell Olivia – who would then obviously tell Matt – about why I needed to move so fast on it. Besides, she told me you two would be far too busy to do a quick sale,' Tom says.

'Not true,' Hannah says. 'That lying little ... sorry. I know I'm not supposed to speak ill of the dead. Look, obviously it's unlikely given everything that the original bidder still wants to go ahead, but I'll try and find out who they are.'

'Thank you for being so understanding,' Tom smiles. 'You're a very real person, Hannah. I don't think I've ever met a woman quite like you.'

Hannah feels herself blushing slightly. Was that a come on? Is he coming on to her?

'I've got some ideas I think might help,' she says, trying to stay cool.

'Hit me,' Tom says, running his fingers through his hair and leaning a little closer to her.

'I was thinking what might be great is if we use the house in some standard videos so people can see it in a different light. Really show how gorgeous it is. Just videos like the dos and don'ts of selling a house, that kind of thing? Keep the house visible in the background, so when it comes time to sell people already know and love it. They've seen it, they've drooled over how perfect it is, now they can have it. That sort of thing,' Hannah says. 'And if you need extra cash, you might be able to rent out the inside for location shoots?'

'I knew you'd have great ideas,' Tom says, giving Hannah such a winning smile she feels her knees weaken.

It's as though she's forgotten she thought he might be a murderer just minutes ago. Her eyes catch on the log basket again. She wonders if she should show him – it's his log basket, after all. But even an *investigation* for murder, never mind the certainty that it had happened, would knock hundreds of thousands, maybe even millions off the asking price for the property. Tom couldn't afford that, and neither could she, really. She needs this sale as much as he does.

If the red paint is just one of Brick's stunts, she could be worrying Tom for nothing. Hadn't enough people been appalled by the sculptures on the night of the open house? Someone probably just shoved it in the log basket to get it out of view. She's buried it again and bought herself some time so she can confirm that she's been silly, her memory was playing tricks on her and the red was always there. It was just a bit of symbolistic paint from a man who no doubt considers himself to be a feminist genius on par with Emmeline Pankhurst. And some prude had just taken offence and hidden it in the log basket.

Back in her car and thrilled with herself for doing such a great job with Tom, Hannah opens Instagram. She realised as she was leaving that there was an easy way to confirm if the sculpture was supposed to have blood on it or not, because Brick had posted a picture of it earlier as part of his mourning collection.

She types Brick's name into the search bar, convinced that this is going to relieve her of her fears. His profile loads painfully slowly, and she has to wade through about ten posts just from today before she sees the thumbnail-sized image of the sculpture.

Clicking on the square doesn't provide the relief that she thought it would, though. Instead, she feels hot, and dizzy. Even when she zooms in or tilts the phone the answer is clear. Red is not one of the sculpture's original features. Feeling her breath catch in her throat, Hannah looks up through her windscreen at the house and the window to the sitting room, where she fears she may have just covered up a murder weapon. A murder weapon that now has her fingerprints on it.

Chapter Nineteen

Amanda sits opposite Marcus Fritton, trying not to let on that she's got absolutely no fucking idea what he's talking about. She's used to Marcus being demanding and making everything about him so when he requested a meeting with her about Bella after she died – despite Bella barely having even started on his new listing and her death being nothing to do with him – she wasn't surprised. But she hadn't seen this revelation coming.

'With so much money at stake, you can see why I was more than a little concerned when I heard our lovely little Bella had passed away. May she rest in peace.' Marcus does the sign of the cross, holding his palms together while he continues to stare at Amanda with expectation.

Amanda thought she'd managed to catch up on everything that Bella had been working on, but she's got no recollection of seeing anything about the property or deal that Marcus is talking about right now. It's weird because Bella had always been very vocal about what she was doing, always shouting about her achievements – something Amanda thought more women should do – so it didn't make sense that she'd keep a massive deal like this to herself. A house with acres of land ready for development would have been an easy and massive sale, and yet she doesn't remember seeing even so much as an email about it in Bella's inbox.

'Did she message you about it, Marcus?' Amanda wonders if she can just get him to forward the chain to her.

He'll get a bit stroppy about it, as though pressing the forward button is an inconvenience he shouldn't have to weather, but it would get the deal done quicker.

'Oh no, this was all strictly off-market and under the radar. Bella was very secretive about it all, which felt a little odd but exciting. Exclusive.' Marcus stretches out the word *exclusive*. 'Just for me, she said.'

Professionally the whole thing's ringing alarm bells to Amanda. Why was Bella doing secret deals? On a personal level, Amanda also found it really embarrassing. If Marcus realises she knew nothing about it, he'll spread word round the industry that she's lost control of the business. Amanda knows she's been spending a bit more time on the mumfluencer side of things lately, but she was a woman who prided herself on having it all and she worked hard to keep it all too. Couldn't the universe just let her have this one?

'She was good like that. Always knew what people wanted before they did. Matched people to properties perfectly,' Amanda says solemnly. 'What about text messages? Did you go and see the property? Did she send you an address?'

'She phoned me and drove us both to see it,' Marcus says. 'I'd sent her an offer the day she died, but obviously she was distracted with this other mega property. My invite to the open house must have got lost in the post, by the way, I assume.'

Amanda knows this'll be a sticking point for Marcus; if he perceives someone might have been considered more important than him, it will be a huge issue for him. He'll have been sulking over that all weekend. She stirs her coffee with a steady hand, despite feeling extremely unsteady within herself. In fact, she was feeling more than slightly on edge today. Maybe it's perimenopause? The internet would tell her it's perimenopause. Or it could of course be because one of her employees has just died. Amanda feels a lump start to form in her throat. Bella had such a bright future ahead of her. She would have been such a great agent.

'It's so sad,' Marcus nods, doing a slight sniff, reaching up to wipe a small tear from behind his Tom Ford glasses. 'She was a godsend. I was going to build some very high-spec, luxury flats there. Obviously, it's in your interests to find it. We could have all made a fortune.'

'Leave it with me, Marcus. I'm sure it's all in hand. I'll check her notes and get back to you ASAP. I'm sure one of the others is already across it.' Amanda's lying. If she didn't know about it and there's nothing about it in Bella's emails, then she can ask, but it's unlikely the others know anything, either. She needs Bella's work phone, really, but the last time she saw that it was in the fountain, drowned and useless next to Bella's body.

'I was expecting someone to have been in touch with

me sooner, to be honest,' Marcus says. 'But I understand you probably had more important things on your mind.'

Amanda knows Marcus thinks he's special and he has high expectations. To be fair, they do a lot of business together. But is he really expecting an apology for her not calling him the moment Bella died just in case they were working on something together she had no idea about?

'I'm so sorry, Marcus, it was an oversight on our part,' Amanda says. 'You're always our top priority. I promise.'

She needs to keep him on side, because she's got a feeling that working out where this property is might be impossible.

'Honestly, it'll all be sorted before you know it.' Amanda gives him as positive a smile as she can muster. 'All we need to do is get the contact details for the seller, which I'm sure will be in her notes, and I promise you the deal will run smoothly. I'd love to see those plans for the flats you've been working on by the station too, by the way. That sounds like such a brilliant development.'

Amanda swishes her ponytail, hoping she's got him off the subject of her own perceived incompetence and onto something that she's heard on the property grapevine has enraged him.

'Oh god, don't.' Marcus throws his hands up. 'Have you *heard* the latest?'

'No!' Amanda says, leaning forwards enthralled and pleased to have distracted him.

Marcus gasps. 'My god, that planning committee. You know that poisonous-looking one with the round glasses?

Small, always wears a tweed suit like he thinks he's some kind of maverick?'

Amanda pretends to recall who he's talking about when she knows exactly who it is because it's the same member of the town's planning committee that he always falls out with. They have a tense rivalry, which causes great amusement to everyone else.

'Oh yes, I think so.' She strings it out.

'He tried to stop the build! Said he was sure he saw a rare butterfly in the area. Tried to halt works until someone had come and looked at the butterfly in case construction ruined a natural habitat. Well! Someone eventually came – some kind of butterfly expert nonsense – and obviously there were no rare butterflies to be seen. I'm telling you – he just does this to wind me up,' Marcus fumes.

Amanda suspects that Marcus is right and, to be fair, it's funny.

'Anyway, all gone now. We're pouring the foundations tomorrow, only a week late. You should have seen his face when I got the sign-off again. Such a bitter little man.' Marcus's face contorts with spite.

'Gosh, so pleased it's sorted now,' Amanda lets out a sigh as though relieved for him. 'What a palaver! Let us know when they're ready to sell of course, we'd love to do that for you.'

'Of course. I'd never go anywhere else! We're a dream team,' Marcus grins.

Amanda wants to make sure she keeps it that way.

Chapter Twenty

Hannah doesn't know why she's driven to Bella and Brick's place. She found the address in the company WhatsApp from when Bella invited everyone for 'drinks and nibbles' last year. (Obviously Hannah didn't attend. She's not two-faced.) The whole way here her brain's been going from nought to a hundred.

Claire had told her and Olivia that Bella and Brick were on the rocks at the open house. But Brick wasn't behaving like anything was different, especially when Bella went missing. Almost like he was in denial? Could he have been so determined that their relationship wasn't over that he killed her? Then wanted to make sure he was with them when they found her to make it seem like he was innocent? A crime of passion? He was certainly a passionate guy (and keen for everyone to know about it). Sure, it would be pretty fucked up of him to post the murder weapon in homage to her the next day. But she imagines he'd have to be a pretty fucked-up guy to kill Bella rather than accept a break-up.

A wave of nausea sweeps over Hannah as she looks up at the glass-fronted Modernist property. She's not sure whether it's guilt about hiding the sculpture or raging jealousy at the simple perfection of this cube of glass and steel that was apparently Bella's house. She knew this was a nice street, but she *had* hoped Bella's would have been a rogue shitty house; maybe something with such a bad case of mould that it was almost uninhabitable, with anyone who lived there encountering those spores that burrowed into your lungs and brain? It would certainly have explained why Bella was such a prick.

But there was no denying – from the outside, at least – that this house was utterly perfect. If it really is where Brick and Bella lived together, then Hannah thinks she might hate Bella even more in death than she did when she was alive. She must have been doing really well; either that or Brick's shitty phallic art was far more successful than she'd realised. It's possible, she supposes. After all, if her job had taught her anything, it was that rich people can be incredibly tasteless.

The sight of Claire's disgusting bright orange Fiat 500 makes Hannah's stomach drop, which isn't an unusual reaction for her when seeing the car, but today it's accompanied by a kind of panic. If Brick had killed Bella, he was dangerous, and no one, not even Claire, should be alone with him.

Parking her car discreetly between two imposing four-by-four tanks of motherhood, Hannah takes a deep breath and checks herself in the mirror. She looks herself in the eye and gives herself a stern talking to before getting out. Closing her car door and walking up the long, winding driveway, she feels shaky remembering Bella's body in that fountain, her brains splattered against the Victorian stone, being washed away by the creepy cherub spewing water. She can't believe she's going in there with him now, willingly. It's against all natural common sense, and yet she carries on, despite impending doom increasing with every step.

The huge floor-to-ceiling glass stretches over two floors and looks even shinier and more impressive the closer she gets to the house. The sun's position means you can't see inside in too much detail, but she bets that Brick and Bella are the kinds of people who have matching Eames chairs that they sit in at night-time, lights on, their fabulous house and lives a stage for all to see. She knows Bella's dead and Brick's an absolute prick – if not a murdering psychopath – but she can't help envying them. She stands in the entrance porch created by the top floor jutting out, like a canopy.

She presses the hideous Ring doorbell (not at all in keeping with the style of the property or its mid-century modern front door) and stands back, afraid that Brick might come at her with another one of his hideous creations the moment he opens the door. There's no noise from inside so she rings again with a shaking finger.

What if she's too late? What if Claire's shitty orange Fiat 500's done its last journey? Knowing Claire, she was probably offering Brick a shoulder to cry on, or a bosom for a pillow. It's so obvious she fancies him. It's obvious Claire fancies a few people, actually – like all of the boys at Sanders. She literally flings her shoulders back and her tits out every time they're near, but that's beside the point. What if Claire's pathetic crush has been her downfall?

The door finally opens and Claire stares back at her, surprised. Her face isn't nearly as tear-stained as it was at the office. If Hannah is being cynical about it (which Hannah does like to be, especially because just seconds ago she'd imagined that Claire was dead), she'd wonder if Claire had been milking it a little in the office.

'Hannah?' Claire tries to recover herself smoothly after an initial shock. 'What a surprise. Are you here to see Brick?'

'I am. I assume if you're here, he's up for visitors,' Hannah says. Claire looks hesitant, but Hannah pushes her way past into the house. She doesn't know what else to do apart from insert herself into the situation to suss out Brick. 'Is he up here?'

'Yes, go up,' Claire says, although Hannah was already halfway up the stairs when she asked the question.

Hannah can't help but notice that Claire looks furious about her presence. If only she knew that Hannah being here might well actually be saving her life.

Upstairs on a very hard-looking sofa, Brick is curled up in the foetal position, a huge woollen jumper over his knees, making him look as though he's curled himself into some kind of knitted amniotic sack. His tiny beanie is still defying gravity on top of his head, even in the throes of grief.

'Brick? How are you doing?' Hannah asks gently, assessing his form for killer vibes at the same time.

He looks up at her with red-ringed wide eyes, almost

childlike. But she doesn't buy it. Of course, he would make himself as vulnerable as possible if he wanted to avoid suspicion that he'd killed Bella.

'Hannah?' His voice is weak in a way she suspects is quite forced, another tick for her theory.

'I'm so sorry for your loss,' Hannah says, standing respectfully in front of him while Claire swoops back onto the sofa, her arm round Brick's form like an eagle covering its young. Maybe she doesn't need to be so worried about Claire after all. She seems almost aggressive right now.

'...Thank ... you ...' Brick sniffs. 'I don't know ... what ... I'm ... going ... to do ... without ... her.'

'I know,' Hannah says. 'It's so terribly sad. Could I get you something? A sweet tea? Might be comforting?'

'I'd ... yes ... please ...' Brick says, holding his jumper up to his mouth, muffling his words as he speaks.

Hannah walks over to the kitchen, keeping one eye on Brick. She's not going to buy his scared-little-boy routine, no matter how hard he pushes it. Popping the kettle on, she opens and closes cupboards, trying to find the mugs and tea bags, while Claire wraps herself round Brick in a way that she may consider comforting, but which Hannah considers quite predatory, actually.

'I've just been at the house with Tom,' Hannah says. She can feel Claire glaring at her for mentioning it. 'We were going to arrange a courier to get all the work you loaned him back to you. I just wanted to make a list and make sure that I've got everything he borrowed. He wanted to pass on his gratitude too.'

'That's OK.' Brick pulls his head slightly away from Claire's clutches and blinks at her.

'I've made a list on my phone.' Hannah walks over to him with the mug of tea in one hand and her phone in the other, open on the Notes app where she'd put the list together earlier.

'I can take a look,' Brick says.

'They were just the pieces that I could see around,' Hannah says.

She knows that she's deliberately left off the *Bella's Vulva* sculpture and she also knows there's no way Brick won't notice. She wants to see what he does, whether he reacts to the lack of the sculpture in any way. She watches him rub his eyes and then stare down the list, his tattooed fingers gripping her phone, the B from Bare on his left hand prominent. It takes a few moments, with Claire glaring at Hannah like she's an absolute monster, but eventually he looks up.

'I think it's all there, but there's just one missing. It's really important . . . It's . . .' Brick starts crying like she suspected he would. '*Bella's* . . .'

'I know. It's such a lot.' Claire rubs his back and shoots Hannah a furious look. 'You don't have to do it right now. Hannah, can he not do this another time?'

'No . . . it's . . . *Bella* . . .' Brick sniffs. '*Bella's Vulva*. It's missing from the list.'

'The sculpture of . . . Bella?' Claire repeats slowly, as if she's having trouble understanding.

'*Bella's . . . Vulva!*' Brick gets increasingly annoyed trying to communicate. Hannah shoots him and Claire a puzzled, innocent look. 'It's of sentimental value! I can't lose it!'

'Oh yes, I remember,' Hannah says, chewing the side of her cheek. This isn't the reaction she was expecting from him. If he killed Bella with it and hid it, then why was he desperate to have it back again?

Brick's phone materialises from somewhere inside his vast motheaten woollen sheath and he taps at the screen a bit. He passes the phone over to Hannah with one hand while his other presses on his weeping eyes.

The screen displays a picture of the sculpture that Hannah doesn't really need to see as Brick starts wailing, and she knows she can't stay here much longer. Her patience for hanging out with Brick is expiring fast and she might do a murder at this rate.

'Right, perfect,' Hannah says. 'I can go and find that for you now. I'll get this sorted ASAP. Don't you worry.'

She does need to go and meet Olivia anyway, but she also doesn't want to leave Claire here on her own.

'Claire, I should head. Maybe we should leave Brick on his own for a bit?' Hannah suggests.

'Oh no, I don't think that's a good idea,' Claire says. 'I think I should stay. I'm really all he has. He knows me so much better than anyone else, and I'm sure you didn't mean to, but I think your visit's unsettled him a little more than he's letting on.'

Hannah tilts her head, aware that she can't tell Claire to fuck off right now.

'OK, I'll head off and leave you to it, then,' she says.

Fuck it, if Claire doesn't want saving, she's not going to put herself in this position any more. Let Brick murder her with a sculpture of a tit for all she cares.

Claire walks her to the door like the bloody queen of the modernist castle, irking Hannah even more than she thought possible.

After seeing Hannah out, Claire sits back on the sofa with Brick. She's trying to comfort him, but most of his words are obscured by either his wool or his wailing.

'I don't get it, man ... My Bella.' Brick shakes his head, the tiny beanie not shifting an inch no matter how vigorous his movements. 'My Bella.'

'I know.' Claire dry sniffs. 'It just doesn't feel real.'

'Bell ... a ...' Brick wails, his head in his hands as Claire scoops him up.

She squashes his head tight against her chest and holds it there, stroking his hair and making soothing noises. She looks around the house, taking in the views from the second-floor modernist living room and the giant sculpture in the centre of the room, a pair of melted cherries that look uncannily like bollocks. She imagines what it would be like to live here, to wake up every morning to this much light and space and all of the lovely things around that make it so homely and nice. It would be quite the comparison to the small room she lives in now where she wakes up every morning able to see both her toilet and her oven from the bed and reach them in just two small steps.

Brick coughs and wheezes into her bosom before trying to talk, and Claire reluctantly releases her grip on him, disappointed.

'I just ... I feel like I can tell you anything, Claire, and I feel like I need to tell you some stuff ... about Bella ... I need to make sense of things ...' Brick sniffs, his brown eyes boring into hers like sexy lasers. She watches him wring his tattooed hands and feels emotionally and physically horny for this man. She can't help it. His sadness has just made her so hot for him. Sure, she knows this makes her a terrible person, but no one will ever know.

'Of course, you can tell me anything.' Claire clutches his hand tight and stares meaningfully into his eyes.

'We fought before she died, you know. We were ... we'd talked about breaking up the night before she died. I don't know if it was really happening,' he says.

Claire tries to look surprised, or inquisitive at the least, but she knows that as far as Bella was concerned they were done.

'I was just ... She was behaving so weirdly. So unlike her? Like she's always been so gentle and kind and, you know ... like an angel ...' He pauses to weep again. 'But she had this stuff that was going on that I feel like no one knew about. Like, this ... Can I show you something?'

'Of course,' Claire says, looking him deep in the eyes, and brushing a tear from his cheek. 'You can tell me anything.'

Brick extracts himself from Claire's overbearing clutches and walks over to the open-plan kitchen where he pulls a small Cath Kidston decorated box out from under the counter. He brings it back over to the sofa.

'Open it.' Brick hands Claire the box and she puts it on her lap, lifting the lid. She gasps in shock, knocking it over.

A picture of Amanda drifts out, fluttering to the floor face up, and stares at them both.

'I found it last week. They're all of her,' Brick says.

'All of them?' Claire asks, staring at the avalanche of photos that have landed on the static-filled shag-pile rug.

Claire leans down to pick up the picture and flicks through the rest of them, gathering them as she goes and putting them back in the box. There are so many, some newspaper cuttings from earlier in Amanda's career, press interviews and profiles on her. Headlines declaring her some kind of queen of property. Then there are pictures of her family.

'I mean I like Amanda as much as the next woman. She's an inspiration, but this feels ... obsessive,' Claire says, looking up at Brick.

'Right?' Brick sniffs. 'It's unhinged. And Bella wasn't like that? She was so ... together.'

'You're right, this isn't like Bella at all,' Claire agrees. 'I guess she really liked Amanda?'

But Brick's face is saying something different. He looks at her wearily.

'I mean ... she wasn't ... like ...' He's pausing again but this time it's not to cry. This time it's more tentative, like he's not sure about telling her something.

'You can tell me anything. I'll never tell anyone,' Claire says.

'She kind of hated her.' Brick seems relieved the moment it's out. 'She used to call her Whore Harrington.'

'WHAT? That's not even proper alliteration!' Claire can barely contain herself. 'How can someone hate Amanda? She's a woman who literally supports women. She does so much good. She's so kind and ... powerful ...'

'I think she wasn't always that kind to Bella?' Brick says, rubbing his face again.

'Yes, she was!' Claire knows it's ridiculous to get defensive over the opinions of a dead woman. 'I literally saw her being nice to her pretty much every single day.'

'At Harrington's she was,' Brick says. 'But before that.'

'Before that?' Claire asks. 'They knew each other before?'

'Bella met Amanda, years ago. She was new to agenting, she'd only just been working a year or two, and Amanda was working for one of the big firms in London. Bella had an interview to work for Amanda at that firm, but Amanda dismissed her straight off the bat saying she wasn't experienced enough. She was absolutely crushed by it. I couldn't understand why it meant so much to her, but she'd sort of followed her for years on Instagram, I guess.

'I'd never heard of her before, but for Bella working for Amanda was a big deal. After that, she spent years trying to prove herself and get better at her job. She was obsessed with one day getting the chance to work for her. She wouldn't let it rest until she got the job.'

'Oh my god,' Claire says. 'I had no idea. She never mentioned that she'd had anything to do with Amanda before.'

'She wouldn't. She was a very proud woman. She'd never

tell people about her failures, only her successes. She wore a mask every day . . .' Brick says wistfully, staring into the middle distance and crying some more.

'But this obsession seems to carry on past her working with Amanda?' Claire says. 'Surely, she couldn't have still been harbouring resentment while she was working for her? They got on so well.'

'I mean I thought so,' Brick says. 'But some of those articles are recent. There's a profile from *The Times* that was only published two weeks ago in there.'

'That was such a great profile,' Claire gushes. 'I thought she came off so well in that.'

'There's other stuff,' Brick says. 'Stuff she told me about. But I can't betray her by sharing it.'

'Why did you show me this, though?' Claire asks, wondering if Brick knows about Esme's house. If that's what he's talking about.

'Because I don't think Bella's death was an accident,' Brick says. 'I think somebody pushed her into the fountain. I think there's even more that I don't know about. She wasn't just out to get Amanda – it was all of you.'

'Not me, though?' Claire looks at his sad and confused face, tears falling once more. If he does know about Esme's house, she wants to make sure he doesn't twig that she does too, because that could be a problem for her.

'Errr, sure,' Brick says, but he's distracted – she can tell he's not paying attention to her.

Claire follows his gaze over to Bella's rose-gold laptop

sitting on the coffee table, with its *'Live, Laugh, Be a Strong Woman'* sticker on it. He stands and walks over to it.

'Want me to make us another tea?' Claire asks, desperately trying to keep his attention as Brick grabs the laptop from the coffee table and heads back to his seat.

He's like a zombie. Claire's not even clear if he's heard her at all as a long, awkward silence stretches between them. He opens the laptop and starts tapping away at the keys before eventually speaking.

'Nah, something I gotta do for Bella,' he says, not even looking at Claire. 'You OK to see yourself out, yeah?'

'Oh yes, absolutely,' Claire says, standing up. She doesn't want to let on that she's embarrassed by such a blatant brush off. 'Bye, then. I'll see you at the vigil later?'

Claire leans down, peering over the laptop screen to try and get his attention. But Brick's already so absorbed in whatever he's looking for on Bella's laptop he doesn't even look up to say goodbye.

Chapter Twenty-one

Olivia sits in Mabel's wine bar opposite the office, flicking between her latest unread message to her husband and the FindMy app where his face is still firmly logged at the hotel. Every time she looks up from her phone and out of the window, the pile of flowers for Bella seems to have expanded and from the looks of the post about the vigil on the Harrington's Instagram account, it's going to be busy tonight. She can't help but wonder if Bella really touched that many people's lives or if people are just clinging on to the drama.

From the discreet booth where she's been trying to hide away from the prying eyes of the locals, Olivia can see Mabel approaching.

'We're so sorry for your loss,' Mabel says. 'How are you doing, doll?'

'We're OK,' Olivia says, hoping she looks sad enough. Obviously, she *is* sad, of course she is. But there feels like this kind of pressure every time someone offers their condolences to give them the right amount of grief and upset. Anything less and she fears their commiserations may turn to judgement.

'We're just getting ready for tonight. I thought people will probably want to come back here after the service to chat over their memories of Bella. It's such a good idea – so many people loved her. I'm guessing there won't be a funeral for a while if there's a post-mortem happening?' Mabel asks, and Olivia knows she's only asked because she's fishing for information.

Olivia tries to ignore the question, instead looking over to the stage, where a huge easel has been set up with yet another massive A0-sized picture of Bella, taken from her LinkedIn profile. She watches one of the barmen putting up bulb-style fairy lights around it so it looks like she's some kind of Hollywood starlet.

'That's so lovely,' Olivia says, pointing to the picture. 'It really means a lot to all of us to have your support. Thank you.'

'The whole town is thinking of you.' Mabel rubs her arm. 'We'll make sure tonight's as special as possible.'

Olivia tries to offer the right kind of smile. Gracious and grateful but not happy.

'Thank you,' Olivia repeats, feeling incredibly awkward.

Mabel walks away with a sympathetic head bob, leaving Olivia to stare at Bella's picture, remembering the last time she saw her alive. The smug look she gave her like she knew a secret about her marriage that Olivia didn't. She's barely slept all weekend, picturing her husband shagging Bella, and she's fed up with feeling like she has no control over her life any more. She thought she could bury it all, and never think about it again now that Bella's dead. But after the morning she's had, she can see that Bella's still tearing her marriage apart even from beyond the grave.

Relief floods her body when Hannah walks through the doors of the bar. Finally, someone who isn't going to be some kind of simpering wreck in the name of Bella Radcliffe.

'Heya!' Hannah waves perhaps a touch too cheerfully. She's just relieved to be back in a public place away from Brick.

'Hey.' Olivia jumps up and gives Hannah a huge hug. The two of them really need each other to get through this.

'There are pictures of her all over this town,' Hannah whispers in Olivia's ear, through clenched teeth while they hug. 'Massive ones; it's like she's always watching.'

'Don't look now.' Olivia nods towards the stage. 'I'm sure either Claire or Brick is definitely going to say something cheesy about hoping she's looking down on us all. I feel we need to be prepared for that.'

'Christ, it's like Godzilla,' Hannah whispers, pulling away and putting on a sombre expression. 'Hey, Mabel.'

'Hey darl,' Mabel says from the next booth along where she's cleaning the table. 'Sorry for your loss.'

Hannah doesn't know how to respond to this because it really doesn't feel like *her* loss if she's being realistic. So she simply nods instead.

'You guys here for lunch? It's on us,' Mabel says. 'What'll it be?'

'Oh, thanks babe. I'll have a Kale Caesar, please,' Hannah says.

'Make that two,' Olivia says, feeling a bit of a fraud getting a free lunch for Bella's death. 'Thank you, that's really kind of you.'

'Great, I'll bring them over. Maybe I'll try and get some of these prying eyes to stop gawping at you as well,' Mabel says pointedly to the three old men at the bar who sit there all day every day from open till close.

Both women had been too distracted by the ginormous picture of Bella to notice them all, lined up, staring at them open-mouthed as though they're real-life unicorns.

Hannah startles Olivia. 'So I stopped by Brick and Bella's place earlier on the way back from Tom's to offer my condolences.'

'I didn't realise you cared so much,' Olivia says, the words coming out as sarcastic as she'd intended.

'I need to sort out getting his "art" back to him.'

'Ah, that makes sense.' Olivia breathes a sigh of relief. Her friend hasn't had a personality transplant; she hadn't gone to Brick's house for a completely selfless reason.

Hannah wants to tell Olivia what she found at Tom's and her frightening theory about Brick, but she knows Olivia's going to tell her to go to the police and she's too scared. What if she gets done for hiding evidence? Or if it turns out the sculpture is a murder weapon, and her fingerprints are all over it. And what if she tells the police and then it turns out it's just some paint or rust, not even blood? She will have delayed the house sale even longer for a rusty vulva and Tom would be furious with her. Especially when she hasn't even flagged the vulva to him yet.

'Guess who was already at Brick's place when I got there? Claire,' Hannah answers her own guess who because she can't bear when people do that. Just tell or don't. Don't waste people's time trying to make them guess to make your life more exciting.

'Oh interesting,' Olivia says, eager to get out of her own relationship drama and involved in someone else's. 'I always thought she fancied him.'

'Oh, she's incredibly obvious about it. Crying one minute, and then all over him the next. It's given me secondary emotional whiplash. And poor Brick has no idea what she's up to,' Hannah says. 'He's so wrapped up in his grief he wouldn't notice if she thrust her bare tits in his face.'

'How was Tom this morning?' Olivia can't help feeling a nervous kind of jealousy about their meeting.

She can't see any signs of dishevelment on Hannah, though, and she's pretty sure she would have told her by now if Tom had banged her over the Aga. She'd definitely have led with that over the story about Brick.

'Yeah good,' Hannah says, not wanting to give away that anything weird had happened while she was there. 'He had a Zoom meeting he needed to do so I wasn't there long.'

Olivia's relieved, but also confused. Maybe he really meant what he said to her last night. After all, the Tom she knows would have shagged Hannah in a second. What if he really has changed? What if Tom's changed and it's her husband who's a big cheating whore of a man?

'Meant that I had time to go and check in on Brick, though and find out what Claire was up to,' Hannah says.

'What are you up to before the vigil tonight?' Olivia asks. 'Are you just going straight from the office? I was just thinking if we've got time in between maybe we could head to yours for a bit. It's closer than mine and we might want to escape all of . . . this.'

Olivia gestures towards the picture of Bella on the stage as evidence, but Hannah immediately clams up. Olivia can't come to hers. She can't see where she's living.

'Oh, I was thinking we'd probably be roped into helping Amanda with set up?' Hannah says. 'Don't want Claire behaving like some kind of martyr that's done everything?'

Olivia does a loud sigh. 'Oh god, you're right.'

'Tom said he'd come tonight,' Hannah says.

'Oh, did he?' Olivia says. 'I didn't realise.'

She already knew he was coming because he'd texted her, asking if they'd have a chance to talk. She'd deleted the text straight away without replying and congratulated herself on her restraint.

'You really don't like him, do you?' Hannah says, watching her friend's troubled face. 'I'd have thought you'd love to have your two friends getting it on? We can be a foursome!'

Olivia screws up her face slightly at the word foursome and Hannah giggles.

'It's not that I don't like him. I just don't think he's really the girlfriend type.' Olivia scrolls on her phone to distract herself, eager not to give anything away with her facial expressions. 'I don't want to see you get hurt. I've never known him settle down with a woman. You deserve better than that.'

'Yeah, you said. But surely it just takes the right woman?' Hannah's quite offended at her friend's lack of faith in her prowess.

'Yeah ... maybe.' Olivia's so distracted Hannah feels like she's barely engaging with her about this. It's fucking rude and annoying her.

'Cool, thanks for the confidence boost,' Hannah snaps, but Olivia barely hears her. She's too preoccupied, staring at her phone as if Hannah's chat isn't even important to her.

A discomfort settles over the two of them and Hannah's glad she didn't tell Olivia about the sculpture. She probably would have only judged her for it or continued staring at her phone, barely paying attention to her like she's doing right now. She feels a distance forming between the two of them right when she needs her the most. Because if the sculpture is a murder weapon, even without her fingerprints being on it or the part she's played in hiding it, Hannah's starting to feel a bit scared now.

Chapter Twenty-two

Claire's thrilled to see that her single bunch of white roses earlier has multiplied. Throughout the day, people have been adding to the pile, and now there's a sort of blossoming sea of white over the green that looks kind of magical. Obviously, Claire's sad that all of this is for someone who lied and betrayed her, but it's the first time in her life that she's ever started a trend. She feels quite powerful.

Illuminated pictures of Bella smile out at Claire from the window of every shop, cafe, bar and restaurant in Wellingden. The square and the bandstand, usually used for more cheerful events like carol singing and switching on the Christmas lights, are covered in flowers, notes, candles and teddy bears. All of it for Bella. The women of Harrington's Estates – minus Amanda, who's busy sorting the sound – are at the centre of it all, wearing black and solemnly thanking a constant stream of people who've sought them out to offer condolences. Hannah's not even sure most of these people live in the town, she barely recognises any of them.

'How are you feeling, Claire?' Olivia asks, smiling politely and nodding at another passing grief tourist.

'I'm OK,' Claire nods.

She's managed to make herself look even more sad by simply not putting any concealer under her eyes when she redid her make-up. And using about half a bottle of eye drops to make sure that she looks overly watery.

She shoots them both a conspiratorial look and realises that this could be her time. Her chance to get in with them.

'There's something I need to tell you both. It's about Bella.' She hopes she looks earnest.

'Oh?' Olivia asks, but Hannah carries on greeting people.

Whatever that expression is on Claire's face, it's a clear indication to Hannah that she probably won't be arsed with whatever Claire's about to say.

Claire can tell that neither of them are interested. She's going to have to up the ante, pull them in by making it sound as juicy as possible.

'I don't think Bella was who we thought she was.' Claire leans in to them both, whispering before stepping back again hastily to smile and greet another well-wisher. As soon as they walk away, though, she leans back towards them once more. 'She had secrets.'

'Huh?' Hannah and Olivia's heads snap up like meerkats.

It's the kind of attention Claire's wanted from them for years. She relishes their stares and takes her time to spill the goods.

'Claire, speak,' Hannah says, confirming that Claire's revelled in it a little too much.

'She had this box – Brick showed it to me earlier. It was filled with pictures,' Claire whispers. 'Of Amanda . . . I think she was obsessed with her.'

She'd thought long and hard about whether or not she was going to tell Hannah and Olivia but, at the end of the day, Bella had screwed her over. Now she's gone, Claire has a chance to be in control of Bella's narrative, and there's nothing Bella can do about it. So why not? Claire couldn't wait to show people who Bella really was. She just has to be careful about going too far. She's always known she can't tell them about Esme because that might look like she was biased. But at least the box has provided her with proof that she's an impartial witness to. She can tell people about it as an innocent observer. Tearing Bella down is going to be her ultimate and final revenge.

'So?' Hannah asks, looking a bit irritated. 'I mean obviously she was. She was constantly trying to impress her. She basically lived up her arsehole for the last couple of years.'

'What she says,' Olivia says, turning away from Claire.

'No,' Claire says, eager to keep their attention and annoyed that she might have fucked it. 'I mean . . . more like she hated her. Brick said she had beef with her. She was obsessed with everything she did because she held some kind of grudge against her.'

'That's . . . weird . . .' Hannah says while Olivia just stands there, assessing Claire.

'Are you OK, Claire?' Olivia asks. 'Has this all maybe got a bit much for you?'

Amanda comes over in a black Erdem dress and Jimmy Choo heels, forcing the women back into silence. She looks classy, elegant, but not overdone. They marvel at the way that she always seems to know what to wear no matter the occasion.

'I know it's bittersweet, but isn't this magical? It's so nice to feel the support of the whole town even though it's such a sad occasion,' Amanda says. 'I was going to start by making a speech, but I haven't seen Brick yet? I wonder if we should wait until he's here? He might want to say something himself if he feels able to. Have any of you seen him?'

Hannah hasn't seen him, but she can't imagine a world in which Brick would not want to say something to a large crowd of people, grieving or not.

'Not yet,' Olivia replies. 'Maybe he's finding it all a little overwhelming, struggling to get himself together? It must be hard.'

'Oh, look! Matt and Tom are here.' Hannah waves to them in the crowd.

Olivia feels her stomach drop at the sight of her usually dependable husband in his black suit, next to the man she kissed in their kitchen just a few nights ago. She's annoyed at how normal Matt looks, like he's just arrived back from work, when she knows that in fact he hasn't been anywhere near the office. All day he's been just minutes from her. Olivia offers a small gesture of a wave back, her eyes slightly glazed over.

'I can give Brick a call if you like, Amanda? See where he's got to?' Claire offers.

'If you could, Claire, that would be great,' Amanda smiles. 'Maybe we should start soon before people get restless, though?'

Olivia and Hannah nod in agreement.

'Brilliant. I thought I could welcome everyone, then I know Claire wants to say something a little more personal about Bella and their friendship. I'm sure Brick will want to come up after that, but do either of you want to say something as well?'

It feels like Amanda's staring into their soul, challenging them both to admit out loud that they didn't like Bella and they'd barely be able to scrape together a sentence of kindness about her. But that didn't mean that they weren't sad she'd died.

'I think we should probably leave plenty of time for Brick,' Hannah says diplomatically.

'And we should leave people time to have their own reflections too,' Olivia agrees.

'He's not answering.' Claire joins them again, locking her phone.

'OK, I think maybe we just start. Let's head over to the bandstand,' Amanda says, looking around at the small candles dotted around the town square, glinting in the darkness. 'I hope we've done her proud.'

'It looks beautiful,' Olivia says while the women pick through the crowd, clasping hands and accepting offers of condolence as they go, like local celebrities. Hannah's never felt like such a fraud in her life.

As they climb the stairs, Olivia gets a clearer view of Matt and Tom, laughing and joking together. For a second, she wonders if Tom knows what was going on with Matt. But surely he'd have told her? He'd have used it as a reason why she should pursue things with him. Surely?

Hannah watches Claire across the stage, blotting her eyes with a tissue as they wait for Amanda to make a start. It's a laughable gesture to Hannah, considering Claire's behaviour with Brick earlier and the glee with which she told them about Bella's box just moments ago.

Amanda signals for them all to move in closer. As they come together, she leans in like a coach giving a pep talk. 'This is going to be hard, but you're all doing so well. You've conducted yourselves impeccably in such difficult circumstances over the last few days. I'm proud of you and I know Bella would be too. We just need to go up there and do this, for Bella.'

'For Bella,' Claire repeats, and stares at Olivia and Hannah, who find themselves also muttering a 'for Bella'.

Amanda taps the microphone and the gathered crowd silences, staring back at them with expectation, for a woman that none of them, even the women on stage ever really knew. Blinking under the bright lights on the stage, it's Claire who moves in first, closer to Olivia, but when Hannah sees Olivia reach out for Claire's hand for comfort she immediately feels as though she's being left out and grabs Olivia's. Her grip's tight, but Olivia's feels slack, as though she's barely even noticed Hannah taking her hand.

'Good evening,' Amanda says into the microphone, her

voice projecting across the crowd. She's normally a good public speaker, but she finds her voice shaking. 'I wanted to thank you all for coming and celebrating Bella and her extraordinary-but-far-too-short life with us tonight.'

Olivia watches Matt, searching his face for any kind of reaction that might be out of the ordinary, maybe a rogue tear or something. As Amanda speaks, he bows his head respectfully. Solid, dependable Matt. The beacon of politeness that she married. Always appropriately dressed, never disgracing her. She watches Tom next to him, also solemn, but staring at Bella's inflated image on the easel.

Dave, Felix and Ron from Sanders are right at the front. All three of them standing in a line, with matching shiny suits and hands clasped in front of them, their heads lowered. They remind Hannah of little boys that have been made to sit at the front of assembly to stop them from misbehaving.

She notices that Marcus is dangerously near the steps to the bandstand, as though he might climb up and start giving his own eulogy about Bella; she wouldn't put it past him. She already heard him earlier telling people how close he was to Bella, and how tragic it is that they'll never again talk about the importance of a solid brass knocker. She feels stressed out just looking at him, aware that if she wants Amanda to think she's management material she's going to have to take on one of his fucking projects.

With all the pictures of Bella staring at her from easels and shop windows, Hannah feels the walls closing in. She's everywhere she looks, each image giving her a knowing stare, as though Bella can see what she's done. She knows she brushed the weapon that probably killed her under the logs. But surely Bella would understand the need for Hannah's every-woman-for-herself attitude? The inside of her head is like a seesaw. She knows she can't just leave the sculpture there – it can't stay in the basket undiscovered forever. After all, she found it, didn't she? It would only be a matter of time before someone else did too. But she can't decide what to do for the best.

Maybe she could tell Tom. They could come up with a plan to dispose of it together? Tom needs the money as much as she does, after all. Then they can sell the place and no one would ever be any the wiser. She'd get out of the property guardian scheme and back into a flat of her own. With Bella gone, she'll never get herself in that situation again.

Or there's the other side of the seesaw, where she confesses about the sculpture, and hands it in to the police. Tom will hate her for fucking up the sale, she'll hate herself for fucking up the sale and police will probably find her fingerprints on it. All the second option seems to offer is wildly fucking up her life even more than it already is. But she worries that she'll never sleep at night if she continues with her current plan. She'd always thought she was more devious than this.

'Bella touched so many lives, whether she sold a house to you or for you, or she simply spoke to you around town. She was full of light and goodness. We were so lucky to have her for the time that we did . . .' Amanda continues, her hand clasped round the microphone as if it's the only thing keeping her upright.

Amanda's annoyed with herself. She needs to keep it together. She's tougher than this. She built her business from nothing, for fuck's sake, scrabbled her way up. She's known harder times than this.

She can't help feeling if her husband had been here she'd feel better. His message said that he had to work late, but it doesn't wash with her any more. She can't believe he couldn't give it up just for one night. Doesn't he realise how his absence might look to the rest of the town? Her own husband not being here to support her?

Her voice falters again as she sees a figure approaching the stairs to the stage out of the corner of her eye. She tries not to be as jumpy as she feels, swivelling her head as though expecting danger. But when she turns, it's just Brick that she sees, ambling up the stairs, unsteady on his feet, his tiny beanie the steadiest-looking part of him.

Claire, Hannah and Olivia spot him too, all three women watching as he trips up each step, one after the other, somehow maintaining his balance despite looking like he's about to lose it. In the audience, Matt and Tom twig that something's not right and start trying to move through the dense crowd towards the stage. As Brick stumbles up, knocking over one of the displays of flowers, his face red and puffy, Claire breaks away from the group and goes to help him, but he pushes her away. Olivia rushes to steady Claire, and Amanda stops talking, having previously thought she could carry on, class and poise doing some incredibly heavy lifting.

Brick goes to kick the other display of flowers, his rage now unmistakable to everyone in the audience as well as those on stage as he repeatedly swings his leg and misses. He strides up to Amanda, snatching the microphone from her, and barges her out of the way. Hannah and Olivia lunge to grab Amanda and protect her, but Claire just stares open-mouthed. The women cower, afraid of him, apart from Claire who finds his angry, emotional state quite sexy.

'What Amanda neglects to mention in her lovely fluffy speech is that these women –' Brick holds the microphone against his spittle-covered lips with one hand and gestures to the group with his other – 'are bitches. She hated all of them. Absolute bunch of cunts.'

There's a gasp from the crowd.

'Harrington's is the most toxic office in this entire town, maybe even the entire world .' He gestures dramatically with his arms out. 'The whole time Bella worked there she was constantly being judged, mocked and stabbed in the back. Now she's gone and it's because of them. She kept pushing and pushing herself, trying to impress them all, trying to feel like she fitted in, while all these women tried to tear her down. And as for "women supporting women",' Brick does bunny air quotes. 'Yeah well ... is it supportive to drive each other crazy with gaslighting and competition?'

He pauses, stumbling slightly. Olivia can see Tom and Matt still trying to break through the crowd to help while Marcus edges away from the situation.

'And you, Amanda!' Brick points to Amanda, almost tripping over his own feet. 'You're the worst! It's your fake nice-y, nice-y mummy persona that started this whole thing. These women may look normal but they're nothing more than a bunch of Botox-filled liars and cheats. She was driven into the ground by them. Destroyed. It's a fucking cult! A cult where they'd screw each other over for the last Rolo if they could, just to impress high priestess Amanda.'

On the road at the edge of the crowd, Hannah sees police cars arriving and nudges Olivia. There are at least five of them in total. The police officers get out and begin heading for the stage, led by DI Knight. Oblivious, and barely able to see straight, Brick continues his rant.

'If you even care who's to blame for Bella's death, it was them.' He points to Amanda, Claire, Olivia and Hannah, all of whom are too busy staring at the police approaching the stage, clearing a path through the crowd far more efficiently than Matt and Tom were obviously able to, due to the sheer volume of them. 'These women are to blame for Bella's death. It was no accident. I know one of them did it, and somehow I'm going to prove it!'

DI Knight climbs the stairs to the bandstand and Brick finally seems to register the police's arrival. Amanda creeps across the stage to meet DI Knight on the stairs, hoping to prevent any more of a scene.

'Clive?' Amanda whispers, aware that many members of the crowd are holding their phones aloft, filming the action. After all, Brick's given them such a spectacle that they can hardly resist. 'Can I help?'

'I'm sorry, Amanda. We're going to need to shut this down,' DI Knight says. 'There's been a development. We need you and your employees to come to the station.'

'What kind of development?' Amanda whispers while Hannah, Olivia and Claire lean forward to try to hear better.

'I'm afraid we think Bella was –' DI Knight leans in towards Amanda the same time that Brick stumbles, falling into him while holding the microphone – 'murdered.'

The word is amplified, ringing out across the whole town.

Chapter Twenty-three

The women sit in the Harrington's Estates office, sipping tequila from a fancy bottle that Amanda keeps in her desk for big celebrations. The town square was empty by the time they'd all finished their interviews and emerged from the police station, but even so Amanda's pulled the blinds down to stop any rogue prying eyes.

'I just can't believe they're saying it was murder,' Claire says, crying as usual.

'Me neither,' Olivia says, sipping the tequila and passing it on to Hannah.

'It's just beyond belief,' Amanda says.

'They told me someone hit her over the head. Is that what they told you guys too?' Claire weeps.

Hannah raises the tequila bottle to her lips, trying not to let anyone see how much she's shaking. She's not going to dignify Claire's question with an answer. Of course, the police told them all the same thing. The police don't lie. Unlike Hannah.

Bella's cause of death had been blunt force trauma to the head. Someone had hit her with something heavy. After

Brick's performance on stage, Hannah had been far too afraid to tell the police what she'd found at Tom's house earlier today. After all, Brick had already made it look like they were all guilty. The police would immediately suspect her if she led them to the weapon.

'Yeah,' Olivia says.

'Thanks to Brick, everyone probably thinks one of us did it.' Hannah passes the bottle on to Olivia.

She's pretty sure what she's just done makes her some kind of criminal. She feels too stressed to even think about how Tom must be feeling right now. He's probably beside himself.

'Oh god, do you think so?' Claire practically shrieks. 'Do you think Brick thinks *I* did it?'

'I don't think he was singling anyone out. He was making out we were all as bad as each other,' Hannah says. 'We should sue him for slander. It's bad for business.'

'I wouldn't worry.' Amanda tries to keep her voice positive. 'Anyone could see that Brick wasn't stable up there tonight. He was all over the place. People know us and they love us. They won't jump to conclusions based on the ramblings of a drunk man. I'm more concerned about all of you. Tonight's been a terrible shock for us.'

'It's just unbelievable,' Claire says, never missing a chance to garner sympathy.

'Yeah, like you say, a total shock,' Hannah says, nervous that if she doesn't say it was a shock one of these women might twig that it *was* less of a shock for her than it was for the others.

Olivia's surprised at Hannah's response, considering she prides herself on being unflappable.

'It must be hard for you too, though,' Olivia says to Amanda.

'Oh, that's very kind of you, Olivia, but I'm fine.' Amanda smiles to her.

'Do you think one of us should talk to Brick?' Claire asks.

'Not when he's behaving like that,' Olivia says.

'Olivia's right. I don't think that's a good idea,' Amanda says. 'I'll offer him a contribution for counselling from the business. A kind of family liaison situation as she died in the line of duty. But I don't think any of you should approach him. He seems very angry and not particularly stable right now.'

Olivia relishes Amanda telling her she's right. Amanda's approval never gets old for her. With Bella around, it had just been so long since she'd had it. She considers the manager's position that Bella was going for before she died and imagines herself as Amanda's second-in-command. Olivia's phone lights up with another message from Matt, but she ignores it, turning her phone face down on the desk.

'It must be hard for Brick because they were breaking up before she died,' Claire says. 'Well, I mean, she told me they were.'

'I'm not sure we should speculate about the status of their relationship,' Amanda says. 'It's not something we should do as women when she's alive and certainly not when she's dead.'

'Sorry, Amanda,' Claire says, chastised. 'I wasn't thinking.'

She feels annoyed at herself for getting the tone so wrong. She thought Amanda would have wanted to know about Brick and Bella. She's sure Hannah enjoyed that. Hannah loves watching other people getting told off by Amanda.

Hannah's actually so wrapped up in running through scenarios in her head that she's not even listening. She knows she should hand in the sculpture – the weapon now, she supposes it would be called. But, if she does, then there's no way of her ever getting out of her financial hole, there's no way of Tom ever getting out of his. What if Tom blames her? And, besides, how's she even supposed to accidentally 'find' it now without incriminating herself in some way? Especially after Brick's very public accusations.

'Maybe we should head home? Get some sleep. Tomorrow's a new day,' Amanda says. 'I'll get you all taxis.'

'Thanks,' Claire says, thrilled again because Amanda's never even so much as offered to pour her a glass of water before now.

'Me and Olivia are OK,' Hannah says. 'Matt and Tom are coming to meet us.'

Olivia shoots her a look that Hannah can't place. Like she wasn't aware that they were coming. Tom has texted Hannah to let her know so she just assumed that Matt would have messaged Olivia too. Hannah looks over to where Olivia's turned her phone face down.

'Yeah, we should be fine,' Olivia says, grabbing her phone and looking at the messages from Matt she's been ignoring. 'They're going to meet us outside.'

'You don't think we need to worry, do you? If someone's

murdered Bella, should we be nervous?' Claire turns to the other women, wide-eyed, her tears stemmed, at least for now.

Hannah simply stares back because she realises she assumed it was Brick who did it. But then, if he had, would he really have been up on stage trying to convince people it was murder before the police had declared that it was? Surely, he'd have been keeping his head down? Going with the tragic-accident line? And if it wasn't Brick, then who was it? And why?

'I don't think we need to panic just yet,' Olivia says. 'The police didn't say we should worry, did they?'

'Exactly,' Amanda says. 'I would say be alert, but stay calm ... Claire, your car's going to be here in one minute. Let's get you home safe and sound.'

'You think I'm not safe?' Claire shoots back, not at all eased by Amanda.

'I don't think you're unsafe,' Amanda says, as clearly and calmly as she can.

'I'm sure you're fine,' Hannah says. 'People don't just kill people for no reason.'

'Exactly,' Amanda agrees.

But Hannah can't help wondering if they'd have all been safer if she'd told the police about the sculpture. And now she knows she's going to have to make up for hiding it, somehow.

'OK Claire, your car's here,' Amanda says, closing her phone.

'We'll follow you out,' Hannah says. She can see Tom

and Matt waiting for them outside and she wonders if she can get Tom on his own. Maybe she can tell him about what she found and the two of them can address it together.

The women stand and head towards the door, where Amanda embraces Claire tightly in a hug. As she heads off to her taxi moments later, Claire thinks this might be the closest the four women have ever been, bonded by trauma.

'Just got a few things I want to take care of here before I leave,' Amanda says, standing in the doorway as Hannah and Olivia approach.

'OK,' Hannah says, giving Amanda a hug. 'See you tomorrow. Let us know if you need us to help with anything.'

'See you tomorrow.' Olivia takes over the hug from Hannah, before they disappear out into the night where Tom and Matt are waiting for them.

Amanda locks the door, pushing against it twice to check that it's secure, then walks across the office, back to her desk. She pours a double shot of tequila into one of the Harrington's Estates mugs and turns on her computer. Feeling unsettled, she stands again, walking to the toilet and double checking the window is locked in there too. Satisfied that everything is secure, she sits back down at her desk, takes a sip of the tequila, puts her head in her hands and starts to cry.

'I feel quite sorry for the guy, actually,' Tom says as they all walk to their cars. 'He's lost the love of his life and he's in turmoil.'

Olivia almost snorts with laugher. When Matt reached out for her hand earlier, she'd whipped it away pretending to have an itch on her face, and he doesn't seem to have noticed that she didn't grab it again.

'It's all very tortured artist,' Hannah replies.

She's impatient for Matt and Olivia to head off so that she can talk to Tom alone.

'Well, quite, he's clearly already a sensitive chap,' Tom says.

Olivia thinks of the 'Suck My Dick' neon art that was above Tom's bed for the open house, a previous product of the 'sensitive chap's' brain. Matt starts to laugh.

'What?' Tom asks.

'Well,' Matt slaps him on the back. 'I mean I just don't know if you could really call his art all that sensitive? Although I guess fisting would *cause* sensitivity . . .'

'Ew!' Olivia giggles, despite herself.

'Matthew!' Hannah shouts.

'On that note,' Matt says, stopping in front of Olivia's Mercedes, 'this is us.'

Hannah's first instinct is to reach out to give Olivia a hug. It's a gesture usually so normal between the two of them, but, for some reason, today it's awkward and she can't quite work out why. Olivia's still got that distracted look to her that's starting to make Hannah question if she's annoyed with her about doing Tom's listing on her own, after all. She didn't seem bothered the other night and, if she is, Hannah doesn't know why she wouldn't just say something. She does feel a little guilty about it, though. As much as she needs the money, she knows that Olivia's going to need it soon too, especially once Matt tells her what he's done. They both pull away, relieved the moment's over and Olivia gets straight into her car. Matt gives them both a little wave then jumps into the car next to her.

Tom and Hannah watch them drive away, an awkward silence settling over them. She knows she needs to talk to him about the sculpture. But now, faced with the perfect time to tell him, she can't think of a single way to broach it. 'It's funny they think it was murder now because I also think I found the weapon in your logs but I buried it back under them because I was initially worried you might have been the killer.' Doesn't feel like the right way to bring it up, to be honest. There's no way to tell him about it in which she comes off well.

'Where are you parked?' Tom asks Hannah. 'Can you drive?'

'Just round the corner,' Hannah says, feeling the start of an imaginary clock ticking. 'And yes, I barely touched the tequila, your honour. It's not my favourite drink, I know that's basically blasphemy for some people.'

'I'll let you into a secret,' Tom says, winking at her. 'I feel exactly the same way about tequila. I'll walk you to your car, lest you get accosted by any crazy artists.'

'Where are you parked?' Hannah asks.

'Oh, I'm not. I've been walking to the station every morning trying to keep fit,' Tom says. 'Matt reckons he's 'pulled a hamstring' so my squash partner's out of action for a bit. Besides, it means I can do my bit for the environment, saving the world one car at a time.'

Hannah knows exactly why Matt hasn't been playing squash and it's nothing to do with pulling a hamstring. She gives Tom a sideways glance, studying his face to see if there's any hint that he might know why Matt hasn't been playing too. There's no indication that he does.

'You're the Greta Thunberg this town needs,' Hannah says. 'I'm sorry about the house. All this means that it'll be even longer before we can sell.'

'I know. Matt and I had to go back to mine earlier to let in the police. They've cordoned off where we found her in the garden, so it's obviously not exactly viewings ready. I know we'll have to put the price down. I'm guessing you haven't had any luck finding the person who put the offer in, either?' Tom asks.

'Nothing,' Hannah says. 'Bella was pretty secretive about it.'

Hannah knows this is her chance. She can see her car in the distance so she needs to tell him about the sculpture now.

'There was something I wanted to talk to you about, actually,' Hannah takes a deep breath.

'Oh?' he asks as they approach her car, and she wonders about pretending she hasn't seen it and carrying on a lap around the block to give them more time. 'This is yours, isn't it?'

'Oh yes,' Hannah says, pretending to have only just

noticed the lilac BMW and cursing herself for driving something so distinctive.

Hannah stands at the car door, hesitating. The longer she leaves it without saying anything the more she knows she's coming across as weird. The idea comes to her in a flash. She looks up at him, leaning against the door in a way she hopes is sultry. Really, it's killing two birds with one stone.

'You've had a bad night. I could give you a lift back to yours if you like?' She leans over and touches his arm. It's only the same way that he was comforting her earlier.

It's inevitable, the two of them getting together – even Matt said it. They can kiss, go back to his and she can somehow lead them into the living room at some point (obviously after they've had sex) then they can accidentally discover the sculpture. She's a genius. She's sure there'll be a chance at some point for her to quickly wipe her prints off it.

'I'm more worried about you getting back to yours OK,' Tom says. 'Why don't I come with you to your place? Then I can be sure you're home safe and I'm sure I can get a taxi back from there. Liv and Matt would probably kill me themselves if you encountered a violent artist because I hadn't done my job properly.'

Hannah hadn't anticipated this. She stalls slightly. Even if she didn't live where she does, she needs to go round to his house, not the other way around. She's going to have to try a different tact.

'Honestly, I'm a big girl. I can look after myself,' Hannah says as she walks her fingers up his arm.

He looks down at her hand and then up again, their gaze meeting. She feels herself pouting slightly in expectation. He goes to reach out round her shoulder and Hannah's sure there's no room for misinterpretation. His signals are clear. She leans forward, pressing her lips against his, her hand round his neck. For a second, she thinks her lip filler's migrated or something – the kiss feels odd. But then Tom pulls away, his lips pursed.

'Sorry, I . . . I think there might be a misunderstanding. I've got a girlfriend . . .' Tom says.

Hannah feels her face burning, glad of the darkness. She's embarrassed for two seconds before she bats it away, replacing it with rage. Rage at Olivia. How could she not have told her? All that stuff with Matt last night saying that he was sure Tom was into her. How could Matt not have told her, either? They said he was a player – they lied to her. They could have just said he had a girlfriend. Surely that makes more sense?

Why does her friend suddenly have an aversion to telling the truth? She's lied about a lot of things lately – including having a meeting this morning, because Hannah drove past Olivia sitting in the window of a cafe twice after she said that and both times she was alone and hadn't moved.

'A girlfriend?' Hannah repeats the words slowly, trying to stop herself from running away crying hot, mortified tears.

'Yeah, I'm sorry. I should have said sooner,' Tom says.

Hannah grips her car keys so tightly she can feel her knuckles whitening.

'Some girlfriend, she hasn't even shown her face while you've been dealing with everything?' She wants to get in the car, but she also wants desperately to find a way to save face.

Hannah analyses him through the darkness, confused at how she could have misread the signals. After all, the other night, Tom was encouraging her, hugging her, flirting, 'comforting' her. And why would Olivia and Matt say he was single when he wasn't anyway? What if they weren't lying, Tom was? Maybe Olivia's right, he's just been playing this whole time. He's a womanizer who's messing with her emotions to feel good about himself. Stringing her along just so he can reject her and feel like the big man.

'I know,' Tom says. 'She works away. She can't get back. She's with Doctors Without Borders.'

Doctors without borders? Really? That's it, she knows he's lying. All the meaningful glances, the touching, the flirting. She didn't imagine it. She's not going to allow herself to be tricked into thinking this was all on her.

She takes a couple of seconds to think before she speaks because she wants what she says to come out calm and in control so he can never turn it round on her. She doesn't want him to know that he's bothered her, that secretly she's hurt and blinking back the tears.

'Sounds like bullshit to me,' she replies, clicking the car key in her hand, before spinning on her heel and getting in her BMW.

It takes her precisely ten seconds from slamming the door to speeding off, leaving Tom speechless in her wake. She won't be texting to let him know she got home safe, either.

Chapter Twenty-four

Claire reaches over to the small kitchen counter in her studio from her bed and puts her empty wine glass down. She leans over to open the fridge and gets a small drunken headrush. There isn't room for the fridge door to open fully. Instead, it smacks against the side of her bed and she slides her hand in through a gap just wide enough to prise the bottle out and top up her glass before sliding it back in again. It's not as bad as when she tries to use the oven and she has to post whatever she's cooking through a tiny crack at the top of the door, and then try and scrape it back out again with a long-handled fish slice.

Glass of wine now topped up she returns to her phone. She's been lying prone for hours, reading through all the text messages that she and Bella have ever sent each other, trying to work out at what point Bella went from a friend to someone who was intent on screwing her over and selling her inheritance from under her.

Claire had invited Bella round to meet her great-aunt Esme and show her that she had friends like Fliss and Saff. She'd wanted Esme to think that she was a chip off the old block. That they could be two businesswomen together. That was Claire's only shot at getting a property. Her only chance to own a home. It's not as if she was about to go from barely scraping together the money for a bedsit to home ownership before she was thirty any other way.

Bella must have really had Brick under her spell for him to show up tonight and publicly accuse *them* of stabbing *Bella* in the back? Bella was the worst one of all – she *made* Claire toxic. And now she was gone. Without her, Claire felt like they'd all become more of a unit. Amanda always went on about how they were family, but Claire had only really felt that way since Bella died; she felt like Olivia and her were definitely becoming closer.

Brick had always deserved better than Bella anyway. Claire knows thou shalt not covert thy friend's boyfriend or whatever, but she stopped feeling bad about masturbating over Brick the moment she found out thou's friend had been betraying her quite so monumentally. She hopes Brick is all right, all that stuff he was going on about. It didn't make any sense. The grief must have got to him, poor guy.

The others have him all wrong. He's a nice guy. A *good* guy. Claire swigs away at her wine, thinking about how he deserves someone who isn't like all the others, someone real, someone who would love him and cherish his talent the way Claire does. He deserves ... Claire, actually. And it's not like anyone's going to stop her now, is it?

Claire stands at the top of the driveway, staring into the huge plate-glass windows, just watching Brick. The inside of the house is fully lit up like a stage against the dark of the night as Brick throws himself against furniture in various stages of grief.

Claire's overcome with desire watching this tortured, troubled man. She's itching for his tattooed fingers to unzip her dress, the B A R E L O V E knuckles grazing against her skin. She wants to hear him tell her that she's not like the other girls – she already knows she's not – but she wants him to confirm it. She knows he can sense that. Surely he can? He wasn't angry with her earlier – he was angry with everyone else. He'd spent the day with her peacefully talking about Bella. The two of them united in grief. They have a special connection; the way he opened up to her just proved it.

Unable to resist him any longer, Claire heads towards the house, heels clacking against the path. She reaches the front door and presses the doorbell, the sound of the ding vibrating throughout the house. For a second, she wonders how on earth it could have been possible that she didn't hear Brick shouting and raging against the glass. The sound of his feet coming down the stairs excites her. The others were so afraid of him, but she knows there's nothing to worry about.

He pulls open the door. 'Claire? What are you doing here?' He seems surprised to see Claire, maybe even slightly disappointed. As if his display could have been for the purpose of someone else.

'I wanted to come and check on you,' Claire says, holding her mac tight around her. 'I was worried about you after earlier. You seemed in such a bad way; not like yourself at all. I didn't want to leave you on your own.'

Brick stares at her, tears rolling down his cheeks. Claire moves into the house uninvited and envelops him in a suffocating hug.

'I'm so sorry, I didn't mean to make it worse. Here –' Claire strokes his back and sniffs his hair, not that Brick notices in the pit of his grief – 'shall we go upstairs and have a drink?'

She pulls away and takes his hand, seductively leading him up the glass stairs with a small portion of lacy bra poking out and 'come to bed' eyes that she put a lot of effort into.

Upstairs, in the main living area, Claire takes a look around, noticing the state of the place. The box from earlier is open, its contents strewn across the room, empty beer cans and a small half-finished bottle of vodka cover the coffee table where Bella's rose-gold laptop sits, open, the light from the screen illuminating the mess. Despite this, she stalks across the room towards the retro bar cart on the edge of the kitchen and mixes two gin and tonics, double gin, light on the tonic. She hands one to Brick, before sliding onto the sofa next to him, her legs bent at an angle, feet up on the cushions, her elbow resting on his shoulder as he cries and takes long chugs of the gin. Gradually, she leans on him more and more. Subconsciously, he slides away but she's like Velcro. She cannot be detached from him. Eventually, Brick succumbs to her as she cradles his head in her bosom for the umpteenth time that day, her black lacy bra on display.

'Let it all out,' she says, stroking his hair as he cries. 'Let it alllll out.'

He slides further away and the two of them topple off the sofa to the floor with Brick wailing. Lying on the thick, shagpile carpet, Claire seizes her chance. She reaches up and touches the exposed edges of his bald head, not covered by the tiny hat, and strokes it gently, seductively, like petting a cat. She walks her fingers down from his head to his cheek, wiping the tears away with her thumb. It would be effective if there were just the odd tear, but a single thumb cannot absorb Brick's ocean-like grief. Her drenched thumb slides slickly across his face. She moves her head, trying to make eye contact, but his eyes are mostly shut. In the end, she pulls up an eyelid with one finger and stares deeply into his surprised eyeball.

'I'm here for you,' she says before letting go of his face and allowing his eye to close again.

She moves a hand down to stroke the exposed bit of chest peeking out from his low V-neck T-shirt. The patch of skin tattooed with the word 'heart'.

'Brick?' She whispers, trying to get him to look at her again. 'Brick?' She says it louder. 'BRICK!' She almost shouts it in his face and his eyelids finally fly open, petrified.

She foists herself towards him, red lips puckered, as he does a sudden jerky army-style roll away across the shagpile. She topples, mac flying open and winces at the definite carpet burns such a drastic movement must have made.

'Brick?' she whispers, her face smushed against the shag,

mac open, underwear exposed, towering Primark heels still on her feet. She tries to peel herself up attractively, but stumbles.

Brick stands, eager to get away from her, and sits on the sofa, grabbing Bella's open laptop from the coffee table as he does. But Claire simply follows, taking a seat and sidling up to him, stroking his arm. He slams the laptop shut on his knees, putting his head in his hands.

'Let me comfort you, Brick. I'm sad too. I can make you feel better. I was Bella's friend. I'm not like the others. I care. We're grieving together; we can connect in our grief.'

'You weren't her friend!' Brick snaps, standing abruptly, clutching the laptop. He stumbles away from her. 'She hated you! She hated all of you. She didn't trust any of you and now I know why. I've been going through her emails, her texts ... everything. It's very illuminating, Claire. And I'll keep digging until I figure out which one of you bitches did it.'

'Brick ...' Claire's gasps, shocked. Her face is a picture of confusion.

'Save your performance. Just go,' Brick says, standing in front of the window, laptop hugged to his chest. 'I probably don't have long until the police come and take this from me, and I'm so close to figuring out who killed my Bella. When I do, I'm taking you all down.'

Brick faces the window to avoid looking at Claire, watching her reflection in the glass, waiting for her to leave.

'She wasn't *your* Bella. She'd dumped you, remember.

You were nothing to her, Brick,' Claire shoots back to him. 'You think she hated me? She hated you too.'

There's nothing more savage than a scorned woman, especially when she's been scorned her whole life.

Chapter Twenty-five

'Finally come home, then?' Alastair's voice startles Amanda from the dark of the living room.

'Jesus,' Amanda stops in the doorway and clutches her chest. She stares suspiciously at him for a moment before walking in and switching on one of the lamps. 'Why are you sitting in the dark like some kind of serial killer?'

'You won't talk to me. I thought the only way I might finally get your attention was via surprise ambush,' Alastair says, raising a crystal glass of whiskey to his lips.

'Maybe it's because I've got enough going on without having to deal with your stupidity,' Amanda says. 'I'm not one of your minions; you can't manipulate me. I'll talk to you about what you've done when I'm ready. We're on my schedule, not yours.'

'That would all be fine if it wasn't for the fact that we have two children. And they can't just wait around while you sulk. This isn't just about us,' Alastair says. 'For the sake of them if nothing else, we can't keep behaving like we're at war. And, besides all that, there's been a development.'

'What kind of development?' Amanda asks, narrowing

her eyes and walking over to the bar in the corner of the room.

She pours herself a brandy and takes a sip before padding over to the sofa with it, making sure she's a fair distance away from Alastair. She needs the space as a buffer between the two of them.

'Well?' Amanda asks again, while Alastair stares at her. 'You're surely not about to tell me a man with a cleaning fetish has got an STI, are you?'

'Oh, very mature,' Alastair says. 'You know I take great measures to protect you. Protect us.'

'Except for the bit where you were exchanging pictures with one of my employees,' Amanda says. 'Fuck it, maybe I am ready to talk about it, actually. You're lucky Bella didn't realise who you are. I suppose I should be grateful for you doing the bare minimum and using a fake name . . .? This was a warning, Al. it needs to stop. I can play you those TikToks of the women cleaning their flats if you want, we can invest in some kind of Dettol porn, but you need to stop it! For the sake of the children! Imagine Rupert and Maisie on the school playground being bullied with fucking Marigolds because of YOU, for god's sake!'

'It's a little bit worse than that,' Alastair says. 'And, as much as you want to blame me, this time it isn't my fault.'

Amanda tries not to show that she's rattled by this as Alastair leans forward on his seat, putting his phone on their herringbone wood floor and giving it a push. The phone skates across the floor with a scratchy noise that sets Amanda's teeth on edge. It comes to a stop in front of her bare, manicured toes. She tries to read what's on the screen from her seat, not wanting to give her husband the satisfaction of watching her lean down to pick it up. But it looks like Bella has sent him messages today. How is that possible?

Amanda bends reluctantly and lifts up the phone. She tries to remain expressionless reading the messages, but they're more of a series of accusations. And, unfortunately, they're accusations that she knows are true.

'You told me I knew everything.' Alastair holds his whiskey glass in front of him like a shield. 'I trusted you. I even helped you. And now this? Is it true?'

'No,' Amanda replies.

'I know when you're lying. Your face guy isn't *that* good.' Alastair takes a sip of his whiskey. 'Now, the way I see it, we've only got one option. You can leave and I stay here with the kids. You never come back and you never have anything to do with any of us again. Our children don't need a mother like you.'

'That's not fair!' Amanda shouts. 'What are you going to tell them?'

'At first, that you've gone away, then I'll tell them you've left and you're not coming back. You need to leave the area. Start somewhere new,' he says.

'With what?' Amanda asks. 'What will happen to the business? People will ask questions. I'm too much of a personality online. People will wonder what *you* did because everyone always knows if a woman leaves, it's the man.'

'What do you expect me to do, then?' Alastair asks. 'I can't risk staying with you if this all comes out.'

'Don't you worry about me. I'll pay off whoever this is,' Amanda says. 'If anyone's leaving, it's going to be you. Especially given your little fetish. The minute I tell everyone you like to be called Mr Muscle in bed and wiped down with a microfibre cloth, you're done for! Your reputation will be ruined! If you want to leave me, then leave me! But I'm not abandoning my children!'

He takes a sip of his whiskey, already detaching himself from her and their marriage. Amanda's long wondered if her husband might be completely dead inside, but this just proves it. He never loved her at all. Among all the fear and stress, she can feel her heart breaking as she clings firmly to the house and children she knows she'd rather die than let go of.

Chapter Twenty-six

Hannah enters the six-digit code into the rusted keypad on the first door, a solid sheet of steel with holes in it. She wrenches it open with a clatter before sliding inside, sure to close it behind her with more certainty than she normally would. At the set of broken automatic glass doors, she fumbles with her keys, her hands shaking as she finds the correct one and inserts it into the lock. Once unlocked, she slides the heavy panes apart just enough to squeeze through and locks them behind her again.

She looks around the communal area of the old disused library, miserable at the thought that, despite her efforts, this is still going to be her home for the foreseeable future. Her eyes land on the old shelves, housing a mixture of torn and faded books and empty beer cans used as ashtrays. What used to be a thriving community hub is now filled with the stench of rotting takeaway, weed smoke and the constantly blocked or overflowing toilets. For £50 a week, it's a bargain, but at what cost to Hannah's health? She worries she'll catch Legionnaires' disease if she's in here much longer, but it seems her only way out has been totally scuppered.

As she traipses past one of her fellow guardians, unconscious on the sofa and clutching a supermarket-own brand of vodka, Hannah tries not to think about what her night could have been. The sheets she could have found herself sleeping under, the man she would have been sleeping under them with, the scented candles and solid walls she could have breathed confidently around without boaking at the smell. All this, and she could have unburdened herself of her worries over the sculpture. Instead, she's here alone, embarrassed and, because she's very unlikely to be invited round to Tom's again, even more anxious about *Bella's Vulva* than before. Brick was right after all: they all had secrets.

Sneaking past the noisy makeshift rooms around her, Hannah slips into the small old staff room that she's made her own, locking the door firmly behind her again. That's three locked doors between her and the outside world yet she still doesn't feel safe. Refusing to turn on the stark overhead strip light – she may have fallen, but she'll never stoop to being an overhead light person – she finds her way in the dark to the small lamp next to her mattress and switches it on, dumping her bag on the table next to the bed. Everything has to go on tables here, she's not placing the last vestiges of her old life on the damp, mildewed carpet.

For years, Hannah's faked it since she made it. It's been almost fifteen, since she decided that she wasn't going to let the bullies at her school be right. No way was she going to let her childhood, and the poverty she grew up in, dictate the person that she was going to become. She'd been determined to make something of herself, and so she did. That's why Amanda has always been so inspirational to her. Both of them have come from nothing, and just like Amanda she was going to succeed. She swore she'd never be a failure again. But here she is, almost back where she started in life, thanks to Bella.

She doesn't have the energy to get undressed or take off her make-up tonight. Instead, pulling the sheets over herself, she just lies on the lumpy mattress in the low lamp light, staring at the old Save Our Libraries signs on the wall, feeling ashamed. She knows this place will eventually get turned into luxury flats instead of a library that kids like her would have taken solace in. And, when it does, she'll jump at the chance to sell them at the highest price tag, all for the money. She doesn't recognise the monster she's become. She'd give anything to sell these flats just to save herself. The same way she left that bloody vulva in the logs just to protect herself. Now, if the police find it, it might be the undoing of her. Everything's such a mess. All she wanted was to get her life back on track.

Music from one of the rooms starts up for the night, accompanied by the unmistakable sounds of sex. A cruel reminder of the fact that she isn't having sex with Tom right now. She could have been if she'd been better. She really needs to be better. Hannah grabs a pillow and shoves it over her head. She can't believe she's let herself become a loser again by being arrogant. Now, she's got no money, no boyfriend, no flat, she's not even good at her job any more. Her skin burns when she remembers her 'kiss' with

Tom. She's made such a fool of herself, thinking that she was something when she's not. She's nothing.

She feels the tears start to come and then slaps herself round the face. She can't keep living like this, thinking like this. Things won't get better if she carries on. All of her self-pitying reminds her of her mother, a woman who blamed everyone else for her drinking and bad decisions about men. Everyone apart from herself. When Hannah was growing up her mum's poor choices and dependence on awful, undeserving men, got them into so many bad situations and she swore she'd never be like that – never reliant on a man. She's clawed herself out of the hole before when she broke free of her mum's self-destructive cycle and made a better life for herself, and she can do it again. But not like this. Not by lying to the police – or, at the least, omitting details – and not by doing nothing about that sculpture.

It's not just the Bella situation that makes her feel like a failure, either. She hates the friend she's become too. She's just going to tell Olivia about Matt tomorrow. He's had long enough, and he's done nothing. Olivia can't blame her, can she?

It's not her fault she found out from a date, but it is her fault if she keeps it from Olivia. She's going to fix that and find a way to fix everything else too, even the bloody sculpture.

First thing tomorrow, she'll go round to Brick's and find out what he was talking about earlier. After his speech, she knows there's no way he did it. If he'd killed her, he would have left people thinking that her death was an accident. He wouldn't have been screaming on a stage to the whole of Wellingden about how she was murdered. Maybe the two of them can figure out who *was* responsible and go to the police. She's never going to get out of here with all this hanging over her. She needs to do the right thing – or as close to it as she can – and then she can focus on selling houses again. It'll take her a bit longer to get out of here without Tom's house sale, but she *can* do it. She's going to get back to how she was and show Tom what he's missing out on. And then he's going to regret rejecting her every single day of the rest of his sad little life.

Chapter Twenty-seven

Olivia slips out from under the cool white linen sheets as quietly as possible, trying not to disturb Matt. Although, she needn't have worried – he's snoring so loudly nothing would wake him in his current state. He fell asleep as soon as his head hit the pillow, not noticing that Olivia had barely spoken to him since they got back, choosing instead to watch a reality show about strangers being paired off together into couples and left out in the wilderness to survive for a week. Matt always claimed he hated the show, but had certainly seemed to have a lot of loud opinions about it tonight.

Olivia turns on the light in the kitchen and grabs a glass from the cupboard, filling it from the tap. So many times, she'd been on the verge of pausing the TV and asking him outright what was going on, saying she knew something had happened between him and Bella. But every time she started to, she became too afraid of what his answer might be to follow through, especially now the police think Bella's death was a murder.

The one thing that she kept coming back to was why

does he still have the hotel room? And how is he paying for it? Even a hotel as grim as the Welling Inn was going to start costing serious money if he'd had a room there for that long. It must be making a dent in their finances somewhere, surely?

She scans every single statement from the last year, trying to see if she can pinpoint the moment when her husband started his deception. But there's nothing abnormal, nothing she doesn't know about on there. Could it have been going on longer than a year?

The only other place where they have enough money is the IVF fund Olivia set up a few months back with Matt's encouragement. She'd hoped she'd never have to use the money, and Matt had always been so positive about it, saying it was great to have it there anyway, because then when they did fall pregnant, they would have all these savings for the baby. He was always so practical, she didn't question how eager he was that they start the savings account.

On the banking app, she navigates out of their joint account and back to the list of savings pots and sees it instantly. The fund's balance is five thousand pounds lower than it was last time she looked. She stares at the figure, hoping it might change, or that she might be imagining it, but when she clicks into the account her worst fears are confirmed. Five thousand pounds was withdrawn a couple of days before Bella died. But it's not been paid into their mortgage fund or even to Matt himself. It's been paid to Caspian Smith, Brick.

* * *

Olivia's outside Brick's house within twenty minutes, banging at his door with a level of rage she doesn't think she's ever felt before. She knew the sensible thing would be to wake up Matt and to ask him about it but if she does that she suspects her marriage is over. She wants all the facts before she decides to implode all her chances of a family and a nice life. She needs to know why Bella was calling her husband so often before she died, and why he sent Bella's boyfriend thousands of pounds. Every time she closes her eyes, she can see Bella's smug face telling her to 'ask your husband'.

'BRICK! GET THE FUCK UP! I NEED TO TALK TO YOU RIGHT FUCKING NOW!' Olivia screams, pounding at the door with her fist and kicking the bottom with her running trainers.

Olivia creeps back in through the front door just as the sun's threatening to rise outside. She closes it behind her as quietly as possible, remembering to reactivate the Ring doorbell as she tiptoes up the stairs. What she's wearing will at least convince Matt that she's got up early to do a yoga class. If he wakes up, that is. He was sleeping so soundly when she left. He's always been a heavy sleeper; it's unlikely he's noticed anything amiss. He'll be completely oblivious to the fact that he's done anything wrong at all.

In the guest bathroom, she puts her nightie back on and folds up the yoga clothes before padding down the hallway and back to bed. Matt's still asleep as she folds herself into bed next to him and tries to go back to sleep.

Chapter Twenty-eight

Claire's never been first into the office before and she's finding it quite thrilling. Obviously, she's spent plenty of time alone at the office while everyone else was at appointments or with clients, idling away the time playing on Instagram. But this is the first time that she's ever actually opened the shutters herself. She feels great pride watching the metal clang and whir upwards.

Inside, she'd been expecting to have to clear up their tequila debris from last night but, of course, Amanda's already done that. Instead, she puts her bag on her seat and goes straight over to Bella's desk. Relieved, she notices Amanda's cleared Bella's last coffee away too. She really wasn't sure how much longer she could carry on with that debacle. It had started to get pretty gross. To be fair, she thinks she might have gone a little far with the coffee-cup thing but she was just being thorough. She didn't want anyone getting wind of how annoyed she was with Bella when she died.

Opening the first drawer in Bella's desk to grab the thin metal ruler she used to break into the second drawer down last time, she notices Bella's got far more paperclips than Claire herself ever would have sanctioned. No one needs an entire box of them. Just twenty per drawer is Claire's recommendation. She can see that she's got three black Sharpies in there too. No one should have more than one in her opinion, they're expensive.

She closes the top drawer before she gets a rage on and uses the ruler to open the lock on the one below. She knows that Bella had a brochure for Esme's house in here somewhere. She found it the day Hannah and Olivia caught her snooping. She's been meaning to grab it since Bella died, but there's always people around. Flicking through the papers, though, she can't see it. It was definitely there a couple of days before Bella died, so where has it gone now? Unless, she fears, someone else has been in the drawer and found it.

Faster now, she rifles back through the brochures, intent on finding it, but stops when she hears the click of one of the other women's heels outside. Slamming the drawer shut, she jumps away from the desk and races across the office towards the kitchen. By the time Amanda's come in the front door, Claire's casually inserting a Nespresso pod into the machine under the neon sign reading 'Never apologise for being a powerful woman' like nothing happened.

'Morning, Claire darling,' Amanda shouts from the front door as Buster trots to take up residency on his bed. 'How are you doing?'

'Morning, Amanda! I'm OK ... still in shock after last night ...' Claire shouts back over the noise of the machine. 'How are you doing? Coffee?'

'Terrible isn't it? Honestly, hard to believe anyone could want to harm Bella. I'm OK! Yes please to coffee,' Amanda says, walking over and placing her handbag on her desk.

Claire doesn't think she's ever seen Amanda drink a coffee before let alone one that Claire's made for her. The tide really is turning. She watches the first coffee come through, trying to remain calm, before putting in a second pod and taking it over to Amanda.

'Thank you darling. No one else here yet?' Amanda asks, yawning into her hand.

'Nope,' Claire says, trying to hide how proud she is of herself. 'Just me.'

'Gosh, I'm exhausted,' Amanda yawns again, turning on her laptop. 'Busy day ahead?'

'A few meetings and valuations,' Claire lies. She hasn't got anything in the diary but this conversation is already more exciting than her average morning. 'I should be able to send you those videos and pictures of Bella for the awards later too.'

'Fabulous, thank you, darling. I know it can't have been easy and I really appreciate it.' Amanda grimaces, taking a sip of her coffee, because she can see Marcus's massive Range Rover with his personalised number plate pulling up outside the office.

After yesterday, she hasn't had a chance to figure out which mystery property he was talking about. She hoped she might have a bit longer. She hates the way he just drops in like he owns the place, always expecting them to tend to his every need.

Claire watches Amanda sip her coffee and panics because she seems dissatisfied. Is it possible she's made a bad coffee? What if she's ruined all her chances of Amanda ever thinking she's a capable person by making a bad coffee?

The door to the office opens as she's mid-panic, wondering if she should offer to make another one.

'Morning, ladies!' Marcus shouts, interrupting Claire's coffee-based meltdown. 'How are we all doing this morning? Quite the night last night.'

Of course, Amanda realises he's probably not even here to ask about the property, he just wants the gossip. She saw him trying to follow them to the police station and being ushered away. At least she can use it as an excuse if he asks her about the house. Rather than having to admit that she thinks Bella was pulling some kind of fast one and not running the deal through the agency.

Claire's relieved that Marcus has come in to distract Amanda from the coffee, which she's now sure – judging by her face – is career-ruiningly bad.

'Morning, Marcus!' Amanda sweeps from behind her desk and goes over, kissing him on each cheek.

She's not going to tell him anything, but if she makes him feel special enough then hopefully he won't even notice.

'Morning!' Claire smiles at him in the hope that he'll register her presence even though he never has before.

'You all did such a good job yesterday. Very moving service. It can't have been easy to hold it together with all that went on. First the stage invasion and then the police ...' he says, staring at her expectantly.

'Thanks, Marcus,' Amanda says, smiling at him. 'It was lovely to see everyone come together for Bella.'

'So many people there. That announcement was just such a shock, for everyone,' Marcus continues, fishing.

'For us too,' Amanda says.

She can see Marcus register that he's not going to get any further with this line of enquiry.

'So what news have you got for me?' he asks, perching his arse on Bella's desk in a way that Claire finds incredibly disrespectful to the dead, actually.

'I'm afraid I haven't got much further with the investigation since yesterday. What with everything going on here,' Amanda tries not to look him in the eye in case he can sense her stress about it. 'Although, Claire, you might be able to help us here. Do you know of a property that Bella was working on before she died belonging to an old lady who was trying to sell it off for development?'

Claire stops mid sip of coffee, the mug resting on her newly plumped bottom lip. She gathers herself quickly so as not to arouse suspicion.

'No, sorry,' she replies, putting the coffee cup down. 'She didn't mention anything like that to me.'

'It's so strange,' Marcus says. 'Because I made an offer the day Bella died, and she was supposed to be coming back to me once she'd spoken to the lady who owns the place, but, obviously, other things happened . . .'

'I can't think of anything. I'm so sorry,' Claire repeats.

No one's sorrier than Amanda, who knows how desperately the agency – and her – needs that money now.

'Ah well,' Marcus says. 'I've got a property you might be able to help me sell if you're up for it!'

Amanda notices Marcus sizing Claire up like he's a shark and she's a tiny lunch sardine. Nonetheless, Claire looks thrilled, lapping up the attention like a dog inhaling peanut butter.

'Of course!' Claire says.

Amanda's shocked by the excitement in Claire's voice, as though she's never had a listing before.

'Great, come round this morning. I'll email you the address. What's your name, darling? I don't think we've met before?' Marcus asks. 'Are you new?'

'Claire.' Claire grins at him and Amanda smiles encouragingly, not answering his other question.

It's probably better if people do think she's new here. She's a new version of herself anyway. Claire 2.0, now with added lip filler and visibility.

'Great, I think I already know how much it's worth, so you let me know how much you think it is and I'll let you know what I think, and we'll work out an answer from there,' he says.

Amanda knows that this is Marcus's way of saying that they'll sell it for the price he wants and he won't negotiate. She can see what he's doing and Claire's a total pushover, but she doesn't have time to go with her and stop him from steamrolling her. She's relieved when she sees Olivia walking through the door.

'Olivia! Morning! You could probably help with this too!' Amanda says, barely able to conceal how eager she is.

Olivia jumps slightly, startled by Amanda's energy, and the three sets of eyes on her the moment she steps through the door.

'Oh?' Olivia asks. She looks from Claire to Marcus, puzzled and then back to Amanda, all three of them eyeballing her like she's breakfast.

'Claire's going to do a valuation for Marcus. I was wondering if you might be able to join her?' Amanda says. 'That way you get the benefit of two sets of eyes and experience, Marcus.'

This at least seems to have placated him for now. He just likes to know that he's important. Amanda hopes it's not too obvious that it's also because she thinks Claire's entirely incompetent, and she doesn't trust her to keep Marcus's delusions on price in check. She needs them to sell this house in good time, not have it languishing on the website for months at a price that suits Marcus's ego. Especially considering the business's current reputation and financial state, not to mention the state of her marriage.

Chapter Twenty-nine

'Hello? Brick?' Hannah feels ridiculous shouting that stupid name into the giant glass hallway that's ironically devoid of bricks.

She wonders if he knows he's left the door open. Judging by the state he was in last night, she's surprised he even managed to find his way home. But he must have done because there's a record playing upstairs that seems to have got stuck, repeating the same line over and over again. Maybe he's in the shower or something. She doubts it, though. She braces herself for him to be in a really bad way.

She hates how nice this house is. It makes her current predicament feel even worse. Sure, Brick has brandished his luminous swear words everywhere – even in the entrance hall – in his trademark basic font, but for the most part Hannah doesn't actually hate the decor. She's furious about it. How dare Bella have had a nice house and have decorated it well too. Although, Hannah thinks, she doesn't have it any more. As the saying goes, you can't take it with you. She starts climbing the stairs.

'BRIIIICCCK?' Hannah sings up ahead of her. 'OK, I'm coming up. You better have your clothes on, buddy!'

Naked Brick would be the giddy limit for her right now.

'Caspian?' she tries a different tack. 'Caspian Smith where are you? Are you OK?'

She walks into the living room and looks around. Locating the record player, she goes over to that first. The repetition's really started to grate on her. Lifting the needle and stopping the turntable, she feels a sense of calm and relief at the silence, which only lasts a few seconds before it becomes eerie.

'Brick? Are you in?' she shouts, wondering if she should just leave.

It's unsettling that there's absolutely no noise at all. She looks over at the kitchen for signs that he might be around. It's a mess but none of it looks fresh. At a guess, she'd say it's the sort of kitchen that cost in excess of £50,000. The irritation that abated when she turned off the music is suddenly back with vengeance. She walks towards the units that mark the start of the kitchen space, to get a better look, but, rounding the corner, she sees a red stain on the floor. Her palms immediately go clammy yet she continues walking towards it. The closer she gets, the more the stain is exposed stretching across the floor and cupboard doors. She wonders if she should call the police, but she feels like she should at least find Brick first. She follows the trail of red, which stops in front of the wine fridge. Despite knowing it's a bad idea, Hannah's curiosity gets the better of her. She leans down and opens the fridge, peering inside. She feels herself become dizzy, almost as though travelling outside of herself. There, next to a bottle of Kylie Minogue Rosé is an ear. Registering the jewellery on the dismembered appendage, it only takes seconds for her to know it's Brick's.

Hannah's hands start shaking on the fridge door and she stands up slowly from her crouched position. Her head spinning. She looks around, trying to work out what to do next.

'OK, Brick,' she shouts, her voice quivering into the still silent house. 'I've found your ear . . . I'm guessing wherever you are you've probably passed out from blood loss, so I'm going to call an ambulance, OK?'

Hannah pulls out her phone and dials 999. She starts talking to the person on the other end of the call, explaining the situation as she walks through the house. She feels as though she's on autopilot, as though none of it is real.

'I'm just trying to find him now. I don't really know the house layout well, though, so I'm not sure where he could be. I was just checking on him because his girlfriend died a couple of days ago and now it looks like he's had . . . well, I guess some kind of episode? BRICK? IF YOU CAN HEAR ME, THEN SHOUT!'

Hannah continues walking through the flat, following trails of blood, checking in rooms as the woman on the other end of the phone talks calmly to her. She pushes open another door, seeing the bathroom tiles first, fuming that they're exactly the ones she would have chosen for a house like this. She knows how expensive they are. Pushing into the room further, she sees Brick's feet. Lying in a pool of blood.

'I've found him!' she shouts, racing in towards him. 'He's ...'

She looks down at Brick, leant over a golden bidet, his head floating in its rust-coloured, bloody water, eyes open and vacant.

'He's dead,' she whispers into the phone before falling onto the floor.

The police arrive faster than the ambulance, an officer guiding Hannah out of the house and into the street. He tells her that they need to make sure not to contaminate the scene further. Out in the fresh air though, despite her steely exterior, Hannah vomits.

'Is there someone I can call for you?' the officer asks as Hannah leans over into Bella's impeccably designed flower beds.

'My best friend,' Hannah replies, handing the phone to the police officer with Olivia's name on the screen as she vomits again.

The officer takes the phone, nodding to her, and she crouches, hunched in a load of bamboo that someone has foolishly planted straight into the ground. In between waves of queasiness, she's pleased to have found fault with the house. They'll never get rid of that bamboo now it's in the ground. It's invasive, unstoppable. A pest that people often make the mistake of planting themselves. It'll plague them, or it would have, if they weren't already dead.

Chapter Thirty

Olivia mutes the call from Hannah. It's the third one she's rejected. She wonders what's up with her, but she can't just take calls when Marcus is showing them around the house. Especially when he's mid-flow, explaining how he lovingly redeveloped the detached Edwardian house to the highest spec 'with love'. She can tell there are parts of it where he feels he's been particularly artistic; those are the bits that she thinks are the ugliest.

Olivia knows Marcus well enough to know that 'lovingly redeveloped' means that he's done it to his taste and style, and he'll be mortally offended by anyone who tries to suggest that his decor may not be to everyone's taste. As far as Marcus is concerned, his opinion, his style, his word is the best and everyone else is wrong. It makes working with him hell. He's also a terror for trying to insist that he's spent more on things and made them higher spec than they are.

'I went to great lengths to ensure that this kitchen was sympathetic to the time of the house's original build,' Marcus says, gesturing around.

Olivia didn't know that IKEA was doing kitchens as far

back as Edwardian times. She's a bit offended that Marcus doesn't think she'd be able to recognise a standard Metod unit and wooden surface.

'It looks just like an IKEA kitchen,' Claire says. 'Wild that things haven't changed so much since Edwardian times, after all.'

Olivia smirks, wondering if Claire's being thick, but when she catches her eye she can see she clearly knows exactly what's going on. She's impressed she's not been taken in by Marcus's patter.

'Shall we go upstairs?' Claire offers. 'I'm dying to see the bathroom. These houses always have such cool bathrooms.'

'Of course,' Marcus leads the way ahead of them. 'The rolltop bath is from the original period. You can just sense all the scullery maids that have bathed in it over the years.'

Both women shudder at his statement, then Olivia rolls her eyes and Claire smirks back at her. Both women suspect that it's going to be a claw-footed tub recently purchased from victorianplumbing.com. Olivia looks around, thinking it's a perfectly nice house that would make a perfectly nice home for someone sold at the right price. But all of this extra bullshit that Marcus is putting into his pitch suggests that he wouldn't be happy with that. She doesn't know why he feels he has to lie all the time.

Upstairs, as expected, there's a modern claw-footed bath probably less than a couple of weeks old. It's never even seen one scullery maid, let alone the hundred Marcus professes to have bathed in it.

'So, there you have it. My little Edwardian mansion,'

Marcus says, having taken the tour around the three-bedroom house, spun some terrible lies and then brought them back to the front door again. 'Any questions?'

'What kind of price were you hoping for?' Olivia asks, eager to cut the crap and get out of there without too much of a fight, especially as Hannah's calling her again.

'One million,' Marcus says without laughing or flinching, which frankly both Olivia and Claire (even in her limited experience) would have expected him to do, considering such an outlandish ask.

'OK, what about if we say eight fifty at a push,' Olivia says. 'I know it's turnkey, and it's three bed, but some of it's quite ... won't be to everyone's taste. And, it's not quite as high spec as we'd need for seven figures. I'm sorry, Marcus but I must be realistic. It wouldn't be fair to raise your expectations.'

'I beg your pardon?' Marcus looks appalled.

Both women can see that he's about to object and Claire's anxious that Olivia's been too aggressive there. The last thing she wants is to lose her first proper chance at a listing in god knows how long.

'There would be no point in putting it on the market only for it not to sell and to reduce it later. You know that as well as we do. The longer it lingers the less likely it is to sell,' Claire intervenes.

'Plus, you've got a railway line across the back garden,' Olivia points out. 'So you have to allow for a fair bit of money to be knocked off for that.'

She knows he probably only bought the place because

it was cheap due to the trainline. He probably paid seven fifty for it and now he's assuming he can raise the price with a low-rent makeover.

'Why don't you have a think about it and get back to us this afternoon?' Claire says, and Olivia nods.

Claire feels like the two of them are riffing off each other, like they're really working as a team on this. She's having the time of her life.

'I could always go to the boys at Sanders, you know,' Marcus says.

Claire feels her heart leap in her chest. She'd been enjoying Olivia's confidence right up until that point. Now she doesn't want to lose Mr Fritton's business to Sanders, the first time she goes to look at a property for him. Amanda would be furious.

'How about nine?' Claire butts in, anxious that she might be about to fuck up so monumentally that Amanda will finally fire her. If she's going to do it, it'll probably be this week after all.

Olivia isn't angry with Claire – she knows she's trying to prove herself – and nine hundred thousand isn't the worst for this. She really needs to learn to be a bit steelier but, overall, Olivia's noticed a shift in Claire's attitude and behaviour. She would never have been so cheeky before now.

'OK, fine. Nine hundred thousand,' Marcus says.

'Great news,' Olivia says, giving Claire a congratulatory smile.

Claire never seems to have much confidence, but maybe

that's just because no one's ever really encouraged her. After all, Bella wasn't exactly the best friend to her. Or to anyone for that matter.

'Great.' Claire sticks out her hand for a handshake and Marcus actually obliges rather than ignoring her. 'Thank you for showing me round your lovely home.'

She knows she's laid it on a bit thick there and she can see Olivia wincing a bit, but she's thrilled.

'Lovely to see you again, Marcus,' Olivia says, shaking his hand with far less enthusiasm than Claire before wiping the sweat off on her skirt.

The two women walk down the driveway towards Olivia's car under his watchful eye. They get in, but Olivia takes a look at her phone before switching on the engine, wondering why on earth Hannah has called her a total of ten times.

'You did well there,' Olivia says.

'Thank you.' Claire is excited but she tries to play it cool. 'Sorry for coming in with the nine there. I panicked.'

'No, you're OK. Nine is where I thought we'd end up. You just got there quicker, with less messing!' Olivia says, tapping away a text to Hannah to find out what she wants.

'Oh, Hannah's been calling,' Claire says, looking at her phone.

'She's been calling you too?' Olivia asks, surprised. 'Don't worry – I'm texting her now. I'll find out what's up. Maybe she's just locked out of the office or something.'

Before Olivia finishes the text, both women's phones beep with a message in the Harrington's WhatsApp group from Hannah.

Harrington's Group Chat
Hannah: Hey guys, sorry to be the bearer of bad news but Brick's dead. I found him at his house. He's drowned in the bidet. His ear has been cut off.

Next to her in the car, Claire gasps and throws her hands over her face. Then begins wailing.

Chapter Thirty-one

Hannah doesn't know where Olivia is or why she isn't answering her phone. It's been ages since she found Brick and she hasn't been able to get through to any of the women to tell them. Not even Claire is answering her phone and she only rang her as the absolute last resort. She didn't want to send a text message, but if she can't speak to any of them, what other choice does she have? The police have already taken her statement and let her go. It'll be all over the town soon enough. The last thing she wants is for them to hear from someone else.

In the back of the taxi – she hasn't felt stable enough to drive after everything – she resigns herself to using Claire's Harrington's WhatsApp group for the first time in her life. It's against all her key morals and principles, but she knows she needs to tell people.

After typing and retyping the message numerous times – each of them reading as more and more hysterical – she sticks to the basic facts and presses send.

Speaking to the police has been intense. She knows – yet again – that she should tell them about *Bella's Vulva* in the log basket, but she's left it too long now. It needs to be a fresh discovery, or they'll wonder why she didn't present the evidence to them immediately. She's spent the entire interview trying not to trip herself up or fuck herself over. She'd told them she was only at Brick's house because she was worried about him after last night – an excuse that anyone who actually knew her would see straight through.

Every time she catches sight of her face in the Uber driver's rear-view mirror, she swears she can see the word 'liar' branded on her forehead. She can't go on like this. Which is why she's decided to put last night's shame and rejection behind her and go to Tom's. Under the guise of telling him about Brick's death, she's going to rediscover the vulva and get it off her conscience.

Hannah rummages in her bag for her mirror and lipstick as the taxi drives down the wide avenues of Wellingden. She might be in shock and Tom might have rejected her only twelve hours ago, but she's still going to make sure she looks her absolute best. She feels the sting of paper slicing through the fleshy pad of her finger and winces. Yanking her hand out of the bag again she shoves the papercut into her mouth, sucking on it to ease the sting.

Boldly reaching back into her bag, she pulls out the brochure she'd found in Bella's drawer yesterday. It had gone completely out of her head after finding the sculpture. She looks at the pictures again. It's an incredible house. Absolutely gorgeous, and a great opportunity. She can't work out why she's never seen it before. Bella told them everything: she bragged about every listing and every sale. Why wouldn't she have told them about this? And why wasn't it on the website?

There's a number that Bella's written down hastily in the margin. Hannah wonders if that might belong to the seller. It's the only thing other than the sculpture she's really got to go on, so what harm could calling the number do? She types it into her phone and presses call. It barely rings once before the person on the other end answers, old and croaky-sounding, sort of fragile.

'Hello?' The voice enquires.

'Hi, my name's Hannah. I'm calling from Harrington's Estates.' Hannah's confident despite being surprised by how weak the woman on the other end of the phone sounds.

'Finally,' the old woman sighs, sounding more annoyed than vulnerable now. 'I've been waiting since the end of last week for one of you to get in touch with me! Will you be taking on my house in Bella's absence? I heard what happened so I'm assuming the fact that you know about it means Bella spoke to you about it before she died? And you understand the need for secrecy?'

'No.' Hannah realises that honesty is probably the best policy here. She's already got enough secrets that she's trying to unpick. 'I found the brochure in Bella's drawer after she ... passed ... and thought I'd better get in touch. See if I can help.'

'Oh for goodness sake, I can't believe she just left it lying around like that! So careless!' The woman tuts, but Hannah doesn't tell her the drawer was locked. 'Well, *Hannah*, you'd better come round and we'll talk it through. When you get here, ask for Esme, and don't tell anyone else that you're coming. This afternoon works for me around three pm, after my nap.'

The woman – presumably Esme – gives her the address and hangs up abruptly. Hannah stares at the handset for a while. She writes the address in her Notes app. If Esme hadn't sounded so old, she'd wonder if the reason there's so much secrecy around this property has something to do with what happened to Bella, and now, in turn, Brick too. But she certainly didn't sound like a stone-cold killer.

'Wow.' The taxi driver lets out a low whistle as they pull into Tom's driveway.

'Client's house,' Hannah says hastily, keen to make sure that the taxi driver doesn't expect some kind of mega tip from her.

'Oh, I know,' he says. 'I saw this place on the news this morning. That woman was murdered here, wasn't she? You ought to be careful.'

Hannah's taken aback.

'Sorry? Did you say in the news?' she asks.

'Yeah,' the taxi driver says. 'Not just local news, either. National.'

Hannah swiftly types Bella's name into Google, seeing the headlines appear straight away. She clicks on the first one: *'Home Sweet Homicide? Could estate agent's death be murder?'*

'Shit.' Hannah whistles as she scans down the article about last night's vigil and the police's sudden and accidental announcement. Underneath that she sees a live amendment, a picture of Brick and Bella's house with news of Brick's death this morning.

'Tragic Bella's Boyfriend Dead.'

She's confused. How can they know about it so quickly? How have they seen it, but Olivia hasn't yet? She goes back to Google and finds that the police have put out a statement in the last couple of minutes, reacting to several media outlets releasing the news about Brick already. They've described him as a 'Male in his early thirties', 'found deceased this morning', and the circumstances as 'suspicious'. Hannah scans for mentions of herself and feels a little let down when there aren't any.

Messages from Claire start popping up at the top of Hannah's screen as the taxi pulls to a stop outside the house.

Claire: What do you mean dead? How do you know? How can you be sure?
Claire: He can't be dead. We saw him last night.
Claire: Why do you know and not the rest of us?
Claire: Hannah, you can't just write something like that and then not reply.

Hannah can't believe she might have to explain the concept of someone dying suddenly to Claire, this week of all weeks.

'Sorry, love, are you getting out or what?' Hannah realises the taxi driver has just been sat here, waiting for her to leave, while she has an existential crisis, but you would have thought in the circumstances he might have understood a bit.

'Sorry, yes, of course. Thanks,' Hannah says, flustered and gathering her things as she gets out of the cab.

Hannah walks across the gravel towards the house, typing back her response to Claire. She can hear the taxi driver calling his mate from his car, already telling whoever's on the other end that he's just dropped someone at Murder Mansion.

Hannah: I found him this morning at his place.
Hannah: His ear was in the fridge. He was floating face down in the bidet.
Hannah: I'm sorry, Claire.

She'd added the third message to make sure no one thinks she's being insensitive. But, really, *she* was the one that had found his body, and yet she knew it was going to be Claire that everyone was consoling. She can see Olivia's read her message but still hasn't called her back. It pisses her off. If this was the other way round, she'd call her straight away. This combined with how weird and distant she was by the end of the day yesterday is really annoying Hannah.

At least she realises she's distracted enough by all this not to worry as much about seeing Tom. She pulls the knocker back and drops it again, letting it thud against the door in a lacklustre manner. She doesn't want him thinking she's too eager after last night. Just as she can hear Tom coming towards the door, her phone finally starts vibrating with a call from Olivia. But it's too late now. Hannah's far too annoyed to answer. She needed her hours ago. What if the murderer had been coming after Hannah and she was calling for help? What then? Would her best friend even notice? Or would she finally call two hours later only to discover it was too late, and she was already dead? She cancels Olivia's call out of spite.

Chapter Thirty-two

Olivia stands outside the hotel room, right in the spot where the FindMy app shows Matt can be found. She's raised her hand to knock multiple times, the same as she's raised the key to unlock the door a few times too. But not one of those times has she actually pulled the trigger, because she knows that the moment she does their relationship's going to be changed forever.

She came straight over here as soon as she saw Hannah's text. It doesn't bode well for her relationship that her first thought was to wonder whether Matt was involved. She knew Hannah would be expecting her to rush straight to her, but she tried to call and didn't get an answer. Now, she can't rest until she looks her husband in the eye and is sure that he's not the one who killed Brick. She's terrified that she's missed the last time that they'll look at each other the same.

Key card in hand, she reaches out for the handle only to be startled by it moving from the other side. The door flies open before she has a chance to run or hide and she's not prepared when she comes face to face with her husband.

'Liv,' Matt gasps, the colour draining from his face.

Olivia stands there silent. She'd practised a whole load of things she was going to say to him, but now she can't remember any of them.

'What are you doing here, Liv?' Matt asks.

She goes to answer, but his face changes, becoming angry, and he cuts her off before she's even started talking.

'Were you following me?' He's defensive, like he's about to turn this round on her and make out like she's the one that's done something wrong here.

'Don't you fucking dare,' she hisses, her voice full of venom. 'I know about the money you gave to Brick, and I need to know why. Was it something to do with the affair you were having with Bella?'

'Affair? With Bella? There's no way ... It's ... That's not what's happened ...' Matt's jaw drops and Olivia cuts him off, pushing her way into the room.

'I'm not buying it. And now Brick's dead, you'd better tell me everything.' Olivia plonks herself down on one of the crusty, stained armchairs by the smoky net curtains at the window.

'Dead?' Matt asks, rubbing his eyes. 'Brick is? How?'

He stares at her for a bit, but she just stares back, her head tilted.

'I know you haven't been going to work,' Olivia says, her eyes narrowing. 'And I know something's going on so you might as well fill me in on everything. Starting with why you sent five thousand pounds to Brick a couple of days ago.'

'Hannah told you, didn't she,' Matt says.

'Hannah?' It's Olivia's turn for the colour to drain from her face. 'Why would Hannah know anything?'

'Forget I said anything,' Matt says, realising that he's fucked up even more.

'How and what does Hannah know? Before me ...' Olivia clasps her hands together to stop them from shaking, her head spinning. She'd been scared when she got here – now she's just infuriated.

'Look, it's not her fault. She found out from a Tinder date,' Matt says.

'FOUND OUT WHAT FROM A TINDER DATE?' Olivia shouts.

'I've lost my job. I made some bad investments, and I did some stuff that maybe might be considered as not exactly legal,' Matt mutters before finishing in almost a whisper. 'And I might go to prison.'

'WHAT?' Olivia shouts. 'And where does Bella fit into all this? Was she consoling you through it all with her vagina or something? I can't believe you fucking cheated on me. I thought I could trust you! And why are you giving Brick our savings?'

'Wait!' Matt says, holding his hands up. 'I never cheated on you. Especially not with Bella. Why would you think that?'

'She was calling you over and over? You're checked into this shitty hotel as a 'long-term guest' according to the one on reception! You sent Brick thousands of pounds? Was that to stop him telling me about it or something? Did he figure it out and threaten to tell me? And now you're saying you don't even have a job any more! So how were you going to pay for that?' Olivia starts crying, releasing all the pent-up aggression and stress that she's been keeping in for over a week now.

'I wasn't having an affair with her!' Matt cries. 'I'd never do that! I had the hotel room because I needed somewhere to go in the days where you wouldn't find me and realise that I wasn't at work. I sent Brick money because I'd convinced him to invest with me at your Christmas party last year. I knew I was in the shit, so I used the bulk of their money to try and pay some people off. And I thought the little bit I'd invested for them would pay big. But I fucked up, I lost that too.

'Then Bella found out what Brick had done and she was furious. It turned out it was her money, not his. She wanted the receipts for the investments, but I didn't have them. She got in touch with the office, spoke to my boss and found out what happened. Then once she knew she was threatening to tell you everything if I didn't get the money back to her. So I sent Brick some money from our IVF fund. It wasn't all of it, but it was enough for Bella to give me a few extra days to figure something out. I'm so sorry. I always intended to pay it back.'

'And now they're both dead . . .?' Olivia asks.

'I know it looks bad,' Matt starts. 'But you know me. You know I'd never do anything like that.'

Olivia stares at him. She barely recognises him. Her responsible and dependable husband doesn't exist. Has he always been like this? Is she such a bad judge of character that she had no idea her own husband was a monster.

'I promise,' Matt says. 'It wasn't me.'

'Where were you the night that Bella died, then? You said you were at work drinks? You didn't come in till late?' Olivia asks.

'I went to the cinema,' Matt says. 'I'd had that work event in the joint calendar for months. I didn't want you seeing it was cancelled and getting suspicious so I went to the cinema. That's why I didn't answer. I watched a Lord of the Rings marathon and got wasted.'

'The lies!' Olivia says. 'The way you've covered it all up! Jesus, Matt!'

'I was trying to fix it so that it'd be less of a worry for you,' Matt says, putting his head in his hands and starting to cry.

Olivia stares at him. He looks so small she almost feels like comforting him.

'And Hannah knew about this the whole time?' Olivia asks.

'Not the whole time. She found out like last week. She was on a Tinder date with this guy called Dan from the office. And he was blabbing about it – which by the way he shouldn't because it's confidential. But I know Dan – he's a fucking weasel,' Matt says.

'Sure, Dan's the problem here.' Olivia rolls her eyes. 'I thought you'd almost taken accountability for something then.'

'I *am* taking accountability!' Matt shouts then calms

himself. 'My point is, I swore Hannah to secrecy. So don't blame her.'

'Whatever. What about Tom?' Olivia realises it matters even more to her if Tom knew and didn't tell her. In a way, she's kind of used to Hannah's selfishness. Hannah probably forgot about it instantly because it wasn't directly about her; all this time she could have saved Olivia so much stress. The money is the final straw, but if Hannah had told her she would have known it was – in a very roundabout way – to protect Olivia. At least now Olivia won't feel at all guilty going for the manager's position that she knows Hannah definitely wants.

'Tom didn't know. Hannah literally only knew by accident ... I know I've fucked up, but I can't believe you'd think I'd kill someone.' Matt's appalled.

Olivia stares at her husband, not registering any more of his words, just knowing that she needs to get out of this hotel room. She can't stay in here with him, making out that her suspecting him of murder is worse than him losing his job and thousands of pounds, then lying about it. Plus he doesn't even know the half of it.

For one thing, Olivia would never have slept with Tom last night on her way back from Brick's if she'd known what the real story was. While Matt's still talking, Olivia stands and walks out of the room.

Chapter Thirty-three

'I can't believe it,' Tom says, handing Hannah a brandy and coming to sit next to her on the sofa. 'So they think Brick's death was murder too?'

'The police just said 'suspicious circumstances', and that's what the press are reporting.' Hannah shuffles slightly away from him, the awkward memory of last night still very fresh in her head despite everything that's happened since.

She keeps refreshing Google with Brick's name as the search term and every time the results multiply.

'I'm guessing that's why the police haven't been round to the garden again this morning,' Tom says. 'They took samples from the fountain last night.'

'Did they look around the rest of the house?' Hannah asks, eyes on the log basket.

'No. They only really seemed interested in the garden,' Tom says, leaning back against the cushions. 'I thought this was supposed to be a quiet town.'

'It is,' Hannah says. 'I just don't get *why* someone would kill them both?'

'Someone who hated penis art?' Tom says.

Hannah can tell that he's trying to lighten the mood and break the tension, but he's not the one who's just found a body in a bidet.

Silence falls between the two of them. Hannah needs him to leave the room so she can 'discover' the vulva and wipe her prints, but, if anything, he seems intent on not leaving her alone. Any other time she'd have loved that.

'Is there no chance he could have done it to himself?' Tom suddenly pipes up. 'The ear ... the absinthe ... the bidet? Could it not have been a cry for help gone wrong?'

'You think he Van Gogh-ed himself?' Hannah gulps. 'What about Bella, though?'

'God, you're shaking,' Tom notices, leaning in and putting his arm round her.

She feels her pulse kick up a notch and her breath deepen. She can't help herself; she's still so turned on by him. She looks down at his big, strong hedgefundery hand on her leg. All the numbers those fingers have dabbled with. She wants him to play with her clit like he would a rich man's assets.

'It must have been a terrible shock. What were you doing over there anyway? Especially after how angry he was last night! You shouldn't have gone on your own,' Tom says, like a teacher telling her off. She can't believe he's trying to tell her what to do. Who does he think he is? Quite sexy though.

'I wanted to check in, see how he was after last night,' Hannah lies, feeling every one of his fingertips against her shoulder.

She knows she could just tell him about the sculpture

– it's right in front of them; she'd only have to point at it. But she doesn't want him to move, especially when he's touching her. And she doesn't want him to think badly of her.

'That's very kind of you. I didn't know you cared,' he says, stretching his legs out in front of him and looking around the living room. 'God, someone somewhere really doesn't want me to sell this house, do they?'

'I'm afraid not,' Hannah says. 'It's not a bad place to have to stay in, though . . .'

'Yeah, besides, two people have actually died,' Tom says. 'You have to be some kind of complete psychopath to complain about a murder investigation impeding your finances, don't you. And after the morning you've had, I think I'm more worried about how you're doing.'

'You are?' Hannah asks.

'Well, yeah,' Tom says. 'I know I said . . . last night . . .'

Hannah looks away from him, already feeling her cheeks burning at the memory of last night's rejection.

'It's OK – we don't have to talk about it,' Hannah says.

'No.' Tom leans towards her. 'I want to. I need to explain myself. Look, I've been a bit confused. But I like you . . . I'm just in a complicated situation.'

'You do?' Hannah looks up at him.

'I do,' Tom says. 'Just . . . like I said, I'm in a complicated situation. I feel like it's important to tell you, I struggle to control myself around you.'

'Oh,' Hannah says, keeping her tone even. She's heard the 'complicated situation' thing a hundred times before from men. Maybe Olivia was right, after all, and he's just a player. But she can't help but be a bit thrilled by it.

'I don't want you to think it's you, though, because I don't think you realise how amazing you are.' He leans towards her. 'I have to hold myself back every time I'm with you.'

Hannah can feel herself getting hot, but she couldn't bear another rejection after last night.

'Anyway, hold myself back, I must!' Tom says. 'It looks like we'll be working together on trying to sell this house for a while yet.'

'Obviously with the investigation, the house sale is on hold indefinitely. But we can still record those videos I talked about,' Hannah says. 'In fact, I'd planned to do one tomorrow if you're game.'

'Sounds good to me. We're a team!' Tom says, looking her in the eye, his arm draped over her shoulder, pulling her in tighter to him.

Hannah's stomach drops. How is she going to explain why she didn't tell him about the sculpture now? He's going to think she's weird. She's going to have to go back to her original plan and find a way to discover it accidentally.

Outside the living room of the mansion, in the hallway, Olivia stands listening in, the key she used to let herself into the house now heavy in her sweaty palm. She could hear voices the moment she opened the door, so she took off her shoes and crept across the parquet flooring on tiptoes.

She'd come because now she knows the truth, that she can't trust her husband, and she can't trust her best friend who'd kept his secret, she needs Tom more than ever. But as she listens to Tom and Hannah, bile rises in her throat. Through the gap in the door, she watches them, his arm round Hannah, pulling her closer to him.

Her eyes mist over with angry, confused tears while her stomach twists anxiously. They slept together just last night, and now he's coming on to her *best* friend. She needs to get out of here right away. She spins on her heel, and creeps back out the way she came, her tights slipping against the shiny wooden floors. She feels like Bambi in a hurry, not even stopping to put her shoes on before racing out of the door, and accidentally slamming it behind her.

On the sofa, Tom and Hannah jump at a banging noise from the hallway. Tom leaps up and walks straight over to the window.

'What was that?' Hannah asks as he watches Olivia's electric Mercedes flying down the driveway as quietly as it must have driven up it.

'Not sure,' Tom lies.

Hannah's phone vibrates.

Amanda: Oh gosh, Hannah I'm so sorry. I hope you're ok. Here if you need anything xx

Amanda: Guys, on this, there's press outside the office. Brick's death seems to have leaked quickly and added to last night's drama, they're keen to get some kind of quote from us. Obviously don't give them anything but I think we should work from home for the rest of today. Make sure we're not encouraging them to hang around.

Amanda: We'll reconvene at 9am for a team meeting tomorrow but I'm here if you need anything in the meantime xxx

Hannah can also see a text from Esme asking her to come half an hour early because she's awake from her nap. But the earlier time means Hannah needs to leave ASAP. She hadn't realised she'd been here so long and she needs to pick up her car from outside Brick's place.

'It's Amanda,' Hannah says. 'I need to go. I've got a client I need to see. But I'll let you know what time I'll be over tomorrow to record those snapshots of the house. We can just use them for promo stuff until we're able to sell. Get everyone lusting after your place and then they'll be delighted when it comes on the market.'

'Great,' Tom says, turning from the window, his face suddenly fixing into a smile. 'God, you're amazing! Even after finding a dead body, you're off to a meeting!'

Hannah tries to look humble, demure, but he's right. She's pretty great. The alternative would be going to the library for the rest of the day or trying to work out why Olivia was being so shit.

'I'd better go,' she says, standing and nodding towards the door.

'OK, let me show you out,' Tom says, glancing out of the window once more before guiding her towards the door. He seems keen to get rid of her now, and she can't work out what's changed.

Chapter Thirty-four

Thirty minutes later, Hannah stands on the doorstep of the house from the brochure, surveying it. It's even better than the pictures in real life. It's small – a cottage really – but even better than the pictures, with large gardens stretching around the property on both sides. Her sales pitch would describe them as sprawling. She can feel herself getting excited, because this much land attached to a small property is an absolute goldmine anyway, never mind how great the house is.

With there being no chance of selling Tom's place any time soon, this could also solve a lot of her problems, unless she was being lured to her death by the old voice on the end of the phone. The secrecy element is still pretty weird, obviously.

Following instructions, Hannah hasn't told anyone where she is. Even if she wanted to, she has no one to tell because she's still too angry with Olivia for ignoring all her calls to call her back. Besides, Olivia's only tried to call her back once, she hasn't even texted or run to find her or anything. It's an insult. If this was the other way round, Hannah would have been straight over to Olivia, frantic about how she was. For all she knows, Hannah could be traumatised right now. In fact, Hannah thinks she *might* be slightly traumatised. She probably should have told someone she was coming here, given everything.

She knocks on the door and stands back. It doesn't look like the house of a killer. She doesn't get any bad vibes from it, and Hannah feels like she's usually a good judge of vibes. She knew the vibes were bad at Bella and Brick's before even walking through the door, to be honest. Besides, this place is an Instagrammer's wet dream – covered in lilac wisteria. No one gets murdered in a house covered in lilac wisteria, do they? But she *has* already walked into one dead body today – why's she putting herself through this? Maybe she should go?

The door opens a crack and Hannah expects an old woman to come out flanked by dogs, wearing a Barbour jacket, long pleated skirt and wellies with one of those 'ample bosoms' men write about in books. But what greets her instead is a woman around five years younger than Hannah, Beats headphones round her neck, in a full matching Juicy Couture tracksuit. She stares at Hannah as though she's just interrupted her doing something very important, an iPad in her hand displaying the bare arse of one of *Bridgerton*'s male leads.

'What's up?' she asks furiously. She's definitely not the person Hannah spoke to on the phone.

'I'm here to see Esme, from Harrington's Estates?' Hannah ventures, wondering if this is it. Maybe this angry-looking woman in sweatpants lured her here pretending to be old on the phone and now for whatever reason she's going to kill Hannah just like she killed Bella and Brick. Although what's she going to do? Bludgeon Hannah with the iPad?

'Right, yeah,' the angry sweatpant-wearer says, opening the door wider and then getting annoyed when Hannah doesn't immediately follow her. 'Come through. She's in the garden.'

Hannah follows her through the hallway, taking in the key sales points, mostly as a distraction exercise to stop herself worrying about her impending death / kidnap / possible torture. She realises there's stories about this sort of thing: people's ambition killing them. She'll be a cautionary tale. Estate agent wanted more so went to mysterious house and was killed.

At least it's a lovely house to get murdered in, though, she muses: black-and-white floor tiles, original wood-panelled walls and a giant oak staircase with portraits hung above every step. It's a little tatty around the edges but, judging by all the family portraits with titles underneath, the owner's some kind of aristocrat.

Hannah often finds their houses can be like that: tatty but full of heirlooms, antiques and secrets. It warms her terrified cockles just thinking about the stories the owner may have about all these family members. Maybe that's what this is, the house of an old aristocrat who needs to go into a home or, at the very least, somewhere smaller. Perhaps the secrecy is because she considers her life to be more public than the usual seller? That's probably it.

Hannah continues following the woman, noticing that at no point does she take off the Beats from round her neck, clearly planning on getting right back to it once she's dropped her off. Hannah peers into a living room on the way past with gorgeous wood tables and a chaise longue, the perfect setting to watch the *Bridgerton* fingering scene, to be fair.

'So is Esme the owner?' Hannah asks.

'Yes,' the woman says, clearly not one for many words and more into getting back to Regency filth as quickly as possible.

They walk into a country-style kitchen complete with Aga and terracotta floor tiles, and out of an old lead-windowed door into a modern back garden, slightly at odds with the rest of the house.

'She's under the parasol over there,' says the woman, pointing towards a striped umbrella where an old woman sits in a wheelchair, sunglasses on, blanket over her legs. 'I'll bring you out some tea.'

Hannah feels the old woman staring at her from under a pair of Dior sunglasses as she crosses the lawn. She can see her red lips and long, bony, red-nailed fingers reaching over and tapping the end of a thin cigarette into an ashtray on the small side table next to her, and relaxes. This isn't a trap. There's no way this woman's killing her. And, as an added bonus, this house will be an incredible sale.

Hannah can't help thinking that her luck's changing despite finding Brick's body earlier today. She feels the bounce returning to her step and smiles at the glamorous old lady, admiring her Ganni co-ord with Hermès scarf tied round her neck. She's a style icon. Hannah wants to take a picture of her that she can use for reference later in her life.

'Esme?' Hannah enquires, unsure whether this woman's eyes are actually open under the sunglasses. The woman doesn't seem to hear, but she's smoking so she knows that she's definitely awake. Is she ignoring her? 'ESME?' Hannah says it much louder this time.

'Yes, I heard you the first time. I just don't shout,' the old woman says without turning to look at her. 'Come and take a seat and talk to me like a civilised person.'

Hannah immediately feels sheepish, her confidence dwindling slightly as she sits down and does what she's told. She feels being told off might be a theme with this lady, but she's honestly so in awe of her ensemble that she'll take it. For a while, neither woman speaks. Hannah's not sure if she should, and she doesn't want to risk the wrath of the old woman again.

'So, what do you know?' Esme asks, tapping her cigarette slowly and looking Hannah up and down as if assessing her.

'Not really anything. I found the brochure when I was helping sort through Bella's desk after she passed,' Hannah answers, as close to the truth as she can manage. 'I thought it was odd that no one else knew anything about the sale at the agency and it was off-market so I decided to take a look for myself.'

'And you haven't told anyone else?' Esme asks, her thin,

drawn-on eyebrows raising above her sunglasses momentarily.

'No,' Hannah says.

'So, you're like Bella, ambitious, out for yourself. I like it.' Esme's eyebrows relax as much as they can when they're pencilled in so severely.

Hannah doesn't argue with the assessment. She *is* ambitious. She *is* out for herself. Who else is going to be out for her, after all. Clearly not Olivia if today's anything to go by. She resents being told she's 'like Bella' in any way, but she'll let it slide for this style queen.

'Bella was selling this place for me before she died,' Esme says, eventually, drawing it out as though she has all the time in the world, when Hannah suspects she may not. 'She had a developer lined up. I think his plans were to knock the place down and build flats.'

Hannah's not sure if she should look sad, surprised or just professional. She tries to keep her face neutral.

'Don't give me that look,' Esme snaps, taking a drag of her cigarette. 'I read the papers. There aren't enough houses for everyone. It's the least I can do. I don't want this place to exist after I've gone. I can't bear the thought of someone else walking around my space. They'd only do something hideous with it. I've seen those white shutters everyone has in houses these days. Drapes! I'm telling you. Drapes are beautiful! Warming! People these days are tasteless monsters.'

Hannah quite likes a white window shutter, but nods in agreement anyway. Esme's a woman who definitely has moths in her drapes, but she still admires the fuck out of her.

'I'm going to sell the place to a developer, create houses for those that don't have them and give all the money to Extinction Rebellion,' Esme announces. 'I've got a year left, max. Least I can do in that time is give other people homes and donate the money to save the planet. I don't want my legacy to just be a bunch of stuff that someone else has to sort through and throw out.'

Esme's so sure of what she's doing and Hannah admires that even though giving all the money from a house sale to charity sounds absolutely batshit to her.

'Bella had already found a developer and, seeing as you've got the brains to be here, I think you'll be more than capable of finishing the deal. You in?' Esme doesn't mess around. She lights a new cigarette from the end of her last one, replacing it in the cigarette holder before staring at Hannah expectantly.

'Of course,' Hannah tries to keep the glee out of her voice. 'I've just got one question.' Actually, Hannah's got many questions, specifically about how she can end up like this sweet-housed icon when she reaches Esme's age. 'Why the secrecy?'

'Bella was doing it off the books. Kind of a freelance agreement,' Esme says.

'So the money wasn't going through Harrington's?' Hannah asks.

She's pretty sure her contract prohibits that kind of thing and so did Bella's. Maybe this is dangerous territory, after all.

'Oh, the money might have been – I'm not across that. I told her she can tell her boss when the sale's done. I just needed to make sure that nothing was going to be said until it's been finalised.'

'Why?' Hannah asks.

'We have one of your co-workers in common.' Esme rests the cigarette on the ashtray.

'Who?' Hannah's brow almost furrows in thought.

'My great-niece, Claire.' Esme picks up the cigarette without looking down, studying Hannah's expression as she inhales.

'Claire?' Hannah tries not to gasp in shock. How can Claire be related to this woman? Wait, is *Claire* aristocracy? She didn't think the day could get any weirder than finding Brick ear-less, but here we are.

'Claire,' Esme confirms.

'So why not get Claire to handle the sale? Or at least tell her?' Hannah asks.

'Well,' Esme inhales and exhales the smoke through her red lips. 'Honestly, I think she'd try and stop me. I did once tell her she'd be getting the house when I die. But there are more important things going on in the world than her inheritance. The world can't carry on as it is. Extinction Rebellion needs our support. Maybe she'll understand that when it's done, but I can't risk her jeopardising it.'

Hannah is extremely unsure that Claire *will* understand. Bella really was a piece of work, planning to screw her over like this.

'Why go to Harrington's, though, if you're trying to keep it secret from her?' Hannah asks.

'Well, my alternative was Sanders ... and I don't think so, do you?' Esme gives her a knowing look.

'Fair point.' Hannah nods.

'It's my dying wish. I don't want Claire interfering before I get a chance to carry it out. Will you help me carry out my dying wish?' Esme stares her dead in the eye.

The lack of emotion in Esme's voice as she talks about dying makes Hannah love her even more. She feels a connection with this old woman that she doesn't think she's ever felt with anyone before. Except for the Extinction Rebellion stuff, which Hannah knows she's far too selfish to bother with. She wonders if she and Esme might be kindred spirits.

'Of course,' Hannah says. 'I will help you carry out your dying wish.'

'Great!' Esme says excitedly. 'We should celebrate with a whiskey. I'll get Sarah to get us one.'

Esme rings a small bell next to her ashtray.

'Can you remember how much Bella was selling for?' Hannah asks, keen to get some specifics before Esme hits the bottle.

'There should be a sales pack she put together for me in the study. That had all the information on it. Be a dear and go and get it?' Esme asks.

'Of course,' Hannah says, eager to have a reason to nose about the place anyway.

* * *

In the study, Hannah can't see the sales pack that Esme was talking about on her desk. But she does find awards, newspaper clippings and photographs of her with famous supermodels from the eighties and nineties displayed on the study's walls. Here is a woman who's really done something with her life and Hannah can't believe she's related to Claire.

A small, blue flash catches her eye from the fire grate as she looks around to see if there's anywhere else the pack could be. Walking towards it she can make out bits of paper in there, charred at the edges, but still unmistakably Harrington's Estates blue. The sales pack has been burned. Clearly by someone who's presumed that the sale was as dead in the water as Bella was.

Chapter Thirty-five

'Come through, Mrs Harrington.' DI Clive Knight ushers Amanda through the reception and into the nicer of the station's two interview rooms.

'Thanks, Clive,' Amanda says as the man puffs out his pink-shirted chest, his matching pink face beaming at her.

'I'm so sorry about Bella. Alastair told me how fond you were of her when we were playing golf over the weekend. I want to reassure you that we're doing everything we can to work out who's responsible.'

'Thank you, Clive,' Amanda repeats, taking a seat on one of the grey plastic chairs with the chewing gum of criminals stuck to its bottom and legs. 'That's actually what I wanted to talk to you about.'

'Of course,' Clive says, taking a seat opposite her and fanning his tie out as though it might have somehow changed state or shape in the sitting down. 'I'm sure you've got a lot of questions. I'll do my best to help you with as many of those as I can.'

Amanda pauses, she looks down at her freshly manicured nails then looks up at Clive, tears in her eyes.

'Oh, Amanda, gosh let me get you a tissue.' Clive stands again, slightly embarrassed to witness such an outpouring of emotion from someone he's only ever really seen to be incredibly stoic and together. 'Here.'

He places a box of tissues on the desk in front of her. Clive's not what could be considered a warm man – he's worked in the police force for too long for that – but he does hate to see a woman cry. It makes him uncomfortable.

'I could call Alastair for you?' he asks, hoping for an out or someone else at least to take the burden.

'No.' Amanda looks up at him, alarmed. 'That's kind of what I've come about. Clive, maybe we could keep this off the record, for now at least?'

Clive doesn't say anything for a while, shifting uncomfortably in his seat.

'I mean, it really depends, Amanda. This is a murder investigation now. So I'm not sure I can promise that. But if you have something important you need to tell me regarding the case it's your legal duty to do so.'

Amanda feared this would be the situation, but she doesn't see what choice she has other than to tell Clive. He's going to realise eventually anyway, and she can't keep information from him. She suddenly feels very trapped in this greige windowless room.

'It's about Alastair. I found out something last night that really ... well, it's worried me. But I need to know that this won't become idle gossip. My family is at stake here.'

'Of course, anything you tell me as part of the investigation isn't gossip,' Clive says, raising his hands from the table.

He seems impatient, but Amanda needs to know he'll keep her secret. It's bad enough that she has to tell him anything, but she knows it could be important, for Bella's case.

'I found messages between Alastair and Bella on a dating app on his phone.' Amanda can barely bring herself to look at Clive, but she still hears him let out a tiny gasp.

'Which dating app was this?' Clive asks.

'Scrubbr,' Amanda says, feeling common.

'I'm not familiar with that one . . . Do you have access to these messages now?' Clive asks.

Amanda pauses, shaking her head, her throat closing with the effort of trying to keep in her tears.

'He's left me, Clive . . .' the tears come again, embarrassingly hard. 'I confronted him about the messages last night and he's disappeared. He's blocked my number. I can't get through to him. I don't know where he's gone.'

'Why?' Clive gasps, shocked. 'I'm so sorry, Amanda. I always thought Alastair was a fine man. I can't believe it. He has a golf handicap of six, for goodness' sake.'

'This isn't the first time Alastair's been on a dating app,' Amanda says, a tissue to her face so that she doesn't have to deal with seeing Clive's face while she recounts the most embarrassing details of her marriage. 'It's something that Alastair's done for a few years now, says that there are things that he can't get from me he needs to get elsewhere. We had an arrangement . . . he does that, but I don't have to hear about it or have it affect our lives in any way.'

'What kind of things?' Clive asks. 'It might be important for the investigation.'

'You can't tell anyone,' Amanda says.

Clive stares at her. 'I promise, Amanda. I have great respect for you and Alastair. I would only share what was completely necessary.'

'He's into cleaning ... the products, the sponges, the gloves, special mop heads and attachments ...' Amanda weeps into her tissue again. 'I had to book the cleaner to come on days when he wasn't in the house.'

Clive's face turns a shade of puce.

'I don't think he realised who Bella was. She met him at the open house. I introduced the two of them not realising they'd met before,' Amanda says.

'Do you think he worried she might expose him?' Clive asks, stroking his chin.

'Maybe,' she manages to sob. She can't believe she's broken down like this and had to tell Clive of all people her most intimate secrets.

'OK, don't worry, Amanda,' Clive says, reaching across the table and putting his hand on hers. 'You did the right thing coming to tell us. I think the first thing I need to do is talk to Alastair. He's a person of interest in the case now. I'll give him a ring. We'll flush him out wherever he's got to.'

'But, please, be discreet?' Amanda says. 'Can you do it yourself? I don't want anyone knowing.'

'Amanda, I promise,' Clive says, squeezing her hand. 'I'll only tell people when strictly necessary and it won't leave this station.'

'Thank you,' Amanda says. 'I really appreciate it, Clive.'

She stands from the desk, checking her face quickly with her mirror so there's nothing for the crowd outside the office to notice when she stops by to grab her laptop.

'Any time, Amanda. I'll let you know how I get on,' Clive says, guiding her towards the door.

'Oh, there was one more thing,' Amanda says, turning back to Clive at the door to the interview room. 'When you check Bella's phone records, she got a call from someone making an offer on the house just before she died. It was why she was in the garden. But none of us have been able to find anyone who made the offer. Probably worth seeing who made that call.'

'You don't think there was one?' Clive suggests. 'That someone was just trying to lure her into the garden?'

'Maybe,' Amanda says.

'Definitely worth looking into,' Clive says. 'Thanks for the tip.'

Chapter Thirty-six

Hannah gets back in her car and tries to figure out what she's going to do next. She sits in Esme's driveway contemplating her options. It feels like she's entered some kind of twilight zone. One in which it was possible that Claire could have known about Bella selling her great-aunt's house and gone to huge lengths to stop it from happening. Which surely can't be true.

Could Claire *really* have killed Bella to stop her selling the house? She looks around, suddenly worried that Claire's somehow watching and now she's also in danger for simply being here. She reverses out of the driveway at top speed.

What if she just never returned Esme's calls again? Or she could just say something's come up and she can't do it now. That way, if Claire ever found out she was there, then she won't kill her like she did Bella? Is she being a bit silly, though? It's *Claire*. Surely there's another explanation. Maybe the old lady burned the details by accident? She was very old – maybe she didn't realise what she was burning? Maybe Claire knew about it but didn't kill Bella? Of course, Claire didn't kill Bella.

Hannah finds herself automatically driving to Olivia's, still curious about why she hasn't heard from her all day and eager to share this new information. Whatever's going on, Olivia's going to want to know about this, and it's not like she can't trust her to keep the secret. Even if she is being properly weird at the moment.

At first, she wondered if Oliva was cross about Hannah selling Tom's place, but she hadn't said anything at the time, and she hadn't looked like she even really wanted to sell it, either. Besides, it was more of a headache than a gift now, what with it being the site of a murder investigation. She can't be annoyed about that.

She tries once more to call Olivia. But it only rings twice before going straight to voicemail. A fury comes over her, she can't believe Olivia's screening her calls and she knows there can only be one reason for it. Matt must finally have told her about his little predicament and he's dragged her down with him. The little shit. Hannah can't believe that's the thanks she gets for keeping his secret all week. She puts her foot down harder on the accelerator, knowing that she needs to sort this out ASAP.

Hannah swerves into Olivia's driveway and leaps out of the lilac BMW, shoulders back, ready to plead her case if needs be and make sure that Olivia forgives her. She knocks on the front door repeatedly, until finally she can hear Olivia huffing and telling her to chill out on the other side.

'So, you're alive, then,' Hannah snaps as the door opens.

'Evidently,' Olivia replies, her eyes steely.

Immediately, Hannah knows that she's right: Matt must have told her everything. Still, at least Olivia's not dead.

'Considering you haven't been killed by the Wellingden ripper, I'm guessing the only reason you haven't responded to me or even *checked in* on me after I found a dead body this morning is that Matt's finally told you the truth,' Hannah says. She's unexpectedly angry. She didn't ask to be told his secret; it's not her fault he didn't tell Olivia right away.

'How astute of you,' Olivia says dryly.

'Look, he swore me to secrecy,' Hannah says. 'I told him he needed to tell you. I said I didn't want any part of it, and it was none of my business. I told him that. I still don't want any part of that. This is between you two and it's not fair to blame me for anything.'

'Well, good for you, shame you didn't realise that as my *best* friend *you're* supposed to tell me,' Olivia says.

'Olivia, he told me he was going to. He promised me he was. It's not my fault he took so long to get up the courage to do it,' Hannah says.

'That's not exactly the apology I think I deserve,' Olivia says, even more pissed off that she actually has to explain this to Hannah.

There's a pause between the two of them and, ultimately, Hannah knows she's come at this on the defence. She'd got so worked up on her journey here and she's been so annoyed this whole time about even being in the situation in the first place.

'I'm sorry,' Hannah says.

Olivia shrugs, but says nothing, staring Hannah down.

'I hated keeping a secret from you. Please forgive me?' Hannah pouts in a way that Olivia finds really irritating.

She knows she's got to at least pretend to forgive her or she'll never stop talking and making excuses for herself. 'Please, Livvy?'

Olivia can't tell Hannah that it's not just Matt that she's annoyed about. She's annoyed about Tom and seething with jealousy after seeing the pair of them earlier. She's furious with Tom and can't help also being furious with Hannah by default.

'It's going to take more than that,' Olivia says. 'You've betrayed my trust and then you've come round here with the gall to have a go at *me* about it. What the fuck, Hannah? I know you double-cross other people, but I never thought you'd do it to me.'

'Oh hey, Hannah!' Claire pops out of the kitchen door behind Olivia, looking oblivious when Hannah knows she's not.

Hannah can't help staring at her, analysing her movements after what she found in Esme's grate.

'Livvy, I opened a new bottle of rosé – hope that's OK!' Claire trills.

'Course,' Olivia smiles over to her while Hannah's left on the doorstep getting angrier by the second.

'Cool, I'll head back outside. See you in a sec!' Claire darts back inside the kitchen with the bottle of Miraval in hand.

'What's *Claire* doing here?' Hannah realises that she's screwed her face up just saying her name.

'She's had a bad day, Hannah. Unlike you, she really liked Brick and she was friends with Bella. It's been hard for her, so I thought I'd invite her round, seeing as I've had a pretty bad day myself.' Olivia glares at her.

'Right, but that's *Claire*? Like are you two friends now or something?' Hannah asks, the familiarity of a playground-style rejection, being cast out by people she thought were her friends, starting to build in her chest like a lump.

Coming face to face with Claire, Hannah almost laughs at herself for thinking she could have been smart enough to know what Bella was up to, and not only that but kill her because of it.

'Claire hasn't lied to me this week from what I can tell and she hasn't kept secrets from me, or colluded with my husband behind my back. So yes, Claire,' Olivia says.

'Well, good for Claire,' Hannah says. 'Claire must be thrilled to finally have a friend.'

She was right. Claire's far too boring and needy to be a killer.

'Don't be a bitch,' Olivia snaps back.

Hannah turns to leave, but feels a wave of sadness hit. She can't just leave like this. She turns back to Olivia, her face softer now.

'Are you seriously not going to forgive me?'

'Maybe if you showed a bit of remorse I would,' Olivia says. 'But you never take accountability for anything. You rip the piss out of people all the time, lording it above everyone like you're so superior. Never recognising any of your own *many* flaws.'

'What the ... fuck ...' Hannah mutters. 'You're not even making sense. Maybe it's best if we talk tomorrow when you've chilled out a bit. What have I actually done here? Not told you something that I knew should come from your husband? Kept my nose out of something that wasn't my business? What are you actually annoyed at me about? Trying to do what I thought was best for you?'

Olivia sighs and looks at Hannah, her voice softening. She realises that she's more annoyed about Tom than Hannah keeping Matt's secret, and Hannah doesn't know anything about that.

'Let's talk tomorrow,' she concurs. 'I'm just angry, and I'm tired and I don't really want Claire to hear all my business right now.'

'Sure,' Hannah says, the rejection now burning inside her. She wants to go home and just be by herself.

Behind Olivia as she closes the door, Hannah sees Claire poking around in the kitchen, completely oblivious to anything. She thinks the idea of her knowing about Bella selling her great-aunt's house and killing her because of it is, surely, laughable.

Inside, Olivia stands leaning against the kitchen counter for a second, catching her breath. She didn't mean to snap at Hannah, or let on that she was so annoyed, but, honestly, if this situation was reversed, Hannah would have let her have it with both barrels. She doesn't understand why she thought she could come round here shouting the odds. Besides that, she almost gave away to Claire what's going on when this is obviously something Olivia really wants to keep quiet. It's certainly not the sort of thing she wants to get back to Amanda, that's for sure. She takes a deep breath, grabs a packet of nuts from the cupboard to snack on and heads back out into the garden.

Outside, Claire's stretched out on the sofa when Olivia comes round the corner to the seating area.

'Oh, is Hannah not staying?' she asks innocently. Claire heard their argument and she's thrilled.

Obviously, she's curious about what they were arguing over, but crucially, if they *have* fallen out, it's an opportunity for her and Olivia to get closer. And that's something she's wanted for years. Finally, Claire can see there's a divide between the two of them and it looks just about big enough for her to worm her way in.

'She was just dropping something off on her way past,' Olivia says, forcing a smile and sitting down next to Claire.

Chapter Thirty-seven

'Morning, Claire,' Amanda says walking into the office at eight thirty am, surprised to see her here first for the second day in a row. 'You're here early!'

'Morning! Lots to do! Coffee?' Claire asks, standing over by the kitchen.

In truth, both women had wanted to get there early because of the group of TikTokers that have replaced the press, watching the office and posting videos from outside. Amanda wanted to be seen by the judgemental social-media detectives to be doing everything she possibly could to help her employees, while Claire just wanted to be seen by them, full stop.

'Love one, thanks!' Amanda replies, letting Buster off his lead so he can go and get in his tiny prince's bed.

Amanda's really noticed that Claire's not just getting here earlier, she seems to be looking a little better too. She suspects Claire might have had some Botox and maybe a bit of filler. It's almost like Bella's death has prompted her to seize life. Whatever it is that's prompted the transformation, Amanda's delighted by it. Obviously as a woman supporting women in business Amanda can never say any of this out loud, but she does judge by appearances.

'Thanks,' Amanda says as Claire puts the cup down on her desk. 'How are you feeling today? I know you and Brick were close?'

'I just feel really sad all the time,' Claire says, walking back to her desk. 'But I think the best thing I can do is to just try and keep myself busy. You know?'

'That's generally what I do when I'm having a difficult time,' Amanda says. It's no accident that she's here so early, letting the nanny take the kids to school. She wants to do something to take her mind off her missing husband and the fact that her personal life, her entire brand, in fact, is crumbling slowly before her eyes. And all she can do is plan to be a single mum bossing life. She just needs to make sure she's ready for it before she pushes out her rebrand more publicly.

'Predictably, Marcus pushed back on price yesterday,' Claire says.

Amanda is distracted by the group of TikTokers – all women in their early twenties – gossiping by the bench and watching the office. She recognises one of them from a video she saw last night captioned 'Real Estates, Real Nightmare', which *had* referred to them all as glamorous, to be fair, so she didn't hate it. It had also estimated roughly what each of the women make a year, thankfully without mentioning Claire's turnover.

'He's a devil for that,' Amanda nods, turning on her computer and scowling at her emails as Claire talks.

Claire's noticed you can never get Amanda's full attention for long – it's fleeting – and you have to keep her impressed to keep it. It's almost a game: the better you do, the longer you last. In order to get to the next level, you need her to pay attention to you for at least five minutes without getting bored or finding someone more important to talk to. If she wasn't so impressed by Amanda, Claire would consider it arrogance.

'But we managed to land on nine hundred thousand for a three-bed mid-range Edwardian reno in the lanes. It's turnkey, but it's not high spec,' Claire says, stealing Olivia's phrasing. She's sure she won't mind, though, especially after yesterday.

'Gosh, well done.' Amanda looks up from her computer briefly, actually making eye contact with Claire. 'Getting Marcus to agree on a realistic price is really half the battle – you'll sell that in no time.'

Amanda's never been so relieved to get a listing for the business. She doesn't know what she'll do if she loses this place as well as her marriage.

Claire feels as though she's just been bathed in light. Amanda looking her dead in the eye and saying well done feels like the equivalent of being baptised by Jesus himself. This and the suspicion that Olivia and Hannah are on the rocks? It's going to be a blessed day! And it's not even nine am. Amanda's head's back down staring at her emails now. It's a clear act, dismissing Claire from her desk. So she heads back to her own computer with renewed purpose.

'You're looking well by the way, Claire,' Amanda adds as

a bonus comment without looking up from her computer. 'Something new with your skin?'

Claire's good mood ascends from a baptism by Jesus to a god-tier disciple status.

'Aw, thanks, I had a facial,' Claire says.

They both know it's more than a facial, but neither woman will say anything. It feels more polite to pretend you've invested in a good moisturiser rather than injected poison into your face, after all.

'Morning!' Olivia says, coming through the office door, and closing it firmly behind her.

She's pasted an overenthusiastic smile on her face in the hope that neither woman will notice she was up all night crying at the state of her absolutely ravaged personal life. At least with her phone on 'Do not disturb' she can no longer see the calls and texts from Tom and Matt. She doesn't want to talk to either of them right now.

'Morning!' Amanda and Claire chime back.

'Have you seen the news?' Olivia asks, sure that they have.

'No?' Claire sits up at her desk like a meerkat.

'News?' Amanda mumbles, head in her emails.

'Ron's been arrested,' Olivia says, throwing her bag down on the desk. 'The TikTok ones outside were all talking about it when I walked past. They're filming Sanders.'

Amanda and Claire both squint out of the window, surprised to notice that Olivia's right: Sanders is the target of the crowd's attention outside, not Harrington's.

'How strange,' Amanda says. 'I'm going to text Clive.'

Claire immediately picks up her phone, searching TikTok for the videos that are no doubt already up. Olivia stands behind her, watching a TikTok live that they can also see happening out of the window, as a woman talks to camera, explaining that as far as they can work out Ron's DNA was found on the body. She proceeds to give various theories about how this could be, but Claire bursts into tears, drowning out the woman's chat.

'I can't believe it . . .? Ron?' She races out of the room towards the toilet.

'I'll go after her,' Olivia says.

'Actually,' Amanda interrupts, really needing the women to focus on work. She'll find out more from Clive when he texts her back, but she's never considered Ron to have much about him, especially not murder. 'I could do with talking to you about something, to do with the agency. I'm sure Claire will be fine in a minute.'

Olivia feels a jolt of excitement. This is it. Maybe Amanda's going to make her manager. She is the most responsible one, after all. Some days she feels like her and Amanda are the only grown-ups in the office. Bit odd of her not to talk to Olivia about it privately first, but it's been an odd week. The sort of week where anything could happen.

'Morning!' Hannah breezes through the front door, and over to her desk smiling. 'How are we all this morning?'

Olivia throws her a filthy look, fuming that Hannah's interrupted them. She sees Amanda moving away and knows whatever it was she was going to say to Olivia, Hannah's ruined it.

Hannah can see Olivia's still in a mood with her and she's certainly not hiding it with the glare she's just thrown across the office at her, but she's got important news.

'Everyone outside's saying that Ron's been arrested?' Hannah announces, sitting down and taking her laptop out of her bag.

'Yes, we just heard,' Amanda says, checking her phone to see if there's anything from Clive, but finding an empty screen. 'We should all head over to the sofa, start the morning meeting. We've got a lot to discuss. Just need to wait for Claire to—'

Claire emerges from the toilet, crying. 'I just can't believe it . . . Ron . . .' she sobs.

Hannah can't believe Claire's crying about this. If Ron did do it, then that's weird and she never thought he'd have it in him, but crying over it's a bit fucking much.

'I heard,' Hannah says, no longer as eager to talk about it if Claire's going to cry.

She looks at Claire's blotchy, tear-stained face and can't believe that yesterday she was questioning whether or not she should be taking on Esme's house, all because she briefly thought Claire was a killer. She's no killer.

'Shall we all go to the sofa and start the morning meeting?' Amanda presses.

'I can't believe they think it was Ron,' Claire sobs again.

'I don't think he did it,' Hannah says, cavalier, on her way to the sofa. 'He's too soft. The man's a walking tissue.'

Claire does another sob into a bit of toilet roll as Olivia guides her to the sofa.

'Not helpful, Hannah,' Olivia whispers. She sits next to Claire with an arm round her shoulder, trying to offer some comfort.

Hannah can't believe Olivia's still so annoyed with her this morning. She'd hoped she might have mellowed or that her joke about Ron might have eased the tension. But she's not budging.

Amanda sits on the other sofa, with Buster jumping up next to her stretching out. This leaves Hannah with nowhere to sit but the small white bean bag on the floor, usually reserved for Claire and their clients' children. She crouches down in her four-inch heels, trying to make the move elegant, but instead simply falls back into it a bit like a beetle. There's a constant scrunching noise as she tries to get comfortable.

'Whenever you're ready,' Amanda says, placing her hands together as if praying for strength.

'Sorry,' Hannah says, the beanbag crackling further underneath her as she tries to stop herself weirdly sliding off to the side. She can feel everyone getting annoyed. Amanda seems particularly tense this morning. 'I'm ready now.'

She sinks slightly to the side again, but Amanda ignores it and starts speaking.

'Do you think they can see us?' Claire butts in, pointing to the gathered group of TikTokers outside who are still facing in the direction of Sanders anyway.

'That is a window, Claire,' Hannah points to the big pane of glass at the front of the office. 'So, yes, they probably can see through it.'

'I'd really like to get on with things regardless,' Amanda says, feeling her temper rise. 'In fact, that's very much what I need to talk to you about. The agency's struggling and I know it's not great timing, but if we don't start getting a few more sales under our belts we might have to think about making some cuts or maybe even ... moving into the lettings market.'

The women's heads all snap round to face her at the same time. Finally, she's got their attention – she just has to use shock tactics.

'Lettings?' Hannah repeats slowly.

She feels herself startle, sitting upright in shock, but trying to maintain balance on the bean bag,

'It's an option,' Amanda says. 'We'd do high-end lettings, of course. We've got standards. But we really need some big listings and big sales.'

If it weren't for Claire, Hannah could tell Amanda about Esme's house now. That would definitely ease some of her worries. And she fully intends to tell Amanda about it, unlike Bella, who was screwing over Amanda as well as Claire. Hannah keeps telling herself she's not really screwing over Claire so much as helping an old lady live out her dying wish. It's got nothing to do with Claire really. She's just selling the old lady's home, and carrying out her wishes, and she's getting herself out of the property guardianship at the same time. A win for everyone except Claire. And it's not Claire's property anyway – it's Esme's. While she's alive she can do what she wants with it.

Olivia knows this is her chance. She can prove herself

here, and then she'll be agency manager. She's been helping Claire with Marcus's property, but maybe she should suggest she takes it on all by herself and Claire could shadow her on it? She's got a couple of other things in the pipeline, but nothing confirmed yet, so it's not like she doesn't have time to find a quick buyer. And it's an awfully big undertaking for Claire, really, considering she hasn't sold a house at all yet this year.

'Well, I've got Marcus's house,' Claire says, thrilled to have something to bring to the table and enjoying that neither Hannah nor Olivia have offered anything yet. 'That's going on market today.'

'I thought you said earlier that you'd agreed the price yesterday? Why the delay getting it up?' Amanda asks, crushing Claire's earlier built-up confidence.

'Sorry, Amanda,' Claire says, and Olivia shoots her a sympathetic look.

'I can help you get it up on the website, Claire,' Olivia says. Then she'll also sell it herself quickly in the interests of the agency and make sure Amanda knows it was all her work.

'Thank you.' Claire tries to hold back a bout of actual tears this time, not ones for show. A cross word from Amanda really hurts.

'Obviously, I've got Tom's house, which we can't do anything with until the investigation is over. But I've had some ideas for it in the meantime and, now I think of it, they might actually help the agency as a whole,' Hannah says proudly.

She could have sworn she saw Olivia rolling her eyes, but Amanda looks interested at least.

'Ooooh! Did you try finding out who phoned Bella with an offer the night she died? They might still want to buy it!' Claire suggests.

'Yes, Claire, I looked into it. No one knows who they are,' Hannah says.

'Well, that's annoying. So close to selling, but . . . so far,' Claire says thoughtfully, as though offering support when she knows what she's really doing is winding up Hannah.

Hannah's going to sell the absolute shit out of Claire's inheritance. She's asking for it.

'Annnyyywayyy, I'm going to go over to Tom's this morning. I thought it would be good to use the house to film some content for social media.' Hannah ignores Claire's stupid comment. Like she wouldn't have already tried to find the buyer? She can't believe she thought Claire might be some kind of criminal mastermind.

'I'm thinking lifestyle images, videos like "five tips to selling your house" and "how to draw in buyers" that kind of thing. Maybe you could all come and we can do a set of talking heads about the agency and what we do? We could focus on being a female-owned business, the women-supporting-women element? How we're a family?' Hannah knows Amanda will love that last bit. 'That way we keep the house on our channels, looking impressive until it's ready to sell.'

'Oh, that's so smart! I love it!' Amanda's practically clapping her hands together with joy.

Hannah's thrilled with herself and it makes her new plan to have the sculpture found by someone else even easier – plus it'll distance her from the weapon even further. For the sake of her conscience – something even she's surprised at – she knows she'll feel better once it's in the hands of the police. She just needs to duck into the living room, wipe off her prints and then she can set it up so that any one of them can find it. Just not her. Sure, she might wipe someone else's prints off in the meantime, but she knows whose fingerprints definitely *weren't* on it – Ron's. She doubts he's ever touched a vulva in his life.

'It also sounds like just the thing to get us all out of this goldfish bowl.' Amanda nods out of the window at the ever-growing crowd.

It seems to Hannah that the internet detectives are still far more interested in watching what's happening at Sanders as the boys arrive to work one after the other in their matching cars, having to face a day of questions without the dickhead leader-in-chief, Ron.

Olivia won't look at Hannah. It's a great idea, but she doesn't want to let on to Hannah that she thinks that.

'This is a good start,' Amanda says. 'But I also need you all to be on your A-game, getting new clients and listings.'

'We'll get on it, Amanda,' Olivia says. 'Don't worry.'

'Absolutely,' Claire agrees.

'It's in the bag.' Hannah nods, feeling a bit sick. If this place closed, she'd have to find another job, and she can't find another job on top of everything else that's going on.

She needs to focus and get new listings ASAP. Now's her time to shine.

'Good, I want us to be able to walk into the Estate Agent Awards tomorrow night with our heads held high. People are going to be gossiping about us, but we're professionals. We want to be known for selling houses, not anything else. *Capiche?*'

'*Capiche.*' The women nod in unison.

'I was going to head to the house now, if it's a good time for you all to join me?' Hannah asks.

'Great,' Amanda says.

'Claire, why don't you come in my car?' Olivia says, so pointed it would feel like yet another knife in Hannah's back if it wasn't so pathetic.

'Love to!' Claire grins.

Hannah and Olivia lock eyes across the sofas, Hannah trying her best to look pitying of Olivia's transparent digs, and Olivia trying to look unbothered by Hannah just in general.

'Oh my god.' Claire gasps suddenly at her phone in her hand.

'What?' Olivia asks.

'The *Daily Mail* have done a piece on us.' Claire holds in a smile. She never thought she'd see the day she was in a national newspaper. Although it's obviously a shame it's under such tragic circumstances.

'Oh god,' Amanda groans.

Hannah feels her head start to spin as they all tap away at their phones to bring up the article. What if they've uncovered stuff from her past that even Olivia doesn't know?

'*Who are the women of Harrington's Estates? The small town estate agent and its women, haunted by tragic murders.*'

It's a breakdown about all of them, their lives, their families ... In some cases they've managed to speak to people that went to university with them or school. Never real friends, always acquaintances, and, even then, people that they've barely said two words to in their lives. Hannah notices that the talking head they've got for her is John, the man who she once faked her own death to avoid. They couldn't have possibly found a worse one.

Amanda scrolls down, petrified at what they might have uncovered.

Amanda Harrington: owner and mumfluencer with a life straight out of a dream. 'I've wanted to be Amanda Harrington since I was twenty-nine,' Sarah, fan and thirty-year-old mother of two.

She feels herself buoyed by this. People still want to be her. She was keeping up the illusion and she could keep it going. Sarah, fan and thirty-year-old mother of two had no idea how much Amanda needed to hear this right now.

Olivia: a perfectionist homebody whose own Instagram is full of posts titled things like #renoinspo despite her house looking immaculate, if a little pedestrian and beige. It's always a shame when someone who so clearly has money doesn't have the vision to use it wisely. She has the potential to be a mini Amanda in the making.

Olivia ignores the bit about her taste, just quietly thrilled with this description of her as a mini Amanda. Surely if a stranger could see it, Amanda would be able to as well. That's got to help her cause to become manager. Surely?

Hannah: *A driven go-getter who's loose with the truth and her morals. 'Sure, she's sexy, but she's also mentally unstable,' John Attwood, ex-partner. 'She faked her own death in a bid to get my attention.'*

But then the personal breakdowns stop and it moves on to talk about the history of the agency. Claire scrolls up and down and up and down again, but she can't see her name anywhere. She's not been included.

'I don't think that's very fair,' Hannah says. 'I barely dated John. He doesn't know me at all. And as *if* I wanted his attention.'

Claire sees another Google alert pop up, this time for a Substack by someone called 'RealLifeInternetDetectiveBitch'. The headline reads: *'Whodunnit: the unhinged women of Harrington's'*. She clicks on it, hopeful that this time she won't have been left out.

'OK, that's enough,' Amanda says, stern and trying to keep her head in the game, no matter how flattering she'd found the article. 'We need to get on with things. No more googling yourself, Claire!'

'I wasn't googling myself . . .' Claire mutters as she grabs her bag and the women head for the door.

'No, you have an alert set up, don't you,' Hannah smiles, sweeping past with her handbag. That'll be killing her.

Outside the office as they lock the doors, the women ever so subtly take a minute to stand still just in case any of the TikTokers want to get footage of them.

Chapter Thirty-eight

'Hi, Marcus, it's Hannah. I've inherited a house of Bella's that I believe you were in talks with her about before she died. It's got a plot of land attached to it and the seller – a lovely lady called Esme – says that she thinks the plan was for a developer to buy and build flats. It sounded like your sort of thing to me, so I thought I'd get in touch with you first and see if it was you that she was talking to about it. Anyway, she's asked we keep this one quiet – it's a bit of a complicated one. I'll explain when I see you. Hope that's OK. Speak soon!'

Hannah ends the call as she pulls up outside Tom's house. Since Bella's death, Hannah's only ever felt a sense of impending doom rolling up the driveway towards the house, but today leaving the message on Marcus's answer phone she feels positive for once. She's going to sell Esme's house, and as soon as someone discovers the murder weapon today she'll have that off her conscience too. She's finally going to regain control of her life. And not only that but Tom said he *did* like her yesterday. She's choosing to focus on that and ignore the stuff he said about a complicated situation.

She does a quick face check in the mirror, eager to look her best when she's seeing Tom, but aware that she's looking tired after an extremely poor night's sleep last night. How *does* one sleep after finding a man's dead body and his ear in separate rooms? Reaching over, Hannah grabs her bag from the passenger seat and jumps out of the car. She had worried this morning that her bag had started to smell a bit of weed smoke, but as she's already had to sell her other bigger Chanel and Burberry ones, this Mulberry's the only one left that she can fit everything in for work. She's starting to worry people might notice her lack of variety soon, but hopefully Esme's house will sort that little problem out. She can't see Marcus dragging out a sale. He'll be in touch with a list of his demands as soon as he's heard the message.

Hannah leans against her car, raising her hand up to shield her eyes from the sun as Olivia's car appears through the gates, and travels down the driveway towards her. Even from here she can see Claire's smug face. It's really perturbed her that this woman – who up until just yesterday she considered too inept to even dress herself correctly – is becoming Olivia's new best friend, worming her way into Olivia's life during her time of vulnerability. She doesn't even know what's happened between Olivia and her husband but she's benefiting from the fallout. Maybe Claire was slyer than Hannah thought, after all?

It's probably for the best that Olivia offered her a lift, though. At least it means Claire's tangerine Fiat 500 won't be garishly polluting the driveway while they try make content. How many times was she going to have to apologise to Olivia for the whole Matt situation? She's sent her three voicenotes and eight text messages. It isn't her fault. She didn't ask to be told about what Matt had done, she didn't go looking for that information. It was something that happened to her, outside of her control. Surely Olivia has to see that? Hannah's sure, at the very least, eventually Olivia will get bored of Claire and come crawling back.

The door to the house opens as she walks up the driveway and Tom emerges in a shirt and black trousers. His sleeves are rolled up, suggesting to Hannah that he does have an understanding of the power of a man's exposed forearm, and, not to slut-shame him, but he was pretty much asking for her to throw herself at him. She feels as though she's only just got her sense of dignity back after being rejected by him, though. The next move must come from him.

'Hey!' Tom waves, as Amanda's black Range Rover turns into the gates of the driveway.

'Hey!' Hannah reaches the doorway and leans over to kiss him on the cheek.

Across the driveway, Olivia's climbing out of her car, watching Hannah and Tom greet each other with a kiss and a hug. Claire's chattering away next to her like she has been the whole way there, but Olivia's not really paying attention. She's trying really hard to like Claire, especially because she knows it'll fuck Hannah off, but she really is quite annoying. She's not sure how much more of it she can take, even out of spite.

'Hey, Tom! I'm Claire!' Claire stumbles across the gravel towards Tom like a thirsty goat, hand outstretched in premature greeting. 'We met before at the open house, but obviously a lot's happened since then! I thought I should probably introduce myself again!'

'Hi, Claire, of course I remember you,' Tom says, looking overwhelmed by her.

Olivia can see that he's trying to look around Claire to see her, but she's not interested. She wants to talk to him in real life about as much as she wants to talk to him on the phone. If Hannah hadn't made it so that they all had to come or risk not looking like a team player, then she would have ducked out of this.

'How's it going?' Tom asks politely.

'There was drama!' Claire says. 'Ron from Sanders has been taken in for questioning! I think they think he did it!'

'Oh yeah, I just saw that too,' Tom says, backing away slightly from the force of Claire's manic energy.

'We've heard they found his DNA on her body, which is pretty vague, though,' Hannah says.

'I can't believe he could be the murderer,' Claire replies as though Hannah asked her.

Hannah seriously doubts Ron did the murder. He wouldn't even be able to lift *Bella's Vulva*. He's so sweaty from all the coke he's ingested it'd just slip straight through his fingers. But she guesses she's the only person who actually knows about the statue.

'They must think he killed Bella and then maybe because Brick knew he did it and was so close to telling everyone at the vigil the other night, he killed Brick to protect himself,' Claire says, as though she's the estate agent Miss Marple.

'Hello! Sorry for the delay,' Amanda says, walking from her four-by-four with Buster trotting joyfully in front. 'Children's school phoned, bit of an emergency, but all sorted now.'

In fact, Rupert had shown up to show and tell with a tampon he'd taken from the bathroom, saying it was one of Alastair's Cuban cigars. Amanda had been given a stern ticking off by his teacher and told that neither option was appropriate for a six-year-old's show and tell. At this point, Amanda went on a rant about how children should learn about periods far earlier anyway.

She's been a single parent for around twenty-four hours and already forgotten show-and-tell day. Everything was completely falling to shit. She just wants to get these video ideas of Hannah's over with so she can get back to sorting out the train wreckage of her life. She wouldn't have even come, but they can't exactly film talking heads without her and it was quite a good idea to try and get the narrative around the agency away from murder.

'Gosh, I don't know how you do it all,' Olivia says.

'You'll be doing it all soon enough,' Claire says, and then clamps her hand over her mouth.

'Oh my god, Olivia!' Amanda rejoices prematurely. 'Are you pregnant? Bella told me you were trying before she passed! But I didn't realise you were already there!'

Olivia's cheeks burn. She can feel Tom staring at her. She can't believe Claire's done this to her. What the fuck?

'No, not pregnant,' Olivia says, embarrassed and angry

that anyone can just ask this question whenever they want. 'Still just trying.'

'Sorry,' Claire says. 'Bella told me before and I just ... sorry ...'

'No worries,' Olivia says, wondering again how Bella even knew.

Now she knows the truth about Matt, she doubts he would have told Bella. She must have heard her and Hannah talking about it in the office. Seems like she was more aware of everyone's business than any of them realised.

Hannah's loving this. She would never let out one of Olivia's secrets like that. Although she knows it's exactly her ability to keep a secret well that's caused the problem between the two of them here.

'Shall we go in and get on with it?' Olivia says, pushing past Tom without looking at him. There's no way she's going to just stand here while he makes puppy dog eyes at her like he hasn't also been making them at Hannah.

'Of course.' Tom follows her into the house. 'Maybe we should get some coffee downstairs first.'

The other women file into the house behind them with Amanda looking around, seeing beautiful details she hadn't noticed before. Maybe she should be doing this listing? Maybe it's time she took some power back in this agency? She's going to talk to Hannah about it later. She's sure, given the circumstances, she'll understand.

'We could do some lifestyle shots!' Claire suggests as they head down the stairs into the kitchen. 'We can make it all hygge or something!'

'That's such a great idea, Claire,' Olivia says, praising her like a child that's just produced a hideous finger painting.

Hannah can't help but think that was for her benefit because 'lifestyle shots' when they're filming 'lifestyle videos' isn't exactly ground-breaking. Also hygge? What year is it? 2014?

'I'm just going to make sure the living room's ready for the shoot,' Hannah calls from the doorway. 'The light's really hitting the Dead Salmon beautifully.'

The rest of the group file down into the sun-drenched kitchen, but Hannah heads into the living room. She's pleased to note that she wasn't wrong about the Dead Salmon. The light coming in from the back window is reflecting pink around the space. Even the grey marble mantle has a peach tone to it like an Instagram filter. This room's going to make her skin look amazing on camera too.

Hannah looks behind her to check that no one's followed her in here before heading over to the log basket. Grabbing a tissue from her bag she wraps it over her hand and prods the logs on top, pushing them to the side. After a few seconds of digging, she's relieved to see the bronze gleaming back at her where she left it. She reaches in and takes out the sculpture giving it a thorough wipe with the tissue to remove her prints while making sure she doesn't rub off the red bloodstains before placing it back in the basket.

She re-covers it with the logs a little looser than before. She knows that they don't have too long before Amanda gets bored or has to go to another appointment. She makes a point of being the kind of busy woman whose attention you can only have for a limited amount of time. And Hannah really wants everyone to be there when the vulva's found.

For extra insurance, she grabs some dog treats from her bag and crumbles them over the logs. She suspects Buster isn't the kind of good guard dog who will sniff out blood or anything like that, but she does know he'll do anything for a treat. She walks away, the logs generously dusted with liver and checks around her to make sure everything else is set up and perfect for filming.

Trotting out of the living room in her Louboutins, Hannah feels relaxed about her plan. She feared that when she got to the log basket, the sculpture might not be there any more, which would indicate that Tom knew about it and was hiding it further. But this proves he didn't know. He'd never have left it in such a shit hiding spot. It's more likely that whoever killed Bella and Brick had got themselves caught up in something weird or dodgy. Maybe in the art world.

Hannah spends about an hour filming outside the house with the office camera, trying to make sure that she gets every angle right and that she has her plan clear in her mind. She sees them all through the living-room window chatting and laughing and tries not to let the jealousy consume her.

Every time she's walked into a room with them today Olivia's glared at her, still seething with rage in a way that Hannah's more and more sure she doesn't deserve. It's starting to feel like school again, like she's being pushed out. Distracting herself with work, she moves around to the other side of the house where she can see Tom in his study window, frowning at his laptop. The way his brow furrows under his glasses is deeply sexy. Absolutely nothing about this man's job is hot to her, but she'd definitely bang him over his desk, with loads of numbers probably on a spreadsheet or whatever blinking away in the background. She doesn't realise she's staring until he looks up and smiles at her. Immediately, she averts her gaze, but it's too late, he's caught her mid-lust.

He strolls over to the window and she tries to look nonchalant. But, as he pushes up the sash, she's distracted by his still-uncovered filthy forearms, the tease.

'How's it going?' he asks, leaning on the sill and smiling at her.

'Just grabbing some outside shots,' Hannah replies, snapping a photo of him as she talks. He clearly knows how hot he looks right now and Hannah's fuming with herself for not simply walking away and pretending to be too busy to talk to him.

A huge laugh comes from inside the house and Hannah finds herself wincing.

'I can't help but notice you're not in there with them. You OK?' Tom asks.

'Oh yeah, someone had to do the outside. It's a dirty job, but you know ...' Hannah says, gesturing to the camera and smiling, but she can tell Tom doesn't buy it.

'I hope you don't mind me saying, but things seem ... a little off between you and Olivia?' he presses, taking off his glasses.

'Oooh yeah, well . . . I think she's cross with me,' Hannah says, busying herself by flicking between pictures on the screen of the camera.

'About the Matt stuff?' Tom asks.

'You knew?' Hannah asks, looking up.

'Not till yesterday,' Tom says, his fingers wrapped round the lintel as he swings slightly on it, leaning towards her through the open window.

'Ah, still just me that was a shit friend, then?' she asks.

'I don't think you're a shit friend at all,' Tom says, reaching out and touching her arm. 'Don't beat yourself up. You didn't do anything wrong. Matt did.'

'Really?' Hannah asks, looking up at him.

'Really,' Tom nods, making eye contact. 'You're a good friend. She'll realise that eventually and come round.'

'Thanks, Tom,' Hannah says. 'You are too.'

'Sorry to interrupt.' Olivia appears round one of the white pillars framing the front door as both Hannah and Tom lurch away from each other. 'But, Hannah, we're ready for you to do your talking head now.'

As quickly as she appeared, Olivia's abruptly disappeared back into the house again. Hannah rolls her eyes at Tom, before turning and following her. The women are only a few steps into the hallway when a shriek rings out from the sitting room. Olivia looks back at Hannah as a reflex before turning back round and racing towards the scream. Tom emerges from his study, rubbing his eyes in confusion.

'What on earth . . . ?' he asks, holding his glasses floppy in his right hand.

'It sounded like Claire to me,' Hannah says as Tom races past her into the sitting room.

But she doesn't need to race She walks into the living room knowing exactly what she's going to see there. The bronze statue is lying on the floor with the blood-coloured stains clearly visible, and Buster the dog stood next to it, guarding it like the bad omen it is.

'I'm calling the police,' Amanda says, grabbing Buster and clutching him to herself before bashing away at the keypad on her phone.

Amanda can't work out why these things keep happening. Why, no matter how hard she tries, does everything keep turning to shit?

Chapter Thirty-nine

Olivia can't believe she's stuck down in this kitchen again with Hannah and Tom making eyes at each other, and Claire crying, as per usual. At least Amanda's here. She's the only other person who seems to be retaining any kind of normalcy at this point. Albeit her and Buster are out in the garden making calls while he leaves small pea-sized shit pellets around.

Olivia watches Tom and Hannah flirting while they make teas and coffees for everyone. It's cringeworthy. As if them congratulating each other earlier for being such 'good' friends to her wasn't bad enough. God, he's just thanked her for passing the milk and she's behaving like he's given her an OBE. She might as well be fellating him right now while the police search and dust for prints upstairs. She hopes Buster gets anxious diarrhoea all over Tom's garden and he has to spend the rest of the day hosing it out of the cracks in the brickwork.

Next to her, Claire's snotting her way through a triple-quilted toilet roll. Olivia watched a TikTok earlier in the week about something called compassion fatigue, and she feels Claire might have prompted it within her.

'Here we are.' Tom brings over two sweet teas.

He places one in front of Claire and the other in front of Olivia, putting a gentle hand on Olivia's back. The firm feel of his fingers through the back of her silk blouse makes her heart thump. He leans over her, so close to her face she can feel the heat of his breath against her cheek.

'Are you OK?' he asks, the words tickling her skin as he lingers there for a moment too long.

Just for a second, Olivia doesn't care what he may or may not have been doing with her best friend (if she can still even call Hannah that). She wants him to throw everything off the kitchen island and have her right across it. Once the stove top's cooled down a bit anyway. She knows she needs to sort things out with Matt, fix their perfect (or not so perfect) marriage, have the life she's always dreamed of having. But every time Tom's near she's overwhelmed with the desire to recklessly throw it all away.

'Fine, thank you,' Olivia says, teeth gritted as she fights to maintain her composure.

'Don't worry, Claire. The police will have it sorted ASAP. If that's the weapon used to kill Bella, they'll be able to find out from DNA, won't they?' Hannah says, cheerier than she's been all week, Olivia notices.

'Well . . .' Tom moves away from Olivia's frostiness and heads back over to the island to stand next to Hannah. 'Maybe . . .'

'What do you mean?' Hannah asks.

'I mean the fingerprints might have been rubbed off. Anyone could have touched it that night too. It was just on display really?' Tom says.

Hannah feels her perkiness fade, realising Tom's right. She's been an idiot. Why hadn't she thought of that? She could have just said her prints were on it from the party. Now she's not only wiped off her prints but probably the killer's too. She feels like a fool.

'At least they can check the log basket where it was found too, though,' Hannah says.

'Log basket?' Claire screws up her face between sobs.

'What log basket?' Olivia asks. 'That's not where it was found.'

Hannah feels the panic shoot through her like an ice pick. She tries to hide it, but she knows her cheeks are going red.

'I thought Claire said she found it in the log basket?' Hannah asks.

'No,' Claire says. 'Buster found it. He was barking at the fireplace, and when I went over there to see what was up, he sniffed it out from under the grate.'

'I could have sworn you said log basket.' Hannah stares at Claire, confused.

If it wasn't found where she left it, that means someone else moved it after Hannah did, which also means someone else knew it was there in the first place. And that can only have been one of the other women or Tom. She stares around the kitchen with a renewed sense of fear.

'Well, she didn't,' Olivia says, standing up. She's unsure

whether she's being defensive of Claire or she's just fucking sick of Hannah's arrogance.

'I didn't,' Claire says, staring her dead in the eye.

Hannah stares back, studying her. Wondering if there's something there she hasn't seen before, a determination, a calculated nasty streak that she's brushed off? Claire could have been the only one of them with clear motive if she knew Bella was selling her house. And, looking at her now, Claire seems to be the only one of them doing well after Bella's death. She's got new listings, she seems more confident, Amanda's being nicer to her, she's definitely had work done.

'Unless you've got something to tell us about the log basket, Hannah?' Olivia can tell when Hannah's lying. She's already suspicious.

'No,' Hannah says, unable to take her eyes off Claire, sure that maybe it's Claire that has something she needs to tell them about the log basket, not her. 'So it was Claire who found it, then?'

'It was Buster who found it, really,' Amanda says, coming in from the garden. 'He was sniffing around by the fire grate then he just started barking. It was behind the grate.'

'He'd been sniffing around the basket, though. Maybe he knew whatever Hannah seems to know about the basket ...' Claire says, her gaze on Hannah now feeling more like a threat.

There are footsteps on the stairs as DI Knight comes down into the kitchen and the women grow silent.

'OK, we've had a look around the area, taken fingerprints

and swabs,' DI Knight says, his hands in his pockets as he addresses them from the bottom of the stairs, completely oblivious to the terrible atmosphere. 'We've sent the sculpture off for DNA testing, but I'm afraid it does look like blood, which would certainly suggest it could be the weapon used in the murder of Bella Radcliffe.'

Claire gasps and Olivia rubs her back, distracted.

'But you've got Ron in already, right?' Olivia asks. 'You think he did it, don't you?'

'We released Ron earlier today. We don't believe he had any part in the murder,' DI Knight says.

'But his DNA was on the body?' Amanda asks. 'Wasn't that why you arrested him?'

'It would appear that Ron had earlier been to the toilet in the fountain when he was drunk. And the DNA had got on to her body that way,' DI Knight says.

None of the women or Tom says anything, all of them too grossed out to speak. Eventually Tom clears his throat.

'Would it be OK, Detective, if I were to get the water cleaned out of the fountain now then?' Tom asks.

'Yes, I think we've got everything we need from it and everything from the house, actually,' DI Knight says. 'We'll take the sculpture back for analysis now.'

'Thank you, Detective,' Tom says. 'I'll come and show you out.'

'I think we should head back to the office,' Amanda says. 'I'm sure Ron will be telling the whole town about his ordeal by now.'

Olivia follows Amanda up the stairs while Hannah puts

their mugs in the sink to help Tom. She doesn't realise Claire is still there until she turns almost bumping into her.

'You know, it strikes me, Hannah, that you should stop poking around near fires,' Claire says before walking out of the kitchen. 'After all, people who live in libraries probably shouldn't start throwing books around.'

The realisation that Hannah's drastically underestimated Claire hits her like a train. Maybe all of them have. Panic immediately courses through her veins as she tries to keep her voice level.

'No idea what you're talking about,' Hannah replies. She edges away from her, but Claire just continues her advance, backing her against the marble island.

'I know all about the library – Bella told me before she died. We laughed about it. I also know that Olivia doesn't know. Stay away from my great-aunt's house,' Claire hisses her breath all over Hannah's face. 'I know you've been there, talking to her about selling it. Sarah the carer told me. She tells me everything. Stay away or you'll regret it. And stop trying to turn Olivia against me. She's *my* friend now. You blew it.'

Hannah stares into Claire's cold eyes, afraid of her for the first time ever. Eventually, Hannah breaks eye contact and brushes past her, saying nothing but trying to look calm as she heads for the stairs. Despite her best efforts, she finds herself looking over her shoulder more than once, even more sure now that Claire's plenty capable of killing Bella and, if she killed Bella – and probably Brick too – over her great-aunt's house she'd have no problems doing the same to Hannah.

Hannah's phone beeps the moment she reaches the safety of the hallway where the other women are still talking to the police. She opens it, seeing an email with Amanda's name on it, despite her standing just feet away from her.

From: Amanda@harringtons.co.uk
To: Hannah@harringtons.co.uk
Subject: Tom's house
Hi Hannah,
I'd like to start this email by clarifying that I do believe you're a brilliant agent and more than up to the task. But considering everything that's gone on at Tom's property I'd like to take over on that listing. As CEO it only feels right for me to be the one he works with now. Hope you understand.
 Amanda xx

In the space of just five minutes, Hannah realises she's lost any chance of getting out of the property guardianship.

Amanda was right about Ron. By the time they arrive back at the office he's giving exclusive interviews to the internet detectives about his incarceration, telling anyone who'll listen about the perils of public urination. It was a display that Hannah would have usually revelled in and taken the piss out of him for. Unfortunately, she's too busy rejecting Marcus's calls about Esme's house for her own safety while feeling deeply depressed about losing Tom's. Not to mention watching her back every time Claire leaves her seat.

Chapter Forty

Hannah races up the steps to the police station, wearing a disguise of sunglasses and a black scarf over her head. She's waited until it's dark so no one sees her, but she's also nervous enough to inhibit her own vision for anonymity. She looks around anxiously from the top step to check that Claire's not watching from a bush somewhere.

Since their run-in at Tom's place, all Hannah can think about is the fact that Claire's the only one with motive to kill Bella and that Claire might be coming for her next. The only bit she can't quite figure out is why Claire would kill Brick when she so clearly fancied him. But maybe he rejected her? She ignores another call from Esme, far too afraid to take it, and wonders if she might just block the number? But Marcus wouldn't be so easily dealt with.

Only when she's safely inside the police station's reception with its holey metal chairs bolted to the floor, daubed in chewing gum and graffiti, does Hannah deem it safe enough to take off her sunglasses. She knows she's taking a risk being here, but she has to tell them what she knows. She can't say anything about the sculpture moving, but she can tell them that she's sure Claire knew that Bella was selling her inheritance from under her. Claire needs to be stopped. Especially when Olivia's spending so much time with her – she could be in danger.

'I'd like to speak to DI Clive Knight, please,' Hannah says. 'It's about the murders of Bella Radcliffe and Caspian Smith.'

The woman on the reception desk gives her a funny look and tells her to sit and wait while she notifies the detective inspector that Hannah's here. Dutifully, Hannah walks over to the seats and slumps down, putting her sunglasses back on just in case someone she knows walks in.

For the last few hours, while she waited for it to get dark, all she's been able to do is anxiously watch TikToks about the case. She tells herself it's not self-indulgence, more self-preservation and keeping herself informed. It's mostly been interviews with Ron, though. The internet is not yet aware of the discovery of a possible murder weapon.

A door opens by the reception desk and Hannah's shocked to see Amanda come out, also in sunglasses, looking very much as though she's trying to avoid being recognised. The two of them startle and look down at the floor.

'Oh, hi, Hannah, just had to come and talk to Clive,' Amanda mutters, scuttling towards the door.

'Oh yes, hi, Amanda, same,' Hannah says hastily, studying her shoes.

'See you in the office tomorrow,' Amanda says, heading out the door.

'...s tomorrow,' Hannah mumbles trying to get the words out fast as Amanda exits the building.

'Hannah?' DI Knight stands in the doorway that Amanda's just left.

'Yep.' Hannah stands and follows him through the door into a greige corridor and an even more – if it's possible – greige interview room.

'Take a seat,' he offers, pointing to the plastic chair on the other side of the table.

She sits, the seat still warm from Amanda's arse, and wonders what she was here for anyway. Maybe Amanda suspects Claire too. She's not stupid.

'What can I do for you?' DI Knight asks.

'I'd like to talk to you about Claire who works at the agency?' Hannah begins. 'I think she had motive to kill Bella and Brick.'

It's an hour later when Hannah emerges from the police station. The town's completely empty as she walks down the steps hastily to get back to the library and into safety. Every rustle from a bush makes the skin on the back of her neck prickle. She tells herself it's just birds, maybe even mice or squirrels, rooting around in there, and keeps walking as fast as she possibly can.

Behind one of the trees outside the station, Claire's watching everything, waiting for Hannah to move far enough away so she can head into the police station undetected herself. She knows Hannah's probably been telling them about Bella selling Esme's place. But that's OK. She's got a lot to tell them about Hannah. She bets the police don't know about Hannah's rivalry with Bella, or that she hated her because she kept stealing listings from her and that Hannah blames Bella for the fact her career's gone so far downhill she's had to give up her flat and become a property guardian. And, as far as she can see, Bella fucking up Hannah's life is more than enough motive for Hannah to kill.

Chapter Forty-one

Amanda sits in the living room, looking around her at all the things her husband's left behind. Clive called her in earlier to tell her he hadn't been able to get hold of Alastair at all and to ask if she wanted the police to launch a missing person's investigation as it's now been over twenty-four hours. But Amanda can't bear the embarrassment of other people knowing she doesn't know where her husband is. Much like with his extra marital cleaning, she didn't want the kids to have to face it as much as she didn't want to have to live it down.

She knows that in a couple of weeks, when things have died down, she's going to have to start telling close friends that her husband's left her. She can carry on making videos and content for a couple of months before she has to make it any more public than that. But she's going to need to be prepared. Her life is the thing people want – her house, her family, her business – and all of that includes her husband. Her husband was instrumental in the creation of Amanda Harrington the brand, and now she's not going to let him be the reason that it falls.

The flames lick at the door of the log burner and she knows she's doesn't have long before one of the nosy neighbours knocks on the door to tell her off for using it and killing the planet or whatever. She stares at the birth certificate in her hands. People are going to want to know what her maiden name is when they realise that Alastair's just upped and left her. They'll expect her to change her name back like Cheryl from Girls Aloud. But she isn't going to. It's just a name after all. It doesn't mean anything about her character, unlike the maiden name on her birth certificate.

In one, fluid and decisive movement, she reaches over and opens the little door of the log burner. She drops the certificate into the flames and watches as the maiden name that could ruin her life turns to ashes.

At the library, Hannah sits on her bed, every sound making her jump. Every so often she gets up and checks the door is definitely locked and that the windows really are so stuck they'd never open in a million years. She can't believe she's this scared of *Claire,* but maybe it really is always the quiet ones, after all.

She's worked so hard to keep the library a secret and now what was it all for? For Claire to expose her anyway? She got the impression that if she left Esme's house alone, Claire wouldn't tell anyone, but she couldn't rely on that. Maybe Claire has told Olivia already? Either way, Hannah's decided she's going to be honest with everyone and just tell them tomorrow. She can't keep trying to claw her life back like this and with Esme and Tom's houses gone, she's truly out of options. She doesn't want anyone's charity or pity, or even any help. She just wants to have to stop lying all the time, to stop having to chase her own tail to catch up. Maybe if she finally confesses what's going on she'll have more chance of getting herself out of this hole.

Hannah craves comfort, someone to tell her everything's going to be OK. But she knows she's not going to get it from Olivia, and she certainly doesn't have any family she'll get it from. She opens the messages between her and Tom. So far they've only discussed business in them but she starts typing.

Hannah: I'm sorry about everything earlier. You must hate us all now.

She wasn't expecting a reply immediately, if at all, but the three dots appear straight away and Tom's message pops up. She's never known a man text so fast.

Tom: Of course I don't! It's not your fault is it? How are you doing?
Hannah: I'm ok! How about you?
Tom: Same. Bit of a day!
Hannah: Amanda messaged after we were round. She's decided that given everything that's gone on, she wants to take on your listing herself. I was going to email you tomorrow properly but I figured I could just tell you now. You're a friend after all.
Tom: That's a shame. I've really enjoyed getting to know you.
Tom: I hope that doesn't have to change . . .

Hannah hovers over the message. She wasn't expecting it and yet she'd messaged him to feel comforted, hadn't she? She just hadn't expected it to be so easy. Maybe he was a good guy, after all? All the stuff about his complicated situation and holding back was frustrating to her at the time. But maybe he was just trying to protect her?

Hannah: Thank you.
Tom: Here if you need anything, anytime. After all, I've grown quite fond of you.

Hannah feels a smile spreading across her face before she can stop it. Just knowing that Tom's there for her makes her feel safer. Maybe he's the first person she should tell.

Hannah: I've got something I need to tell someone. I haven't even told Olivia. But keeping it to myself is just making it worse.
Tom: Consider me your confessional.
Hannah: I'm living as a property guardian. Things got tight at work, and I couldn't afford my flat anymore. I've been hiding it from everyone because I'm so ashamed.
Tom: Is that it? I thought you were going to tell me you had a verruca or something hideous like that.
Hannah: I don't think I have one of them, but probably will soon if I keep living here.
Tom: Well I still think you're pretty great, and it sounds like you've been under a lot of stress. I like that you felt you could tell me.
Tom: If you get a verruca I'm out though. Sorry.

Out of what, Hannah wonders.

Tom: I also don't think you're the killer, for what it's worth.

Hannah stares at the message. Why would he think she was a killer?

Hannah: Um thanks? I think?
Tom: I just mean because of the video that was posted about you . . .
Hannah: ???
Tom: Link: Hannah Tomkins – the lead suspect in the murder of Bella Radcliffe and Caspian Smith.

Hannah nearly drops her phone. She sits up and screams before pressing play. There's just one woman, in questionable make-up, talking to the camera and explaining that a 'source close to the deceased' has said that a murder weapon was uncovered today and that one of Harrington's estate agents 'namely Hannah Tomkins' was behaving suspiciously and seemed to already know more about the weapon than the others. Almost as if she already knew it was there. Hannah's quite sure she knows exactly who that source is. Claire, trying to frame someone other than herself.

Olivia does feel a bit bad for telling that TikToker about the way Hannah behaved when they found the weapon earlier. She knows that video's going to go viral instantly, what with it being the first mention of a murder weapon.

But, when she saw Hannah walking into the station she knew she had to do something to retaliate. God knows what she'd gone in there to tell them. Olivia tries to tell herself that her anger towards Hannah has nothing to do with Tom, but deep down she knows that she wants to get back at her for all her flirting with him earlier.

From her car across the square, Olivia's watched all of them – Hannah, Amanda and Claire – going in and out of that police station tonight. She's been sitting here for hours. In a kind of teenage dreamlike state, she'd left the house earlier thinking she'd see whether she found herself drawn to either visiting Tom at his house or Matt at the hotel and that would decide the course of the rest of her life for her. But, despite everything, she'd driven to Tom's house only to find a strange car in his driveway, realised it was probably a date and she was being an idiot, and reversed back down the drive with her headlights off. She was furious with herself for even going there. He'd shown her time and time again he was just a slut of a man, and yet she'd fallen for it, all because he said he loved her.

She'd driven into town, in a rage at herself, and parked up, unsure what to do. Seeing Amanda go into the police station was a nice distraction, then she'd sat and watched everyone going in and out, all of them looking like they were trying to sneak in undercover. Was there no one in Olivia's life who wasn't keeping secrets? At least Matt had kept his trying to protect her and protect their life together. And Olivia still loved him, didn't she? Maybe Matt was the only person she could trust, after all, and maybe it was time to try to repair their marriage. She heads to the hotel to bring her husband home, where he belongs. Everyone else's lives might be a mess, but she and Matt can fix theirs.

Chapter Forty-two

Hannah's spent most of the morning watching Claire across the office. She's exhausted after spending the night anxiously hiding in bed, afraid of every tiny sound in case it was Claire coming to get her. It seems wild to her now, though, looking at the same Claire across the office, that she could be the person responsible for all this. But the evidence was mounting:

1. Yesterday's confrontation in Tom's kitchen where Claire had really shown another side of herself and actually threatened Hannah.
2. Claire's the only one of the Harrington's women with a solid motive, and at least one of them – apart from Hannah – knew about the sculpture because someone other than Hannah moved it from the basket to the grate while they were there yesterday morning. It *has* to have been Claire.
3. It was clearly Claire who's feeding information about Hannah and the case to the TikTokers outside, trying to frame Hannah for the murders. She has no actual proof of this, but she knows she's right.

Surely the police will be dragging Claire in for questioning soon, especially after what Hannah told them last night. DI Knight seemed pretty interested in what she'd had to say. And at least if Claire gets arrested before the awards tonight people might stop gossiping about the TikTok theories that Hannah's the murderer.

Claire looks up from her screen and Hannah immediately looks back down at her own computer. Hannah is anxiously awaiting a reply from Amanda after she emailed her first thing this morning suggesting all the reasons Amanda should promote her to manager. She thinks a hierarchy at the agency would be a good thing and she even said she wouldn't expect a pay rise right away because she knows the agency's struggling, she'd just be happy with the title change. She's outlined all the ways that her managing the other two would make this ship run a little tighter and, with Olivia barely talking to her anyway, it's not like their friendship will muddy the waters when she's in charge. Hannah is completely alone in this office with a possible serial killer watching her every move.

At least she's got Tom in her corner now, though. Things feel brighter after their texts last night. His replies slowed down because he said he was hanging out with a friend, but this morning he'd messaged asking how she was and how she'd slept. She can't remember the last time someone did that. At a basic level, Hannah realises that, despite how hard she tries, she's just like everyone else. All she wants is for someone to consider her in their day.

Next to her, Olivia's tapping away at her keyboard with

the kind of loud passive aggression that signifies she's not really doing anything of any meaning or worth, but she really wants Hannah to think she is.

Actually, Olivia's just adding the finishing touches to a strategy she's sending over to Amanda about the team, suggesting that she should take a manager role within the agency in order to help things run a little smoother and improve sales. She knows Hannah's going to be going for it too, but Hannah can't have everything she wants, and she's pretty sure she's put together an airtight pitch for herself. It's all part of her new plan; she's sorting things out with Matt, she's going to get promoted and she's going to get pregnant. She just needs Claire to stop sending her direct messages about nothing. It's really distracting to have them pinging up in the corner of her screen every five seconds.

Claire's typing away a hilarious message to Olivia about Marcus's latest request that they throw an open house for his place just like they did for Tom's. He doesn't understand why they wouldn't do for his nine hundred thousand place what they would for Tom's ten million mansion. She knows Hannah keeps watching her and she's not stupid – it's no coincidence that DI Knight suddenly received information about Bella selling Esme's house after Hannah's visit to the station last night. But she told him she had no idea about any of it and he believed her. She'd like to think Hannah got the message about Esme's place yesterday, though. She's not about to let Hannah carry on where Bella left off and she's not going to be underestimated any more.

Across the office, Amanda's responding to Instagram

comments from followers telling her how fabulous her life is but doing it on her computer so none of the other women can tell she's not doing work. She can see Hannah's still fuming with her for taking over the mansion listing, but the atmosphere in the office in general today feels pretty frosty. She should probably do something about that before tonight, but she also just wants the women to get on with their fucking jobs because she can't hold everyone else up right now when she's barely able to hold up herself. As for tonight, they're just going to have to learn to be fucking professional.

'I've sent over the final presentation for Bella's section at the awards, Amanda,' Claire says, solemn despite the bouncing efficiency that's been coming off her keystrokes all morning.

'Brilliant, thank you, Claire,' Amanda says, looking up from her screen and taking off her glasses. Does she want a biscuit for doing a basic task? 'While we're on tonight, I know that we've all got a lot going on at the moment. Maybe there are some differences between us with regard to the things that have happened in the last week or so. But, please, could we at least try to put on a united front in public?'

'Of course, Amanda,' Claire says.

'Absolutely,' Olivia says, and Hannah nods.

'Hannah, I know there's a lot of rumours swirling around about you in particular. Obviously, we all support you,' Amanda says. 'And we know you're not a killer.'

Hannah looks from Olivia to Claire knowing full well

that Claire's dobbed her into TikTok's finest detectives and probably *is* a killer, and Olivia's being a prick to her right now. But she's going to be gracious. Claire can't exactly kill her in the middle of the office, can she?

'Thanks, Amanda. That means such a lot,' she says, maintaining her stare from one of them to the other, smiling.

Amanda can see the tension between the women is stretched to absolute breaking point. It's bad enough that she's going to be there without Alastair just when everyone's looking at them. She needs to make sure she looks good and in control at all these events so that no one can look back on them when they find out about the split and suggest that this was when she 'let herself go' or some other shit.

'Brilliant, so everyone has an early mark this afternoon to head home and get ready before the ceremony,' Amanda says, standing from her desk and walking towards the toilet. 'Remember, we've got nothing to hide.'

As soon as Amanda's in the toilet and out of earshot Olivia turns to Claire.

'Claire, do you want to come and get ready at mine?' she asks, glaring at Hannah the whole time.

'Sounds good!' Claire chirps.

'Pathetic,' Hannah mutters under her breath.

'Sorry, did you have something to say, Hannah?' Olivia asks, throwing her shoulders back defiantly. She's sick of Hannah's bitchiness.

'Just that you're only inviting Claire round to piss me off and make some kind of stupid point. Claire, she's using you,' Hannah says.

'Don't listen to her, Claire,' Olivia says. 'Hannah's such a massive bitch she wouldn't know genuine friendship if it smacked her in the overinflated lips.'

'Oh, that's rich coming from the woman who once had so much filler injected she could only drink through a straw for two months.' Hannah rolls her eyes.

'Is that all you've got for me? Digs at my appearance and some filler that faded two years ago? I thought you prided yourself on being witty?' Olivia asks.

'I don't bother wasting my wit on people who don't deserve it,' Hannah replies, her voice raised.

'Oh no! Hannah doesn't think I'm worth it!' Olivia shouts.

'I just think you're being a massive bitch about nothing! And I don't understand why you were being so fucking weird and unsupportive about Tom liking me before!' Hannah shouts back.

'Because he doesn't fucking like you! He's a player! He'd shag anything that moves, it's just that you're moving so much in his face he can't avoid you!' Olivia shouts.

'Mummy, the children are fighting,' Claire whispers to herself as Hannah screams at Olivia, calling her a stupid bint.

'What the . . .?' Amanda comes back into the room and tries to gain their attention, but Hannah and Olivia are too far into their fight to notice what's going on.

'FUCK YOU!' Hannah's screaming. 'And fuck your fucking mug that you bought me which is actually really fucking hideous!'

Hannah launches a pink mug with the word 'friend' on it, which corresponds with Olivia's pink mug with the word 'best' into the bin next to her desk with a smash.

'Literally the cringiest thing I've ever seen in my life.' She turns to Claire. 'Sorry, Claire. I should have just given that to you, seeing as you're my replacement.'

Claire stands up, on guard and ready to defend her new best friend.

'Stop being so mean to Olivia! She's had a really hard week! HER HUSBAND MIGHT GO TO PRISON, YOU KNOW!' Claire shouts.

'CLAIRE!' Olivia shouts back. She can't believe it. She only told Claire about Matt last night and she's already spilled it at the first opportunity. She knew she shouldn't have been so trusting, but she just really needed someone to talk to now she can't talk to Hannah. 'I TOLD YOU THAT IN CONFIDENCE! DON'T TELL THE WHOLE FUCKING WORLD!'

'I'm not ...' Claire looks confused. 'You said Hannah already knew?'

'BUT AMANDA DIDN'T KNOW!' Olivia shouts back, furious.

Amanda says nothing, partly relieved this is happening now and not tonight.

'WELL, SORRYYYY,' Claire shouts back.

'Great secret-keeping, Claire.' Hannah finds herself clapping sarcastically, her fear of what Claire might do momentarily paused.

'At least *she* wasn't keeping secrets from me about *my* life!' Olivia shouts.

'This is so fucking unprofessional. Everyone sit down and shut the fuck up!' Amanda suddenly explodes, swearing uncharacteristically to get her point across. 'NOW!'

She slams her fist on the desk in front of her and accidentally kicks her chair back. It shoots off behind her, smacking against the wall, hard. The trophy shelf that sits above her head, filled with her years of accolades, wobbles then falls off the wall. Her awards from previous years, all twenty, glass and metal, vicious-looking statues come raining down on her as she dives under the desk just in time, avoiding being pummelled in the head by them.

'AMANDA!' the three women gasp, and run to her aid while Buster stays in his dog bed, watching the drama unfold, but not giving a tiny shiny shit about it.

'Oh my god.' Amanda emerges from her cover under the desk.

'Are you OK?' Olivia grabs her hand, helping her up.

'You could have died!' Claire gasps.

Hannah studies the shelf that's just come clean off the wall.

'Someone's sawn through these screws,' she says, rubbing her fingers against their flat edges. 'This was a ticking time bomb waiting to happen.'

'You could have died,' Claire repeats, blinking.

'Are you OK?' Olivia asks, bending down to help her.

Amanda shakes herself off, and stares at the women, blinking in shock.

'Yeah, totally fine. I'm sure it was an accident. Alastair put those shelves up, you know, and he's never been good at DIY.' Amanda's voice shakes even as she tries to convince the other women that it's nothing to worry about. 'Absolutely fine, really!'

'You should sit down,' Hannah says, grabbing Bella's chair from her desk, Amanda's own covered in the remnants of her broken and dented trophy shelf.

Amanda does as she's told, trembling from the shock.

'I'll get you a glass of water,' Claire says, rushing over to the kitchen and filling a glass before trotting back over like a golden retriever with a ball.

'I think we should tell the police,' Hannah says, still staring at the screws while Claire passes Amanda the glass. 'It really looks like someone did this on purpose. And what if it was whoever killed Bella and Brick? What if they're after you too now?'

Olivia and Claire stop what they're doing. Amanda's eyes meet Hannah's briefly, wide, like a rabbit caught in the headlights, and no matter what she says Hannah knows that she's rattled.

'Hannah,' Olivia whispers. 'You can't just say stuff like that – you're scaring everyone.'

'Yeah, Hannah,' Claire echoes, and Olivia wishes she wouldn't. Claire's only bonus was that she was loyal. Now Olivia knows she can't trust her to keep a secret she's just irritating.

'Honestly, Hannah, my husband is very bad at DIY. Let's

just leave it at that, shall we?' Amanda says, her eyes glazed over somewhat as she sits sipping the water.

The women stand around her trying to work out what to do for the best when Claire whispers in Olivia's direction.

'I'm really sorry about earlier. I wasn't thinking. I didn't mean to tell Amanda about Matt ...' Claire starts, but Olivia's been burned too recently. She's too pissed off to listen to any kind of apologies.

'Whatever,' Olivia hisses back. 'It's done now. Maybe it's best if you don't come round tonight. I think I need a bit of time to myself before the awards.'

Hannah lets out an involuntary snort of delighted laughter that Claire's fucked up now too.

'Not sure what you're laughing about,' Claire whispers back to her, the three women inching closer to each other in anger as Amanda just sits startled in the chair. 'She didn't even invite you to begin with.'

The women jump as the door opens and Ron's head peers round.

'Hello! Just a welfare check, ladies,' he says, his face giving sympathy with an edge of smugness. 'I just wanted to say I know none of you are murderers and I'm always here for your protection whenever you need it. Think of me like a condom, a sexy, sexy condom, saving you from murder.'

'Fuck off, Ron,' Hannah, Claire and Olivia shout back at him while Amanda hugs Buster close.

Chapter Forty-three

Claire gives up knocking and eventually accepts that no one's going to answer the front door. She hasn't got a lot of time. The awards start in an hour and she planned to come tomorrow, but she was just so cross she couldn't let it go. Besides, she wants Esme to see her looking fancy for an awards ceremony, prove to her that she's got her all wrong because she doesn't seem to have the faith in her that Claire wishes she did. If Esme could just see her like this maybe she'll respect her opinion on the house and stop this stupid business of trying to sell it behind Claire's back.

She heads round the back of the house to see if Esme and Sarah the carer are out there but it's empty. She walks up to the kitchen doors and finds them unlocked, tutting. She's already had to have a word with Sarah about security, although, it's not as if Esme has ever been any better at it. Esme has always assumed that if someone tried to break in, she could probably take care of them and, to be fair, the woman was an absolute weapon with a croquet mallet. All the same, she's old now and Claire thinks better care should be taken.

'Hello?' Claire calls.

She walks through the old terracotta-tiled country kitchen, judging each messy surface she walks past. She can't believe Sarah lets it get this bad. If Esme were more with it, she never would have let this happen. If this were Claire's house, the kitchen would always be spotless, ready for her to entertain the no doubt countless guests that she would be having round all the time. Claire's always believed that confidence would come in a house like this. She goes to see people in their properties ready to sell all the time, and every single property feels like a step closer to getting her own. It's just that often those steps are scuppered when the owners decide to go with a different agent.

'Hello? Sarah? Aunt Esme?' Claire walks into the hallway still calling out to them. 'Guys, it's Claire?'

She wonders if maybe they're out, but she can't think of anywhere that Esme would go these days. Everything becomes clear when she walks past the living room and sees the back of Sarah's head, her headphones on, a particularly filthy bit of *Bridgerton* playing on her iPad screen. Claire watches her from behind and realises she's completely oblivious that there's even someone in the house. Anything could be happening and all Sarah would hear is the ASMR Regency snogging noises. Claire could be anyone – she could be a dangerous intruder. She can't see Esme, so presumes that she's probably upstairs having a nap. And maybe the best thing to do would be to leave Sarah down here, watching her smut so that Claire can talk to Esme, just the two of them. The last thing she needs is Sarah sticking her nose in or claiming she's stressing Esme out.

Creeping up the stairs, Claire looks at the pictures that she's always found so ridiculous, but will absolutely keep and claim as her relatives when Esme's gone. She looks down at the worn, threadbare stair runner, that she's planning to replace, and at the panelled walls she'd already decided to paint Farrow & Ball Jitney. She needs to tell Esme how much it would upset her to lose the house. Maybe she'd understand and stop trying to sell it if Claire just explained.

On the landing, Claire sees Esme's door is ajar. She can hear her on the other side of it making huffing noises.

'Aunt Es?' Claire shouts.

'Fucking finally,' Esme says from behind the door. 'I've been awake ages and that dozy cow hasn't noticed.'

Claire rushes into the bedroom, finding Esme struggling to get her walker across the room. Claire's always loved her bedroom with its old Liberty print bedspread and cushions, the doilies on the side tables that were dreadfully trendy at some point and the ticking pelmets around the bed with matching ticking curtains, scraped back so that the evening sunlight streams onto the bed.

'Are you OK?' Claire asks, rushing to her aid.

'That fucking carer, never here when I need her. What's she doing? Watching her fucking filth again? Not sure why she thinks she has to hide a few heaving bosoms from me,' Esme says, lunging forward with her walker.

'Where's your chair?' Claire asks.

'Left it downstairs. I couldn't be doing with all the faff. I just need to get to the stairlift,' Esme sighs. 'Anyway, to what do I owe the pleasure of this visit? I thought you were working today and then you had some kind of fancy awards? Is that what you're wearing. It looks like Chanel – is it Chanel?'

'It is,' Claire says proudly.

'You look good,' Esme says.

The words boost Claire's self-esteem more than years' worth of therapy or confidence mantras ever could. She feels ready to dive in and talk to Esme about the house, once and for all. She'll appreciate her honesty, she's sure of it.

'Aunt Es, I thought I should talk to you about this face to face, before . . . well, it just seemed urgent.' Claire gets annoyed with herself for already fannying around too much and not articulating herself properly. 'I'm just going to come out and say it. I've heard you're trying to sell the house to a developer and I just can't believe you'd let this place be torn down.'

Claire feels herself getting angry again at the thought of this perfectly good house and all her childhood memories, simply being destroyed and replaced with shiny new flats. She can't let her do it. She helps Esme and her walker across the landing gradually, towards the top of the stairs.

'That fucking woman! I knew she wasn't as trustworthy as Bella,' Esme says, incensed. 'I told her not to tell anyone!'

'I was going to find out eventually,' Claire says. 'Why didn't *you* tell me?'

'I knew you wouldn't approve. And you might try

and talk me out of giving your inheritance to Extinction Rebellion. But think about the big picture!'

'Sorry, what?' Claire stops at the top of the stairs. 'You're doing what?'

'Donating the money from the sale of the house to Extinction Rebellion. You were telling me yourself you're doing well at work, so I can only assume you don't need the money,' Esme says. 'Give it to those in need I say. And Extinction Rebellion is such a good cause.'

'Extinction Rebellion,' Claire says again, her eyes glazing over.

A red mist settles over her, something she can't shake off. Esme carries on talking about saving the planet for the next generations. But Claire's too far gone to truly hear the words. All the work she's put in. Everything she's always wanted, the future she's imagined herself having in this house, all of it given to pissing Extinction Rebellion? She pushes Esme with one fluid movement, almost without effort. Esme goes tumbling down the stairs, a small scream escaping her before a series of bangs echoes in the hallway, as she hits each step, her Zimmer frame bumping down after her.

After what feels like an eternity, she stops. Claire stands at the top of the stairs, in her heels and gown, her make-up perfect, not a nail chipped or a hair out of place, staring down at Esme lying at the bottom of the stairs, twisted and unnatural-looking on the cold, black-and-white stone floor of the hallway.

Claire pauses for a few seconds, before whipping herself

into action. Slipping off her heels, she tiptoes down the stairs, her footsteps following the path of Esme's tumble. She tries not to look as she passes Esme's body. Glancing into the living room, she can see the headphones still on Sarah's head and the famous *Bridgerton* fingering scene on the screen of her iPad. She'll be at least another hour before she can tear herself away from that.

It's almost two hours before Sarah finally stirs from a *Bridgerton*-fuelled nap. She takes the headphones off, relieved not to hear Esme screaming at her to get up the stairs and do her fucking job. Maybe she's got lucky and Esme's still asleep too? She walks out of the living room, and immediately sees the frail heap of Esme sprawled across the floor, blood pooling around her head, her Zimmer frame lying next to her on its side.

Chapter Forty-four

Hannah and Olivia stand at opposite ends of the steps to the town hall, under the massive Estate Agent of the Year Awards banner. If it weren't for Amanda insisting that they all go in together to pose a 'united front', they both would have just gone in by now rather than standing here feeling like spectacles.

Hannah's never felt so nervous in her life, especially after what happened to Amanda in the office earlier. That shelf felt like a real wake-up call. They still don't know who killed Bella and Brick (although she's sure it was Claire) and, if whoever it was (Claire) can set up something like that in the office, then god knows what she can do out in the open, or at the awards. There could be peril everywhere. She edges away from the banner in case that's a trap too.

What's worse is that she knows everyone still thinks it was her despite the police not arresting her. People are actively shying away from her on the steps. This afternoon, she's been followed by two internet detectives as she tried to get her nails done and she's seen a profile about her on the *Daily Mail* TikTok account given by someone who clearly wants their own podcast, talking about Hannah as though she were a fictional character.

Olivia can't believe Claire hasn't shown up on time. She can see Amanda at the bottom of the steps mixing with everyone, but Claire's nowhere. She's late and keeping them all waiting while everyone stares at them. She's glad she suggested to Amanda that they make her redundant. She felt bad at the time, but now she stands by it.

At the bottom of the steps, Amanda smiles at other agents as she passes through the crowd, aware that they're all gossiping about her and the agency. She keeps her head held high, but feels like screaming when she sees Hannah and Olivia pointedly standing apart like teenagers in a playground feud. If they can't even get it together and be grown-ups at a public event like this, then how are they expecting she'll want to make them managers? Even if there were a manager's position available to start with, which there isn't. She doesn't understand where this idea's come from. Bella was obsessed with it too. Amanda's never said she wants to appoint a manager. The agency's her blood, sweat and tears. She's not about to hand over running it to someone else.

'Hannah! Olivia!' She greets them both at the top of the stairs with a smile and a loud shout to make them come to her. It feels like she's herding feral cats.

'You look gorgeous.' Hannah's first to arrive, like a whippet, showering Amanda in praise.

'Absolutely stunning,' Olivia says on the other side of her. 'Your hair's gorgeous.'

Amanda has gone for a half-up, half-down do, which she loves because it still allows her hair to flow while being classy. And she was going to be classy – despite what happened at the office earlier – she just hopes the other women will follow suit.

'Thank you, you both look wonderful,' Amanda says, then blinks, clearly irritated. 'Where's Claire?'

'Not sure,' Hannah says. 'But we can go in and she can join us.'

'I'm sure she won't be long,' Olivia says, tilting her head as she speaks to Hannah over Amanda.

'I would rather we all went in together,' Amanda says.

She's quite disappointed with Claire. She'd been proving herself a bit for the first time in her entire career this week and this is a huge and irritating slip backwards.

'Oh, there she is!' Olivia spots Claire, but doesn't wave at her.

Another group of agents walk past, whispering and giving Hannah filthy looks. She can feel herself shrinking as she watches Claire climb the steps like butter wouldn't melt. Not arrested for murder yet, not even top suspect among the gathered agents, because that's still Hannah. What's worse is that no one, not Olivia or Amanda – she's obviously not expecting Claire to – has publicly stood up for her and told everyone she's innocent. She wonders if she'll ever live this down. Maybe she could move to another town? Start again? She could find property there for Tom to invest in, lure him away with her. There's nothing to stay for here.

'Sorry I'm late! Amanda, you look radiant. Honestly, you're so brave, pulling yourself together after everything that happened earlier. I'd still be such a wreck,' Claire blusters, looking around her. 'Oh. Is Alastair not here yet?'

'He's away on business, so I'm flying solo tonight. Shall we go in?' Amanda says, ignoring Claire's compliments.

The women form a line, Amanda and Claire in the middle with Olivia and Hannah on the wings, where they can't reach each other to fight. The last thing Amanda needs is for someone to catch footage of them in some kind of bitchy argument. She's always thought they were too classy for something like that, but earlier they were like screaming banshees. Common. It isn't the Harrington's way.

Walking into the hall's lobby, the women are ambushed either side by eager greeters handing out programmes. Hannah, who's already on high alert and convinced that if she's left alone with Claire at any point she'll probably try to off her, jumps and screams in the greeter's face, though still manages to grab a programme. But then almost screams again when she sees Bella's face on the cover of it staring back at her.

'I thought it would feel like she was still here with us,' Amanda says to the women, staring wistfully at the picture.

'Leave no woman behind,' Claire says. 'It's beautiful.'

Hannah and Olivia both feel they might vomit.

The other agents grow quiet at their arrival, everyone watching, scandalised. Hannah can see her face on Felix from Sanders's phone screen as he shows a female agent from the next town along the investigative piece posted earlier today on the local *Gazette*'s website, entitled: ***Home Sweet Homicide Continued: Could Harrington's Hannah be who the police are searching for?*** She'd slap the phone right out of his hand if people weren't then going to use her aggression as proof she did it. A notification sound travels around the room as everyone appears to receive an alert at the same time. Seconds later, a video informing everyone that that earlier today an attempt was made on Amanda Harrington's life at her office follows suit. The reporter's words bounce around the room like gunfire, while Amanda tries not to react.

'Let's find our table, shall we?' she shouts over the sound of multiple phones.

Taking a firm lead, she marches forward through the sea of other agents watching them, towards the darkened hall where the ceremony's due to take place.

'Claire,' Hannah whispers. 'Did you tip off the press again?'

'No!' Claire says. 'Also, what do you mean *again*?'

'Sure, like you're not the anonymous source that made them all think I did it.' Hannah rolls her eyes.

'How do you know it wasn't Olivia?' Claire hisses.

'Because I'm a fucking grown-up.' Olivia tilts her head and the three of them scuttle into the hall.

Amanda scans the hall of round tables covered in white tablecloths – definitely not linen, some kind of polyester blend – trying to find the Harrington's Estates one. She booked a big table eight months ago and now fears that their much-depleted number – especially not having Alastair with her – is going to make them even more conspicuous. At least it's dark in here. The blackout curtains have been drawn so no one can see the sun setting outside and small blue and purple spots of light dance around the room. A big yellow spotlight is directed towards the stage where a glass lectern and huge projector screen are set up. She can't wait to get this over with and get back home to her children. The more of these events she survives without Alastair, the stronger she'll feel.

Olivia spots the Harrington's Estates table at the front by the stage and points everyone to it. Hastily, the women take their seats, leaving a chair between them. Definitely for the best considering everything that happened earlier, and the way Hannah's jaw now tenses every time Claire opens her mouth. They keep their heads down as other agencies file in, finding their tables. Olivia pours herself a glass of red wine and keeps the bottle next to her. She can see Hannah wants it, but she's not passing it over to her.

Hannah glares at her eventually getting up with a great screech of her chair legs, stomping over and grabbing the bottle before heading back to her seat. For once too distracted to pay attention to Hannah and Olivia's dramas, Claire pours herself a glass of white and puts her phone on 'Do not disturb'. She doesn't want Sarah the carer's calls interrupting the ceremony. If she doesn't see them, she can pretend it hasn't happened. She knows she's going to have to face what she's done eventually, but right now she wants to enjoy the awards. She downs her first glass of wine and fills it up again, hoping that Amanda doesn't notice.

'There's a bet going on which one of them did it you know. Especially with the whole sabotaged-shelf business from earlier,' says an agent, his voice floating across the room to the Harrington's table. 'But everyone's pretty confident. Ron's gone hard and put his entire bonus on Hannah as the murderer, four to one.'

'Makes sense. That Claire one wasn't even working there till after Bella died, was she? I never saw her,' someone else's voice pipes up.

'Nope, I never noticed her before, either,' the original voice replies. 'She's way too sweet to be a killer. Looks like she'd thank you after giving a blow job. It could never be her.'

'Have you seen the knockers on the other blonde? Think her name's Libby?'

'Can't say I've ever really looked at her, mate. To be honest, I've always wondered about these rampant feminist types though. I mean that anger's got to go somewhere, hasn't it?'

'Well, murder's certainly an angry sport.'

Amanda tries to pretend she doesn't hear them, sipping at her wine delicately, and texting the babysitter to check in on her children.

'Well, well, well, if it isn't Harrington's!' Marcus says cheerfully, appearing next to them in a blue crushed-velvet suit with a lily pinned to its top pocket.

'Ah, Marcus,' Amanda says. 'I didn't realise you'd be here.'

Hannah feels herself starting to warm up. She's been

ignoring Marcus's calls, too afraid of Claire to even get in touch to explain she's not dealing with the house any more. She hadn't expected him to be here. Why would he be at the Estate Agent awards when he's a developer?

'I *would* say I'm estate agent adjacent! Why wouldn't I be here?' Marcus says, offended. 'I see you've got space at your table. Mind if I sit with you?'

'Of course,' Amanda says, relieved because at least this means there'll be someone saying *something* at the table.

'Wonderful!' Marcus pulls out the chair between Amanda and Hannah. 'Hannah, I actually needed to talk to you! About Esme's house. You left a message saying you were selling it, but then haven't returned any of my calls!'

Hannah clams up. She can feel all of them staring at her, but no one more aggressively than Claire. She can end this now, just tell him that she's not selling it and then she doesn't have to worry about Claire killing her just like she did with Bella. But, as she opens her mouth to speak, Marcus gets there first.

'So just to check we're on the same page, the house is a cottage with land for development, seller is a woman called Esme – sorry I didn't catch her surname. No onward chain as she's going into a home. That right?'

'God, that sounds great,' Amanda says. 'Just what we need.'

'Esme de Vere?' Claire asks. She's not letting Hannah get away with this. Everyone needs to know what she'd be prepared to do for money. Especially Amanda. Amanda lives and breathes loyalty. She pinches herself and her eyes fill with tears. 'My great-aunt Esme de Vere? You're talking about her house, aren't you?' She becomes progressively more flustered and panicked. 'That house is my inheritance. You can't develop it!'

A tear slips down her cheek as she boosts her performance, eyes pleading with Marcus across the table.

'She doesn't really want to sell. She doesn't know what she's doing, Marcus. She's a very old lady, who's not in her right mind! She loves that house; she'd never sell it normally. It's so important to our family!'

'I'm so sorry! I had no idea!' Marcus gasps in shock, for the benefit of the watching crowd. 'Of course, I won't be buying it now I know. I assumed it was all above board!'

He turns to Hannah, an accusatory look on his face.

'I can't believe you'd take advantage of an old woman like that!'

Hannah can feel the agents on the tables around them judging her yet again for her monstrous activity.

'Oh my god, Hannah! That's awful!' Olivia cries. 'What a terrible thing to do.'

'Not very Harrington's-like behaviour, Hannah,' Amanda whispers. 'But maybe we could talk about this later?'

Hannah feels her face growing red with rage as the tables around them start whispering about her once again. She feels her eyes pricking with tears at the injustice of it and knows she has to speak up. She's not having everyone think she's this murderous bitch who sells houses from under helpless old women.

'Oh, give it up Claire. You knew Bella was already selling

it when she died,' Hannah shouts. 'It's *not* your house and Esme is perfectly able to make decisions. You're just pissed off because she wants to give your inheritance to Extinction Rebellion.'

There's barely a beat before Claire responds, her tone savage, the tears now seeming to have ceased.

'Bella was doing it behind everyone's back, even Amanda's,' Claire hisses back, not playing any more. 'She was planning to keep all the money for herself and not even put it through the agency. Is that what you're planning too?'

'No! Of course not!' Hannah cries, turning to her boss, appalled. 'I'd never do that to you, Amanda!'

'Maybe we could talk about this another time?' Amanda whispers, and smiles tightly, aware that everyone's still watching them.

'Welcome to the Wellingshire Estate Agent of the Year Awards!' The lights dim suddenly, and a man appears on the stage, recognisable to everyone in the room as a D-list comedian who's been on a panel show once and now has it at the top of his CV as the headline 'TV comedian for hire'. But no one can remember what his actual name is or what else he's done.

'Wow! Jeez, no one told me that estate agents were so good-looking! Lots of attractively presented property in the room,' says the comedian, and is met with complete and exhausting silence.

Chapter Forty-five

It's been a long thirty minutes for everyone in the audience, forced to listen to the compère endlessly congratulate himself for a series of shit property-based 'puns'. There's a collective sigh of relief as he calls half-time and the lights go up, everyone itching to get to the bar so they can stock up on the strongest drinks available to help them through the next half an hour.

Hannah stands first without saying anything and begins walking in the direction of the toilets, followed by Olivia, Amanda and Claire. Olivia can hear her huffing but ignores her. People still need to go to the toilet. Abandoned at the table, Marcus looks around the suddenly empty seats, confused about where they've all gone.

When the women reach the toilet queue, it's already so big that Hannah debates whether or not to use the men's.

'There are more toilets in the basement,' Amanda says. 'Barely anyone knows they're there.'

The women gratefully follow Amanda through the lobby, relieved that people are drunker now. Someone's clearly been passing around the coke so everyone's more interested in themselves and less interested in watching them. Hannah still sees people move out of the way and flinch as she comes past, though, like they think she'd kill them standing at a bar in front of a hundred local estate agents.

'Just down here,' Amanda leads them to a spiral stone staircase that takes them underneath the old hall.

Downstairs, the corridors are slim and stone, and smell of mildew, but at least they can talk in private here.

'Here we go.' She escorts them through the door marked 'toilet'.

The women crush into the tiny space and stare at its two cubicles.

'You go first,' Hannah says to no one in particular.

'Yeah, go first,' Olivia echoes.

'Don't mind if I do.' Claire slinks into one of the cubicles almost smacking herself in the face with the door.

'Thank you,' Amanda says, walking into the other, far more sober.

At the sinks Hannah and Olivia stand in awkward silence. Hannah notices that her lipstick's slightly worn so opens her bag and roots around for the tube. At least this'll give her something to do in the face of Olivia's clear anger.

'Ouch!' She jerks her hand away, blood coming from a cut on her finger and accidentally drops the bag in the process.

The contents spill across the floor: lipstick, face powder, two tampons and a hairbrush skid across the tiles as the clatter of something metal hits the stone and Olivia's jaw drops open.

'What the fuck?' Hannah sucks her bloody finger, confused and sore.

'Why is there a fucking mini hacksaw in your bag, Hannah?' Olivia stands over the debris and blinks up at her.

'A what?' Claire's voice comes from one of the cubicles, slightly giddy with drunkenness.

'A mini hacksaw, Claire,' Olivia shouts into the cubicle, not taking her eyes off Hannah. 'Hannah's got a mini hacksaw in her handbag.'

'I don't know how that got in there,' Hannah says, squatting and scrabbling around to replace the contents of her bag, aside from the hacksaw, which she leaves on the floor staring back at them. 'It's not mine.'

'So now you're saying someone's put a mini hacksaw in your clutch?' Olivia screws up her face in disbelief. 'Why? Who? Honestly, Hannah, you're just such a fucking ridiculous person. I can't believe it's taken me so long to see it.'

Amanda comes out of the cubicle, her eyebrows raised high.

'Hannah?' Amanda stares at the hacksaw on the floor. 'Hannah, did you saw the shelf?'

'No,' Hannah shouts. 'And I'm sure you'd need more than that piddly thing to get through the screws.'

Claire throws open her cubicle door and stands with a hand on her hip in its doorway.

'You'd only know that if you did it,' she says, head tilted as she walks over to the sink.

'Oh really Claire? And I suppose you're going to pretend you know nothing about it?' Hannah glares at her.

'I think someone better tell the police about this,' Olivia says. 'And it's going to be me.'

'Tell the police about what?' Hannah asks. 'Someone trying to frame me? I haven't done anything wrong.'

'Sure, sure,' Olivia says. 'You know, I've always thought you were kind of dead inside, but I didn't realise it was anything more than just a lack of emotional intelligence. Now I see it, you're not just dead inside – you're psychopathic.'

'Hannah the Harrington's Hacksaw killer,' Claire says, almost amused as she hangs in the doorway.

Hannah's positive now that it was Claire who put the saw there. She'd never come up with that much alliteration on the spot. She's planned this. But, after earlier, she knows no one's going to believe her.

'Fuck this,' Hannah says, walking to the door. 'I'm not staying to be accused of stuff. I'm out.'

'You going to go crying to Tom again?' Olivia says bitterly. 'He doesn't care about you, you know. He's a fuck boy. He'll take anything he can get from anyone.'

'Maybe I *am* going to his!' Hannah shouts. 'Because you've got him all wrong. You're so judgemental you think everyone else has to be perfect and chaste, married before thirty and settled down! Just like you! But maybe you're bitter and jealous because we're still out there having fun while you're fucking chugging Horlicks with the sodding shipping forecast!'

'Oh fuck *off*, Hannah!' Olivia rolls her eyes.

'I'm *trying* to!' Hannah retorts back childishly from the door.

She storms out of the room, closely followed by Amanda, who really wants to contain the argument. They've made enough of a scene tonight. How's it going to look if they don't all come back to the table? Rather than promoting either of them to management, Amanda's pretty sure that come Monday, she'll be firing them both.

'Hannah!' Amanda calls after her. 'Darling, we need to talk about this as a family!'

'Fuck it, I'm going upstairs to get my jacket and then I'm out too,' Olivia says, storming out of the toilet.

'But they're about to honour Bella?' Claire shouts, racing after them.

Hannah storms across the dark car park, her cheeks burning under the occasional streetlamps. She can hear Amanda behind her, but she's not stopping. Not when Amanda's just asked if she tried to kill her.

A gruff, cockney voice comes from behind the trees at the side of the carpark, stopping both Hannah and Amanda in their tracks. 'Amanda!'

Hannah turns, watching as a figure emerges from the shadows and stands under a streetlamp. He's older – maybe in his seventies – wearing a flat cap and tracksuit bottoms. Definitely not Amanda's usual sort of acquaintance. Hannah doesn't think she's met him before, but, weirdly, she recognises him; she can't be bothered to stick around and find out what's going on, though. She's had enough stress tonight. She just wants to get out of here. Free from Amanda's pursuit, Hannah gets into her car and speeds away, getting one last, closer look at the stranger on her way past.

As Hannah's car speeds past, Amanda stares at the man she hasn't seen in nearly ten years. He's older but still the same, even down to his hat and the tracksuit.

'You're supposed to be in prison,' she whispers, hoping there's no one around to hear.

'I escaped. A bloke in the kitchens owed me a favour,' the man replies. 'I saw the news: no prison's going to stop me when my little girl needs me.'

The man opens his arms to Amanda but she doesn't move, feeling a small tear trickling down her cheek.

She tries hard not to crumple on the spot.

In the main hall, Claire sits at the table, taking in every bit of the night, scared to let it end and look at her phone. She smiles gleefully as Bella's name is announced as the Agent of the Year and goes up to accept the award, clutching the glory with all her might.

Chapter Forty-six

Hannah sits in her car, the sky above still dark and stormy, rain lashing at the windows of her BMW.

Ahead of her Tom's house looms large. She looks at it now through the eyes of the papers who've started calling it 'Murder Mansion' rather than the incredible beauty she saw when she first came here. She stares down at her phone, but there are no missed calls, no texts from anyone. No one coming to their senses and realising that she's been set up. That even if she had been the one to saw the screws on the shelf, why the fuck would she carry the hacksaw around with her to the awards ceremony? She's not stupid.

She's come to Tom's because she doesn't want to be alone and, at the moment, Tom seems to be the only person showing her any kindness. Now she's here, though, she worries Olivia might have told him about the hacksaw and he might be swayed into believing she's done something wrong too. But maybe he'd actually listen if she told him what's happened. He could talk Olivia around, make her see the sense that she appears to have completely lost.

Hannah watches the house through the rain, almost too

afraid to go to the door, in case Tom rejects her again. Then she'd have no one. Although, Amanda came after her didn't she? She was just too upset to stay. Maybe she doesn't believe Hannah did it. But then who was that man? She's sure she recognised him ... He looks like someone she's heard of, but never met. Especially the hat and tracksuit combo ... Suddenly, she pieces it together, putting a name to his face. She texts Amanda, because if she's right, how does he even know Amanda's name?

Hannah: How do you know Dennis Sharrington? I thought he was in prison?

She watches her phone, waiting for a response, but there's no sign of one coming any time soon. She's so worked up and confused; maybe she got it wrong? Maybe her emotions have got the better of her? She's not dead inside, whatever Olivia says. Hannah clenches her fist; it had stung when she said that. Surely Olivia more than anyone should know that's not Hannah. They've been so close for so long. It's the fact that Olivia believes it all that stings the most.

She *does* have real emotions, and she can prove it. She's going to cry right now. She opens her phone, goes into the Spotify app and selects Fergie's 'Big Girls Don't Cry', then rests her head against the window, watching the water droplets hitting the glass, rolling down in small rivulets. She blinks, really listening to the words, trying to take them in to provoke an emotional response within herself. She's not dead inside, she's going to cry real tears, then maybe she'll send Olivia a video of it. Undeniable proof. But nothing comes.

She strains, really tries to push out the tears. In a fit of desperation, she tries singing along, slapping her hands hard against the steering wheel when she reaches the chorus, screaming the lyrics. She *is* just like a child missing their blankie. It's a metaphor for the rug that's been continually pulled out from under her, her whole life. This song is her and it's *so sad*. But *still* nothing comes. She remembers Olivia and her less than two weeks ago, arriving at this house for the first time. How together they were, how much of a team. Surely there has to be something she can do? She can't just let their friendship go. Olivia's the only real relationship she's ever had, the only person she's ever truly loved. She opens her phone, types out the first message between them for a couple of days.

Hannah: I'm sorry. I know I haven't been the best friend and I should have told you about Matt, but please can we talk? I miss you. It doesn't feel right not to have you in my life. And I didn't do what Claire's saying. I need to explain about Esme's house, but I didn't do the other stuff. I promise. Please can we talk? I love you.

She presses send and flings her head onto the steering wheel, expelling a dry whimper. The rest of the song washes over her. Maybe it's precisely *because* she's a big girl that she can't cry? She stays with her face smushed against the steering wheel, trying to force out the tears that just won't come.

A knocking against the window startles her. Alarmed, she snaps her head up, walloping her chin on the steering wheel. Through the blurry rain-soaked glass, as she holds her chin, she can see a figure, dark wet hair, one curl set on his forehead, dripping. His eyes pierce the window and she feels butterflies flipping around her stomach, like an amateur gymnastics team.

She opens her door, stretching her right leg out first, into the driving rain. She feels it beating down, harsh against her skin as she gets out of the car entirely, shutting the door behind her to stop her much-adored leather seats getting wet.

'Is everything OK?' Tom shouts over the rain. 'What are you doing here?'

'I needed to get away,' she screams back against the howling wind that's gathering pace. 'I didn't know where to go. Everyone hates me and thinks I killed Bella, but I didn't do it. I don't know how to make people see I didn't do anything they're accusing me of.'

'I know,' Tom says, putting his arms round her. 'I know.'

Hannah pulls back, their eyes meeting through the storm as he brushes the wet hair from his forehead. She bites her lip, and he leans forward. His hand grasps her face the moment their lips connect, their sodden bodies slipping against each other, Hannah leaning hard against the BMW's door.

'I think we should go inside,' Tom breathes into her ear.

'But your complicated situation? The doctor without borders?' Hannah asks.

'She's in a war zone,' Tom says. 'She might not even survive.'

The two of them make brief eye contact before they run, shoes sliding against the sheen of the wet gravel. They race into the porch, kissing under its wisteria-covered bricks as the rain falls around them. Tom opens the door, and they fall inside, their damp footprints trailing along the parquet floor all the way to the bedroom.

'Are you OK?' Hannah asks.

The two of them lie breathless, tangled in Tom's white linen sheets. Hannah sits up pulling them around her, enjoying their freshness against her still-clammy skin. They feel as good as she thought they would. It all does. She looks down to the floor where their rain-sodden clothes are strewn across the room, creating puddles.

'Of course,' Tom says.

But he doesn't seem fine. He seems troubled when she wants him to be post-coitally elated. His phone beeps and she can see a look of concern on his face when he grabs it from the nightstand next to him. She leaves him to whatever work crisis she imagines has popped up and checks her own phone, thrilled to see a text from Olivia.

> **Olivia**: I know, I'm sorry too. I've been so angry about stuff and Claire's such a knob. I love you too. I'm coming to find you. We can't go on like this, we need to talk.

She looks up from the message, relief washing over her. Maybe things are going to be all right, after all. Maybe she can have her best friend back and have Tom. They can double date! But, when she looks over at Tom, his face is sour.

'What's up?' she asks.

'That complicated situation,' Tom says. 'She's messaging. She wants to see me.'

'Oh, should I go?' Hannah asks.

She looks around her, all the elation leaving her body.

'I should really talk to her,' Tom says, seemingly so obsessed with the messages that he hasn't realised Hannah's face start to crumple, tears forming in her eyes.

'Of course,' Hannah says. 'I'll go.'

All at once, she feels small and used. Olivia was right: he's a fuck boy. Now he's had her, he doesn't want her any more. She thought he was the only person she had left on her side but now he's barely even looking at her. She feels like one of his houses, once he's finished with it. He's ready to move on to a better model.

Hannah clutches the sheet around her, grabbing her underwear from the floor and shuffling into it under the covers. She's not exposing any more of herself to him than she already has. She should have accepted who he was when Olivia told her, not waited until he showed her himself. She'll text Olivia on her way out of here. At least she can salvage her friendship tonight.

'I'll just get dressed and get out of your hair,' Hannah says.

'I didn't mean you had to leave right away. I've said I can talk to her tomorrow.' Tom looks at her with a Cheshire cat grin and she can't help but want to punch him in it.

He's made her feel used, made it clear that he really wants someone else and he's willing to kick her out of bed for them. And now he wants round two?

'No thanks,' Hannah says, taking a deep breath, her back turned to him. She doesn't want this man to see he's made her cry. He doesn't need the ego boost.

She lets the sheet fall, now wiggled into her dress again and struts across the room.

'Hannah . . . don't be like that! Come back to bed?' he asks with the wide-eyed expression of a cheeky schoolboy, pulling the duvet back to reveal himself like some kind of tantalising prize.

Hannah gives him a disgusted look and leaves. She races down the stairs two at a time, eager to grab her things and get out of this house. But, at the bottom of the stairs, she realises she's not alone. A familiar face emerges from the living room, clutching a 'For sale' sign. Hannah grabs the cool marble top of a side table in the hallway for stability as the woman comes towards her.

'What are you doing here?' Hannah asks, confused, trying to understand how she even got in.

'What do you think I'm doing here? We need to talk,' she responds. 'I can't have you carry on like this, Hannah. Not after everything you've done.'

She advances towards Hannah with the sign in her hand as Hannah backs away down the hall. She wants to run but she's scared to turn her back on her.

'TOM! TOM! HELP, TOM!' Hannah's screaming for him up the stairs.

'What's going on?' Tom's shouts back are muffled, but she can hear him moving. It's going to be OK.

Hannah keeps backing away from the other woman, but she continues advancing towards her with the sign. Her face is unlike Hannah's ever seen it before, a glazed, dead look behind her eyes, as though she's possessed.

'No. This doesn't make any sense,' Hannah says. 'What are you doing? Why are you doing this?'

'Hannah?' Tom shouts, his feet pounding on the stairs as he comes to see what's going on.

Hannah knows he's a piece of shit, but, surely, he can save her. She sees him registering that they're not alone, but it's too late as the other woman rushes towards him with her sign.

'What are you doing here? What are you doing with—' his cries are muffled by the sign coming down towards his head as he tries to fend it off.

'You should really be more careful who you give the keys to your house to.' The woman pants with the effort of wielding the sign, pulling it back again to take another swing.

'HANNAH, RUN!' Tom shouts, trying to punch the sign away, but it's heavier than he thought.

Hannah races towards the door, making a break for freedom, her hand on the lock. She pushes down on the handle, but it doesn't budge. Behind her, she can sense the other woman getting closer while Tom lies prone on the floor. Hannah flicks the latch, but nothing changes – it's been locked with a key. She looks over to Tom helplessly, a red stain spreading across the parquet from his head. She continues to yank frantically at the door, but it won't open; there's no way out.

Around Hannah, the world swirls as the other woman corners her. Her heart is thumping so hard she can feel it in her throat. She tries to protect herself but the 'For Sale' sign comes down on her head. She can hear the blood rushing in her ears and see it on her hands and arms.

Blinking in pain, she makes eye contact with the other woman, watching as she swings the sign back for a second time, really seeing her for the first time. She pleads with her silently but there's no let up. Relentlessly the sign comes again, smashing into her skull.

Hannah's legs give way beneath her as she falls to the ground, past the swirling colours of the Constable's stormy scene, hitting the parquet with a thud. A small tear cools her warm cheek as with her last bit of strength, she reaches out to the for sale sign that now lies discarded next to her, and smears one blooded finger across it as purposefully as she can manage.

Chapter Forty-seven

Olivia breathes in the post-storm smell of petrichor on the summer breeze, relieved that the rain's stopped. She walks through the darkness towards Tom's house, lit only by the glow of the yellow porch light. Nevertheless, her clutch in hand, heels sinking into the gravel, she advances towards it. Goosebumps litter her skin in the cooler air and she hugs her jacket around her. Pulling the doorknocker back, she recoils at the loud thud of it smacking the wood, slicing through the peaceful darkness.

She stands for a few minutes, but there's no sound from inside nor any lights coming on. A crunching of gravel from behind makes her spin round as a figure in a long dark dress stumbles down the driveway towards her. She recognises Claire from her drunken swagger. As she gets closer, the prickles on the back of Olivia's neck die down at the relief of seeing a familiar face, even if Claire is a prick.

'Claire?' Olivia squints through the darkness. 'What are you doing here?'

'Got a text from Hannah,' Claire says, taking out her phone.

'Oh, me too,' Olivia replies. She'd been a bit annoyed when Hannah's reply told her to meet her at Tom's, but she just wanted to fix things, so she came anyway.

'Like this?' Claire shows her the text.

Hannah: Come to Tom's house we all need to sit down and work this out. It can't carry on like this.

'Similar,' Olivia says, narrowing her eyes.

The two of them stand in front of the door, confused by the almost-certainly empty house.

'Do you think we should see if there's another way in? She did say to meet her here? Obviously, I worried at first what with Hannah being the killer . . .' Claire says breezily but Olivia blocks her out while she thinks.

Olivia knows Hannah's not the killer. She feels bad that she was the one who got the TikTokers suspecting her. That was mean; she was just so angry. And it's not as if the police agreed. They'd have arrested Hannah by now if they thought it was her. The hacksaw in the handbag was weird, though, and it's made Olivia wonder about Claire and whether she was setting Hannah up. Especially after the thing about her great aunt's house, because it all felt a bit, well, hack, actually.

'But, you know, safety in numbers,' Claire chirps, linking arms with Olivia.

'I've got a key that Tom gave Matt and I in case of emergencies,' Olivia fumbles with her clutch.

'Works for me,' Claire shrugs.

Olivia's hesitant at first, but it's not like he doesn't know she has the key, and can let herself in any time. He pretty much asked her to, after all.

'Should we call the police?' Claire asks. 'I mean just in case Hannah's luring us to our deaths?'

'No, Claire,' Olivia sighs, putting the key into the lock and turning. 'It's Hannah – she's not luring us to our deaths.'

She pushes at the door, but it only opens a bit, hitting against something on the other side. She stares at it, puzzled.

'What is it?' Claire asks, creeping behind her.

'There's something in the way,' Olivia says, wincing as she shoves it again and again, making no headway.

Claire joins in, pushing the door alongside her but, even with both their strength behind it, the door doesn't budge. Olivia assesses the gap. She thinks she can probably push through it then let Claire in from the other side. It's starting to worry her that Hannah invited them here, but isn't answering the door and now it won't open. Surely Tom's here too? Maybe they're in the back garden, but she doubts it. It's been raining pretty heavily.

'I'm going to squeeze in through that gap,' Olivia says. 'I'll find out what's blocking the way and see what's going on.'

'OK, I'll stay right here,' Claire says, shivering slightly and she doesn't think it's just from the cold. This whole thing's giving her weird vibes. She was curious at first– Hannah never texted. And she obviously saw messages and calls from Sarah the carer when she got Hannah's text too, but this was the more appealing of the two options. So she ignored those, and came to see what this was about, putting her phone back on 'Do not disturb' to delay Sarah once more.

Olivia turns on her phone torch and squeezes herself in through the gap. Inside, something immediately feels off. The Constable still hangs opposite the door, but it looks strange, and there's no sound or light coming from anywhere else in the house. She reaches behind her, flicking the light switch several times, but nothing happens. Reluctantly, she resigns herself to looking around with her phone torch.

It's the blood that she sees first, smeared along the wall in one giant stripe, past the Constable and into the corner. Lowering the torch light along with her gaze, Olivia turns and lets out a small wail at the sight of Hannah sprawled across the floor in front of the door, a dark red pool around her head, her hand resting on the red-spattered Harrington's Estates sign that was once displayed at the top of the driveway.

Olivia falls to her knees, propping her phone on the console table for light and tries to rouse Hannah, but she can't be woken. She shakes her and pleads with her, but the blood coming out of her head and the way her body's slumped already suggest what Olivia had hoped wasn't true.

'What's going on? Olivia? Are you OK?' Claire's shouting insistently from behind the door.

Olivia tries to talk but instead all that comes out are tears. She crouches over Hannah's body thinking about the last few days between the two of them. The arguments they wasted their last days together having. Claire pushes her way through the gap in the door in seconds but Olivia just screams more as it bashes against Hannah's lifeless body.

Once inside, Claire stands back gasping. She leans down, feeling around Hannah's neck, trying and failing to find a pulse. Olivia's annoyed; she doesn't need Claire to confirm it – she already knows Hannah's gone.

'What's that?' Claire asks, peering at Hannah's hand resting on the Harrington's sign, her finger pointing up. She reaches towards it.

'Jesus, Claire, stop touching her!' Olivia screams but she can see what Claire means.

It looks like a bloody 'S' on the 'For Sale' sign, right by where Hannah's limp hand has come to rest, one finger pointing towards it.

'I'm phoning the police,' Claire says, but when she goes to turn her phone off 'Do not disturb', it immediately starts ringing with a phone call from Sarah the carer. She quickly turns 'Do not disturb' back on. 'Maybe we could use your phone?'

Claire looks over to the phone propped on the console table just as a clinking noise travels up the stairs from the kitchen, making both women jump.

'What's that?' Claire whispers.

'Tom?' Olivia questions.

She stares down at her best friend's body, furious and terrified for a second before taking off in the direction of the stairs down to the kitchen.

'He could be hurt!' she cries back to Claire.

'What if it's not him?' Claire shouts after her. 'Olivia, stop! You could just be running straight towards danger.'

'It's Tom – I know it is. He's probably just fended off the attacker,' Olivia says, not thinking straight, tears clouding her vision as she races towards the stairs. 'I can't lose him *and* Hannah.'

'Or he *is* the attacker . . .' Claire calls after her, following behind and muttering to herself in a high-pitched tone. 'Leave no woman behind, Claire. Fuck's sake.'

At least she's sobered up a little.

Olivia's halfway down the stairs; she's not going to wait for Claire to hurry up and join her. She's already failed Hannah, she can't fail Tom too. The shock makes her shake, her head pulsing with adrenaline as she bounds down the final stairs, hoping for some kind of break in the darkness soon.

Moonlight shines through the garden doors, illuminating the kitchen island that Olivia admires so much. Behind her she hears Claire gasp, a small high-pitched scream coming out of her mouth as a figure moves over by the restored butler sink.

'TOM?' Olivia wants to run towards him, but there's something not right about his silhouette. It doesn't look broad enough.

'We need to phone the police,' Claire says, her phone in her hand, but she knows what'll happen if she turns 'Do not disturb' off. She'll have another problem to deal with and she can only deal with one at a time.

'What's happened, Tom? What happened to Hannah?' Olivia persists hopefully, despite knowing deep down it can't be him.

'Olivia? Claire?' Amanda's voice comes back through the darkness.

'Amanda?' The relief in Claire's voice is palpable, but Olivia can't hide her disappointment.

Claire charges past Olivia in the direction of Amanda, like a toddler eager to hide in their mother's skirt.

'Did you see Hannah?' Claire asks, flinging herself at Amanda.

'I know, love, I know,' Amanda says, sniffing. 'I've already called Clive. He's on his way with a team. I've told Alastair – he's just at home looking after the kids.'

Olivia watches her face in the moonlight. She doesn't look sad. She looks just like normal. She always looks just like normal. Normal, composed Amanda. The darkness of the kitchen suddenly becomes suffocating and dangerous. Olivia wishes there were a candle or something. Anything to help her see a little clearer. She could have sworn Amanda said that Alastair was away on business earlier. Maybe she's confused with the shock of it all.

'What are you doing down here?' Olivia asks, her eyes narrowing in Amanda's direction.

'I wanted to make sure the killer wasn't still here,' Amanda says. 'I thought I heard someone. I was going to try and apprehend them before the police arrived.'

'What are you doing in the house, though?' Olivia asks, backing up towards the strip where Tom keeps his knives.

Something feels off, and it strikes her that she should arm herself. She doesn't want to be taken unawares, like Hannah clearly was.

'Hannah messaged me. Said she wanted everyone here to talk,' Amanda says. 'Why she chose a client's house, I do not understand. We all need to have a stern chat about professionalism on Monday.'

Claire normally admires the way that Amanda's able to compartmentalise and get the job done. A true professional. But something about what she's just said feels weird even to Claire. She watches Amanda in the moonlight. Confident and unflappable even now, despite Hannah being dead and despite the possibility that a killer could still be in the house with them. Claire has read something about Botox hampering empathy. Maybe it also hampers fear? But Claire's never felt her heart race this much in all her life and she's had it now too. She thinks about Hannah upstairs, all that wasted Botox. Had she been trying to draw something with her hand on the sign? Was she giving them a clue as to what happened to her? Maybe a picture?

'I mean maybe wait a few days for us to, you know, grieve Hannah first. Right?' Olivia says, looking over at the knife strip just a few steps away.

She doesn't want to unsettle anyone, but she does think she'll feel a bit safer with something to defend herself in hand. Just in case. She thinks of Hannah's finger, pointed on the sign. It feels purposeful, like she was trying to tell her something. The S next to the Harrington's. Sharrington?

The Sharrington's . . . the dodgy real-estate family from the noughties. But they were all in jail, weren't they?

'What's a Sharrington?' Claire suddenly blurts out, nearly but not quite connecting the dots to the same level that Olivia has and placing them both in danger because of it.

Olivia turns to the knife strip and notices that there's already a vacant space. Without wasting any time, she grabs a meat cleaver, its olive wood handle soft in her clammy hand. She turns just in time to see Amanda heading towards Claire with a bespoke, serrated kitchen knife that Olivia knows for a fact Tom has never once used.

'CLAIRE WATCH OUT!' Olivia screams as Claire dodges out of the way and grabs a huge grey Le Creuset casserole from the counter at her side – again very much for show, never-used, one hungry owner.

Claire raises the lid like a shield, fending off Amanda's knife movements as Olivia rushes to her aid. Amanda stands, the knife raised, eyes shifting between her two employees. Her expression's that of a caged animal, realising that it's two against one. Olivia watches the knife in her hand start to shake, the moonlight bouncing off the serrated blade.

'Jesus, Amanda!' Claire exclaims, moving the pan around to defend herself.

'*I'm* a Sharrington,' Amanda says, panting with the effort of trying to hit Claire with the knife and dodge the pan.

Standing at Amanda's side, Olivia holds the meat cleaver up to her. She kicks out, striking the backs of Amanda's knees with her foot. They weaken, but she doesn't go down.

'Stop it,' Olivia snaps, as though telling off a child. 'Stop trying to stab Claire.'

'It's not very fucking feminist, Amanda,' Claire huffs, still frantically trying to protect herself with the Le Creuset. 'The internet is going to go fucking mental over this.'

Eventually, realising she's not getting anywhere with the threat of Olivia and her giant cleaver getting closer, Amanda finally stops swiping at Claire. Still clutching the knife, her face starts to crumple in a weird way, almost as though each bit of it is a building block attempting to fall down, but being held, frozen by the invisible scaffolding of Botox. She looks constipated, tears rolling down her cheeks, as her shoulders – the only part of her physically able to – begin to sag.

'I was going to say you did it.' Amanda waves the knife in Olivia's direction. 'I was going to say because you wanted the manager's position so badly, you'd killed Bella, then Brick because he knew about it, and then you killed Hannah. I set up the shelf earlier so it would easily look like one of you was doing it all. And I moved the vulva so someone would find the murder weapon and conclude that it must have been one of you that whacked her with it that night after I left. That way you'll already be under suspicion when I call them later tonight, traumatised, and tell them you tried to kill me. I'll say there's been a fight, but I overpowered you, and was – sadly – the only survivor of your little killing spree. Poor little Claire didn't stand a chance.'

Claire gasps.

'No one would believe I'd do that,' Olivia protests.

'Of course they would,' Amanda snaps back, a frenzied look in her eye. 'They'd believe any of you could have done it at this point. The fact is, all of you were so driven, so vicious and bitchy with one another, you barely needed my help. You've made yourselves look like suspects all on your own. Everyone will believe me. I'm the victim. I just wanted to support women, lift them up. I was doing a good thing.'

Despite her conviction, Amanda looks smaller to Olivia the more unhinged she becomes. She almost feels sorry for her, standing in front of them now, a pathetic shadow of who they thought she was. Claire lunges towards her with the heavy Le Creuset lid, trying to smack the knife out of her hand. But Amanda's too fast. She dodges it, laughing loudly in a way that terrifies them both. Olivia advances with her meat cleaver and the three women are in a stand-off, weapons raised, enhanced lips curled.

'Hannah figured out who you were, didn't she?' Olivia asks.

'Yep, and if she'd figured it out it would probably only be a matter of time before you did too, Olivia ...' She turns to Claire. 'Not you so much, Claire, but ... leave no woman behind, you know. So I used Hannah's phone to lure you both here once I'd killed her.'

'So Bella and Brick had figured out that you're a Sharrington?' Olivia asks. 'That's why you killed them?'

'I still don't understand what a Sharrington is ...' Claire whispers, but Amanda ignores her.

'Bella sent me this email a few days before the open house, saying that she wanted to be promoted to manager. She'd been making vague comments for a while that suggested she might know something about my past. But when she sent that email, she'd filled it with odd little sentences that *proved* once and for all she knew everything.

'She was smart, nothing too obvious. It was subtle. But when I didn't reply right away, she leaked the email to the whole company. You all received it, but fortunately none of you were smart enough to pick up on it. I knew once she'd done that, even the manager's job wouldn't stop her. I was right because the email wasn't all she did to try and ruin me. I just didn't find out about the other stuff she did until after she died.' Amanda shrugs then smiles at them smugly. 'Anyway, nothing she can do about it now.'

'Sorry,' Claire says, holding the cast-iron pan over her face. 'I'm going to have to ask again, what's a Sharrington? I don't get the big secrecy.'

'Of course you don't, Claire,' Amanda says.

Olivia stares at Amanda, taking her in. If she's a Sharrington, then why isn't she in prison like the rest of them? How's she out and about, walking free, setting up businesses under a different name? She tries to remember the case studies she'd read when she was first training to be an agent. The things people told her about the family.

'If you're a Sharrington, and you're not in prison, you must be . . .' Olivia squints, trying to remember.

'Tamara Sharrington,' Amanda says.

'The daughter? You were only just twenty when it all

happened. That's why you didn't go to prison. You hadn't been in the business when it all went down,' Olivia says, the story coming back to her now.

'That's what they thought anyway.' Amanda grins, all the trademark class gone from her face, despite the net worth of her Botox pumped skin.

Amanda's jaw clenches and Olivia can see she's losing her nerve, her fingers trembling round the knife's wooden handle.

'I still don't really know who the Sharringtons are, just FYI,' Claire mutters out of the corner of her mouth to Olivia.

'The Sharringtons were a family of property developers and estate agents. They covered everything. Except they were dodgy as ... Mr Sharrington – your dad, Amanda – was put in prison for life last I heard, for a series of murders, and using the properties he was developing to hide the bodies,' Olivia says.

'Oh my god, that was you!' Claire gasps. 'I remember seeing a Channel 5 documentary on that, actually!'

'Channel 5, Claire? Really?' Amanda looks down her nose at her.

'I mean ... your family was *on* Channel 5, not sure you're in a position to throw stones from that glass house ...' Claire puts her shoulders back a little further. 'You're from a family of actual murderers.'

'I didn't kill anyone,' Amanda says, starting to hunch, the persona she built for herself shrinking. 'Well, not until recently anyway.'

'Yeah, then you killed everyone,' Olivia says, her own hand shaking while she holds the cleaver as close to Amanda as she can get while staying clear of Amanda's own knife.

'I get that you're annoyed with me,' Amanda says. 'But you don't know how hard it was to distance myself from them. When they were put in prison, I had no money. I had to start again, work my way up from the bottom. No one would give me a job – not with my family's reputation – and selling houses was all I knew how to do. I couldn't train in something else; I had no money. What was I supposed to do? Let all that knowledge go to waste and go and work in a supermarket or something? None of you could understand what it's like to go from having everything to having nothing with everyone judging you. Even my so-called friends didn't want anything to do with me any more. I was completely alone. I was scared.

'I realised I had options, a way to get myself free of it all. It's not like I wasn't going to take them. There were a few houses that hadn't been seized by the authorities because Daddy had put them in my name. I didn't realise until after I'd done them up that Daddy had hidden more dead bodies in the foundations. By that point I was in too deep. I had no choice. I needed the money . . . I would have been ruined if I hadn't sold them.'

'You sold the houses knowing they had dead bodies in them?' Olivia asks.

'You sold murder houses?' Claire asks, holding the Le Creuset up to her face and peering from behind it.

'We did an exorcism first! I threw holy water all over

them!' Amanda protests. 'It was the last dodgy thing I did! The last thing I did with any link to my family.'

'Surely they started to smell?' Olivia knows she needs to buy some time and find a way out of here. Amanda isn't going to let them leave easily with everything they know. She needs to distract her.

'They did.' Amanda nods, sheepishly. 'But I was out of there before anyone noticed. I'd already changed my name. It was like witness protection, but less legal. I was totally on my own when I set myself up as an estate agent. I worked my way up in other agencies. And I used the money I had from the sale of those houses to build my reputation, and dress myself, make sure I was a prospect for a man like Alastair. I needed that security, insurance. I really did build my career from the bottom up until I could open the agency.'

Olivia blinks. 'Except for all the money you got from selling murder houses.'

'Why did you change your name to Harrington? It's not exactly a huge change from Sharrington, is it?' Claire asks. 'That strikes me as stupid.'

'*That* was Alastair's name. I became Amanda Harrington when I married him. Before that I'd been Amanda Darcy,' Amanda says proudly, brushing her hair off her face with a brave smile, as though trying to keep hold of the last vestiges of that class. 'It was a coincidence, but I felt like with Alastair I was so protected, and it felt good being Mrs Harrington. Classy.'

'What do you mean *felt*?' Olivia narrows her eyes, remembering Amanda's slip earlier. 'Wait ... Where was Alastair tonight?'

'He's away on business,' Amanda says.

'You said he was at home with the kids earlier,' Olivia presses.

'Oh my god, you did!' Claire gasps.

Amanda looks down at the floor. She lowers the knife slightly, but Olivia knows she's not going to let it go completely. She curses herself for leaving her phone upstairs on the console table, next to Hannah's body. She was so convinced that it was Tom down here, hurt and needing her help, that she wasn't thinking straight. Surely Tom will show up soon, though. If not, Claire's their only hope to phone the police, and with a bit of Le Creuset in each hand it's not looking hopeful. She's suddenly terrified that she might actually have to use the meat cleaver.

'Alastair knew that I was a Sharrington. I'd told him that much. But he didn't know any of the other stuff. About how I made the money to get myself out of there – the murder houses – and built myself the career I have now.' Amanda's voice trails off, wobbling with emotion.

'He found out, didn't he?' Olivia asks.

Amanda nods solemnly and sniffs. 'Brick found a message Bella had been threatening to send to Alastair, telling him all about it, on her computer after she died. She never got the chance to send it, but he did, using her account. That's why I killed him, and cut his ear off first to teach him a lesson. He always wanted to be a tortured artist after all. It's the closest to Van Gogh he was ever going to get.'

'How did Bella know?' Claire asks, screwing her face up.

'I didn't realise – obviously – when I hired her, but Bella's family bought one of the murder houses. I guess it sort of ruined their lives or whatever when they discovered a dead body in the floor, and now, years later, Bella was out for revenge. I don't know how she found me, but she was unhinged! Like I said, she was going to destroy me and there was nothing I could do to stop her! She was going to expose my husband's little hobby and everything.'

Claire tilts her head questioningly. 'Hobby?'

'SOME THINGS ARE PRIVATE!' Amanda shouts, leaning towards Claire with the knife, but Claire rebuffs her with the threat of a Le Creuset to the head.

'Where's Alastair?' Olivia persists, pushing her shoulders back as she wields the cleaver, trying to give off the air of someone who would definitely use it.

'Dead,' Amanda whispers. 'Once Brick told him, he felt betrayed. He was going to disgrace me, take the children from me. I thought he loved me. He broke my heart and I couldn't let him take my children as well. So he's dead. Marcus was pouring the foundations for his new flats this week. I buried him in the dirt there in the dead of night. He's under concrete now. At least being a single mother will up my Instagram followers. It's going to be very inspirational for a lot of people when I thrive despite everything.'

'You killed your employees and your husband? All of that just to keep your secret?' Claire asks, feeling deeply ashamed as she starts to connect the dots with her own life and everything she's done to get what she wants. 'Is that thriving?'

'I mean you can't really think Bella didn't deserve it? After everything I gave her, she threw it back in my face! At the open house, she lured me out into the garden to blackmail me. I just came back with a counteroffer – her own vulva to the head – a cunt-er-offer, if you will,' Amanda says, her mouth twitching slightly. Suddenly Amanda's eyes glaze over, a darkness sweeping over her as though she's reliving the moment. 'I had no choice. I had to defend my life. I couldn't let her ruin everything. It's her own fault. She drove me to it. I'm not a bad person.' Amanda puts her head in her hands for a second, before whipping it back up again, just as Claire and Olivia start creeping towards her.

'Not really women supporting women, is it?' Olivia wrinkles her nose. Maybe if they break her a bit more, they can weaken her enough to escape. But Amanda's expression switches from shame to anger.

'Do you really think the kind of life I have comes easily?' Amanda stares at them both with a pitying expression. 'You both want this success? You've no idea how hard it is to keep it. I literally sell my own dream to people every day. I'm the face behind our whole agency; women admire me day in, day out. I love my life and they do too. It's not easy to keep up something so perfect, Olivia.'

'So you killed people just to keep selling houses?' Claire asks. 'Bricks and mortar? They're not a life – they're shells people live in and make their own. You did all this just to make sure people stay envious of you? Well, I don't envy you at all.'

'Trust you to be simplistic, Claire,' Amanda snaps her head round to face her. 'But you know you're wrong about that. *I influence* people to buy homes, to decorate them a certain way. To live a certain life. I have power. I'm leading people to greatness.'

'You're not the fucking Dalai Lama!' Olivia shouts, nervous that Amanda's getting too close to Claire. 'You're an estate agent with a rich husband and an Instagram following. And now you don't even have the rich husband.'

'Oh, Olivia, I don't think you're one to cast stones about husbands. Not after what yours has done.' Amanda backs away from Claire, approaching her with the knife. 'Everyone knows, darling. We talk about it all the time.'

Olivia knows Amanda's trying to shake her, but she's not going to succeed. She knows Claire's got her back in this the same as she's got Claire's. Whatever's going on with Matt has nothing to do with Amanda.

'Do we?' Claire asks, screwing her nose up. 'I mean I know what Matt did, but no one talks about it to me all the time?'

'No one talks to you at all, Claire,' Amanda says, amusing herself.

Claire's face falls and Olivia immediately moves to defend her.

'My husband committed a few financial crimes. You've killed four people in the last week,' Olivia says.

'Five.' Amanda talks over her and Olivia immediately stops. 'I've killed five.'

'Who . . . ?' Olivia asks, but deep down she already knows the answer.

'Tom,' Amanda smiles, watching the devastation wash over Olivia. 'I think you liked him, didn't you? Hannah was in bed with him when I got here, by the way. Anyway, he's dead too now, I'm afraid. Look over in the garden.'

Olivia glances over towards the Crittall doors, but she can't see anything outside except darkness. She's worried this is another distraction technique from Amanda, getting them to look elsewhere so she can escape, or worse. Claire shines her phone light over while Olivia keeps an eye on Amanda, telling herself she's bluffing. But when Claire makes a squeak Olivia can't help immediately looking over. In the beam of Claire's torchlight, she sees Tom's dead body lying in a pool of blood, his eyes open.

Amanda advances towards Olivia and there's a split second where Claire thinks she's going to get her before Olivia's face changes, her fingers clenched around the knife. She emits a roaring sound and charges towards Amanda with the meat cleaver. Amanda dodges out of the way at the last minute and Olivia heads for Claire. Grabbing the Le Creuset lid from Claire's hand she spins and lurches forward in one fluid movement, smacking Amanda around the head with it. Amanda drops the knife. Her eyes roll back and she loses consciousness, falling to the floor like a dead weight.

Olivia moves with speed, leaning down to check that Amanda's still breathing. But, after everything Amanda's done, she's not sure if she's relieved or not when she feels the breath coming from her nose. She collapses to the floor next to Amanda's unconscious body and feels tears start to stream down her face at everything she's lost.

Claire taps at her phone screen dismissing calls and notifications from Sarah before holding it up to her face. 'Police please! Yes, we've caught the murderer! The murderer, murderer!' She clarifies, stamping her foot. 'THE ONE THAT'S BEEN KILLING EVERYONE IN OUR TOWN! SHE'S HERE WITH US NOW AND WE NEED SOMEONE TO ARREST HER BECAUSE SHE'LL DEFINITELY KILL US WHEN SHE COMES ROUND IF YOU DON'T!' Claire screams loud enough to wake the dead in the house. 'Perfect, thank you. Please could you also send an ambulance, just I think she probably has concussion.'

Claire slumps down next to Olivia, holding the knives and Le Creuset for good measure, just in case Amanda wakes up. For once she doesn't cry, just stares into the wreckage of the house as the kitchen starts to fill with blue light and the noise of police sirens.

Chapter Forty-eight

Claire and Olivia sit in foil blankets, staring back at the house, watching the paramedics wheeling a stretcher carrying Amanda over to an ambulance escorted by several police officers.

'I'm supposed to be going on holiday next week.' Claire looks at the mess of police and paramedics racing around in front of them, tears glistening in her eyes.

'I can't believe she did all of this for houses,' Olivia says.

'It's truly not worth it,' Claire agrees, but she's staring down at her phone, feeling shame.

She's got so caught up in everything Amanda was selling, thinks Claire, that she became her without realising. She's done something to Esme that no one can ever find out about, something that will haunt her for the rest of her life. Maybe she wasn't so different to Amanda, after all. It's just that she no longer considers it a good thing.

Knowing she has to face what she's done and try to fix it, she opens her phone and clicks on the notification for Sarah's missed calls. She lost herself briefly, but maybe Esme will be OK? Maybe she survived? She presses the call button next to Sarah's name and holds her breath.

Sarah answers after one ring and Claire listens for a moment as she tells her Esme's had an accident. Genuine tears prick her eyes and she starts sniffing.

Olivia stares at her inquisitively.

'I'll come as soon as I can,' Claire says before hanging up the phone.

'What's happened?' Olivia asks. 'Has Amanda done something else?'

'Not this time,' Claire says. 'It's my great-aunt Esme, the one with the house. She fell down the stairs. She's in a coma.'

'Oh my god!' Olivia gasps, putting her arm round Claire while she cries.

From the back of the ambulance, Amanda watches Olivia and Claire and wonders how long it'll be before they're forced to do things that they don't want to for their family or reputation. Maybe then they'll understand. Actually, she thinks, Olivia might, but Claire never will. She's simply not smart enough.

What will happen to Amanda's children now? Where will they live? Who will raise them? Surely Alastair's parents are too old to be given custody? The image of Alastair's tweed-loving mother raising her children in tiny matching tweed suits is almost too hideous for her to bear. And what about Buster? Who's going to make sure his raw diet is adhered to?

There's a commotion at the house as another stretcher comes flying out of the front door, moving far faster than hers did. Paramedics are shouting and leaping into action. Even the ones that are supposed to be helping Amanda race out of the ambulance to help. She peers through the open doors, watching the commotion around the stretcher as the police keep their overbearing presence either side of her.

'Hannah!' Amanda watches Olivia scream and race towards her friend, wondering how, after everything that's gone on between them, Olivia can still care so much about her.

'She's alive, but her pulse is weak,' Amanda hears the paramedic say.

At least that's one less for the murder charges, Amanda thinks. See, she's barely done anything wrong.

Epilogue

Six months later

Olivia sits at her desk, staring out into the town. Across the road, she can see the old Harrington's Estates office being pulled apart by its new owners.

'What do you think?' Claire asks. 'One of those vegan cafes?'

'Oh, definitely,' Olivia says from her desk.

When Olivia started her own agency, she thought about taking over the old Harrington's office herself, but decided she didn't want to do it in Amanda's shadow. Instead, they took over the old Sanders office when they went out of business a few months back. It turns out they spent longer physically knocking it out of the park with a cricket bat than they did metaphorically with sales.

'Look at her – she's got "start the morning with matcha" written all over her,' Olivia says, watching as a woman across the road in workout bra and leggings bosses builders around. 'I bet she's made numerous TikToks about her morning routine in her time.'

'And definitely a few about why matcha's better than coffee when it's just not,' Claire agrees.

Olivia wishes Hannah was here. She'd have gone right in on the matcha woman with them.

'Do you think Amanda's inspirational quotes are still in there?' Claire asks.

'I mean probably,' Olivia says. 'You want them?'

'Maybe.' Claire shrugs. 'I could send some to her in prison. She'll be there a while. I imagine she needs pepping up. Although now I've moved in at Esme's place I could do with some decoration. I know she could wake up any day, but I can't keep living with dead earls on my walls indefinitely.'

'Oh, definitely,' Olivia says. 'We've talked about this. You spend so long at her bedside, caring for her. You need to have things for you every now and then. Replacing some dead earls with inspirational quotes sounds just the thing.'

Claire smiles gratefully to her friend and business partner as Olivia stands from her desk to stretch, her hands on her lower back supporting her and her now-significant bump.

'Did you get my message about Tom's parents? They called about the house sale,' Claire says.

'Yeah,' Olivia replies. 'They've been notified that they can sell. So I've said we'll do it for them.'

'Oooh! You going to tell Matt?' Claire asks.

'Yeah, I've just sent him a message,' Olivia says.

'It's good that you two are amicable,' Claire says.

Matt might have been spared prison, but Olivia just

couldn't trust him any more. After everything that's happened, she didn't want to waste any more time. She discovered she was pregnant a few weeks after they broke up, but kept it to herself, knowing it wasn't his. At least now she's selling Tom's place, she can use the commission to decorate the nursery in her new house. It's nice that Tom can contribute towards his baby even though he'll never meet them.

'Speaking of things for myself.' Claire stands from her desk and picks up her bag. 'I'm going to go and grab lunch, might see if I can get hold of that Michelle Obama quote while I'm at it. I actually kind of miss it.'

'Cool, see you later,' Olivia says, sitting back down and getting on with the job listing she's putting together.

They need to hire other people before the baby comes, but it's taken them a while to get to it. Truth be told, they're a little afraid of trusting people at this point. But Olivia knows she'll need all the help she can get if she's going to raise this baby on her own and run a business. She couldn't help hearing Amanda in her head, telling her how great being a single mother was for her Instagram profile. She jumps as the door to the agency swings open.

'Hiya, that house I just went to see is *in-cred-i-ble*. Or it could be. I swear there should be a law that if you have rank taste you need to give your house up to someone with good taste who can do it justice.' Hannah swings her holdall onto the desk and unclips Buster's lead, letting him run across the office to his little bed.

'By my calculations, very few people would retain their

properties that way,' Olivia says, letting out a small burp and frowning.

'Ooh, that reminds me,' Hannah chucks a packet of Rennies at her. 'Got you these. Don't say I never think of you.'

'Oh god, love you,' Olivia says, grabbing the packet like it's gold. 'How did you know?'

'You were a smidge percussive this morning . . .' Hannah smirks.

'Oh god,' Olivia giggles, and pops a Rennie.

'Scan's at five, yeah?' Hannah asks.

'Yeah,' Olivia says. 'You coming?'

'Wouldn't miss it for the world,' Hannah says. 'Then I'll cook you dinner and we can curl up on the sofa and watch *Traitors*.'

'Perfection,' Olivia sighs.

Claire emerges from the old Harrington's office with the Michelle Obama quote in hand. She can't believe it was still there and in one piece. She just got there in time too. The lovely woman who's taking over the office and turning it into a raw-food cafe said she was about to start throwing things away. She seemed sweet, and someone that Claire was sure would soon become a firm friend – she'll see to it by going in there every day.

Standing on Wellingden green taking in the sight of the new office and the town in the beautiful spring sunshine, Claire thinks she might have cracked it, the perfect life. No mortgage, living in the house she's always wanted and a great job. She wouldn't mind someone to share it with, of course, maybe a person to start a family with, and carry on her family legacy. But you can't have everything all the time. And she was happy, carefree . . . wasn't she?

The ringing of her phone from inside her bag interrupts her thoughts and she rummages with her free hand until she locates it. The number isn't one she recognises off the bat and it excites her to think it might be a new client.

'Hello, Claire de Vere,' she answers, proud of how professional she sounds.

'Hi, Claire darling, it's Betty, one of the nurses from the hospital looking after your great-aunt? I've got the most wonderful news for you. Esme's awake! We're just doing some tests, but she seems well, and she's asking for you!'

Claire feels a jolt of adrenaline, almost dropping the quote. Her fingers curl round the frame like claws as she takes in the words: *'There is no limit to what we as women can accomplish.'*

'Oh, wonderful news,' Claire says, her knuckles turning white with the intensity of her grip. 'Please tell her I'm on my way in now. I can't wait to catch up.'

Author's Note

I feel I need to make it clear that Hannah's views are not my own. I have both Jitney and Setting Plaster from Farrow & Ball in my home, and I love both colours dearly.

Acknowledgements

Firstly, thank you to YOU for reading it. I'm so sorry you went through that. I hope you're OK.

The biggest thank you has to go to my poor editors Lucy Dauman, Sophie Wilson and Isabel Martin who shaped this book and made it what it is, because without them it would be awful. Thank you for putting up with me and for all your hard work. I have been so lucky to work with all three of you and I'm so grateful for all the time, effort and love you've put into this. And thank you to all at Headline, for all the wonderful things that you do for me and my books. You are a brilliant team and I'm so fortunate to work with you.

Thank you to Chloe Seager, the best agent/therapist/friend there is. Without you my books, and my life, would be utterly terrible. You are a queen, an icon and a hero . . . and you know far too many of my secrets now for us ever to part. Also thank you for introducing me to the TV show *Murder House Flip* . . . Ahem.

My wonderful friend Nick Perry sadly passed away when I was writing this book. He loved a council planning meeting, so it's in his honour that I added Marcus's town-planning woes. He was a wonderful man who would probably have absolutely hated Marcus and his terrible developments, but I couldn't let it pass without honouring him in some way. He was truly special and I miss him.

Thank you to Daisy Buchannan, my new and very wonderful friend, who helped me get through the latter drafts of this when I was convinced I'd simply have to hand back the advance and move into a cave on the beach. Thank you to all the writing friends I've met along the way who have been so supportive. Other writers are the best: Lauren Bravo, Maz Evans, Holly Bourne, Kat McKenna, Laura Steven, Julia Tuffs, Amy Beashel, Josh Silver, Danielle Jawando, Simon James Green, Beth Reekles, L. D. Lapinski, Harry Woodgate, Lucy Vine, Ravena Guron, Hattie Williams, Julia Raeside and Joel Morris. I'm so sorry if I've missed anyone out. Also, sorry if I cried on you.

Thank you to Abi Nightingale and James Goodill who this book is dedicated to, and who I have definitely cried on. You were the best office buddies a girl could ask for and I miss you every single working day. (And the non-working ones too.)

Thank you to Anna, Sarah, Maz and Tal, Debora Robertson, Liz Vater and Jo Adams – the best friends in the entire universe. And thank you to my family.

Lastly but not leastly, thank you to my husband, Nick (and Angus the cat) for being my best person. I couldn't do any of it without you and I love you. X

Their hangovers may fade, but this is a hen party they'll never forget . . .

Lauren, Saskia, Dominica, Farah and Tansy have been friends since nursery. They wonder if that was the last time they all actually liked each other.

Reunited as bridesmaids at Tansy's spiritual hen party in the woods, it doesn't take long before old grudges begin to surface. Not to mention the secret they've been hiding for twenty years.

But what starts as a weekend of macramé and contraband vodka ends in murder when Tansy chokes to death on a poisoned cacao drink.

As the body count keeps climbing, the friends realise that one of their group must be the killer – and if any of them want to make it down the aisle, they need to watch their sash-covered backs.

Available now

RAISING READERS
Books Build Bright Futures

Dear Reader,

We'd love your attention for one more page to tell you about the crisis in children's reading, and what we can all do.

Studies have shown that reading for fun is the **single biggest predictor of a child's future success** – more than family circumstance, parents' educational background or income. It improves academic results, mental health, wealth, communication skills and ambition.

The number of children reading for fun is in rapid decline. Young people have a lot of competition for their time, and a worryingly high number do not have a single book at home.

Our business works extensively with schools, libraries and literacy charities, but here are some ways we can all raise more readers:

- Reading to children for just 10 minutes a day makes a difference
- Don't give up if your children aren't regular readers – there will be books for them!
- Visit bookshops and libraries to get recommendations
- Encourage them to listen to audiobooks
- Support school libraries
- Give books as gifts

Thank you for reading.
www.JoinRaisingReaders.com